IN CONGRESS ASSEMBLED

CORSAC FOX
BOOK 7

BLAZE WARD

KNOTTED ROAD PRESS

To Poke A Third Eye
Corsac Fox, Book 6
Blaze Ward
Copyright © 2025 Blaze Ward
All rights reserved
Published by Knotted Road Press
www.KnottedRoadPress.com

ISBN:
Paperback: 978-1-64470-491-2
Hardback: 978-1-64470-492-9

Cover art:
Jay O'Connell https://www.jayoconnell.com/
Illustration 108050035 © Raffaele1 | Dreamstime.com
Illustration 22850687 © Seamartini | Dreamstime.com

Cover and interior design copyright © 2025 Knotted Road Press

Reviews
It's true. Reviews help. Even a short one, such as, "Loved it!" So please consider reviewing this book (and all of the ones you've read) on your favorite retailer site.

Never miss a release!
If you'd like to be notified of new releases, sign up for my newsletter.

http://www.blazeward.com/newsletter/

Buy More!
Did you know that you can buy directly from the Knotted Road Press website?

https://www.knottedroadpress.com/shop/

ALSO BY BLAZE WARD

The Science Officer Series

Start with: The Science Officer

The Jessica Keller Chronicles

Start with: Auberon

CS-405 (Command Centurion Kosnett, part of Jessica)

Start with: Queen Anne's Revenge

First Centurion Kosnett (sequel to Jessica)

Start with: Encounter at Vilahana

Additional Alexandria Station Stories

Alexandria Station Collection

Handsome Rob (Alexandria Station Universe)

Start with: Can't Shoot Straight Gang

=====================

Corsac Fox

Start with: Flight of the Corsac Fox

Operation Marrakesh

Start with: Trial by Leviathan

Captain Daring

Start with: Revoked

The Hunter Bureau

Start with: Mirrors

Fairchild

Start with: Fairchild

Last Stand

Start with: Lost Dreams

The Lazarus Alliance

Start with: Escape

Shadow of the Dominion

Start with: Longshot Hypothesis

Star Dragon

Start with: Birth of the Star Dragon

Kincaide's War

Start with: The Eden Package

Star Tribes

Start with: Winterstar

Blaze also writes Action-Adventure Here

CONTENTS

PART ONE

NUBIA

ONE

"All hands to action stations," the call came over the speaker.

Vanguard Ulysses Fortier—Uly—was already at his station, listening to his own words echo back out of the speakers with a serene smile that belied a hard bit of grumbliness underneath. He would have preferred not to be doing this.

Not be here at all. Or to send Sterling Huff to handle it, but the young gentleman wasn't back yet from his mission, to say nothing of Dan and her Congress, headed off to recruit Human colonists to join them in Imperial Sector Fourteen.

Today, it was him. Then Uly smiled, because he did have a great crew. And a powerful ship in *Nubia*, the former Skyhawk *Invincible*, still among the most powerful vessels in space.

He looked over, but Haydar Ramezani was concentrating most of his tentacles on his controls, though one waved back breezily. Working left across that line he had Yaqub Zobo on guns, with the everpresent purple stripe across his shoulders, more of a superstition than anything at this point. Del Blakeslee handling communications and sensors to let Haydar be a data nerd.

And Drew Roscoe flying. With occasional maniacal laughter that let Uly know that man was as deep in the zone as few pilots ever achieved.

"Uly, thirty seconds to drop," Drew called over his shoulder.

"All turrets live," Yaqub answered. "Standing by to fin some fool pirate."

"You're making assumptions," Haydar countered. "The intelligence we've assembled suggests more than dumbasses today."

"That's why we brought help," Del reminded everyone.

Uly nodded.

Lots of help. New ships from Isann and Saari, plus Khet and Ononguli vessels. Not that terrible formation of heavier ships that had raided Zhoralong the second time, but only because Uly hadn't had time to get Anna a message to send a fleet.

Instead, he had purchased the entire contents of a couple of heavy cargo freighters and sent them to a rendezvous while he made plans. That would feed crews along the way.

And now, they were here.

Back home at Bastion, Lyra Bondarenko was acting as Governor still, mostly because Uly needed help while so many of his key players were far away. At the same time, the Bondarenko Clan and even the Zehlennko—related to his other wife Katya—had stepped up and put their horns on the line to help.

The Khet Directors at Z'Gosza hadn't wished to be relegated to second place, so they had sent ships, colonists, and trade to make sure that profit flowed in their direction as well.

Today, he missed having Lukyan Chayka with him, either in *Compass Rose* or *Fire Diamond*, but Uly had also made sure that he was doing this on a Thursday.

Because EVERYBODY had developed an allergy to *Tuesdays*.

Nubia dropped out of warp.

And Uly immediately understood why the *Auga Empire* had been so quiet along most of the Ononguli frontier for so many months. He'd thought that they had withdrawn forces to chase Sterling and *Vauquelin*. Or rethink their original plans to start the next war with the Ononguli.

Instead—or in addition?—they'd been building a secret base just inside the outer edge of Sector Fourteen, where they could threaten Bastion and Saari equally. But only after that monster was completed.

"Yaqub, kill that Striker on escort duty," Uly ordered.

Nine 14.7dm wavebolts went downrange almost simultaneously, which you could do with a sharp crew coming out of jump and ready to fire immediately.

After this, reloading times would matter, but he had first-rate veterans handling that, as well.

"Drew, how long until the rest of the squadron drops?" Uly asked.

"I told them sixty seconds, because I wanted all eyes on me for this," Drew replied. "That might have been a dumb idea."

Uly grinned. Drew never had dumb ideas. One of the most gifted pilots Uly had ever known, and technically the only civilian on this warship, with Blair Mitchell traveling with Dan as the galactic expert on xenobiology.

"We'll make it work," Uly assured him. "Haydar?"

"Minimal encryption deployed," the Mazhin First Officer and Chief Data Scientist grumbled with a dejected tone.

A man *deeply* insulted that there was utterly no challenge to hacking your communications, because Haydar liked to tell people that he'd forgotten more about signals encryption than the *Auga Empire* had ever learned.

"Jam them anyway," Uly ordered.

"Oh, doing that," Haydar said, the eyeroll implied by the tentacles in ways that nobody but a Mazhin could probably decipher. "Lots of small patrol vessels about, so they have the opportunity to overwhelm us if they get their shit together."

"Good thing they can't talk to one another then, isn't it?" Uly teased.

One orbital station. That same standard design that Uly had stolen to build Bastion. And the freighter that carried the disassembled parts, plus a number of smaller vessels that were handling various tasks but were generally unarmed in Auga service.

One Striker. What Uly had originally been taught to call a Forward Cruiser, because they were designed to operate away from base for long periods of time.

Several Interceptors floating about. Equivalent to destroyers or corvettes in *Batyr* service. Weapon platforms for the most part, designed as squadron leaders for smaller ships.

Like the three dozen or so Ultra-Bombers and Probes that Haydar and Del had already identified.

"Yaqub, target the nearest Interceptor for a partial salvo while that Striker gets organized," Uly ordered. "If they can."

He missed having Sterling's brutal efficiency at war-fighting, but Uly had also tasked the man with teaching his genius in the form of a new Emro School.

Starfare.

Uly had recorded all the classes on command and diplomacy, at least what he couldn't bribe, swindle, or blackmail others into doing, but Sterling had a pure gift for ship maneuvering in combat.

"Haydar, status on the station?" Drew asked as his delicate fingers hung poised over his keys.

"Negative on wavebolt turrets, Drew," Haydar replied. "Not detecting any scanner or weapon-lock emissions."

"Uly, permission to get silly?" Drew asked.

"Granted," Uly answered, laughing at himself and all the dumb things he had been taught about how to be a naval officer.

Like how a commanding officer had all the ideas and transmitted them to his crew. Or how the crew would have to couch a suggestion in careful terms so as to not offend a superior officer.

He couldn't imagine a *Batyr* Forward Cruiser where the Pilot got a green light and a blank slate to go commit graffiti.

"Yaqub, stand by for a jousting pass down our right flank," Drew called. "Help's coming from what will be behind them when they turn to scream at us."

"Turret three will rotate back," Yaqub answered. "I'll need someone to gaff with the forward pair."

"Oh, I gotcha coming," Drew laughed in an evil tone.

Uly leaned back and watched his team go to work.

TWO

Drew had gotten out of the shower this morning feeling like he had the winning lottery numbers in his back pocket. Like that perfect wave was hiding just out on the horizon until it saw him paddling out into the surf, where they could make music and records together.

The Punks™ had built a base, but were busy doing it by the book.

The wrong book.

Sterling had explained the smarter way over beers at one point, pivoting his engineering teams to get ALL the guns working first, even before crews had somewhere better to sleep than a hammock hung between two stanchions.

The Auga never committed jazz. Gonna cost them today because he could use the half-built station shell to hide from the Striker, forcing that silly git to maneuver and twist around to come after *Nubia*.

Which would leave his ass hanging out all wrong when help arrived.

Drew slammed the engines to the stops and ignored the screams of surprise and probably outrage he was going to hear from Chief Engineer Sadeq Akhtar and that guy's crew.

But generators and engines were supposed to be used up. Uly's words.

Go like hell today. Rebuild it tomorrow.

Or steal something better, except that there wasn't anything better.

Not, at least, until the Yarikh babes built them something that was the next evolution in deadly.

They might. Their asses might be on the line if the Auga decided to charge this way for a generation and ignore the Ononguli.

Bow turned down, plus a butt wiggle like a kitten about to pounce on a mousy toy. Roll a shade to the right, to make sure that all three turrets could elevate enough to continue engaging when Drew got silly on somebody's ass.

Like now.

"Gunnery, all ahead crazy," he said, remembering to use his outside voice for this, because he was IN THE ZONE.

The perfect wave.

There.

Now.

Awesome.

Nubia went low and left like a shark. A big, ugly, beautiful black moon pearl of a shark. Overhead, nine big guns went boom like a drummer waking folks up.

"Haydar?" Drew asked.

"Chickens, Drew," the guy replied. "Headless and headlong."

Drew cackled. Haydar had finally gotten comfortable with Human-isms in communication.

Hard to do, when Mazhin had about five times as many senses going on. Humans were poorly limited in comparison, but had a lot more poetry than Mazhin.

Auga ships, lacking central coordination and attempting to figure out what to do. Chickens with their heads cut off.

And all attempting to rendezvous, because Auga squadron tactics were built around the onion approach, with the smallest ships out front, the medium ships protecting them back a row, and the big ships aft, where their big wavebolt launchers had to travel the farthest to hit some-thing, so often weren't any more dangerous than the little ones that the Ultra-Bombers had.

But them headless and headlong just meant they were firing at him and sailing the wrong way, trying to get over to the Striker so they could form up.

Whoopsie.

A light began to blink on his board.

"Del?"

"This is exactly why I refused to take that bet," Del replied evenly. "Man arrived six seconds early."

"It's Eskil," Drew reminded him. "That's probably late for him. What's he doing?"

"About to maul that dumbass who just turned everything to engage you," Del countered. "You were expecting anything different from that giant furball?"

Drew laughed. His job had been the distraction.

Mission accomplished.

And now the entire Samuur squadron had dropped into place.

Gonna be fun.

THREE

Eskil Haldur had come to appreciate his new Light Striker. *Nikodemus Lindberg*, named for one of the founding explorers of the modern Samuur age, back when the Samuur had first managed to build a primitive Variable Pulse Spatial Generator based on plans from some itinerant tinkers and a lot of moxie.

Today, that man's spiritual descendant was the new flagship of the Samuur fleet, the first Light Striker and heaviest warship they had ever built.

So far.

Eskil had intentions to build something much heavier, as soon as their yards could handle that. Might take a few years, but he was patient. And enjoying his new command.

Two twin 8dm turrets each, paired fore and aft, for a total of eight tubes, all slewed to the left because Drew had ordered *Lindberg* to come in at a hard slant where they could take advantage of that firepower from surprise.

Eskil didn't think Drew had known what was there waiting for them, but he occasionally wondered if the gods themselves had reached down and touched the Human with prescience.

There was an Auga Striker parked almost exactly where all *Lindberg*'s bores were already aimed. Like magic.

Human magic, the most dangerous kind.

"Aava," he ordered, turning to the woman handling guns. "Give the big one everything now, plus the 2dm bolts as well. Hold the 1dm for defense and reload for a second salvo, assuming our escorts will be able to handle incoming fire."

Aava Lehtonen nodded with ears and whiskers, but remained otherwise focused on her boards. Maks had included a specific tone with each heavy barrel, so that folks didn't have to look at a screen to track fire. It sounded almost like someone plunking notes on a piano, but this was a major chord of both hands first.

The Auga was turned away from them almost ninety degrees and already headed the wrong way around another one of those massive stations Eskil had come to know from his visits to Bastion and the Watchtower.

Except that this one wasn't firing anything.

Had they forgotten to arm it? Foolish mistake.

Worse, Uly had apparently been timing things, because *Nubia* belched forth nine of those monstrous wavebolt torpedoes at the same time *Lindberg* did, catching the Auga vessel in a trap from which there was no escape.

That conductor was, at least, smart enough to engage *Nubia*'s heavier fire first, leaving the lighter 8dm 'bolts for his defensive gunners.

It was, however, *insufficient*.

"Hemmo," Eskil said, turning to his First Officer. "What's wrong with them?"

"Haydar Ramezani is currently broadcasting as much of a jamming signal as he possibly can on every Auga frequency in use," Hemmo grinned back. "They appear to be somewhat distracted."

"Somewhat?" Eskil asked, watching four of his wavebolts slam home into the Auga Striker with catastrophic consequences.

About what he could do with a hammer and an empty milk container made of aluminum.

"Orders from the flagship," Hemmo barked. "Come right and aim at the interceptor on that flank where we can gang up on him. Osman, on your number three screen."

Eskil had an echo of his pilot's board and saw where Osman Laine was about to go.

"Aava, bring the rear turrets around and put another salvo into the heavier Striker as we go," he ordered.

"What about the station?" she asked.

"Is Uly engaging it?" Eskil countered. "Has it fired?"

"Negative on both accounts," Hemmo called.

"Then ignore it until otherwise ordered," Eskil ordered. "Pass that along to our escorts as well. Have them stay close and defensive until Uly gives us new orders. There are too many small ships firing things at us around here to duel, but we appear to have just crushed their flagship."

Another salvo, this time split fore and aft at two targets, mostly because that Striker still had mounts that could fire. And had not surrendered to Uly.

Eskil missed the sort of single combat challenge that the Samuur had engaged in before meeting the Auga. Like sailing into Bastion and challenging young Sterling, without understanding that Uly was coming.

Or that Sterling might have been able to take that hunting pack by himself if pressed.

There was less honor here, but the Auga had started to build another one of their stations in space that Uly had claimed. And space that the Samuur would need for their own trade routes later, if they were to be more than a minor stop on the way to greater capitals.

This, then, might be the war that Uly had expected, starting here instead of going horns-in on the Ononguli, as had been the case for so many centuries previously.

And one that directly threatened Saari itself, which was unacceptable.

But *Nubia* had arrived and challenged the moorage by itself, which was another measure of honor, because Uly had not warned *Lindberg* off from firing.

Games were honorable. War could be, but only when everyone was expected to behave in a polite, formal manner.

And Eskil had gotten over himself for expecting such things from the *Auga Empire*.

At least for today.

Today, it was battle. And that Interceptor was about to be crushed by *Nubia*, without Uly sending out a call to surrender, so he had chosen to draw the line.

Here, and no farther.

It was a thing the Samuur knew well.

Eskil's job was to protect the weak from the wicked. The rest of the galaxy from conquest by the *Auga Empire*.

To hold the line.

And he would.

FOUR

Uly studied the screen, dialed back far enough to contain all of the vessels in range.

The Striker was mostly done, having been hammered hard from both directions. The Interceptor that Drew had gone after next was shedding parts and plasma. Several other Interceptors had started to gather, but had a problem because their flagship was crippled and the station apparently unarmed.

Or, as Haydar had mentioned, installing all the turrets and turning them on usually came much later in the construction process, which was why Uly had dropped everything to attack today.

Another month, and they might have been able to hold him off.

"Drew, slew around and head back," Uly ordered. "Draw Eskil and his team in on your flank as a shield so we can harm people."

Because 14.7dm bolts did a lot of hurt.

"Comin' up," Drew replied, typing furiously. "Del, bring them down my left flank on the turn."

"Left flank shield, aye," Del said calmly, also typing.

"Haydar, I need a channel to talk to whoever might be in command at this point," Uly said. "Likely someone on the station."

"Likely," Haydar agreed. "Purple button on your screen and talk."

Uly found the new icon and pressed.

"Attention, Avocur system, this is the Warlord of the *Spinward Reaches*," Uly said, letting his voice go low and heavy. "You will surrender right now, or I will hunt you down and destroy you tomorrow. I am not feeling benevolent, so this will be your only warning. Respond on this channel."

He cut the line and ignored it, save to nod to Haydar's tentacles.

"No, I doubt that they will," Uly replied to the semaphored question. "And yes, we will get ugly on them, because I have had enough."

Even Mazhin could cringe at his tones, but Uly understood. The Auga had chosen to build a new base in a place where they could finally threaten to attack Bastion.

Or Saari.

Or cut trade routes he was building linking the Khet of Z'Gosza with the Ononguli of Rayzian.

Bullies, the lot of them. And they would not recognize anything except strength sufficient to push them back.

Thus, we will.

"Del, how is Conductor Bakirov doing on his wing?" Uly asked.

Uly had divided the overall force into two large squadrons, under Eskil and an Isann gentleman named Danemon Bakirov, who was a distant cousin of the Chief of Chiefs and a well-respected leader among their kind.

Ononguli and Khet conductors had wanted to complain, but taken a look at Uly's mood and refrained.

"Closing like a cloak and forcing about half of the defensive forces to dither, sir," Del replied. "Folks are starting to get organized, now that Haydar left them a channel to talk."

Uly nodded. As planned. They could talk themselves into trouble, or out of it, and with the Striker no longer relevant, he had enough firepower to overwhelm the defensive squadrons and annihilate them.

If they pushed him far enough.

And they might yet. The Auga were still coming to grips with the idea that someone might push back.

Might be able to push back.

Might be willing.

Uly wondered if the time had come to assemble a fleet mean enough to take a world back from the Auga, something they had done to the Ononguli and others too many times.

Maks had ideas that he had patiently worked out with Sterling. They would probably work.

Auga would eventually discover fear.

"Haydar?"

"Seriously ugly argument going on, only semi-encrypted," his Chief Data Nerd replied. "Striker Conductor wants to die to the last man, while the station governor understands that he has nowhere to run to once we chase off or destroy all the escorts."

"Del, those three Interceptors and that block of Ultra-Bombers on the left?" Uly said, highlighting a cluster on his board and sending it to the man. "Hit them with a targeting scanner bright enough to read by at night."

"Coming up."

Nubia had powerful sensors. Bright, using the right vernacular.

Every ship over there suddenly was standing in daylight, if you will.

Uly opened a channel to his own ships.

"This is the Corsac Fox," he said simply. "Everyone pick a target over there and fire your offensive wavebolts at them."

Yaqub was nodding, like he'd seen it coming. But then, there weren't many reasons to shine a light.

Nine whumps as terrible dragons began tracking.

Those were the most dangerous, as smaller bolts didn't retain their violent efficacy over such great distances.

But even a soft impact was dangerous, as more than one hundred joined it. They almost looked like they'd been timed, but that just meant that Auga defensive gunners had to decide which to attack and which to ignore and hope they survived.

"Del, what's the Striker doing?" Uly asked, noting a vector change on his map.

"Think he's trying to run, Uly," Del replied. "Crawl to the edge of the zone we've established with our generators so he can get to hyperspace."

"Drew."

"Gotcha," Drew replied.

Uly watched *Nubia*'s bow suddenly slew around hard on gyroscopes and the engines started pushing with some emphasis.

Variable Pulse Spatial Generators generated a sphere where they interrupted one another. Two ships getting too close to one another canceled the field and dropped them both into real space. In battles, a squadron could trap another that way, unless someone could get outside that range and flee madly.

And even then, *Nubia* could probably run them down fairly quickly.

"Yaqub, reload and put your next salvo into whichever Interceptor looks like they might have a competent commander on their decks," Uly ordered. "Then hold and stand by for Drew to chase."

"Saw that coming," Yaqub replied, firing as quickly as the tubes could reload. "Target will be nullified."

Uly located the comm channel he wanted and Eskil was there a moment later.

"Sir?"

"I'm likely going to have to take that Striker when he runs, Eskil," Uly said. "You assume command here while I'm gone and either accept all their surrenders or finish them off."

Whiskers twitched, but Eskil understood the stakes.

Honor had been served by *Nubia* attacking alone. Surrender had been offered, even after the outcome had been largely decided.

This was war.

"Understood, Vanguard," Eskil said. "We'll hold the line."

That was the one thing Uly *never* doubted about the Samuur. And this one in particular.

He **would** hold the line.

"Uly, he's gone," Drew called.

"Not for long," Uly replied. "Take him."

"On it," Drew said, deadly serious for the first time today.

A few seconds later, *Nubia* vanished as well.

FIVE

Eskil cut the line and looked around. Normally, a Light Striker like *Lindberg* was not a serious threat in fleet actions, being more of an escort for Devastators or a squadron commander on a wing.

Uly wanted the job finished.

"Hemmo, drop the jamming Haydar was doing, but be prepared to ramp it back up," Eskil ordered. "Aava, who's left that feels like five minutes in the penalty box?"

"This one," she said, highlighting a heavier Interceptor on the flank that had largely been overlooked up until now, well out of position to be hit by any of the attacking forces.

Still, it was only an Interceptor. Not much larger than *Tiikeri* had been, though far more modern.

The overload attack Uly had sent had largely worked. Most of the vessels on that side of the field of battle were damaged to some degree, with a few of them out of action entirely, including the other three Interceptors that had been overwhelmed.

He found the channel he wanted and smiled at Conductor Bakirov's Isann face.

Another of Uly's allies, both as a species and the man himself.

"Uly put me in charge while he's gone," Eskil said.

"Who do you want crushed?" Bakirov replied.

"This one," Eskil said. "Bring your force to port and drop down two levels while we circle to starboard and start our run. On the command, everyone will target this vessel with the intention of scoring a single kill."

Most of the time, wavebolt impacts hit shields and weakened them or knocked them down, spreading the energy across a wider face and damaging the outer hull, but everyone built that ring of chambers to be empty in battle and capable of absorbing the damage without the ship losing fighting effectiveness.

"Lance shots?" Bakirov confirmed.

"Everyone, yes," Eskil said, then cut the line and nodded to Hemmo to transmit that to all ships. "Osman, bring us around and take us in."

Wavebolts also had two modes, selected at the moment of firing. Fist was a contained ball of energy that simply detonated on impact. Lance mode sharpened the energy into a spike that could punch through shields and drive a stream of plasma deep inside a ship, but it also had to impact just right or it might carom harmlessly off, like a rock skipping across a still pond.

The remaining defenders were starting to coalesce into a globular formation that might actually succeed, but they simply didn't have enough defensive turrets and neutron omnipulsars to do the job.

Not when everyone was going after one target.

"Hemmo?"

"Everyone is prepared," his First Officer replied. "Bakirov's force is in position."

"All ships: FIRE!"

SIX

Uly watched Drew, Del, and Haydar conduct what could only be classified as black magic, tracking the damaged Striker through warp space by the trail its generators left, wider and brighter than it should have been because the ship had already suffered so much damage.

"Drew?"

"He only thinks he's getting away from me, Uly," Drew said in a deadly sober voice that would be frightening to anyone who really knew Drew Roscoe.

Terrible Vengeance itself.

Uly leaned back and waited. They didn't need him to handle this. Then he had a thought and opened an intercom line aft.

"Security," Inari Johansson replied, the Samuur woman taking over for the moment because Solomon Wyndham and most of his team had gone with Dan aboard *Vauquelin*, both to handle security on new Human colonist recruits and to provide Dan more humans if she needed to make them visible.

"It's Uly," he said simply. "Stand by to possibly board an enemy vessel, once Drew stops them."

"Will they have surrendered?" she asked.

"Do not assume so," Uly offered. "They ran and we're chasing."

"Teams alerted, Vanguard."

He cut the line and smiled a little crooked. Mostly to himself, but he had to wave off an inquiring tentacle.

Eskil had, no doubt, told Samuur Paramount Aarne Kallio what he thought Dan would be looking for in her Combat Team. And potentially in the Congress itself.

The Paramount had made certain to put three interesting Samuur women front and center for him and Dan to get to know. Inari was a close combat expert who was handling bodyguard duties while Dan was gone. The Hudaibirdi sisters, Maikki and Taija, were aboard *Vauquelin*, as Sensors Officer and Damage Control Officer respectively, where Dan and Sterling would see them working.

The Congress had been Dan's idea. Her Combat Team, after Suka Kuri had basically ordered Dan to collect AT LEAST ONE WOMAN of every species they encountered who could learn all the close combat martial arts any of them knew.

It had only been later that those two dangerous women had turned around and decided to make them all *his* wives, as a way for each species to have themselves represented at the highest level of the government that Uly was building in Imperial Sector Fourteen.

The *Spinward Reaches*. Until recently ,something of a dark spot on all known maps, because the local civilizations were all hardly interstellar and only barely starting to expand again after the most recent fall in galactic civilization.

And now he had many wives, but the Congress was all headed to a Human colony on the far side of space to recruit more people.

His job was to hold things together while Dan and her women were off doing things.

So he got to watch Inari at work. Woman had almost a head on him. Not quite double his mass, but she was a jock and a warrior even among the Samuur, which said a lot.

"Uly, I'm close," Drew announced.

"Take him," Uly ordered simply. "We'll see if he wants to surrender honorably or die for his emperor. I don't really care, one way or the other."

Several shoulders in front of him flinched, but Uly wanted to make clear to everyone that he had reached the limits of his patience with the Auga. They could behave, or he would make them.

However he had to do it.

Whatever methods became necessary to train the *Auga Empire* to stop being a bully to everyone they met.

"Got'm," Drew said, and *Nubia* dropped into real space.

SEVEN

Yaqub, having had no orders to the contrary and a pretty good feel for Uly's mood, put six bolts into the Striker as soon as his targeting systems could resolve the ship against the backdrop of space.

And, lacking orders, all of them were fists for now. Uly had suggested that they could surrender. Whether they took him up on it was up to them.

He could score kills here. Ugly ones. Fin you, then float your stupid ass to the top of the tank belly up.

Yaqub turned and sipped from the straw he'd added to his console. Everyone else wanted a lot less humidity in their air, so Khet like him were always dry, and he'd been vetoed on installing mistergates everywhere.

So he needed water. The Auga needed time to understand that they'd finally pissed the Humans off.

Yaqub had been with Uly long enough to understand what an amazingly stupid idea THAT was.

Impact.

Shields took most of it, after four 1dm bolts did a little bit to soften things. *Someone* had lost at least two of his omnipulsar mounts, because only two were left, trying to protect the ship. Not nearly enough.

Aft shields were gone. Knocked down and stomped a bit. Nobody was talking, save little tidbits back and forth.

Uly, trusting him to do it right.

And Yaqub had his Gunnery Certificate hung proudly in his quarters, after Sterling had decided he was good enough to handle this job.

No higher praise.

Yaqub put the next three downrange as lances and counted heartbeats for the first six tubes to be reloaded, wondering if he needed to offer carrots or sticks to those teams.

Except that less than three seconds separated fastest from slowest.

Pretty damned good work.

He put six more in play, all fists because Yaqub had a pretty good idea that only two of the previous batch were going to get stopped cleanly.

Yup. Impact. Aft. Stern hit. Almost EXACTLY square. Oh, that's gotta hurt.

Six more coming. *Y'all ready to die?*

Tracking.

Seriously?

No commentary?

No asking for ransom?

Nothing?

Yaqub shrugged and watched four stupidly heavy wavebolts slam into one dumbass Auga Striker. Already hurt pretty bad.

Utterly done now.

Yaqub figured that he could just crush them like a soup can with his next salvo, but this was that moment that Sterling always demanded more.

Expected you to exercise some mercy on a downed foe, so you didn't turn into another bully punk like the Auga.

He rotated his head aft and looked at the boss pointedly, ignoring the tentacles behind him.

Watched Uly draw a breath. Hold it. Release. Turn to Haydar.

"Order them to strike their colors or suffer the consequences," Uly said simply.

Yaqub nodded and turned back to confirm nine green lights on his board.

Consequences, indeed.

EIGHT

Haydar had their frequency, but that ship refused to answer, so he hacked into their systems and broadcast his signal inside using the emergency circuits.

Lukyan had taught him that trick, back when every Ononguli ship had those sorts of overrides already baked in. A bit harder on an Auga vessel, but he'd taken one apart and The Auga built such things as identical as two welding robots in a dockyard could manage.

"Auga vessel, you will hear me," he said bluntly. "In twenty seconds, the order will be given to destroy your vessel without survivors. You will not make it to any friendly world from here, because you are in a zone claimed by the Warlord of the *Spinward Reaches*. Counting down."

Sure, lay it on extra thick. Most of the crew weren't Auga, after all. Probably half or more of the officers were members of the masters. Maybe some of the senior divisional leads.

The vast majority were all the other species that had generally not been given any choice in joining the *Auga Empire*. Rather, they'd been conquered by a species that had decided to control the galaxy.

And held against their will ever since.

So yes, he might have a few opinions on the subject, but Uly was unlikely to return to *Danumash* space in *Nubia* and let him bombard a few palaces and orbital stations as a political statement.

At least today.

Idly, he wondered if that crew might successfully mutiny in the time given. Or if they were all the sorts of fanatics that would rather die for their emperor than admit that they might be wrong.

You got all kinds in space.

Twenty seconds elapsed without comment.

But this was *Nubia*. Nobody would take it upon themselves. Yaqub sat and waited, ready to turn into a bump on a log from the scent he was giving off. Del was listening on all channels. Drew had a deadliness about him that was almost as frightening as Uly, because you rarely got that sort of contained rage off the man.

It would be like Kit Simonson deciding to cut your throat.

Uly sighed.

"Del, are there any worlds nearby where they might manage to get in a shuttle or something?" Uly asked.

"Nearest is slightly over two light-years, Commander," Del replied.

You might manage it, if you had an emergency Spatial Generator in one of the larger runabouts. The sorts of things a commanding officer might use. The crew itself would be doomed. And were probably just waiting for the ax to fall.

"Drew, track any secondary vessels trying to run," Uly ordered. "Yaqub, fists only, slowly. Let's batter them into submission if we can. Inari, stand by for rescue operations."

Haydar nodded. Even in his rage, Uly wasn't about to simply execute innocent sailors. Casualties in warfare were one thing, but hunting the helpless was the other end of the spectrum.

Haydar smiled when Yaqub only fired five wavebolts. Tracked as they got close, with defensive 1dm bolts trying vainly to stop them. And omnipulsar fire that was insufficient.

But five rolled the vessel onto a flank and lights on the hull went out. Plasma and atmosphere were leaking instead, blowtorches lighting the night, but that was a systemwide failure of conduits and generators.

Nine probably would have destroyed the ship. Five merely killed it, and possibly soft enough to matter.

Haydar approved.

NINE

Uly watched the Striker die.

"Got a shuttle emerging," Del called sharply. "Possibly translight capable. Turning away from us and running. Starting to accelerate. Probably officers. No signals of any kind being broadcast."

Officers, leaving their crews to die. Or to the mercy of the Corsac Fox.

"Yaqub, kill the shuttle," Uly ordered, understanding that it was both necessary and that nobody else would take that responsibility onto their own fins.

One bolt began chasing. The pursuit ended quickly in a small supernova of fire.

"Security, you're on," he ordered, grinding his teeth to keep from howling insults and character assassinations after those officers on that shuttle.

He sat back as Drew began maneuvering closer. *Nubia* didn't have the large bay for assault shuttles that other ships did, but if the Striker had stopped being a threat, they could sail close enough that Inari's people could cross the gap on backpack thrusters.

At some point, they might even dock to take off survivors that he would eventually send home.

"DREW! Back off!" Del suddenly barked. "Reinforce forward shields max NOW!"

Uly had no idea what Del had seen, but everyone in front of him was moving. Reacting. Typing.

Then the Striker detonated. Even then, something of a damp squib, but the hull shattered from a series of internal explosions running bow to stern in slow motion.

That conductor had abandoned ship. Abandoned his crew. And then chosen to kill them.

Uly suddenly didn't feel nearly so bad about sanctioning the Auga with death.

"I have survivors in suits, blown clear of the wreckage," Del called. "Security, routing you vectors. Get all ships in the air and all medical teams on standby."

Again, a top crew. And Del—normally-so-quiet-you-missed-him Del—was barking orders and taking charge of things, so Uly let him.

Not many sailors over there had made it clear of the explosion, but they'd rescue all of them that they could. If nothing else, their bodies could be sent home to their families.

He owed them that much.

TEN

Eskil studied the battleground.

What there was of it, after about a third of the little ships had fled for their lives and he had chosen to let them, more interested in keeping the larger ships under control and dealing with the station, because Eskil had no idea how quickly Uly would return.

He had met Urs Edvin Székely, the Auga who had commanded *Vauquelin* when it had been the Auga vessel *Serene Naddoddur*, so Eskil was prepared for the Auga governor of the station.

Human-like, generally. Furless except on their head, plus jaws for the men. Shorter than humans, but broader and heavier. Stocky. Muscular. Impressive.

But it was the third eye in the middle of the forehead that really looked weird to Eskil. Larger, but generally kept closed except when they were using their supposed mental powers on you. The Emro women, Suka Kuri and Anari Supasei, had explained that they didn't have that much power. Nor anything like the range to Eskil's bridge.

It was generally a public relations ploy on their part.

"What species are you?" the Auga over there asked in a tone Eskil could only qualify as derisive.

"Conqueror," Eskil replied, then relented. "My particular ethnic group, however, is Samuur."

Because everyone was equal in Uly's world, which meant that anyone might marry someone from another species, as weird as he occasionally still found that when he stopped and thought about it. And adopt children from a third or fourth species.

Because everyone was equal in Uly's world.

Even the Auga, if they chose to participate.

"What happens next?" the Auga asked.

"You can surrender formally, in which case we will make arrangements to transport you somewhere safe and eventually get home. Or you can decide to die by making us destroy the station while every one of your crew are aboard. If it comes to that, I doubt that we will bother rescuing people, so choose wisely."

Eskil had seen how angry Uly had been, when the coordinates and potential outcome had become known. The first Auga step in the *War For The Spinward Reaches*, he had called it that day.

At least it allowed the Samuur to aid their Ononguli allies, by drawing some of the Auga ire to the northwest.

At what cost, though?

It did help that there were no more undamaged Auga vessels about, save for another one of those monstrous ships that carried component parts to one of their standard stations, such as Uly had stolen more than one of, selling them on to others to be able to move massive amounts of cargo between major worlds.

All the smaller escorts who could had fled. The others had been pummeled into submission by *Nubia* and *Lindberg*. And a great many friends.

Eskil waited. He had been warned that the Auga moved with far more patience than almost any other species. That had let them build such an immense empire.

It also let faster-reacting species have certain advantages.

For now, he paused the line and muted it.

"Hemmo, let me know if they make a decision before I have to make one for them," he said. "Aava, any threats?"

"Nobody," she replied with a hint of a sneer to her voice, but they had all charged madly into battle today, surrounded by many conductors and ships known only by name and occasional reputation, and not all of them had measured up to her standards.

Or his. But they had all answered Uly's summons, so that meant that they were allies.

"Hemmo, go ahead and order all Auga vessels to dock with the station," Eskil decided. "They might have enough space to evacuate it entirely, saving us from locating a liner to carry them home."

"What if they blow it when they leave?" Osman asked.

"Then we kill them all for violating honor and parole," Hemmo spoke up, a great deal more bloodthirsty than even Eskil usually was.

The Paramount had selected Hemmo Lindholm for this role because the man was the calm, quiet one chosen to balance Eskil's usual crazy.

But they were all growing into new jobs in a new galaxy utterly unlike anything they had been prepared for five years ago.

Hemmo met his gaze with calm certainty, then jolted slightly.

"The Auga conductor has spoken," he said.

Eskil brought the line live again.

"Sir?" Eskil asked politely.

He could always escalate later. If necessary.

"We will accept your terms," the man said. "I note that you have ordered vessels to rendezvous."

"They will take off as many of your people as they can," Eskil nodded. "All of them, if possible, and we will make supplies available to get you home. Food and whatever else you need."

"What did you do with the commander of *Serene Naddoddur*?" the man asked abruptly.

"He's currently working at Bastion, managing a small cargo transportation company, last I spoke with him," Eskil replied.

Then, to be a touch rude, he cut the line.

"Let them fume and wonder," he specifically ordered Hemmo. "Aava, keep watch and stand by in case anyone starts trouble, including any cargo vessels that suddenly arrive, because a system with this many people has to be getting food regularly."

"I'm on it," she replied.

Eskil leaned back and watched.

Waiting.

Uly would be back soon enough. Perhaps he could deliver the man a partially complete station.

"Hemmo, Saari is closest, among the major players, yes?" he asked.

"Saari and Krilic, on the edge of the Ononguli Sphere, yes," Hemmo replied.

"Find me two fast couriers and stand by to detach them," Eskil said. "We'll send messages both directions with requests for repair and construction crews to come here, if Uly isn't back in a few hours."

At Bastion, they had the Watchtower.

Here at Avocur, they might be building their first castle against the *Auga Empire* itself.

Best it be done quickly.

ELEVEN

Uly sighed a little as *Nubia* dropped out of warp and he saw what was going on.

All of the ships close to the station flew Auga flags, surrounded by ships of the *Spinward Reaches*.

Wolves, herding sheep in close.

"Messages from Eskil," Haydar said. "Information pack with everything boiled down tightly. Station surrendered honorably. His words. Ships offered parole to withdraw station crew to safety, pending results of us taking control of the half-finished carcass. Need for supplies, so he has already sent couriers to Saari and Krilic. Everything under control. Again, his words."

And not idle ones. Not from Eskil Haldur.

"Drew, put us in a position to control things supporting *Lindberg*," he ordered. "They have a better hold on the situation. Yaqub, Eskil is in charge for now."

Nods. Professionals. That was the best part about a lot of this, as he usually only had to identify a goal, then get out of the way and let people make it happen, instead of pushing them to get there.

"Haydar, how much work to finish the station?" he asked.

"About two-thirds done now," Haydar replied. "This was almost exactly the point at which Sterling turned around and got all his guns mounted and ready. For the same reason. We've got fully trained crews at Saari, working at Maks's yard, so they could come here and get to work instantly. In fact, a number of the folks who built the Watchtower are there."

"I'll assume that Eskil asked for them," Uly said. "Inform the local governor that I'd like to meet with him before he leaves, then let Inari arrange security here to bring him aboard if he decides to come. Two aides may join him. Fully secured against trouble."

Meaning searched and scanned by extremely paranoid people, but this one would be sent home. Conductor Székely had chosen exile, assuming he would be executed for cowardice, when his ship broke and he chose to save his crew.

Rather than killing all of them.

Here, the Auga in charge could simply claim *force majeure* and be done with it, as an overwhelming plague of barbarian raiders had come over the hill and burned the village.

Or whatever lies they told themselves to justify conquering the galaxy.

TWELVE

Inari understood that her new job guarding Uly was something of a dress rehearsal for larger tasks, but hadn't decided if that was a step she wanted to take.

And didn't think that the Paramount and the First Commander would force her to do it if she balked, but she might be wrong.

For today, her job was dealing with the aliens. Keeping them under control. Making sure they understood that any threat would get them squished. Not merely executed, but made to look bad and get themselves severely embarrassed in the process.

And she had that entire female assault force that had originally gone to Rayzian with her, but she was in charge when bodyguarding, in spite of Aliisa Sekam and Tyyni Salo having more overall rank. They only commanded the ground detachment.

Inari was in charge here.

Auga and two friends came up to her belly button, more or less. And might weigh as much as she did, but none of them looked ready to wrestle with a Samuur. Or twenty.

She didn't bother with names. Primary. Aide One. Aide Two, that latter being a gopher sort of assistant to Aide One, rather than an advisor of any sort.

Normal, she'd come to understand from folks.

"Sir," Inari said as he exited the shuttle that had retrieved him from the station. "If you'll follow me?"

She didn't wait, but did glance back and modulated her strides to a much shorter species than even humans. All of her ladies did, cocooning the three Auga as they went forward to where Uly and Haydar Ramezani were waiting.

That meant Drew Roscoe and Yaqub Zobo would be in charge if trouble started. There were a great many less painful ways to die.

Introductions completed, Inari took up a spot just over the Auga commander's right shoulder, the species being right-handed by design. Her team was all a half-step closer than normally necessary, and everyone ready to go to unarmed combat at the slightest threat.

That would be six on one, if the three Auga started something. Wouldn't last long.

"I am the Corsac Fox," Uly began. "Ulysses Fortier. Warlord of the *Spinward Reaches*. Your foe, as long as the *Auga Empire* is unwilling to live in peace with the galaxy."

Hard words, but folks had whispered how angry Uly was at the whole situation, even as he had spent years maneuvering it to exactly this outcome.

But Inari also understood his opinion on bullies.

"What message for me?" the Auga asked. "Or the Empire? You asked to meet."

"I did," Uly said. "Conductor Székely has served his parole most honorably. He has refused my offer to send him home many times, expecting that he would be executed as a traitor for the crime of surrendering his vessel instead of destroying it and his entire crew. Until now, I had not appreciated how little you thought of the sailors under your command, but the Striker that fled specifically killed their crew after the officers attempted to flee."

"Attempted?" the Auga asked.

"They abandoned ship without terms, after I had warned them, so I killed them," Uly replied. "Their ship detonated a few moments later, so they were sacrificing their crew intentionally. I have had enough. The *Auga Empire* will behave, or I will make it do so."

"You?" the man sneered. "You are one strange alien, who was even a prisoner of the Empire briefly. Our intelligence suggests that you have hardly any naval forces to resist us, if and when we decide to chastise you for your impudence."

"I just destroyed your squadron and captured your station," Uly reminded him in a tone that sent shivers up Inari's spine. "At some point, I suppose I will have to start taking worlds away from the Empire, if that's what it takes to make my point. I have far more resources at my call than you understand, Commander."

"Oh?"

"The Auga see themselves as superior," Uly said. "That all other species are somehow lesser and must be conquered, then controlled for their own good. A great many species have rallied to my flag, because I promise them two things."

"Two?" The Auga's derision was making him reckless, but Inari was forward on her toes, ready to swipe or bash.

"Freedom of existence," Uly stated. "They can develop as they think appropriate, as long as they do not harm others. My nation welcomes all as equals and treats them thus under the law. Ononguli. Khet. Mazhin. Zuath. Ugotha. Emro. Everyone."

"And number two?" the man asked, falling into a trap even Inari saw coming.

"Freedom from fear, Commander," Uly laughed. "The Auga are only powerful when they can bully other, weaker, nations into submission. Or conquer them by sending out immense and implacable fleets of ships to take their worlds. We of the *Spinward Reaches* will be doing something about that, the next time you bother us. You have been warned."

Inari shivered. Calm. Collected. Polite, even, but she had gotten stories from Haldur and others about how mean humans could get when backed into a corner. Or threatened.

Or merely angry.

Uly was angry.

"And that's your message for the Emperor?" the Auga asked, but the smugness had bled out of his voice, leaving it closer to a petulance that even Inari could recognize. "To leave the barbarians alone to destroy themselves and all adult civilizations?"

"Yes," Uly said. "Or you could consider turning yourself into the sort of civilization where people demand that you let them join, because the benefits are so amazing. When was the last time someone asked to become a member of the Empire?"

Inari squeezed her lips together and worked at keeping ears and whiskers still, because that was the sort of body blow that philosophers lived for. Knock someone down—metaphorically, usually—and start stomping. Verbally.

Still, the three Auga all looked stunned into silence.

"I thought so," Uly nodded, then turned and looked up at her with a warm smile.

"Inari, could you see them back to the shuttle?" Uly said. "They'll be returning to Ajorn shortly, no doubt to brief the elders of the empire how this encounter went."

Knock them down, then start kicking. Mentally.

All three Auga staggered to their feet. Inari put on her best, most helpful, smile.

"This way, gentlebeings," she said politely, gesturing and walking.

Get them off Uly's ship and out of her fur. Send them home, infected with one of the most dangerous diseases ever discovered.

Doubt.

Inari saw herself as a warrior. Knew the others saw it as well.

She had, however, read their founding legends, and understood why the Isann saw Uly as a demigod made flesh.

Or, to quote that Ononguli pirate, "Uly got shit done."

She was looking forward to what came next.

PART TWO
VAUQUELIN

THIRTEEN

Sterling studied the latest cartographic updates on his screen as *Vauquelin* blasted through warp space.

He already had existing regional maps from the Auga, taken when the ship was captured. To that, he had added more detail than any conductor probably ever needed, but Sterling understood it to be almost a compulsion at this point. And he understood Haydar a lot better.

Better to have those answers than to need them.

Especially in the middle of nowhere, potentially being pursued by the entire Auga fleet. Or at least the one tasked with trying to outthink a Human attempting to evade them.

Flight. Careful to avoid any stars that might be inhabited. And steering clear of transit lanes where some patrol might accidentally cross their trail and alert the authorities.

Not that a Probe or even an Interceptor might threaten *Vauquelin*, but they'd run immediately, and shrink the circle the bad guys needed to scan to find them.

Sterling was pretty sure they were pissed over Stradosha. That, and him getting away afterwards.

Maikki Hudaibirdi had command at the moment, as Sterling was sitting here watching. Training her and the others to step up and handle things, to be prepared for that dreaded *Pop Quiz* he'd learned from his mentors to make people better officers.

How you trained was how you sailed.

Izaskun Zabala, a new Ugotha crew member who had heard Uly's call and answered, was piloting at the moment, with the Khet Jatau Kaita off duty.

Everyone was available quickly in an emergency. Sterling had arranged his crew to have their quarters closest to their duty station, regardless of status. He himself had the quarters of a common sailor, albeit not shared with anyone else, but only a tenth of the size of the space the previous conductor had been given.

Sterling had turned that space into a ship's library.

"Sir?" Zabala asked, causing him to stir because she was glancing over her shoulder instead of looking at Maikki.

"Yes?"

"We're coming up on a nexus point, Commander," Zabala noted. "You've noted three paths we could take from here, depending on circumstances."

Sterling paused and dialed the travel map in closer.

Oh. Yeah. He'd lost track. They were that close, weren't they?

"What's your suggestion, Zabala?" he asked, watching her and Maikki automatically nod to themselves.

Pop quiz. But if you were prepared for them, then surprises in combat were just another pop quiz to deal with.

"Option one takes us on the most direct path to Bastion, Commander," she replied. "I would presume that the Auga would concentrate most of their patrols along that road, since this is closest to five systems they control. Option two heads out lateral, on a reciprocal closer to a flight to Z'Gosza. Useful as a backup, but doesn't gain us ground and forces us to double back later to rendezvous with our next cargo ship. Option three takes us closer to the Auga core again, after we've gotten distance, but that might be worth evading patrols that have headed farther out."

Sterling nodded. All of his people were smart. That had been one of the first criteria for service aboard *Vauquelin*, given this mission. And then smarter to be sitting on his bridge, learning Starfare from him and everything Uly and the others had recorded.

"I'm detecting a *'yes, but...'* in your tones?" Sterling prompted.

Another flinch. Another pop quiz. A glance from Maikki that looked an awful lot like *'I told you so.'*

Sterling grinned.

Then his screen changed to a larger map again. And a line appeared. A most interesting line, studying the path. Not straight, but straighter than they had been running since dropping Dan and her second mission off.

"You'll note that the far end of this emerges not all that far from Krilic, sir," Zabala offered. "A week's hard sail lateral and we're in friendly space. Presumably safe, but we can't be sure until we talk to the Ononguli we find, as the Auga might have lashed out again."

"Skip one rendezvous?" he asked, checking her path.

"They'll have orders to abandon the mission and make their way home by alternate routes if we don't appear within a certain time, sir," she offered. "Assuming they're still safe with all hell breaking loose around them. We have supplies to make it that far with a solid margin, even bypassing."

And she'd done the math. The cartography. The planning. The logistics.

Sterling ignored everything and dug in hard, presuming that she had something here he'd missed. Easy to do when any turn was possible and you had no way to tell which was better.

At least ahead of time.

Somewhere behind him, Stradosha and neighbors would be a while recovering. After all, it was probably a unique occurrence that an Auga Heavy Striker raided an Auga world, even a pirate like him in disguise.

And it drew all eyes inward to Sector Three, while he was trying to get home and Dan was running to Sector Seventeen.

Chaos, injected into the body politic of the *Auga Empire*. Haydar had explained how much damage that sort of thing would do, though

Sterling understood that he wasn't worldly enough to really grasp the finer details. He was, after all, the son of a Gentleman, rather than the scion of nobility like most of the officers aboard *King Hewitt II* had been.

Or even Uly, when you considered who his dad was. Not that he'd ever mention it without being specifically asked.

"What's this point, Zabala?" he asked, highlighting an icon on the map.

"Patrol station, sir," she replied after a moment. "Easy enough to avoid if we pass under them."

"Agreed," Sterling said. "But what happens if we take it out as we go by?"

"Doesn't that defeat the purpose of hiding, sir?"

He grinned, but both women were facing away from him.

"Look at this," he drew a blue line on her map. "The most likely vector of flight afterwards, wouldn't you agree?"

"Or one of these two," she countered, surprising and delighting him by adding them in purple.

"Yes, and what happens if we go straight up for roughly three hundred light-years?" he inquired. "Then roll over and head home on the path you've outlined?"

Long pause as she did some math.

Everyone saw the galactic disk as a flat thing, because maps tended to render it that way. They forgot how thick it was, more than a thousand light-years top to bottom with most of the stars and mass in the central quarter.

"We speed up, Commander," she said. "And avoid almost all folks looking for us, assuming we get away clean in those first few hours."

"Assuming, yes," he replied. "Maikki, I need you to start thinking about how we can best evade everyone."

"Because we're going to go blow up a small patrol base in the middle of nowhere?" Maikki answered.

"We want them distracted, Lieutenant," he said. "This will do it. Uly and Dan will both appreciate our efforts to damage the Auga in the one place they are vulnerable."

That certain superiority that they were the most powerful, most dangerous civilization in the galaxy.

That they were safe, even.

Right up until the humans emerged from Imperial Sector Seventeen.

FOURTEEN

Maikki had come to appreciate that Sterling Huff was far more dangerous than even her cousin Eskil. That the Humans had a ragged, slashing edge to their biology that went beyond mere culture and made them lethal to anyone they encountered.

Sterling occasionally spoke aloud of some of the things *Danumash* or *Batyr* might do in various scenarios, just so she knew why nobody else wanted that many humans running around, beyond the few hundred Dan was recruiting initially.

The *Auga Empire* would have mass on them, but only until the strangers brought their technology up to modern levels from hardly better than Samuur at present.

Today, that deadliness was on her side. Maikki had plotted the most likely zones where trouble or interference might originate. Sterling had reviewed them, added a few tidbits from his own thought processes, and created an attack pattern.

Now, they just had to execute it.

"Pilot, call the countdown," Sterling ordered.

Oddly, Sterling had insisted on Izaskun Zabala being here on the bridge today, with Jatau Kaita down in the secondary bridge space backing her up, instead of the other way around, like normal.

But it had been her idea, somewhat.

"Twenty seconds to expected emergence," Izaskun replied loudly, crisp and sharp because this was her mission, at the end of the day.

In spite of Sterling modifying her original escape path.

"Gunner, everyone loaded?" he went on.

Andrii Dovzhenko. Ononguli. Semi-reformed pirate, at least by their standards she had come to appreciate.

"Locked in and ready, sir," Andrii replied. "We're zeroed on the forward turrets and starboard on the aft one, with an expectation of a port turn when we arrive for the first salvo."

"Sensors, I'll need a hard scan, maximum targeting data possible as soon as possible," Sterling continued. "Jam them after you're sure what we're facing, but I'd like there to be no surprises today."

"Aye, sir."

None. She had every sensor unit tuned and ready, with no idea who might be present, though the manual suggested a place like this as a base for a handful of Probes that patrolled the wider region, and three or four Ultra-Bombers for defense.

Ships that would have absolutely no chance against a Heavy Striker. Especially one coming out of warp hot and heavy and firing as soon as they located targets.

Victims, really.

There was little honor in it and she kept herself still.

Or thought she did.

"Yes, Maikki," Sterling chuckled. "Honor will be served."

Worse, the violent, dangerous, lethal humans understood that Samuur didn't want to act that way.

And would still adjust their own, Human behavior.

At least Sterling and Uly would, and that would be the standard everyone else was trained to.

"Emergence," Maikki called. "Scanning now."

"Order them to surrender, too," Sterling said.

She blinked, then typed that message, unwilling to trust that her voice wouldn't break while speaking, because even a cursory scan showed how badly outclassed those people were.

One Probe, docked. Three Ultra-Bombers, also docked. One small station that didn't displace as much volume as *Vauquelin*, to say nothing of mass.

Or firepower.

"Guns locked, standing by to fire," Andrii said. "Optimum range in twenty seconds."

"Coming around to broadside," Izaskun answered. "Stand by."

Maikki had her jammers running on every frequency save the one she'd sent orders to the station on.

"What's going on?" a Zuath woman replied from the station, full audio and visual.

Low-ranking officer by uniform. Utter shock from the way her headcrest was flopped over sideways.

"You are ordered to surrender," she repeated. "Failure to acknowledge and we will open fire."

"Is this some sort of a joke?"

A message scrolled across the bottom of her screen.

** Their shields are coming active. Gunner, fire EXACTLY one bolt at them. – Huff **

Because honor would be served.

Maikki heard the thump. Watched the woman on the screen panic and start ordering her defensive crews into action, but they were no more prepared for today than their commander was.

Worse, it was a Tuesday. Maikki had heard all the Ononguli stories about *Tuesdays.*

And those superstitions growing into terrible legend.

Today was not likely to alter that. Expand it to the Auga, perhaps, which might not be the worst outcome.

Sterling Huff could be a terrible foe when he chose.

The bolt impacted. Square. Heavy. Ruthless.

Shields went down over a wide facing.

"Station, you may surrender," Maikki repeated. "Or we can destroy you. Choose wisely."

Also ruthless, but honor had been served. Would be served. Any of the smaller vessels undocking at this moment would draw the next bolt. Or a bevy of them.

"What do you want?" the Zuath commander shrieked.

"We're destroying the station," Maikki replied. "If you choose to surrender, you may load all your crew aboard the Ultra-Bombers and Probe, then flee. If anyone turns back, we will destroy all of you. If anyone fires on us, we will leave no survivors in our wake."

Her whiskers shivered, but those were the words Sterling had impressed on her in planning this raid.

In three days, this system would be swarming with enemy forces, assuming there was any warship close enough to threaten *Vauquelin*. There might not be.

And even three days was enough of a head start.

"We surrender!"

"Excellent news, mistress," Maikki replied. "You will begin to abandon by detaching the first Ultra-Bomber when it is fully loaded, then fleeing, one at a time so there are no misunderstandings about your intentions, because you should have none about ours."

She muted the line and sucked a hard breath deep into her bowels.

All of the Auga fleet would know where to find them shortly.

Hopefully, it would be worth it.

PART THREE

THE FAR SIDE OF THE GALAXY

FIFTEEN

Dan Chastain had taken to having her planning meetings in a conference room large enough for the entire Congress and everyone else that needed to be involved.

Today, that included Rabiu Khadijan, Elias Ioannidis in his role as Historian to the Court of the Yarikh and resident elder, and Dionysia Stavrou as unofficial head of the Yarikh Young Hotheads.

"Have you decided which one to visit?" Dionysia asked as folks settled. "The first one?"

Dan shrugged.

Not a lot to pick from, save that she had traveled to all three worlds in her previous life. More years ago now than she liked to think about, but not much would have changed.

"Gorge is primarily a vacation world," she said in answer. "Known for that great rift valley that gave the world its name when settlers arrived. Fantastic views and hiking, but hardly anything bigger than light industry. Iethert is mostly farming and primary goods for export, both foodstuffs and minerals extracted from the ground because they are pretty shallow there. Masym has the most industry of the three, absorbing a lot of imports from Iethert and producing finished goods. It also has the largest population, but also is the most likely to have piracy and smuggling problems locally, as well as a risk of *Batyr* warships to be in harbor."

"Is that a bad thing?" Elias asked, leaning forward.

"They are less racist than *Danumash*, sure," Dan said. "But they'll have questions we can't answer."

Humanity ran across an entire spectrum of skin tones in ways most other species didn't. She'd heard suggestions that maybe they had been isolated from one another on different worlds for long enough to start splitting into new species, before everyone was jumbled back up again today and largely in a range generally medium brown like Uly. At least compared to the paler folks in *Danumash*.

Or the extremely dark brown skins like hers and her Yarikh cousins. She would have liked the opportunity to sail as far around the curve as Aurtan, but that would have added a month or more to the journey. And tempted her to not just recruit people her color, but to maybe grab a bunch of kinfolk for the adventure.

Next time.

Rabiu leaned in, his headcrest bobbing.

"So let's say some dumbass pirate jumps us," he offered. "Or a Human warship who doesn't know any better. We surrender immediately, right? Let them dock and attempt boarding? Are you telling me that any *Danumash* or *Batyr* ship is really going to be ready for your assault battalion, pouring backwards through their locks and shooting everything that moves?"

That stirred the crowd, but Dan wasn't surprised. She'd brought that force to help keep colonists from getting restive on the long voyage home. Someone would object when more of the truth came out, most likely.

The Congress could handle even a handful of fools, but one hundred and fifty killers could take just about anything smaller than a Heavy Striker. Except that these would be Human ships, so Forward Cruisers. More likely Destroyers or Corvettes.

Terms that the wider galaxy had never heard.

"Any *Danumash* vessel that came along, I'd happily capture and steal," Dan replied. "*Batyr* is a bit more of a problem, if only because technically I'm Unlawful Absent, along with several of my crewmates also aboard, and a vast collection of prisoners we were supposed to capture aboard *King Hewitt II*."

"So drop those sailors on one of the three colony worlds and let them find their own way home," Dionysia offered. "If they only ever see Humans, because the combat troops keep their helmets on, they won't know what they are facing. Let them think there's some new pirate base in the region. That keeps them bottled up in these backwoods and swamps, right?"

Young Hotheads, indeed. Dionysia looked seventeen, but was only a little younger than Dan. The Yarikh could live for more than three centuries, so they had programmed their genetics to hit young adulthood then slow their aging extremely.

Still a different species, as far as that went, but more compatible with humans, when you got down to it. But most of the bipeds were able to find ways to enjoy themselves.

It was for all the men save Uly that she wanted to do this. To give them the opportunity to have families, biological instead of adopted because Anari and Sterling would adopt at some point.

Or something. Wasn't Dan's problem to solve.

"We hope it keeps the humans safely bottled up," Suka Kuri replied. "At some point, it is likely that someone comes looking, if only because Uly and Dan have mentioned to others the far reaches of Sector Seventeen. One only has to find a way to sail that distance safely to reach them."

"And Uly still thinks that's a bad idea?" Elias asked.

"We are barbarian hordes, as far as the Auga are concerned," Zamira noted with a wry grin, her Isann face among the closest to Dan's in bone structure, though silvery gray. "The humans are, as Dan and Uly will remind anyone who asks, a veritable plague. A wildfire racing down a hillside in dry grass, destroying everything in front of it. Can you outrun it to the river?"

Dan kept her chuckles inside. The Yarikh had, until Anari and Kit had arrived to jar them out of their complacency, lived lives of artistic pursuits comparable to Suka Kuri's other student, Hiko Seiichai, Moss School Adept who might become an Exemplar himself, one of these decades.

Then the barbarians had pounded on the front door. Kit had used the imagery of poor cousins showing up out of the blue with friends, hoping for dinner. It wasn't entirely wrong.

Elias looked like he'd sucked a lemon by mistake. Dionysia nodded grimly.

"How long will it take to recruit several hundred young, hungry, crazy humans?" Dionysia asked.

Biologically, similar. Culturally, a gorge as wide as Gorge between them.

Rabiu chuckled. All eyes rotated to watch the friendly fishman.

"He's not here, but I believe it is my duty to speak up for him," Rabiu grinned at everyone.

"Who?" Suka Kuri asked, mock-glaring at the man while both smiled.

"Ethir," Rabiu said. "After all, most of the Legal Department needed to stay home to advise Uly, leaving you with one middle-aged accountant who ran off to become a pirate."

More laughter. She remembered the pudgeball he'd been when they first arrived at Z'Gosza.

"And your suggestion?"

"Give them that old time religion," Rabiu replied. "Full-on tent revival stuff. Offer them a new world, way off in the darkness where *Danumash* and *Batyr* will never find them again. Never bother them. Let them live lives of hippie fulfillment working the soil and toiling in factories without the old masters. I'm pretty sure that the lack of a legal aristocracy will draw *Danumash* folks like moths to flames. Dunno what entices *Batyr* citizens."

Dan leaned back and listened as the group discussed it, split pretty evenly down the middle on the idea. After a few minutes, everyone turned to her.

This was her mission, in the end. Her way of getting most of the way home and growing the colony at Bastion by making sure that future generations included humans.

"There is risk," she reminded them. "Most of the species aboard this ship are unknown in Human space. If we get taken, we're prisoners.

Possibly slaves, because those *Seven Kingdoms* punks will want to know more."

"I'll personally destroy the nav computer, Dan," Rabiu sobered. "I've got people sharp enough that they could sail us home from memory if it came to that. Or I can navigate us around the curve to Khet regions easy enough. It would take longer, especially if we're stealing a ship to do it afterwards, but it can be done."

She nodded, accepting their intense commitment that they had come this far, and intended to see it through.

As she would.

SIXTEEN

Suka Kuri had a space where she could train, both herself and the various Emro aboard. Everything cleared out and scaled up to her needs, when usually she had to adapt to smaller people spaces.

Dan entered while she was meditating, having just completed a full training sequence of all the various katas and systems that Dan had assembled over the last several years.

It made for a most interesting thing, though Dan hadn't begun to synthesize it down into a singular school. Might not.

Suka Kuri would have to prod her a bit harder, one of these days, as Dan was certainly an Adept of Sabre, likely on her way to becoming an Exemplar herself, though Suka Kuri kept that tidbit to herself.

Didn't want to frighten the woman, after all.

Still, Dan was here. Suka Kuri smiled and unfolded herself, rising from the floor and moving to a comfortable table where bar stools had been installed for smaller people. There was hot water in an insulated pot, so she went ahead and began making tea.

No words had yet been exchanged. That wasn't entirely uncommon when dealing with Dan, who enjoyed solitude in ways that many people did not.

It steeped. They waited. Watched.

Smelled.

Good tea started by enticing the olfactory senses, long before you got to taste it. Today was caramel and vanilla, with brown sugar notes underneath that slowly trailed off to a faint citrusy taste clear at the back end.

Exactly what the seriousness on Dan's face probably needed.

Suka Kuri poured. They toasted. Sipped.

Waited.

"It can't be that bad, can it?" Suka Kuri finally asked.

Dan shrugged.

"Rabiu's suggestion on the potential for piracy," Dan replied. "Been thinking about the odds and he's probably right."

"Wondering if we should have brought more of a warship?"

"We'd have never been able to disguise something like that," Dan shook her head. "Especially not as big as it would have had to be, to have the extra space for passengers we need. Wondering if we can justify offering the same deal to idiot pirates, if we do end up capturing them."

"Would they later try to defect?" Suka Kuri pressed.

"Nowhere for them to go," Dan laughed cruelly. "Uly's allies on all four sides, plus the *Auga Empire* beyond that. Some might decide that they could make money by selling the Auga information or something, but it would be from inside a prison cell. If the Auga would listen."

"The second time they had Human prisoners, they will probably pay more and better attention, Dan," Suka Kuri replied. "You folks that joined us on *Iron Wasp* might have just been random strangers, washed up on a distant shore after a terrible storm. More would suggest that they were closer than they are. Perhaps close enough to send an exploration fleet."

"Which would immediately run into *Danumash* and likely overwhelm them, at least initially," Dan nodded. "After which, all the humans are more likely than not to suddenly make common cause and decide to take on the Empire."

"They cannot win," Suka Kuri noted.

"Won't stop 'em," Dan shrugged. "We're not the most sane species out there. Even after Auga captures all those Human worlds, they'd have a hell of a time controlling them. Worse if they decide to impress humans into the Empire, not understanding that they'd taken the wolf into their house."

Suka Kuri shuddered. She understood how unique and special Uly and Dan were. One only really had to compare them to Emil and Gennady, who were supposedly more like common Humans, to understand how far Uly could go. And how badly things might have turned out, had Uly decided that he needed several million humans to help defeat the *Auga Empire*.

Or several billion.

"Then you make any pirates you find the same offer," Suka Kuri decided. "A fresh start, far from any warrants or bounties, on the exchange that they behave. You can always imprison the worst later if they refuse to change their ways. From what I know, however, you are quite likely to find any number of humans who look on such an adventure with the same excitement as the Isann."

"*Sailing Into Darkness*," Dan nodded. "You are not wrong there. And none of these people are likely to be able to return home later."

"As long as you make that clear up front, the onus is upon them to understand that you were not lying," Suka Kuri reminded her. "They can have a fresh start at a new life."

"If they are willing to pay the price of losing the old one forever," Dan completed the phrase.

"It seems to have worked rather well for you and Uly," Suka Kuri grinned. "And Sterling, Solomon, and several others, not the least all the Mazhin you've met and seduced with your anarchistic ways."

Dan did laugh at that. Uly was practically Mazhin, with his ability to communicate with them. Just as the Isann saw him as a demigod sailor and the Ononguli had married into his clan for his might.

And all the others.

"Now we just have to go do the thing," Dan nodded.

"You'll do fine," Suka Kuri reminded her. "And I'd like the chance to walk on a Human colony, at least once."

"I'll see what I can do."

After all, how much potential for greatness had been hidden away from the rest of the galaxy, deep in Sector Seventeen?

SEVENTEEN

Technically, Rabiu was the conductor of the *Free Trader Polat*, but only on paper. And then, only when operating in the northwest corner of the map, though he'd really only recently expanded his horizons that far.

Yalwa Emeghara was First Officer. And a far better pilot who had managed to teach Rabiu what commands to give and when for the ship to fly correctly. That had been useful when there had only been a dozen of them as crew.

Now Dan was here, along with her Congress and her assault battalion. Yalwa still made him give the orders, but was fine listening to her give them as well.

All part of that much deeper cover that would see Yalwa promoted to something big and important later, assuming they managed to pull off the swindle of the century.

Bridge would have been crowded, but they'd selected a ship with extra space up here specifically because this mission was going to be big and long and painful and whatever else.

Lots of bodies. Rabiu had put Dionysia Stavrou in the command station, mostly as a statement. She wasn't the youngest person aboard, but would outlive everyone else here presumably. Best she get used to making her own decisions when this entire generation was gone.

"All those stars?" Dionysia was asking Dan. "Human?"

"Not all of them, but that cone, yes," Dan replied. "We may never know which of us was the lost tribe, but at least there are a great many new cousins to meet out there, when the Yarikh might later introduce themselves."

Rabiu did know a few secrets that were the sorts you took to your grave, but that was Uly using him as an insurance policy. Potentially, all the humans and Yarikh had originated on the far side of Sector Forty-One, as far beyond Rabiu's old home in Fifteen at Z'Gosza as the Auga capital at Ajorn, just in the other direction where it would take someone nearly a year to sail over to investigate.

Presumably, the humans had all come from that direction, but Uly suspected that to be thirty or fifty thousand years in the past. Some ludicrous number of lifetimes.

Forever ago.

Dionysia looked up at him and Rabiu smiled indulgently, like a favorite uncle.

"And you want me to take us in?" she asked.

"They will be expecting a Human face," he reminded her simply.

There were other options, but all of those would make people nervous. Better if someone they recognized arrived. At least by species, as they might not like deeply brown folks, as he was given to understand.

Fortunately, they had a lot of firepower handy if things got out of hand.

"Yalwa, how soon?" Dionysia asked the man who actually knew these things.

"Four minutes to the outermost marker we should be expecting, based on Commander Chastain."

Rabiu snorted. He doubted that Masym followed standard Auga imperial practices, but anything was possible.

Dan had been an enlisted sailor on boarding teams when she'd come through here, and Uly had only been aboard that particular vessel for a matter of weeks, apparently.

Still, act like a professional. Or fake it appropriately.

Everyone settled in and waited as the clock ticked down.

Free Trader Polat emerged into Human space and Rabiu drew a breath of wonder. They had made it to the far ends of the galaxy, at least as far as his old chums at work would have seen it.

And they would not have been entirely wrong.

"Anything?" Dionysia asked.

"Passive signals inbound and being processed," Yalwa replied. "Stand by."

Rabiu held himself still and waited with the rest.

"Three tiny stations in orbit," he finally said. "Not a lot of orbital traffic and all of it small. Smells civilian."

"Human colony in the middle of nowhere," Dan spoke up. "That's actually busier than the last time I visited. And that largest station is new from ten years ago. Used to only be the smaller two."

Rabiu had heard the words, but not really internalized them until now. Humans really were hardly any more advanced than the Isann or the Samuur, unlike the Khet or Ononguli.

It was their potential for violence that made them dangerous. Uly and Dan were just a whole bunch more civilized.

But they were here.

"Drop us in closer," Dionysia ordered, which she could do, since she was seated in the big chair.

"Coming up."

Blink. Blink back. Stars, and the planet much larger.

"We're being hailed," Yalwa announced.

EIGHTEEN

Dan stepped up and looked around the group, making sure everyone was out of the shot except her and Dionysia.

"I've got this," she announced simply.

Nobody else had ever been here except her, Emil, and Gennady, so nobody else would have any clue how things operated. And she had only the haziest ideas, having been a punk who was more excited about shore leave, bars, and sunsets than politics and the like.

"Masym Control, this is *Free Trader Polat*, out of Bastion, looking for docking instructions," she said as the line came live.

Dan hit transmit and waited to see what kind of response that generated. Word would get around, but Bastion would only be suggestive of a concept. It didn't tell anyone where to find it.

And if pressed, she'd do the same thing that Kit had done to the Yarikh on Day One, pointing in a particular direction.

Save that she would leave out the part about how it was eleven thousand light-years away. They didn't need to know that until later.

If ever.

Then a Human face appeared on the screen and she had to catch her breath. It had been a great many years since she had seen a strange human, her distant Yarikh cousins notwithstanding.

"Bastion?" the man asked. "I don't have that registry anywhere in my records."

"We are a long ways from home, Masym," Dan replied. "Long sail to make it this far."

"Hauling cargo, *Polat*?" he asked.

"Negative," Dan shook her head. "Hoping we can recruit some folks to return home with us and help expand bloodlines and build out our colony. Growing, but we'd like it to get bigger now, rather than in a century, ya know?"

"Understood, *Polat*," he agreed. "Your timing is pretty good on that measure, as we've got a solid population boom going on. What currency will you be using?"

Dan took a deep breath and willed all those dark gods that had smiled on Lukyan to smile on her today. Sterling had found the data, copied originally from *King Hewitt II* to *Iron Wasp*, then retained when that ship turned into *Corsac Fox* and later *Batyr*.

A set of numbers. Special ones, referencing a particular account that the *Danumash Navy* had created at Masym, just as they had similar ones at Gorge and Iethert, among a few others.

Because *Danumash* believed in keeping slaves. Usually aliens they had captured for one reason or another. Or Mazhin ships that had strayed too far from their usual haunts while hunting business.

This account was for secret operational funds when a ship called that didn't want to identify itself as a *Danumash* fleet element.

She read the sequence to the man without any inflection or emotion, even as everyone around here was vibrating with energy.

"Confirming that, *Polat*," he said, reading them back to her with two digits flipped that she corrected.

"Understood, *Polat*," the man said. "We've cleared you at this end for dock seventeen, level three. How many crew will be debarking at present?"

"Only a handful, while we study the lay of the land, Control," Dan said. "I'm the only crew member that's ever been here, so the others aren't entirely sure what to expect. Nor was I after this long."

"Well, you're welcome, *Polat*," he offered. "And we'll have a deeper chat about needs when you dock."

Of that, Dan had no doubts whatsoever. The question was, how would they react to an undercover *Danumash* operation arriving? Even if she was lying?

Dan's best hope was that the *Seven Crowns* got blamed for everything that happened from here. Served them right.

And if shit went sideways, she had a plethora of killers immediately at hand to deal with it.

That might not be an accident.

NINETEEN

Dionysia had spent the entire journey absorbing everything Dan and Solomon could teach her about being human.

At least as they saw it. It was rude to think of them as mayflies, but perhaps not entirely wrong, as they would all be dead in less than a century.

She had several ahead of her, and Rabiu the Deadly Khet Accountant™ had quietly reminded her that she would likely outlive everyone else in this solar system.

Today, she presented as Second Officer, with Solomon Wyndham pretending to be First. Yalwa and Rabiu were handling the actual duties, but Solomon looked like the locals and could talk to them on the comm. That left her and Elias free to accompany Dan to the station. And eventually the ground.

Suka Kuri had expressed her jealousy about not being able to do those things. At least for now. Later, there might be a chance, but things were far too amorphous at present.

Free Trader Polat was docked finally. The ship had not been built with Human docking mechanisms, but had been modified later, based on the Human Engineer Kolya Roux's memories that were probably close enough. What a rough colony in the darkness might do if they had to repair something themselves, rather than relying on imported parts.

Dionysia found herself with a better appreciation of her cousins and all their friends, who lived in a universe where chaos was an everyday thing, rather than a black swan event that disrupted things.

The Scholar herself, Nomiki Marinos, had warned Dionysia to pay attention to how the galaxy was likely to change, now that the Yarikh had emerged from their den and their slumbers, but Dionysia hadn't appreciated that imagery until she was looking out a porthole at a Human station that struck her for its primitiveness, when Dan had mentioned that it was newly constructed and better than they'd had before.

Frightening, really. But they were cousins and meant well, as long as you socialized them early and kept those lessons reinforced.

And Kit Simonson really had been the perfect choice for an ambassador, even when Anari had held the title. Kit's nerdy enthusiasm for life had won him a lot of friends he didn't even know about.

And now, she was about to board a Human orbital platform.

Dan was armed. Dionysia was, as well. Emil and Gennady were here, ready for mayhem. Blair Mitchell rounded out the team about to face the barbarians.

Solomon would remain behind, as would Kolya for now, available when someone needed to talk to the ship and were expecting humans.

"You'll do fine," Dan muttered, glancing over.

Dan was tall. Dionysia was a little smaller, both in height and scale, but that was Dan's size. Most Human women, she knew, would be as much smaller than her, while the men would generally fall in between them. More like Uly, though much heavier.

Less than Solomon. He was the wall holding everything, as he had seen it. Dionysia did not doubt that Human for a minute. Truly impressive in what he had accomplished, both physically as well as mentally. And emotionally mature, especially for his age.

They all were.

Then the hatch opened on the far side of the airlock and Dionysia saw her first new humans.

TWENTY

Dan walked first. She knew the system. And was the only officer, as she saw it. Dionysia was good, but she was an actress playing a role. As were most of them.

Dan was in charge. Of the ship. Of the mission. Of the Congress.

This was her charge to expand Bastion and make certain that there were humans living there a century from now. Helping turn back the Auga, assuming Uly didn't succeed in his lifetime.

Station Control stood there. He had a name, but she thought of the man by his title.

Middle-aged Human male. Beard and hair black with hints of white along the edges. Fairly pale skin more like *Danumash*, at the other end of things from her.

She watched him absorb things. Two black women in charge of three white men, as his kind might judge things. Dan had a lot of experience with the natural racism that even *Batyr* hadn't gotten entirely over, though nowhere nearly as bad as that punk Thorley Eldridge had embodied.

"Welcome," Control nodded in a perfunctory kind of tone.

Professional, but not really meaning it. Dan wasn't surprised. Nor offended.

"Been a lot of years," Dan reminded him.

And another ship. In a different uniform, since she had her and her people wearing the medium blue uniforms Omid had designed, baggier than *Batyr* did it and trimmed in scarlet and mint. It made her people look good.

And less like pirates out for a jaunt.

Blair stepped up first, smiling as he usually did. And even wearing a uniform for once. Handed the man a clipboard thick with papers.

"Medical records for the five of us," Blair informed the man. "I'm a trained nurse, so these should be adequate for your medical teams to handle."

They were leaving out the part where Blair was the only one from *Danumash*, with her, Emil, and Gennady from *Batyr*. And Dionysia much farther from home.

"That answers one set of questions," Control said.

"And we're prepared to answer more," Dan replied. "Here or on the station. Which would work better?"

Everyone was armed. Control was by himself, but it was two packs of dogs sniffing at one another.

"Let's go into my office," he said, studying all of them.

At least Solomon wasn't here, where the young man's immense size and bulk would likely cause other issues.

Dan followed him deeper into the station, past folks who were surprised by her skin tone, from the looks of disdain that immediately followed.

But this planet was closer to *Danumash* than *Batyr*, so she'd been expecting it.

And that racism would filter out a lot of folks she didn't want, anyway. A pair of black women in charge? You sure you want to go live on that world?

Yeah, useful filter.

Control left Emil and Gennady in the hallway, since it was obvious what their role was. Blair joined her and Dionysia in the office, three of them on this side of the immense desk and Control over yonder.

"I've checked into the account number you transmitted," he said simply, obviously wanting her to fill in more details.

"Was there a problem with it?" she countered, reminding herself and everyone else by her tone that this was a secret naval mission that didn't need to be broadcast to everyone.

"It's a bit out of the ordinary," he replied. "And hasn't been used in many years."

"As I said, we're a long ways from here, and haven't had a lot of communications with folks closer to civilization in a decade."

Had she and Uly really been gone that long? It boggled the mind.

But they had a lot of road ahead of them yet.

"And your recruitment intentions?" he pursued doggedly.

"We'd like to range possibly as high as about sixty/forty female," Dan said. "Currently, we have an imbalance the other direction that we'd like to offset. Colony is small, so an extra four hundred folks would greatly help with bloodlines, especially as nobody originated from this vicinity, so they won't be remotely closely related to the folks they'll meet over there."

"And where is Bastion, anyway?" His eyes glittered.

"West and a little coreward," she lied easily, expecting this question. "Little under four hundred light years around the curve, in a space where there are only a few stars and not many inhabitable planets."

Sterling had handed her excellent maps of the region, like all the others.

"How'd you end up out there?" he asked, a touch of confusion evident now.

"Honestly, we had some troubles with pirates," Dan shrugged. "Got away from them and kinda kept going. Set down roots and started building our new colony, then got to a point where we figured that we liked the place and wanted more folks."

Most of what she said from here in would be lies trimmed with bits of truth. Uly specifically didn't want humans emerging from Sector Seventeen randomly. Not if they might run into the Auga first by going coreward.

The Khet would be a better solution, but that would be the long run clockwise out to Sector Fifteen, where Sixteen in between was largely mapped astronomically, but hadn't ever been subject to deeper surveys by anyone, at least according to Sterling's records, which would be as good as anyone's.

Rather like Seventeen.

Control studied her. Turned to Dionysia, who had remained largely silent up until now and might pass as Dan's younger sister, just learning the business. Or daughter, had Dan started extremely young, which you sometimes did on new colony worlds.

He finally focused on Blair.

"Bloodlines?"

"Currently, roughly an even mix between ethnotypes normally found in *Batyr* versus *Danumash*," Blair said. "Boss was actually born on Gralbo of all places, but left for a lot of reasons. She's from Aurtan. I was born on Husni in the *Seven Crowns*. Whole colony is like that."

Dan smiled inwardly, while remaining a dour and professional face. Blair was leaving out lots of details, but nothing he'd said was a lie, which made everyone feel better.

"And you want to only slightly imbalance female?" Control pressed.

"A few too many men right now," Blair nodded. "Need more women. Not enough to make harems, but enough to give the guys hope of kids, ya know? Less likely to get into trouble if they can turn into family men."

Not that those men were a problem. At least not that way. Most had gotten over their specism to see Ononguli and Isann women as women, rather than aliens. Khet and Zuath might take a bit more work, but there had been no discipline problems that way.

Helped, when everyone understood that Dan and her Congress of Wives would be in charge of investigating any complaints. Kept the boys focused.

And Kit had worked out some sort of relationship with Mel, though Dan hadn't asked. Nor had she dragged those two along on this mission, the Yarikh Engineer doing better work at Bastion and Saari to make those places safer from the Auga.

"You haven't been back in a decade?" Control turned to ask her.

Dan smiled.

"You hadn't even started this station, last time I got shore leave," she replied, hinting that she'd been on a warship at the time from her vocabulary.

She didn't specify which ship. Nor would she, unless really pressed. Aurtan already told him *Batyr*. That was enough.

His eyes did get cagey.

"You running a pirate base?" he asked, point blank.

Dan couldn't help but laugh.

"Oh?" Control seemed surprised.

"My husband, the governor, hates pirates more than just about anything in the galaxy," she said. "If he had the power, he'd hunt them all down and blast them out of existence without mercy. Smugglers generally get a pass, but those pirates that attacked us pissed him off to the point that he's got a bounty for the top five leaders of that ship. Dead. Not alive. Just their heads on stakes will satisfy him. We're hoping to build something new out there. Something neither *Seven Crowns* nor *Institutional Republic*. Need bodies. Would prefer dreamers."

"Dreamers?" Control was lost now, but that was fine.

"Run away from all this forever and build a new home," Dan nodded, gesturing to the room about her.

Control processed all that, including the tidbit that her unnamed husband was the governor of this unknown world. Which he was. *Warlord of the Spinward Reaches* would just frighten folks around here, if they knew that title.

Best to keep it simple.

"Any aliens out there?" Control asked after a long moment in thought.

"Couple," Dan allowed. "We've traded with some of them. Run others off. Part of the reason we want more humans, so they don't overwhelm us eventually. Generally friendly enough if you're armed and dangerous."

That got a blink. A look at Blair—the medical expert—who nodded once soberly.

Yeah, buddy, there are aliens out there. A whole shitload lot of them. Trillions of beings, once you get beyond the desert that divides Sector Seventeen into two pieces and has protected the Human realms for this long.

Dionysia leaned forward at that moment and drew the man's eye.

"We need them young and hungry," she said simply. "Ready to work a lifetime at building a new paradise light-centuries beyond anything you folks have. Not *Danumash* and not *Batyr*. Better."

"Better?" Control asked, locked on her and seeing her as a teenager, instead of a young-looking adult.

"No gods, no kings," she said, surprising Dan because that was much more of a *Batyr* way to frame things.

Danumash had one god that ruled a whole raft of angels and saints. And *Seven Crowns* for seven kings by blood.

Control studied Dan with new eyes. Surprised eyes. Curious eyes.

"What's out there?" he asked.

"You have no idea," Dan smiled.

TWENTY-ONE

Solomon didn't really understand starships. His job was Security. Third behind Dan, then her Congress.

Today, he was a Human face when folks called, because nobody was ready for a Khet or an Ononguli to answer the comm.

That put a smile on his face.

"*Free Trader Polat*," he answered, bringing the line live.

Yalwa had put him in an office so Solomon didn't have to worry about non-humans accidentally wandering into view of the camera.

"Are you really a colony ship?" an older woman asked as soon as the screen came up.

Older? Middle-aged, maybe. Older than him.

Solomon nodded to her. Dan hadn't even made it back from her interview with the authorities, so someone had leaked. Or talked. Or looked at the hull and done some basic naval architecture.

"Aren't you a little young to be a ship's First Officer?" she asked, sounding rather a lot like his mother, the Duchess.

Solomon wondered if a beard would make him look more mature.

"I was an officer at fourteen, mistress," he replied, studying her.

Face had the same age marks as his mother, so he put her between forty-five and fifty-five. Solomon was twenty-two, and a fourth son who wasn't useful for anything except naval service, scholarship, or marital alliances.

He'd chosen ships. Sterling could have been a professor by now.

She studied him closer, perhaps seeing past whatever image she'd conjured up.

"When will you be departing?" she asked bluntly.

"When we have a full load," Solomon told her, wondering what desperation might drive such a woman.

But he'd been born the son of a duke. Never to want for anything except something to give his life meaning.

Lucky for him that he'd met Dan, and then Suka Kuri.

More than enough purpose there.

"How soon?" she demanded.

"You'll need to talk to Dan Chastain," he said. "She's in charge. We'll have an office at some point and you can register. If too many people show interest, there might be a lottery for slots. Past that, I don't know."

Which was not a lie. Middle-aged women would probably be welcomed. Bearing children was probably unlikely, but such folk would provide a stabilizing force on the younger colonists. And could help in the child-rearing.

Not that he understood such things, but Solomon had been listening in Dan's planning meetings with Uly.

And, maybe, he might meet a future breeding partner. He didn't want to go so far as to say *wife*, finally grasping that physical shape had little to do with capability. Or attraction. And Dan and Uly were going to establish a different way of thinking about such things. The Congress, for instance.

Solomon had no idea if it might work, but he knew better than to bet against those two when they set their mind.

The woman was studying him in ways that made Solomon a little uncomfortable. Less like his mother and more like an older woman on a street. Hungry looking.

"What about you?" she asked, voice softening. "Are you single?"

Solomon wasn't sure he wanted to answer that question. Felt like a trap.

Still, he understood that lies or prevarications were inappropriate.

"Yes, mistress," he answered.

"How old are you?"

"Twenty-two Standard, mistress," Solomon offered.

She studied him some more. Hungry eyes.

"We'll talk more," she said, then cut the line, leaving him almost gasping for air.

He understood that life on the outer worlds could be hard. Not enough people. Law sometimes either too heavy or too light.

And most people lacked the financial security to go somewhere else easily. Solomon had never really had those sorts of problems in his life, save for the day that a wavebolt killed the bridge on *King Hewitt II* and took all of the officers and Sailing Mistress Hylda with it.

Uly and Dan had altered the course of his destiny. And that of the rest of the survivors.

And, if he wanted to be honest, probably the galaxy as well.

Solomon wondered what a trip to Masym was going to do to change it yet again.

TWENTY-TWO

Dan had established an office with Station Control's help.

And it was on the station. Easier to control things, once *Polat* was shifted around to a long-term docking station hardly ever used. Longer walk to get anywhere, but they were out of the way.

Mostly.

And all of this was new, so she had taken her team—her five-person Human team—and gone on long walks. Everything around here still retained the shininess of new construction, rather than the oil stains and rust of the older stations.

Masym was a busy world, and it didn't spend a lot of time and effort on making things pretty. Too occupied banging out new things from various factories.

Station Three was alive with smells of trade and bodies from many worlds. Most of the station was dedicated to warehousing goods coming up from the ground or in from the stars. Every hue and size of humans running around, but few others. Occasional Zuath in the corridors, of a subspecies she didn't know. A few Ugotha. Both species she had known from before.

Rumors and gossip had led her to a different deck. An arcade dedicated to trade offices, like the bigger, brighter one up a level, but this place gave off hints and suggestions of a rougher lawlessness.

Not bad. Just darker in here, like the lights were set at a lower level. And the people she could see in her immediate vicinity had an implied seediness that was more like what she'd been expecting from Masym.

Dan wondered how many of them were criminal fronts. Scouts for pirates. Or fences disposing of pirated goods.

Then she saw a man standing behind a counter in something of a forgotten corner and immediately started that way with a smile on her face.

Emro. She wouldn't have known that before. Big and green. Not as tough or dangerous as Anari or Yanouk, but he had the size and mass of his species. And locked eyes with her as she got closer.

Dan watched a hand twitch like he wanted to be grabbing a pistol. All of them were armed, but only with stun weapons, Control insisting that they didn't need anything and negotiating to land in the middle when she demanded something more than nothing.

Dan smiled up at the Emro when she got close.

"You are not from around here," she began as she came to rest.

His eyes scowled, but his mouth remained in a polite grin. Brittle and frosty.

"You have no idea," he replied darkly.

"Actually, I probably do," Dan countered. "I have a dear friend who is an Exemplar of the Moss School."

That rocked him back on his heels, which was an impressive feat, as big as he was.

"And two Adepts learning both Moss and Sabre simultaneously," Dan continued, just to watch his eyes cross in confusion.

"But you're Human..." he managed.

"Also not from around here," she nodded, watching him grow cagey.

"How is that possible?" he asked, voice hardly a whisper now.

"There is life beyond Seventeen," she said carefully, watching acknowledgment in his eyes.

And surprise. Maybe a touch of fear, as well.

"Dan Chastain," she introduced herself. "Captain of the *Free Trader Polat*."

"The new colony ship," he muttered, confirming to Dan how fast and how far the rumor mill had carried things in just two days.

"The same," she replied. "How did an Emro come to Masym?"

"That might require several beers to explain, madam," he said sourly.

"I am happy to take you out to dinner to listen."

He paused. Considered. Nodded.

"Odan Sume," he introduced himself. "Emro, as you know. Far from home, as you guessed. Intrigued at your friends. And if you are that far from home, you should probably meet Madam Abdolahean."

He pointed one enormous finger and Dan rotated to look. And gasped herself, because the person indicated was Mazhin. She wondered if that woman knew any of her friends that had been rescued aboard *King Hewitt II*, the ten having originally come from six different ships.

"I was not aware of any Mazhin in the region," Dan said, turning back and surprising Sume again. "I also have friends there that she would probably like to meet. You should, however, consider keeping certain things quiet for now."

"Are you spies or pirates?" he asked bluntly.

But then, knowing an Emro and a Mazhin on sight put her in rare—and dangerous—company.

"Worse, Sume," she grinned. "But there are limits to what I can tell you at present."

"Blood oaths unto death, like humans tend to do it?" he teased.

Dan turned deadly serious and watched him blink.

"Yes."

He gulped. Studied these five strange Humans. Nodded.

"Normally, I close in about four station hours," he offered carefully.

"Happy to treat you to dinner, sir," she softened. "And catch up on news from home."

He would know many things Dan would find useful. And neither of them were from around here.

"I look forward to it."

Dan bowed her head and gathered her folks up to cross the arcade.

What was a Mazhin woman doing in a place like Masym?

TWENTY-THREE

Dan approached the Mazhin woman like she would any of the tribe back on her ship. Or at home at Bastion. Walked right up on the other side of a table displaying fabric and related wares and stopped, smiling at the woman in complete silence.

The four with her did as well, though Dionysia was uncomfortable. Still getting used to Humans.

Madam Abdolahean watched her with eyes as well as tentacles, both ranging up and down as Dan stood there, waiting.

And waiting.

"Oh!" Madam Abdolahean finally said. "How?"

Dan wondered if the woman had smelled Nasrin on her skin. Or recognized a Mazhin hand in designing and sewing these uniforms. Because tailoring was one of Omid's love languages, once you got her relaxed.

"Friends," Dan replied. "Mister Sume suggested we should talk, possibly having friends in common."

How and which friends was left to the imagination, though Mazhin might be able to read all manner of things from their scents.

Humans hardly ever appreciated how many things Mazhin tentacles could detect.

"Your friend?" Abdolahean asked.

"Currently aboard my ship," Dan nodded. "And assuredly quite interested in meeting you, because she belonged to a group of ten that had all been captured off of six different clanships. My Human husband *Speaks* for their Clan now."

Dan grinned when the woman's tentacles wanted to knot themselves up. Took a fairly good surprise to do that to a Mazhin, but she'd had practice. On one of her best friends in the galaxy.

Abdolahean mouthed the work *Speaks?* without sound. Dan smiled.

A shiver ran up Abdolahean's body, then settled. Dan wondered if the woman represented a clanship, or had been captured by *Danumash* at some point and escaped somehow.

Not many other possible explanations for being here. Especially here.

"I would appreciate meeting her," Abdolahean replied. "Catching up with the news. I have been separated from my kind for a long time."

Dan assumed that.

She decided to gamble.

"How tied are you to Masym?" she asked. "And would closing your kiosk now and traveling to my ship to meet Nasrin be acceptable?"

Abdolahean was already shoveling things into a trunk on her side of the space, so Dan turned pointedly back to the Emro gentleman and nodded to him, one he matched.

She was here recruiting, after all. Might as well rescue a few folks while she was at it.

How many others had been washed up on these shores with no easy way to get home?

TWENTY-FOUR

Nasrin smelled her as soon as the airlock opened. There were a few other Mazhin on *Polat*. Part of Dan's assault battalion.

By dint of a lot of things, Nasrin *Spoke* for them. But that was part of her job, and came with membership in the Congress of Wives.

Dan led her in, standing to one side with Dionysia next to her. Emil, Gennady, and Blair vanished deeper into the ship, leaving silence in their wakes.

But Mazhin didn't need noise to communicate. They had evolved as pack hunters capable of bringing down big, dangerous game because they could move and strike in silence.

Have whole conversations by smell and semaphore.

Like now.

And Dan understood that, standing to one side watching. Possibly listening, but she wasn't as good at it as Uly.

But then, who was?

"Siah?" Ziba Abdolahean asked, finally speaking aloud after nearly five minutes. "Twin boys?"

"Azad and Vahid Siah, yes," Nasrin answered.

The Wrench and *The Spatula*, given their jobs and loves in life. Identical twins, which were incredibly rare among the Mazhin, compared to other species she had come to know.

"I think I knew their family," Ziba breathed.

Nasrin's original clan, the ten of them as *Danumash* slaves, had been forcibly assembled from the slave pens, based on technical and social expectations. Working for the masters and getting better lives than toiling in fields or mines.

One of these days, Nasrin intended to visit those seven worlds. And bomb them mercilessly from orbit.

Payback, as it were.

"Were you aboard their clanship?" Dan asked, interrupting some.

"Yes," Ziba breathed. "We were taken. I was able to earn my freedom later, leaving *Danumash* space and eventually ending up here."

Yes, bombed. Leveled with extreme prejudice. Maybe several times.

Annihilated, once all the aliens were rescued. And not just because those people had expected her to grow up as a whore. None of her clan had ever touched her. Only Uly had ever even kissed her. And he'd asked first.

Danumash simply needed to be expunged from the galaxy. Utterly.

Ziba was reading her emotions and nodded wanly.

"Tell me of this Corsac Fox," she instructed, looking around.

Dan moved them to a nearby conference room and fixed tea. It took two hours to finish, just covering the high points, but Ziba was aghast. And excited. Dionysia watched, astounded, but she was getting it all from a radically different perspective.

"Of course, I'll come with you," Ziba said. "There are others at Bolton and Delcaster. All seven worlds, I'm sure, but I have known kin on those. Or did. But to be free and among my own kind."

"There are not that many Mazhin, yet," Dan countered.

"You are her sister," Ziba said pointedly, smiling. "In spite of being Human. And she speaks of several other species in the same smell. I demand the right to see such a thing for myself. And meet my cousins again, however far removed they are. Kin. All of you."

Nasrin glanced at Dan and got her nod.

"I need to go speak with the Emro gentleman," Dan said. "How soon could you be packed to depart, Mistress Abdolahean?"

"Two days," Ziba said. "Assuming I can pack my wares and transport them. A week if I need to sell everything."

"Omid would never forgive me if you didn't bring all of it with you," Nasrin grinned.

Dan rose and nodded to Dionysia.

"I'll take my team back onto the station," she said. "You introduce Ziba to Suka Kuri and the Congress, then start making arrangements while I'm gone."

Then she left. Ziba blinked in a surprise that reached the tips of her tentacles.

"Just like that?" she asked.

"We are the Congress of Wives," Nasrin replied. "Uly's chief advisors. Dan trusts all of us to handle things. Expects it. It is part of Uly's amazing reach and power."

"I look forward to meeting this Human," Ziba nodded.

"You will be amazed," Nasrin assured her.

TWENTY-FIVE

Dionysia trailed in Dan's wake, laughing quietly to herself that everyone saw her as a mere youngster. Dan's *much younger* sister or possibly even daughter, when they were hardly that far apart in real age.

Yarikh were simply no longer human.

Still, it made an effective cover, given that these humans tended to overlook her. Or ignore her. Something.

It was, however, still strange to Dionysia to be around so many aliens, after growing up exclusively Yarikh. Humans lived short lives, so they were always in motion. Always hurrying.

Never taking time, but they didn't necessarily have time. Dan understood that she had a few decades to make major progress, then would inevitably slow down and need to hand things off to those coming behind her.

People like Dionysia, but also the rest of the Congress and all the others assembled to make decisions.

And the Yarikh needed to be at that table. Should she consider marrying Uly? That wasn't her decision to make, but she would need to speak with the elders at some point. Not just Elias, either. The Scholar and the Engineer. They would know.

For now, Dionysia pretended to be a teenager again and worked on absorbing as much as she could about these distant cousins. Kit had been almost perfectly correct in describing the vector that got here. Free-hand and off the cuff.

But it was Kit. Everyone spoke about how smart he was, in spite of the Yarikh supposedly being more advanced. Better designed.

Improved.

The Scholar and the Engineer had wondered aloud in her presence if they had lost something important as a civilization, and both Kit and Uly had held up a mirror showing them all the flaws they liked to ignore. And Dan.

Dionysia couldn't ignore them. Not surrounded by so many more humans. A lost tribe.

Who was the lost, though? Nobody knew. Nobody would likely ever know, unless and until someone went looking into their own distant past.

If those records could be found. And trusted.

Dan was speaking to someone in the market, waiting a few, final moments until the Emro male closed up his shop. Dionysia found herself turning around, face all scrunched up.

"What are you looking for?" Emil Beranger asked, suddenly standing beside her in spite of having a cybernetic leg from below his left knee.

It was supposed to click, but he always moved so silently in spite of it.

Or because of it.

"History," Dionysia said, uncertain beyond that.

"Ours or theirs?" he asked.

She noted that Gennady had turned his back on them, automatically keeping watch aft while his partner was engaged.

Were all humans that prepared to offer violence at any moment? It was one of the things that marked them different from even her kind.

But Emil had asked a question.

"Who's older?" she pressed, suddenly under some compulsion she'd never expected.

Emil's eyes unfocused.

"Probably Dersingham," he said. "One of the original Crowns, if you go back far enough. Might be a load of hokum, though. Can't say I ever really cared that much."

"Are the crowns older?" she asked him.

"The crowns are a modern thing," Gennady spoke up quietly. "Used to be a whole bunch of places, kinda scattered about. *Batyr* split off about the time they started conquering each other, then had to fight them when *Danumash* got big enough to be a threat. Nobody's made much progress in the last century, though."

She glanced at the tall, skinny man with long arms and a face he described as a troll.

Unexpected that these two would be smart, but maybe they were just quiet most of the time. Watching from the back.

Like she was supposed to do, except that she couldn't.

"Books?" she asked.

"Saw a sign earlier," Emil pointed. "Not down here, but up on the main concourse. Probably a bookstore. Dunno if they have a library for travelers."

That made sense. Better to sell you a license to a book you could download. Other places would let you trade them in for credit, deleting the file or expiring it after a certain period.

Was Dersingham the home of the lost tribe?

A lost tribe?

How many were there, after all?

Dan had turned and was watching her.

"Emil, you go with her," Dan said simply. "Gennady and Blair with me. Check in and either join us for food or plan to eat on the ship."

"Got it," Emil said, looking at Dionysia for direction.

"Up?" she asked him.

"That way," he pointed, obviously expecting her to lead so he could continue his bodyguard job.

What would she find?

PART FOUR

THE SPHERE

TWENTY-SIX

Lukyan looked up when Maks wandered into his office aboard *Fire Diamond*.

Nobody had warned him that Maks had come aboard, but they were docked to a station over Rayzian and he supposed that Maks might have blackmailed everyone into keeping quiet.

He did check the calendar on his wall, but it wasn't Tuesday.

Yet.

"You look like hell," Lukyan offered.

Rather than sass back, Maks shrugged, so he must be exhausted.

"Uly did it again," Maks muttered simply.

Lukyan's turn to shrug. Nicer than *I told you so*.

Probably.

"What do we know about Avocur?" Lukyan asked.

Latest messages home from Krilic, sent by DJ Gross aboard *Tanis Dragon*, after a messenger had gotten to them asking for supplies to repatriate a station full of Auga prisoners.

At least Uly was still trading folks home. Lots of Ononguli prisoners likely serving their whole sentence before being dropping broke on a planet somewhere, instead of the good old days.

Or whatever they'd been.

"A threat to Bastion somewhat," Maks replied. "More threat to Saari and the trade route running closest to Auga lines, if they'd decided to thrust a salient out like that. Uly's going to keep it."

Lukyan whistled. Either he'd missed that in the briefing packet, or Maks was reading the man's mind. Probably the latter, because DJ would have said something in the executive summary he sent Anna. *Wardog Charlie* was probably fit to be tied, to have missed something like that.

Should he suggest to Anna rotating Avhust Holub and his maddog crew over to assist Uly on that flank? *Wardog Charlie* was really only a heavy Interceptor on a scale with *Fire Diamond*, but the hotheads made up for that.

"What's the Empire do in response?" Lukyan asked.

"Something stupid, probably," Maks replied. "That's why I'm here."

Sounded like somebody else facing a *Tuesday* instead, which Lukyan found he was fine with.

Tuesdays were never fun. He'd woken up more than once and spent the whole day waiting for the other horn to hit. Usually, he'd made it through safe, but that wasn't the same thing.

"Define stupid," Lukyan offered, wondering where his best friend in the galaxy might be leading them.

"From what was defending the place, which Eskil sent home with the report, I'm thinking the Auga tried to slip a base in quietly and get it built before anyone could react," Maks said. "Low profile, not really understanding that everyone has been quietly scouting for exactly that sort of behavior."

"The Auga are nothing if not predictable," Lukyan replied. "Bit them in the ass this time. What about next?"

"I'm thinking that they've lost several stations to us along this front, if you go back enough years," Maks nodded. "We haven't really seen the monster war fleets that they could bring to bear if they chose, mostly because those tend to be laid up in ordinary—maybe literally drydocked in storage—a lot of the time. At least until the next war breaks out."

"They're already overdue," Lukyan noted.

"Which is why I think we need to do something rash, ugly, mean, and pointed to them," Maks grinned fiercely.

"How ugly?"

"Nobody has heard from Sterling," Maks noted. "I'm guessing that they've been tying themselves into knots trying to track him, and that's consuming resources, both ships and minds. However, at some point, either they catch him or he gets away."

"I assume Sterling makes it home," Lukyan said simply.

It was Sterling Huff. Most dangerous war-fighting conductor he knew. Even going back to some of the bigger demigod legends. Hell, Uly was better than most, and deferred to Sterling.

But Lukyan had been there to watch the kid work. And he was still getting better.

"He gets home," Maks agreed. "Then the Auga decide to finally do something grand and epic."

"Send a fleet of Devastators to Avocur?" Lukyan guessed.

"Probably," Maks said. "Try to capture it or maybe end up destroying the place before Uly can finish it."

"How do we stop them?" Lukyan pressed, already knowing the answer but wanting *Trade Factor Maks*, formerly Governor Maks, to speak the words.

At what point would he be Vanguard Maks? Or Marshal Maks? Uly would need to finally go ahead and trade Warlord for Fleet Marshal. Or keep both titles, since the former was a political one.

"Pack hunt the punks," Maks said simply. "Take the Ononguli Swarm and push it onto the offensive, instead of relying on it to bother folks invading our worlds like usually happens. We can't afford to lose another world and need to make sure the Auga end up paying instead."

"What's that look like to you?" Lukyan asked.

"I'm planning to ask for a meeting with Anna," Maks said. "Prelude to the full Council, but get her aboard early. And then asking her to send you inward to scout. To find the place where the Auga decide to assemble that fleet so we can harry it before it even leaves dock. If they can get that fleet moving, there's almost nothing we can do to stop it."

"Not even starve it out later?" Lukyan probed.

It had been Maks's idea in the first place.

"The damage will have been done," Maks shrugged. "I need to stop them on their side of the line, not ours."

"Finally going to draw it and enforce?" Lukyan asked, wondering if all he was going to do was ask questions.

But it was Maks. Man was filled with bright ideas. And had made both of them a lot of money along the way.

Plus, best friend. If he ever got married to Anna, his best man.

Lukyan could do this.

Maks nodded.

"I need something bigger than *Fire Diamond*," Lukyan challenged, mostly to see how far ahead of everyone else the guy was.

"How would you feel about flying something built on Saari?" Maks asked, eyes glittering with something terrible. "Eskil's turned in his notes and the yard is updating a few things that didn't come up until now."

"What ship?"

"Sister to *Nikodemus Lindberg*," Maks said. "Light Striker, but long-sailor designed for raids. They wanted to build a whole wing of those first, before moving on to some sort of heavy guardship design for the inevitable Auga raid."

"The Yarikh boats not sufficient?"

"They can be overwhelmed, same as anybody," Maks said. "You just have to bring enough launchers with you. The Auga excel at that."

"Light Striker?" Lukyan was intrigued. Way intrigued.

"Slightly improved," Maks nodded. "And Ononguli require less space and less calories on a daily basis, so more comfortable and stay at sea a lot longer."

"Because you want me commerce raiding behind Auga lines," Lukyan nodded.

"I want you finding their fleet," Maks replied sharply. "Then running like hell home, so you can lead Uly and a force in to hammer the shit out of it while they are all in one place. Lots of dumbasses with horns that can handle the raiding part. Not a lot that I trust to sneak away instead."

Lukyan had to agree with that. Ononguli tended to be linear.

He had been, before he'd turned half-human, according to more than one person.

"I'm in," Lukyan offered.

It was Maks. He didn't ask for much. Never had. Just got the job done.

However it needed.

"You load like you're getting sailing orders tomorrow," Maks replied. "I'll talk to Anna. If she approves, we're both hauling ass to Saari, then I'm probably moving on to Avocur. Or wherever Uly is."

"Send DJ a note to route Sterling to Avocur first, then Saari," Lukyan decided. "Fifty/fifty he shows up first at Krilic, knowing that he's got a safe harbor there."

"Done," Maks agreed. "You good with it?"

"Gonna inflict a *Tuesday* on someone else?" Lukyan laughed. "The Auga need a few of those."

"They do," Maks said, rising and exiting. "Chat in a couple of hours."

Lukyan nodded, then opened a comm when he was alone.

"Yeah?" Dmytro Shvets asked. 2IC, up on the bridge, supposedly in charge with Lukyan in his office.

"We're sailing in twelve hours," Lukyan ordered. "Whatever you need to do to get ready, do it. That includes anything taken apart getting put back together. Long, hard run coming up."

"Twelve hours?"

"At most," Lukyan assured him. "Then trouble's coming."

TWENTY-SEVEN

Anna Shevchenko was still *Vatazhko*. The Lord of the Endless Plains.

Head of the Ononguli Council responsible for the Sphere itself. A few had made noises about challenging her, but those had tapered off significantly once people began to appreciate things beyond their corner bodega.

Especially Uly and Maks and what was coming.

She was in her office in the palace, but sitting on a couch with a glass of hot tea in one hand as Maks finished up his explanation.

"I'm hearing a lot of ifs, ands, and maybes," Anna said as he took a long drink.

"That's because I'm trying to outguess the Auga Emperor and his entire retinue of advisors," Maks replied. "They've already done something out of character by building at Avocur, when in all previous wars they would have gone at one of our worlds."

"But for Uly, you are probably correct," she decided. "Does this stretch them sideways enough to matter?"

It was a long frontier already, with all the worlds the Auga had spalled off the original Ononguli Sphere, flattening one side faster than colonies could be expanded on the other. And all of her advisors had predicted another Auga attack, though if you asked three people where you would get five opinions.

"I think they've grown concerned enough to want to lash out at him," Maks said. "And/or drive a firm wedge between him and us. Avocur lets them do that. Or would have. I don't think their spies have figured out Saari and the Samuur."

"I'm not sure I have, Maks," Anna chuckled. "And I know them better."

He shrugged. But Maks probably knew them best, at least among the Ononguli.

Uly knew them the best. Had figured them out in five minutes.

But that was Uly. He did that.

"So I think we need to attack them, Anna," Maks said simply. "Right now, while they are still recovering from losing Avocur and before they can send a force to take it back."

"That force is chasing Huff," she reminded him.

"Mentally, yes," Maks agreed. "Physically, those Devastator squadrons are docked in various places. At least I think so. I won't know until someone brings me fresh intelligence."

"And that's Lukyan?" she asked.

Not that she was surprised. Those two men went back nearly twenty years as shipmates and friends. And Lukyan was special. Anna had made sure that he didn't get far, not that they could do much now.

And, thinking about it, the war wasn't going to end in her lifetime, so maybe she needed to corner him at some point and make it formal, because Lukyan wouldn't initiate something that big.

Man still thought he was marrying well above his station.

She'd have to fix that, too.

"That's Lukyan," Maks confirmed. "I don't trust anyone else I could send, because Eskil is busy and Sterling's not home yet."

What did it say about the Ononguli that Maks's second choice was Samuur and his third was Human?

Bad things, but at least honest ones. The Horde simply hadn't had time to reform into a proper fleet. But if she sent a swarm forward, they might not have to, because it would play to their strengths.

"And a new ship for him?" she asked, halfway between *Vatazhko* and concerned spouse.

Or both.

"For now," Maks nodded. "At some point, I need you to break out the big beasts and get them sailing. People need the experience. *Storm Crow* might need a whole new crew rotated through, in order to train people."

It was her turn to nod. That was traditionally the call to battle for the clans.

The Summoning, when everyone took their battleships and manned them for the first time in a generation.

And it was overdue, but that was Uly driving the *Auga Empire* onto their back heel, where they were dancing to his tune, instead of her to theirs.

"Will you be in uniform?" she asked him.

Anna had finally surprised him, watching his horns bounce up and back.

"Do I need to be?" he countered, surprising her.

Did he? Probably not.

Trade Factor Maks was building fleets at Saari. And new designs, based on Samuur logic that was different than Ononguli.

And while he was competent enough as a pirate, she had plenty of those folks.

Only one Maks.

"No," Anna decided. "You continue to do what you think is best, acting as my ambassador whenever you need that behind you. I need those fleets and banks that you promised me all those years ago, because the war might have finally begun."

He nodded.

"I'll keep you posted," he said, rising and seeing himself out.

Indeed, the war might have already begun.

How did Uly win it?

TWENTY-EIGHT

Sterling let out a tremendous breath when *Vauquelin* dropped out of warp and was immediately challenged by *Wardog Charlie*.

Even those lunatics, because he'd made it home. After one of the ugliest games of tag he'd ever participated in.

And winning. Barely.

Maikki's head popped up.

"Call from *Tanis Dragon*," she said simply.

"Conference mode, Lieutenant," he replied, waiting for her to raise a hand. "This is Sterling Huff."

"You made it," DJ replied. "Welcome home. Lots of news for you to digest, but orders from on high involve getting you reloaded with cargo and supplies and turning you around as quickly as possible for a run sideways."

As always, DJ would boil it down into diamonds and throw them at you like knives. Sterling processed all that and presumed that his raid had triggered some sort of reprisal from Auga, but not aimed at this quiet corner that had far more ships in harbor than usual.

The War? Probably. It had been a distinct possibility, headed in to Stradosha. Hopefully, Dan and her team could slide sideways around the Empire on their return flight, if the Auga were stirred up.

"Where do you need me?" Sterling asked.

DJ was in charge of this system. At least when Maks or Uly weren't around.

"Dock with the station and get ready to start packing things away," DJ nodded. "I'll come aboard your ship in an hour or so, but I'm sending you Maks's packet now to read. Not sure what it implies, but I have notes suggesting that things are ramping up for major action, as soon as Chayka identifies a target."

"Understood," Sterling said. "Lt. Kaita, take us in and get us in place. DJ, I'll let the wardroom know that you're coming."

He cut the line and dialed up Aibek Sulaymanov, currently aft on the secondary bridge.

"You heard?" Sterling asked.

"Already sent the chef a message," Aibek laughed. "They've got notes on Conductor Gross's favorites. Figure it's worth charming him."

Sterling laughed as well. DJ owned this corner of space. Anna Shevchenko kept him and *Tanis Dragon* here to protect things, and that had turned into anchoring one of Uly's trade routes back to Z'Gosza.

"Message pack arriving," Maikki said.

"Route it to my office, then you take the bridge and get us docked," he ordered, throwing a pop quiz at her. "Aibek, meet me forward."

Sterling rose and headed to the hatch.

He was several months out of date with the state of the galaxy. Sounded like he'd missed a few things.

Time to catch up.

TWENTY-NINE

Aibek still marveled at his amazing luck. At surviving that suicidal-in-retrospect raid on Bastion. And meeting Uly. Introducing him to the Isann.

Becoming part of the team, when he could have just as easily been thrown in prison as a criminal and fuckup.

Except that Suka Kuri had believed in him. And Uly. And Sterling.

They were in the latter's office, rereading the executive summary.

Aibek whistled.

"Agreed," Sterling replied.

"Can we hold Avocur?" Aibek asked.

"I suspect that significant resources are going to be rotated forward to reinforce it," Sterling replied. "Then the station is likely upgraded for front-line action."

"What's that look like?" Aibek asked.

A few years ago, their little puddlejumpers had been considered state-of-the-art back home. Now they were hardly worth scrapping for hull metal, save that they could haul cargo between worlds. And did, as fast as they could load and unload at each end.

"Twelve decimeter wavebolt mounts," Sterling replied. "And more of them. Many more 2dm for defensive purposes. More of everything, really, assuming the Yarikh don't decide to arm us with bigger and more dangerous tools."

"Would they do that?" Aibek asked.

As advanced as the Isann had been primitive. Just quieter and reserved on the topic, but he'd gotten the impression that even a major Auga Sector Fleet assault on their homeworld of Traiffe could be annihilated.

Not just defeated and driven off, either.

Ended.

Just like that.

What kind of technology would that take? And how safe was the galaxy, if they really were cousins of the dangerous folks Uly claimed humans were?

Sterling was watching him with those gray-green eyes that looked so weird to an Isann.

"They could," Sterling said. "But that might require them to conquer the galaxy at some point. Or destroy it to ensure their safety."

It was the calm, deliberate way this *kid* said it that was probably the most frightening part. Sterling was hardly older, physically, than his daughter Zhyrgal.

Aibek still didn't think he knew anybody as purely dangerous in command of a starship. Dan and her Congress had to get close enough to shoot you, so they didn't count.

"How do we stop them?" Aibek asked.

"We don't," Sterling replied. "We deal with them in an honest and polite manner, because they seem to reciprocate behavior. Kit was friendly and agreeable, as he is, so they were. Anari was polite and educated, and that impressed them. We showed up formal and diplomatic, instead of dumbass pirates set to attack the place. They could have destroyed my old ship so fast nobody noticed. I'd rather they didn't have to do more than the minimum necessary to convince people to behave. Uly's the same way."

Aibek gulped and pulled his tunic tighter as a fidget he recognized.

"And Avocur?" he asked in a quieter voice.

"Maybe we defend it," Sterling shrugged, leaned back and looking decades older. It was in the eyes. "Maybe we have to go raid someone, deep behind Auga lines, because that will rattle them again. Or more. If nothing else, Stradosha forces them to defend more worlds with their current fleet, which means fewer ships available to attack the Ononguli and the Samuur."

"And Bastion," Aibek pointed out.

"We protect our friends," Sterling said. "They'll get to Isann itself, one of these days, if we don't stop them. Ergo."

"Ergo," Aibek agreed.

Isann had the bodies. And the experienced sailors. They didn't have the tech and the ships.

Yet.

The Samuur had proven to be good allies and good friends, building as fast as parts could be assembled and shipped. Both Isann and Samuur parts, making new ships. With blended crews that even the Ononguli had started volunteering to serve on.

But that was Uly. And Sterling.

"What does *Vauquelin* need?" Sterling asked, sounding like a commanding officer.

"An overhaul and better maintenance than we can pull in motion," Aibek replied automatically. "If we're parked somewhere, I might start dismantling a few generators aft, one at a time, for rebuilds. Still a few yard tasks, but if we're in a defensive fleet, we can take the time, even without hauling to Saari to do it. Or Bastion."

"Make a list," Sterling stated. "Stack rank it based on an expectation of another hard sail like we just completed, then identify how long the ship needs to be off-line to effect things. Also, in warp, how much can we do, chancing random encounters."

"You got it," Aibek nodded. "Gross will fill us in on the rest of this?"

He waved at the tablet.

"I doubt that he knows much more than this," Sterling replied. "We might be updating him more about what we've done, but I don't think they tracked us on this last run, so anyone showing up here is random, or they were already planning a raid. And *Wardog Charlie* is hyped up."

Aibek chuckled at that. He'd gotten snippets of that ship's legend from other Ononguli crew. That was putting it mildly.

"We'll be ready for Gross," he said simply, rising.

Sterling nodded and Aibek headed for the wardroom.

Time to charm one of Anna Shevchenko's closest allies out there.

THIRTY

Eskil happened to be on the bridge when *Vauquelin* dropped into existence at the outer marker, everyone immediately scrambling because it was an Auga Heavy Striker appearing.

Good practice, too, because they had captured seven freighters hauling cargo and food to Avocur before the Auga had finally managed to stop that run of ships.

Not that he liked Auga food, but it could provide an agreeable change from the usual. For a time.

Did it have to be so bland, though?

Next run home to Saari for supplies better be overloaded with spices on the return.

Still, Sterling was home. Or back.

Safe, which was what mattered. And being escorted in by the Ononguli vessel *Wardog Charlie*. Eskil had heard rumors. Legends. Tall tales, if you will.

Useful, with what rumors suggested was coming.

And the sisters were home, so he could update them on all the things the design team had done while they'd been gone. And probably catch hell from both of them.

That was on him. He'd suggested both for *Vauquelin* before he'd known what was coming. And they no doubt had impressed everyone with their competence.

He was still likely to catch a ration of shit. At least they would both have ideas for him. In between the yelling.

He grinned as the line came live and Maikki smiled at him. Mouth, without ears or whiskers. About what he'd been expecting.

"Uly's at Saari," he said first. "What do we need to know immediately?"

Someone had told Sterling where to travel to, after all.

"We're fresh out of Krilic, obviously," Maikki replied. "They provided a full report, pending updates. How soon is anything happening here?"

"I intend to send Uly a courier inside of an hour with whatever you brought, so he's ready," Eskil said.

"Part one of our mission was an overwhelming success," Maikki said, obviously speaking for Sterling.

Eskil wondered if the young man had gone ahead and made her Second Officer. Smart choice if he did.

"Rescued the Ancyn?" he asked.

"And did a great deal of material damage in-system," she nodded. "Dan's Congress is proceeding on their section, while we distracted and disrupted Auga operations across several sectors."

"We'll have the first big planning meeting when you get to orbit," he promised. "Then another when Uly gets here with Lukyan."

"Looking forward to it," she said, then cut the line.

Hemmo was busy typing.

"Anything I need to worry about?" he asked his First Officer.

"I'll need to digest it," Hemmo replied. "Mostly, they are well behind current news and will need to be updated. Will Uly send them back out on this raid?"

"Assuming we can get the station to the point it can defend itself? Yes," Eskil decided. "They'll have time, though, because Lukyan will have to do things first. That's what the sisters and the rest will need."

"Can we stop the entire *Auga Empire*?" Hemmo asked.

Around the bridge, ears twisted inward subtly.

"Uly can," Eskil reminded them. "We're here because the innocent need protecting from bullies. All the Auga have to do is withdraw to the lines they have negotiated with everyone else and honor them."

"Are they even capable of that?" Aava asked sourly.

"I think so," Eskil told her. "If not, we're simply defending Saari from an invader. And doing it earlier, and with more friends and more firepower than we would have, had *Tiikeri* remained the pinnacle of Samuur engineering."

"What can we build that's even better than *Lindberg*?" Hemmo asked.

Eskil paused to type a few commands on his screen. The main display changed to show *Vauquelin*, slowly rotating horizontally to show all sides.

"This is *Vauquelin*, the Auga's current design for a Heavy Striker," he reminded them. "And we've dismantled and repaired it, so we know exactly what it is capable of. Not all that impressive by itself. Their threat is in the number of them that could be brought to bear, if the Auga decided to finally focus on attacking Uly. Then, it is either any number of these ships, or lines of Devastators sailing to broadside and cutting loose."

"How do we stop something like that?" Aava asked.

"Maks Sobol has a plan," he reminded her. Reminded everyone. "It might even work. Nobody has ever been in a position to test it."

"Because the Ononguli aren't that organized, usually?" she pressed.

"That's part of it," Eskil agreed. "And they've never had friends willing to step up and help. That's us. And everyone else. Uly is in a position to maybe do something about the Auga. We just need to take advantage of it. Eventually, we need to build a few monsters that can take on an Auga Devastator line."

"Or a stupid number of gunboats that can overwhelm them with fours and sixes," Aava offered.

"Casualties in that sort of battle would be hideous," Eskil replied. "How many ships do we lose in the process of stinging them to death? I'd rather pounce and rend, personally."

Nods. It was the Samuur way.

And they would do it. The Ononguli needed help, and had asked. Had acted honorably.

And, truth be told, it was the future of the galaxy itself at hand.

He was looking forward to what the sisters had to say.

THIRTY-ONE

Maikki really wanted to punch Eskil in the snout, but settled for glowering at him across the conference room table. Taija, seated next to her, wasn't much better.

Eskil had the decency to repress his normal exuberance for a time, looking sober and commanding.

They were aboard *Vauquelin*, parked immediately next to both *Lindberg* and the station in case something came up, but *Wardog Charlie* had chosen to patrol at the outer marker most likely to represent an Auga incursion, so they would have warning.

And Maikki had asked Sterling and Aibek to join them today, but to do so as civilian consultants, rather than senior officers. Experts on a topic.

She modulated her growl at Eskil's smile.

"Lukyan's getting the next boat?" she asked in a sweet, polite voice her grandmother had taught her as a warning.

Eskil's whiskers cringed. So did Sterling's and he didn't have any.

"I understand that you will be up for one soon, Maikki," Sterling intercepted her ire. "Personally, I'd like to keep you on *Vauquelin* as long as I can. Not because you shouldn't have a command, but because you're so damned good at what you do."

She paused and rotated her head to study her commanding officer, who had gone so far as to dress in civilian clothing for this meeting.

"And I think that I'll likely be taking command of *Nubia* at some point, when Uly needs to become a permanent politician," he continued. "Retiring to Bastion, as it were."

"And I'm likely to become the Isann ambassador at that point, as well," Aibek spoke up.

Well, shit.

Maikki would have bet that there wasn't anything that could dissuade her from savaging her cousin today. Even with witnesses.

And she'd have been wrong.

She blinked at the two men, Human and Isann.

Did that mean that she would take command of *Vauquelin*, in that instance?

Suddenly, a lot of pieces clicked together in a pattern she hadn't been prepared for. Saari was building Light Strikers. Good ships. The designs they had settled on were excellent, especially compared to what she had been aboard before.

And they were unlikely to start building heavier vessels in the short term, simply because they could turn out three Light Strikers in the same period as one Heavy. Nature of the construction, even with the new modularity that had been baked into the process.

At least Sterling was smiling at her.

Maikki recalibrated her outrage and turned it back onto her cousin. Irrepressible was back. Like he'd known this ahead of time and not warned her.

He was like that.

"So, you'll be flying escort on my wing?" she asked, all sweetness and light and razor blades again.

Taija snickered quietly. Eskil flinched.

After all, he was First Commander.

But that was the Samuur Fleet. The armed might of the *Illuminated Solidarity*. Maikki and Taija had taken a lateral transfer and promotion out of the orange and indigo, into the medium blue of Bastion.

Then it hit her. Bastion was a planetary system.

Uly was building the entire *Spinward Reaches*. And inducting as many species and sailors as would take orders and work for the common good, regardless of species.

She wasn't Samuur, anymore. Well, she was, but she was part of Uly's fleet, and hadn't really processed that at any point along the way, in spite of all the clues being right there in front of her.

Shit.

Eskil hadn't spoken. She turned to Sterling.

"Everybody but *Nubia* will be answering to *Vauquelin*, won't they?" she asked.

His own grin spoke volumes. Humans grinned with mouth and eyes, which had taken her some time to understand and get used to.

He was grinning ear to ear, as they would describe it.

"Until we convince the Yarikh to help us build something even bigger and nastier," Sterling replied evenly. "*Nubia* is a Light Devastator by displacement, and a Heavy by firepower. I am utterly certain that the Scholar and the Engineer could design something for us that is still less than they have, and more than anybody can counter. I'll need squadron and fleet commanders I know and can rely on to do things for me."

Like her. Like Eskil. Like Lukyan.

Because Eskil Haldur was First Commander of the Samuur, but Sterling Huff was probably First Commander of the entire allied force.

Uly would call it a Fleet Marshal. Supreme military commander. First Flag.

Yes. First Flag. That was Sterling Huff. And he was expecting her to raise her own flag at some point. In the near future.

Shit.

Everyone had sobered quickly at Sterling's words. Even Aibek, who would normally be up for some command, but he was a middle-aged pirate thrust into circumstances far beyond what he'd been expecting.

Held his own. Reminded her of Hemmo Lindholm, on Eskil's bridge. Served the same role for Sterling, bringing calm, logical maturity to balance intuition and energy.

She would need someone to balance her. And maybe sooner than she'd been expecting.

Way sooner.

"I feel like I've been had," she muttered.

All of them—INCLUDING HER OWN SISTER—grinned. Like they'd been in on it.

Might have been.

"Now what?" she asked Sterling, ignoring Eskil because he was suddenly commanding a scout wing of Uly's fleet. Of Sterling's.

Like Lukyan would be, in the next *Lindberg*-class ship.

Vauquelin would be the hammer. And *Nubia*.

Had this entire mission been an audition on her part?

"Yes," Aibek said. "It was."

Maikki realized that she'd been muttering with her outside voice and slammed her teeth together to shut up.

"Uly will be back with a force," Sterling said. "Lukyan will be off raiding. We'll be doing an overhaul and finishing the station. Then training and recruiting. Then probably another raid, once Lukyan nails down the coordinates I need."

"Will you be commanding *Nubia*?" she asked, ignoring everyone else for now.

"I believe that I can make a case Uly listens to, yes," the young Human replied, serious and smiling. "He needs to be home, being the Warlord permanently. We're his hands. His fists when he needs them, but open hands for the people who need help up."

Maikki had to pause and parse that. She'd seen the lethal brutality that Sterling Huff brought to the table, but he still stopped and turned it off like a light switch occasionally, in ways that took her breath away.

Because it was a tool in his hands, not a part of his personality. She needed to grasp that. Internalize it.

Master it.

Taija leaned in and scowled sufficiently to cow even a grinning Eskil. It was good.

"We also brought home some new designs for the team," she growled at him. "Both better Interceptors as well as heavier things that Saari, Ononguli, and Bastion might build, now that we're getting serious and in a proper war."

Eskil nodded. Maikki leaned back and listened as her sister started detailing the various designs the two of them—along with Humans, Mazhin, Khet, Thogin, Ugotha, and several others—had come up with while raiding Stradosha.

And what they had learned in the process.

But she needed to rethink a lot of things, apparently.

It was a good thing she liked her cousin.

THIRTY-TWO

Lukyan had seen the specs for Maks's new Light Striker, parked across the way. And all the tweaks they'd added, learning new things in the building of *Lindberg* and fighting it against Auga defense forces.

He might be salivating as they drifted into dock. Just a bit.

Okay, more than a little.

Fire Diamond was impossibly outclassed by this new beast, but that ship was a much older Ononguli design. A commerce raider, sure, but not a warship dedicated to war.

He honestly didn't think any Ononguli vessels really were. Not like the Samuur could build, when they were designing things to Human standards for Uly and Sterling.

But this was the war. Uly's conflict had been brewing for years, but even the Auga needed time to wind themselves up to do things, and Uly had bashed them upside the head several times, each right at the moment when they were planning to get serious.

Apparently, nobody had ever done that before. Not to the Auga.

Slava Tkachenko was piloting, like usual. Horns down and tapping keys with precise care as they finished docking.

"We really selling *Fire Diamond* to the cats?" Dmytro asked obliquely.

"Trading it in for credit against this new ship, yes," Lukyan replied. "Anna is also paying them list price, mostly to inject credits into the system so they can look at expanding the yard."

"Always about the velocity of money," Dmytro muttered, nodding. "What changes for us?"

"We brought a few extra sailors, but mostly we'll be adding Samuur and Isann bodies, from the latest report, so the ship will be multinational out of the graving pool," he replied. "That's by design as well, so that everybody sees this mission as representing Uly and not just the Horde. Gonna need that later, because Anna still thinks that they launch a reprisal invasion against the Sphere, depending on what we do and who we do it to."

"We're docked," Slava announced. "Station power locking in and coming on. Shut everything else down?"

"Yes," Lukyan reminded him. "Just like we talked about. Everybody packed up? I expect that we're departing *Fire Diamond* in the next day at most and transferring over."

Nods. None of them had believed him, of course, so Lukyan suspected that he'd be the first and possibly only Ononguli crew member over there for the first few hours, but he was fine with that, because *Warhammer Rose* already had a partial crew that had been responsible for signing off on everything the yard had done and testing systems.

A couple of quick sails around and a few training missions to confirm that everything met his standards, and they'd be off doing terrible things to terrible people.

Nothing new there, except that they might actually manage to pull it off, for the first time in the history of the Ononguli Sphere.

"Station calling," Dmytro said. "It's Uly."

"Any request for secrecy?" Lukyan asked.

"Negative."

"Main screen." And Uly appeared.

Having never known Humans before that fateful *Tuesday*, Lukyan could still see where some fundamental change had taken place in the man. Possibly moving out of youth and into some level of mature adulthood. Dan had it as well, and she was a few years older than Uly, so maybe something happened to the species at thirty standard, give or take.

Calm. Focused. Serious. More so than before.

Partly, that was probably Dan being gone for a long mission. Lukyan didn't appreciate the time away from Anna, but that was a mature relationship that might turn into something more serious.

If she stayed serious. He was still twitching at their last conversation. She might be. Way serious.

"Hiya," Lukyan said, watching Uly's face screw up sideways into a smile.

"Welcome, Conductor Chayka," Uly said in a voice that wasn't very serious. Nor were the eyes. "You pirates ready for forward military operations?"

"It is not Tuesday," Lukyan reminded him sternly, but still grinning.

That got a laugh.

"Maks is ready for you to take command of *Warhammer Rose,*" Uly nodded. "How soon can you be ready for an inspection, then the first set of planning meetings?"

"The Paramount sign off on the yard?" he replied. "And Maks?"

Nods.

"Then I should do something rude," Lukyan grinned. "Dmytro, you're in charge of the transfer. Last ten crew members who finish packing go last through the dinner line for two weeks. And have my gear transferred over first."

He turned back from Dmytro's wicked grin and smiled at Uly.

"I'm yours," he said.

"Excellent," Uly replied. "I'll grab Maks and have someone fly you over to *Nubia.* Probably easiest to meet there."

He cut the line and Lukyan rose from his station.

There was a hint of disbelief in the air.

"I did warn you," was all he said as he headed for the hatch.

If they hadn't actually believed him, that was on them. Uly believed in moving fast.

Oh, and they never had found the spy on Rayzian that had warned the Auga about the Zhoralong raid. And nobody had been prepared for Stradosha, so the leak was absolutely Ononguli.

If he ever found out who it was, Lukyan planned to grind their horns off flush with their skull.

But right now, he had a mission to complete.

THIRTY-THREE

Uly had half of his team ready, the other half being out there somewhere with Dan.

Her Congress, but still his hands to do things.

Fortunately, he had several entire civilizations in the process of standing up to be counted. That would matter. Starting today.

Lukyan sauntered in and Maks immediately rose and walked over to the coffee robot and started tinkering. Lukyan stuttered off course, then joined him, though neither spoke.

Uly still appreciated the gesture. Haydar did a thing with his tentacles that would have been a snort if he was human. Piruz Kossari—aka *The Used Camel Salesman*—matched it. Melpomeni also caught it and grinned. Kit looked up from his tinkering as if he'd heard something anyway, then went back to whatever he was sketching. Uly liked pulling the young man into these meetings, mostly because he looked at everything sideways from most of Uly's advisors.

And, because things kept getting bigger, Uly had gone ahead and added two more folks to the Legal Department. And messed with the balance of things, because both the Paramount and Chief of Chiefs had found him women solicitors, though neither were likely to impress Dan, but she had different needs.

Both of these women were also married, with families, and practicing law back home before transferring to Bastion to help shape things. Probably both would have been threats to challenge for supreme political authority at home at some point as well.

And might yet.

Adylet Akmatov was the Isann. Mid-thirties equivalent in age. Sharp mind that occasionally jousted with Piruz, though she tended to let Haydar have his way.

But then, his Samuur advisor, Kaarina Koivu, could match whiskers to tentacles with any of them. Middle-aged. Children on the verge of adulthood themselves. Possibly someone to sit on any supreme court in a few years.

Maks and Lukyan joined them after a time and everyone relaxed.

"Gonna go hunting?" Lukyan asked immediately, the first words anyone had spoken.

"My hope is that they are at one of three places," Uly nodded. "Haydar has the data, working from Sterling's notes and things we stole with *Vauquelin*. I need you to find out what they are up to, so we can adjust to it. If it is an attack fleet being assembled, I'll have to respond, and don't have the firepower I need at hand."

"The squadron can get from here to Avocur quickly," Melpomeni pointed out.

"Once we know that the Auga aren't about to pull a fast one on us," Piruz said.

And he was probably the expert on that topic, though that usually wasn't something discussed in polite company.

"Agreed," Haydar added. "We'll hang here, poised to move, but Saari is far more important than Avocur in the short term."

"What about the long term?" Kit asked, then looked down again.

A jeweler, shaping diamonds with his words. But that was Kit.

"I think that long term we have to hold Avocur," Uly said. "Reinforce it sufficient to draw a permanent boundary line separating the *Auga Empire* from the *Spinward Reaches*."

"The edge of space you'll claim?" Kaarina asked, whiskers bristling.

"Draw a rough line connecting it with Krilic," Uly described. "That's outside what Auga claims today. They can choose to be content with what they have, and there are still a lot of systems on both sides of that line that might cause us to negotiate adjustments later. Extend that onward to Khet space."

Adylet nodded at that, but she was an expert in the conference room meeting, rather than the courtroom. Haydar had explained it once as the difference between the combat librarian and the stage actor, in terms of how they approached their jobs and what they could accomplish.

Uly wanted all this to be handled as quietly as possible. Diplomats over finger foods, when it had been warfleets blasting each other for too many centuries.

Let the galaxy grow up. As soon as the primary bully was brought to heel.

"What does Avocur need, in order to be held?" Ethir asked sharply, sounding more like a piranha than anything.

"Defensive firepower," Kit replied, turning to look pointedly at Melpomeni.

She shrugged and nodded.

"We have reviewed your notes," the Engineer spoke quietly. "The sorts of offensive firepower that the *Auga Empire* could bring to bear, if they decided that it was necessary."

Everyone waited, poised.

"Traiffe understands the risk that we could unbalance the galaxy, if we were to supply you with too much technology."

"I only need enough to stop them," Uly replied. "Maks wants enough to hold the current line in Sector Twenty-One. The Empire still isn't evil, so much as misguided. They think of themselves as the civilizing influence, rather than the conquerors. And anything you provide us will eventually be stolen and copied by them, so I'd rather you continued to hold a monopoly on certain things, if only because the Scholar or her immediate successor are likely to see the culmination of this war, one way or the other."

"And if you lose it?" Melpomeni asked.

"Then you have that long to prepare to defend Traiffe itself," Maks spoke up in a hollow voice.

Uly felt the air bleed out of the chamber at those words, but Maks wasn't wrong. Underspeaking it, if anything.

Uly still didn't know if the Yarikh might decide to fight on that day. Might choose to destroy the *Auga Empire*. Or simply withdraw again, possibly deeper towards the Core, where they could gain another millennia or three.

The Auga might fall over and collapse tomorrow, but Uly wasn't willing to bet on that.

He was willing to inflict a few measured blows intended to weaken the structure, though.

Awaken the citizens of empire to things done in their names, when he was certain that they generally lived in ignorance.

Jewelers, shaping diamonds.

"Would the Yarikh be willing to move their defensive squadron from Bastion to Avocur?" he asked the woman. "Probably need to reinforce it significantly, as that is probably going to be a battleground at some point, when the Auga decide to dislodge our hold on it."

He watched her do the math, but none of this was new. And the Auga's implacability had been on display for her and her kind to witness.

Here or at Traiffe, the Yarikh would be facing the *Auga Empire*.

Today or tomorrow.

Unless Uly stopped them. With the help of all of his friends.

"I can talk to Nomiki," Melpomeni replied. "It might require we field a third formation."

Shrugs around the table. Time would tell.

"So," Lukyan said, blowing away all the fog and smoke that might have accumulated. "Let's talk about your three targets, and what you need me doing."

Uly leaned forward and began filling the man in. It would be his horns on the line, without any backup if something went wrong, after all.

PART FIVE

MASYM

THIRTY-FOUR

Dan was on the surface of a Human world. That summed it all up for her. And her other four humans—or three and Dionysia—were down here with her, walking around the city of Brahyrst on a hot summer day, surrounded by hundreds and thousands of other humans wandering about on their lunch hour. Or taking a day off.

Something.

Word had gotten around. And their uniforms stood out, because Masym was an independent colony world, beholden to neither *Danumash* nor *Batyr*, though someone as dark as her and Dionysia weren't likely *Danumash* citizens. Upright ones, anyway.

Only pale folks were important in the *Seven Crowns* region of space.

Folks noticed them. Dan had hired a local firm to handle the actual recruiting and vetting process, to make sure that folks knew that there was no returning to Masym if they chose to depart.

Nor were they told how far away they would be going. Merely that it was a permanent relocation.

Because it had taken her an entire chain of resupply freighters, good planning, and still a lot of luck, just to get here from Bastion. There was another chain home.

Dan was looking for something specific today. Something she had been dreaming about for years. And had brought her team to the edge of town, rather than remain near the center, because what she needed wasn't a city thing.

The address on the board told her she had arrived, so she crossed a parking lot with a few ground vehicles that were all dinged-up flatbed haulers.

Trucks. A farm thing.

"Can I help you?" a young woman asked earnestly as Dan led her folks in.

Rustic place. Wood counter, polished by hands, rather than anything more exotic. Floors scuffed by countless feet that left trails in the tile.

"I have peculiar needs," Dan replied, feeling ancient, but the woman looked more Dionysia's perceived age.

"Oh, the colonists!" the girl suddenly perked up.

Dan didn't think of herself in those terms, but supposed that others did.

An older woman emerged from an office behind the counter. The younger one's mother or an aunt, as similar as their faces were.

"What can we help you find?" the younger one asked, glancing over. "What does your colony need?"

"Chickens," Dan said simply. "And chocolate."

The older woman nodded sagely at those words.

"What's your climate?" the younger one asked.

"We can grow things hydroponically if necessary, but we have a full, global range that can be planted with crops," Dan replied. "I'd like to expand bloodlines on my birds, so any sub-species combinations that can cross-fertilize would be fine. Helpful, even, as we'll need to create new breeds better suited to our home."

Nods. Deadly serious faces, because this was a farm store, serving all the hinterland folks who kept the city dwellers fed on a daily basis.

"Do you have the right insects to pollinate?" the older woman asked, stepping up like a general planning a campaign.

"Unlikely," Dan replied, uncertain and possibly out of her depth. "Virgin world. Our original colony ship was damaged by pirates and we lost certain things."

Both women nodded, so they'd heard the cover story Dan had spread. Useful here, because apparently she needed to look at including farmers or botanists with her recruits. Specific specialists, if she wanted chocolate.

"Oh, and coffee," she added.

"You'll need an entire package," the older woman said in a dark, oracular voice of doom. "Ladybugs. Chocolate midges. Several kinds of bees, especially if you want honey. Wasps and a few other things. What's the native insect life like?"

Dan paused at that. She'd been aboard starships and stations for the most part.

Gennadi stepped to the counter.

"It is not a tropical paradise, where we're planning to build the big city," he replied. "Coastal on a river delta. But there are native species that have a similar enough biomorphology and chemistry. We probably need spiders as well. Omnivores with good stomachs, capable of holding a line against alien incursion."

His grin at the way her mouth fell open was just the frosting.

"Blair, I need your expertise," Gennadi continued.

Dan took a step back as the two men and two women suddenly dropped into a cant so dense as to be almost impenetrable to follow.

She listened for nearly ten minutes, then they started dickering prices from the way the vocabulary changed and she got more involved. The younger one was named Freda, and Ellen was indeed her mother.

"Livestock?" Ellen asked as they wrapped up negotiations for a full package of things to haul.

Plants. Seeds. Insect brood sacks and live specimens. The works.

"We have a small ship, but there is space for some animals, assuming they take well to transport ships," Dan hesitated.

"You can freeze sperm from several bulls," Freda noted. "Thus transporting only cows instead. Same with pigs and sheep."

Pork bacon? Tempting. Oh, so tempting.

"What we don't have are experts," Dan said. "We have the ability to grow crops, but those are native things we have determined are safe. I'm looking to include more Human things in that."

Ellen suddenly got cagey.

"Oh?" she asked.

Dan looked around, but the place was generally empty at the moment. Her five, these two, and nobody really in earshot.

"Perhaps we could talk in your office?" Dan asked.

"Yes, that would be good," Ellen decided. "Freda, you stay on the counter."

"Dionysia, you come with me," Dan ordered. "The rest of you wander and shop, in case there are things we didn't realize we needed before now."

Though what, she wasn't certain. Still, she didn't want to announce that her little colony world, hiding off in the darkness, already had a population of over one hundred thousand, because there were no humans currently on the surface, and only a few humans total, most of them with her on this mission.

And the Yarikh wouldn't count, even if some of them decided to till the soil or raise animals.

Not today.

She followed Ellen in and closed the door.

"You don't act like a woman on the verge of poverty or starvation, in spite of a new colony supposedly escaped from pirates," Ellen noted.

Dan studied her.

"How good are you at keeping secrets?" Dan asked simply.

Ellen got even cagier at that. Not nervous. Sharper.

"What's out there?" Ellen asked.

"More than humans," Dan countered carefully. "Bastion is a new world, but my husband has been recruiting folks more local to help us build it. We do not, however, have nearly enough humans for long-term viability. That's the recruitment. And the leaning into more females, because we might share a few good men in order to spread out those bloodlines."

As opposed to a bull with a harem of cows, but that was one of the differences between humans and livestock.

"And you don't have farming experts," Ellen challenged.

"Not yet," Dan replied. "After this, I think I need to make sure to recruit some, because there's obviously a lot more going on that I never appreciated until now."

They fell into silence, watching each other.

Ellen turned to Dionysia. Studied her closely.

"What's your relationship to Dan?" Ellen asked pointedly.

Dionysia glanced over for help, but that was because it was a Human thing, rather than maturity.

"None," Dan offered. "Very distant relative, if anything. And much older than she looks, but everyone always accuses her of having a babyface."

Ellen didn't need to know about Lost Tribes, after all. Or the Congress. Nobody did, save those folks who would be traveling with them.

"And I've heard that your husband is the governor of the colony?" Ellen asked, turning back to Dan.

"Correct," Dan nodded, leaving it at that.

Warlord of the Spinward Reaches really would frighten people.

"A completely new world?" Ellen pressed.

"Beholden to neither *Danumash* nor *Batyr*," Dan agreed. "Currently, we run just about exactly half and half by national origin. But I wanted to come here instead of one of their worlds, because I needed hardier folks, willing to do the work necessary to build something without having to deal with those two."

Ellen's grimace was tiny, but probably due to skin color. Two dark brown women, the kind that generally faced all manner of racism, but the other three outside were much paler, so the colony had a range.

"What are your limits on recruitment?" Ellen asked vaguely. "Age? Gender? The like?"

"Children accompanying adults are acceptable," Dan said. "Extended families, as well, but we'd like as many single people as possible, so that we have the ability to mix and match later. Uly, my husband, was surprised when I decided he needed more than one wife, but has acceded to my decision."

Ellen blinked at that. Probably expecting a harem. And a bull.

Nothing could be further from the truth, but this woman didn't need to know that.

Or did she?

"Adults past fertility would also be welcome, because we need those folks helping and bringing a lifetime of experience in things," Dan tossed out, just to see where Ellen might take it.

Forty-ish? Not fifty. Possibly menopausal. Possibly not.

Obviously sharp and knowledgeable. In things Dan had discovered she might need, if she was going to have someone grow cocoa and coffee beans for her.

Because chocolate. And chickens.

More silence.

"Never coming back?" Ellen asked.

"It's been a decade since I was here last," Dan replied honestly. "I won't say never, but it would be unlikely in the near future. And there will not be regular trade between these worlds and Bastion, either."

Because that was a long sail. Small ships could pack enough supplies, but she'd brought all her killers with her, just in case.

Ellen nodded. She seemed torn. Dan handed her a card with their contact information, both the recruiting office and her personal one she'd gotten on arrival, then started to rise.

"I might be one of your recruits," Ellen said nervously.

"Oh?" Dan sat back down.

"Freda's not really tied down, and has spoken about leaving Masym for some other place," Ellen offered. "Her father is no longer in our lives, and occasionally resents that. This would be a way to have a completely new start, wouldn't it?"

"Utterly," Dionysia spoke up. "And an adventure."

Dan nodded. That much, she could promise.

"But never coming back to Masym," Dan said soberly. "And not that many humans to know."

"Who else have you met?" Ellen asked, her eyes promising that she had made accurate guesses.

"We're not alone," Dan replied obliquely. "And we have friends. Many of them. I just wanted to make sure humans survive out there, but keep all this under your hat, because I don't need entire classes of folks thinking that their opinion matters."

And she had one hundred and fifty people to enforce that.

"Let me talk to Freda," Ellen said. "And I'll let you know. Either way, we still need to make sure you have what you need on that ship."

She rose and Dan joined her. Allies in certain industries would always be welcome. She didn't need industrial equipment, because even Isann was turning out more advanced things these days.

But chocolate? And chicken soup?

Worth the trip right there.

THIRTY-FIVE

Suka Kuri had taken to listening in to planetary broadcasts. News. Entertainment. Education.

She could see why Uly and Dan had had such atrocious accents when she'd first met them. At the same time, they hadn't known that they were speaking a dialect of Galactic Standard that spanned most known stars.

She wondered how few people knew the truth. Couldn't be that many. She remembered an ancient sage who had believed that a secret known to three was only secret if two of them were dead.

But Masym had things to teach her. Every world did, really. Every person as well, though with some of them, such things might charitably be classified as *bad examples*.

Halyna entered while Suka Kuri sipped her tea and thought deep and philosophical thoughts. Or something. She was still digesting the latest pop song hit that had started getting significant airplay on Masym planetary radio transmissions, comparing it to what Suka Kuri had listened to as a teenager, all those decades ago.

She gestured to the younger woman and Halyna joined her at the table, pouring herself some tea.

"How may I ruin your morning?" Suka Kuri grinned at the woman.

"Might be ruining yours," Halyna replied, matching it.

"Oh?"

"Dan has met Mazhin and Emro on the station," Halyna reminded her. "And we are aware of Zuath and Ugotha, plus suggestions of Mettai, though nobody saw one. All of which suggests that you might be able to visit the station directly. Or possibly even charm your way to the surface, where you, Anari, and Yanouk might join Dan, at least in measured increments."

"I have considered such things," Suka Kuri acknowledged. "Where it breaks down is the possibility that our presence disrupts Dan's careful lies and evasions about Bastion. Yes, she has met and recruited a few aliens, as the humans would see them, but the colony is supposed to be a purely Human thing."

"Which is what brings me here," Halyna replied. "I have been having conversations with Yeong-Suk and Zamira. They raised interesting questions, but didn't feel like it was appropriate, bothering Dan."

"Whereas you might challenge an old woman to social combat?" Suka Kuri teased as Halyna grinned at her.

Halyna Bondarenko fell in the middle of the Congress, by age relative to lifespan, but had an unexpected maturity about her. A calmness.

Perhaps a willingness to poke old women.

But to be Moss School was to demand such challenges on a regular basis.

How else did one learn?

"Me?" Halyna asked, smiling. "Perish the thought. It's Dan that we're looking out for."

"Uh huh."

More grins. All of the Congress had finally grown comfortable as equals. Dan might be First Wife, but that was merely knowing Uly the longest. He shared an equal and unique companionship with each woman, and she had worked diligently to assure herself of that in her role as the elder witch watching over her coven.

Or something equally silly.

"Humans can be tribal creatures," Halyna offered, holding up a hand to forestall interruption. "As bad as any of the rest of us, yes."

Suka Kuri nodded.

"If a few alien women were involved," Halyna continued, "that might induce a subtle and possibly unconscious bias among prospective recruits, further weeding out those that suddenly might be confronted with a non-human-centric galaxy."

Suka Kuri had done similar math, but she was thrilled that the Congress was equally filled with philosophers and warriors. Women who did both.

Saber AND Moss.

Dan had extremely high standards for admission.

"You might also seduce those with more prurient interests," she challenged.

"Would that be the worst outcome, if they met other standards?" Halyna challenged her right back. "Sterling and Anari. Uly and all of us. Even Kit and Mel. Not all future family units will be based solely within species. Granted, it has taken me some time to outgrow my own provincialism, but I can see where Dan is right. And Uly. People comfortable with aliens in a personal sense will better fit in."

"And the risk?" Suka Kuri challenged, channeling her favorite Human scholar and general self-appointed-pain-in-the-ass with his Socratic Method.

"We become exotic and valuable as potential pets," Halyna nodded. "Pirates of one flavor or another decide to attack *Polat* once we depart, expecting to rob us blind of all our supplies and possibly acquire a ready-made sex slave caste. I'll be standing next to Nasrin when they try."

As would the rest of the Congress. And everyone else.

Uly understood what they had done to the Mazhin, but even then Suka Kuri didn't think that Nasrin had told him everything. Plus, she was certain that there were elements Nasrin had simply been too young to understand at the time.

Omid yet retained her reticence, as did Haydar.

Captured *Danumash* pirates, however, might be shoved out an airlock. For extra evil, they might be left in a working suit at the time, so that they had hours or even days to die slowly.

Suka Kuri understood that such acts verged onto evil, but one does not negotiate with a rabid animal. Or an attacking one.

One uses excessive force to end the threat. If chasing the creature away suffices, so be it.

Sometimes, you were better off putting someone down, right up front, though it had been decades since she'd had to kill anyone.

Still wasn't the same as *never*.

"Who?" Suka Kuri challenged deeper.

Not acceding, but not denying. Gauging the depth of preparedness of the Congress, if they felt comfortable bringing a philosophical question to her, the Exemplar of Moss.

"We range an entire gamut of options," Halyna replied. "An Isann like Zamira all the way down to, say, a Guezal like Yeong-Suk or a Khet like Ciah, since both Emro and Mazhin appear to be known here. At that point, scales of ramifications comes into play."

And it would. Giant green women suddenly weren't all that exotic. Nor were tentacles.

Weird, but part of the current milieu.

"Go big or go home?" Suka Kuri grinned.

"That's Dan's call," Halyna replied. "We are tasked with offering her options and executing her plans, but this is a Human world, so the rest of us can usually only guess."

"And Dan and Uly are both exceptional, so they cannot be used to establish anything except one end of a spectrum," Suka Kuri nodded.

"Agreed. How much do we wish to reveal?"

"Let me talk with Dan," Suka Kuri decided. "There is a fine line there, and as you note, we need to play to her plans, rather than forcing her to dance to our tune."

Halyna nodded and sipped. Suka Kuri matched her and they fell into a companionable silence.

What did Dan need?

THIRTY-SIX

Like all the guys, Blair had generally assumed that any wife he found was going to be an alien. Not that he minded, having discovered just how interesting people could be, once you got beyond skin tone and shape.

Being back on a Human colony was just weird, because he was suddenly comparing the average woman on the street, who he should have been lusting after, to the women he knew elsewhere that he did. Or worse, the Congress, but that wasn't fair to anyone.

And he even wore a formal uniform for this mission, instead of the stuff he'd normally have pulled out of his closet. That outfit in bright blue and yellow checks was calling his name, but not today.

Today, he was in the main office, interviewing prospects because the recruiters had finally started locating people that could get past Dan's list of initially high standards to even make it this far.

I mean, when you're talking to the mission's nurse, regardless of the fact that he was probably the galaxy's top xenobiologist, however much by accident, you're serious. He needed to be serious.

So he'd braided his hair back today and tied it off with a clamp that would keep it out of his face. Shaved everything clean and even put on a nice scent that Nasrin had picked out for him, because she had the sharpest...nose.

Looking like a professional, which just put to shame how badly run things had been when Hylda had originally hired him as ship's medic, before she got the contract that killed her. At least a lot of assholes had gone with her, though he did miss the woman occasionally.

Didn't help that today's candidate looked so much like her. Younger cousin, maybe.

That same brown hair, though longer than the crop Hylda had maintained, and without the gray starting to appear underneath. Same green eyes and richly tanned skin Hylda had gotten in the tanning booth. Same lean muscles, though he didn't ask if Miss Jacquel Pery was also into rock-climbing.

It was already almost too much that she was being flirty. Touching when he got close and did the usual medical exam things that no machine could replicate.

At least he had space separating them now, with her on the table and him rolling his chair out of reach. Even of those impossibly long legs.

"Any history of illness that we need to be aware of?" he asked, *pro forma* working his way down the clipboard in his hands.

Using it as a shield if she suddenly lunged at him kept coming to mind.

"The usual childhood stuff," Miss Pery replied. "Great-grandparents suffering the usual ailments of age, but three of them are still alive in their second century."

Impressive. Maybe.

"Where are they living?" he asked, listening to accents now.

She shut down most of the flirtiness.

"*Danumash*," she said, much more quietly. "Bolton."

As in, the capital world of the seven capitals of the *Seven Crowns*.

"Oh?" Blair leaned in, all innocent and shit. "And their social classification?"

Dan wouldn't have even known to ask that question. He doubted that anyone from *Batyr* would have been able to just toss it out there soft and polite.

Miss Pery froze. Deer in headlights. Mouse seeing the owl swooping.

Unprepared for someone to know enough to call her on her bullshit, obviously.

Blair fixed her with a hard gaze, all set to toss the woman out on her ass right now as an impostor. Gennadi and a couple of newly hired toughs were just outside the door. And Miss Pery was fully dressed, so it wouldn't take long to have her on the street.

She squirmed uncomfortably as his smile frosted down.

He waited, counting down in his head.

"It's complicated," she offered.

"No, it isn't," Blair growled simply.

Because it wasn't. Dan had need of people, and trusted him to filter off trouble. Medical as well as psychological.

Miss Pery shuddered. Shrank in on herself a little more.

Pity.

He was just about to check the rejection box on the bottom of the form when she spoke.

And blew everything up in his head.

"Grand Duke and Baron. Duke and Countess," Miss Pery muttered quietly. "And respective spouses."

Huh?

Oh, fuck.

Worse, he probably had the records somewhere close to look up those eight people, if there was a Grand Duke in there. Reserved title, rather than inherited. Only awarded to siblings of the High King himself. Offspring of a Grand Duke or Duchess usually married high in the existing structure, once you were far enough apart for blood disorders and genetic issues to not overlap.

Which meant that Jacquel Pery was the great-great-grandniece of High King Dayton Wakefield himself.

And shit had just exploded well above his paygrade, so Blair rose and walked to the hatch, opening it and smiling grimly at Gennadi.

"I need Dan," he said simply. "Now."

THIRTY-SEVEN

Dan studied the young woman.

Attractive. Pale in that *Danumash* way that half of Dan's and Uly's men had. Athletic. Smart, from the test results. Fit, from Blair's examination.

Blair had rolled himself into the corner and gone quiet. Dan had pulled up a chair that put her a little below Miss Jacquel Pery, but only physically.

They studied each other for a long moment, but Pery had had time to stew while Gennadi had located her. Dan had studied things before making entry into the room.

"I have concerns," Dan began, mostly to see if the young *Danumash* noblewoman would incriminate herself.

But she only nodded. Blushed, which stood out on lighter skin. Pupils dilated. Breathing got shallow.

"I can explain?" Pery offered.

Dan waved a hand.

"Don't care about your family," she replied. "Mostly care about whether you're some sort of spy or trojan horse I need to deal with. Or just disqualify you right now and call it good. Why do you wish to vanish from Human history, Pery?"

Because honestly, that was what you folks were signing up for. Weren't, but they would only learn that truth much later. After they settled at Bastion and got their feet under them and learned how much they had been swindled.

Pery flinched. About what Dan expected. Blair had probably been playing good cop until things went sideways. *Good Enough Cop.* Dan was here for the other end of things.

Bad Enough.

"Because you promise that I can vanish from Human history," Pery countered, drawing her shoulders down and back. Jaw forward.

Tough.

"Why do you want to?" Dan asked.

"Do you have any idea…no, bad question. You're *Batyr*," Pery said, waving a hand negligently at the universe. "I am a **trophy** that they want to collect, Mistress Chastain. To adorn a shelf or mantle somewhere. Or would be, if they could find me. Catch me."

"Who's hunting you?"

"Every mother with an eligible son in the damned *Seven Kingdoms*," Pery growled tightly, showing some serious, honest emotion. "They all want to marry into the royal household and see me as their entry point. I'm not even a *person* to them."

"I understand that feeling, but for other reasons," Dan countered.

"Oh. Shit. Sorry." And the blushing was back.

Dan had read somewhere that a blush was almost impossible to actually fake. Not when it went to the ear tips and someone actually radiated heat at you.

Pery nodded, lips compressed into white lines and jaw muscles standing out.

Dan relented some. Blair's reactions to the woman had been perfectly on point, but he was approaching it as a medical thing. Or had been.

And had been smart enough to call for help when it got bigger than that. And it probably had.

"Forever, Pery," Dan said simply.

"No more *Danumash* noblewomen setting me up on blind dates," Pery practically snarled back, but her venom wasn't aimed at anyone on this planet. "No more seeing the title and rank before they even knew what color my eyes were. Oh. Shit."

More blush.

"Rank?" Dan pressed.

Pery gulped. Sucked a hard breath that looked like it might have inflated her toes.

"Primogeniture," Pery whispered. "You understand what that means?"

"Eldest legitimate child inherits," Dan nodded. "Absolute in *Danumash*, rather than agnatic, so any child, instead of only males, though I'm surprised that they haven't enshrined that in law."

"Oh, they've tried," Pery growled ugly. "Failed every time, mostly because a lot of angry women get up in their faces, every time they raise the subject. Absolute makes inheritance a lot easier, because agnatic forces weird calculations and adjustments constantly."

"So you are the...?"

"Eldest of the eldest of the eldest," Pery grimaced, a lot more subdued. "Technically, the duchy would fall to me and whichever spouse I eventually married, but only in another thirty or forty years, barring plagues, wars, and black swan events."

"How the hell did you end up on Masym?" Dan asked, amazed and aware of the surprise that Blair was doing a pretty good job of hiding on her flank.

"Outside of *Danumash* space," Pery replied with a shrug. "As far as I could run, and still be someplace big enough to hide. Gorge and Iethert are both too small, population-wise. I had access to funds I could turn into liquid for safety and help me vanish. And it still took a lot of planning to make it this far. I live in terror of bounty hunters showing up on my doorstep in the middle of the night."

"As you probably should," Dan agreed.

Hell of a lot of smarts and moxie, for a woman who looked *maybe* twenty-four at the oldest. But she supposed that, like Uly, Jacquel Pery had had far more advantages as a kid than most.

Especially folks like her.

"But then you showed up and suggested I could vanish forever," Pery continued, ratcheting her intensity up another notch and aiming it at Dan like a flashlight. "Beyond any reach of any of them. Sign my ass up."

Dan was surprised by the raw vehemence behind those words.

"If you do this, you should probably send them some sort of formal letter, doing whatever your kind have to do to pass your claim off to whoever is next," Dan said. "Do they do that?"

Pery stopped and blinked at her. Surprised as hell. Probably expecting Dan to push back, rather than offer her that lifeline.

"Yeah, I could relinquish," Pery offered quietly. "Haven't, because I always expected them to drag me back or cut me entirely off."

"You come with us, and you're just another sailor," Dan said. "Just another shopkeeper. Or farmer. Or whatever. Uly's from *Batyr*. So am I. Got no truck with inherited aristocracy and won't allow it to take root. But you also aren't ever returning to Masym, either."

Pery gulped.

There. Raw. Deal with it. Or not.

Dan rose. Nodded to Blair. Turned back to Miss Pery.

"You go home and spend a few days sleeping on it and deciding," Dan ordered her. "If you are still interested at that point, I'll have one more interview for you to pass. That one gets you a guaranteed slot on the ship when we leave."

Pery rose and shook her hand, tentative, but that was the dawning of hope. Not the fear of rejection.

Because *Grand Duchess* Jacquel Pery would have to convince Nasrin and Suka Kuri that she was serious. And could be trusted.

There wouldn't be anything for Dan to add at that point.

PART SIX
WARHAMMER ROSE

THIRTY-EIGHT

Lukyan was back to piracy, but he didn't mutter that too loud. Especially not around these yahoos. Missing Maks, but most of the rest of the folks had been with him on *Compass Rose*, back before *Fire Diamond*.

Warhammer Rose was just the next step up in lethality, and he'd added a larger boarding contingent than usual, because Uly needed him doing certain tasks along the way.

And, hey, free training at the expense of the Auga. Never discount the value of live fire exercises.

"Lukyan, got a signal," Lahja Arifullen said from her new sensors station.

Samuur woman. Smaller than most of them, which made her only the size of Samuur men. Still bigger than most Ononguli.

Her folks still called her *Tiny*. The daring ones.

"What's up, Tiny?" he replied.

"Cargo vessel, moving slowly out of dock with a lot of whining at the station," she said, ears going back and forth as he watched. "Light-speed wave is about an hour old, but nobody over there is bothering to scramble signals, so we're listening in real time, plus delay."

"Got his flight path?" Lukyan asked, feeling his blood start pumping a little harder.

"Affirmative," Tiny replied. "Didn't drive right over us, but close. Headed to Shingi to pick up more supplies. Running mostly empty because they dropped everything at Izabh."

"Because some furless punk is gonna build himself an armada here," Dmytro muttered, using one of Tiny's nicer insults for the Auga. And others.

Furless.

Snort.

"Dmytro, sound the alert," Lukyan decided. "Time to go hunting. Slava, get Tiny's data and plot me a chase. Tiny'll find them for us when we get close."

He leaned back and watched folks explode into action. Well, not explode. Hands and comments into microphones, mostly, but ACTION!!!

Warhammer Rose slipped up into warp, sniffing for the path that an old Auga freighter had left in the aether as it rumbled by. Beast that size sure as hell wasn't moving fast. Not as slow as *Wren* or one of those beasts, but the next size down.

Could you aggressively waddle? That might describe them.

Only a few minutes passed.

"Got their trail," Tiny announced. "Dead on the expected beam. No pirates around here?"

"We're way behind lines," Oskar reminded her. "And the Horde has largely withdrawn from this region these last few years because of Uly. Somebody got lazy over here. You'd think Sterling would have reminded them."

"Bureaucracy has so many letters because it was an imperial project," Lukyan pointed out to much laughter.

Lukyan keyed the line aft to the barracks, where Kairat Sydykov would be organizing his people. A pirate's pirate, one of the folks from the original Bastion Raid that had introduced Isann like him to the wider galaxy.

Them that had survived, anyway.

"Sydykov," he answered.

"Big Auga freighter in our sights," Lukyan said. "Largely empty and small crew aboard. Still a pain in the ass to locate them all, so take everybody when you go."

"Already rounded up the barber and the cooks," the man chuckled darkly. "You folks are getting cold sandwiches for dinner."

Because every body you could lay hands on and arm. Uly did it that way, over and above every one of Dan's combat battalions. An armed mob, that could be turned loose.

Lukyan was okay with heating his own soup in the microwave tonight.

He cut the line and nodded.

"Tiny, bring us home," he ordered.

THIRTY-NINE

Lahja Arifullen had volunteered for duty on what was primarily an Ononguli warship, partly because they needed bodies and partly because she got to be bigger than everybody else for once in her life. Not that she had much of a chip on her shoulders, but even Samuur men were usually taller than her, much to her everlasting embarrassment.

Ononguli were so much smaller than her. Even the big ones. And Isann.

She almost felt like a giant on this boat. It was nice.

And she was working directly for one of the top conductors around. Eskil was wonderful, but august and remote. Way too important these days. And Huff had a full crew that included important Samuur.

Warhammer Rose was a blank slate and she got to commit her own kind of graffiti here.

Heh.

Variable Pulse Spatial Generators left a trail. All of them. Every time you lit one up.

The better maintained your generators were, the smaller your trail was. And the faster it evaporated into the aether.

Ship they were chasing should have seen some serious yard time before this, but Tiny took that as a clue that their yards were busy on more important ships. Getting them ready for something. Or, like Izabh behind them, getting ready to send a warfleet over to do something about Avocur.

Her job, then, to stop them. Cold. Boop them on the snout, as it were, because *Warhammer Rose* was a small ship against a bigger force of things being assembled over there.

Kinda like a small Samuur women punching you in the nose.

Her kinda piracy.

There.

"Slava, slow down a shade," she ordered, studying her boards as they overtook their foe, based on all sorts of calculations.

Lukyan expected her to supervise the Ononguli men around here when she was handling Sensors. They were all older, relative, most of them having been with Chayka for a decade or more.

Old farts, challenged by the dangerous chick suddenly added to the bridge.

Yes. Timing was right. Target was translight, but far enough away that nobody should stumble over them from behind. Someone coming up from Shingi would simply land atop them if they got too close to the field *Warhammer* generated.

Hopefully, another freighter, filled with cargo to steal, rather than a cop, ready to arrest them all.

She'd gotten horror stories from the Ononguli around her about Auga custody and why it should be avoided as much as possible.

Some asshole named Adrian who was apparently related to Governor Maks. Not that anyone one around here remotely liked this Adrian punk.

"Thirty seconds to estimated contact," Tiny called, listening to everyone around her screw it down a notch tighter.

Slava flying. Oskar shooting stuff. Kairat ready to go a-viking with his boarding ax.

And, because Lukyan was the guy he was, it was a Tuesday and they were doing it to someone else.

She hoped.

"CONTACT!"

FORTY

Lukyan liked the way Tiny was working out. Didn't take shit from people, but didn't start shit either. Did the job with a hard professionalism that occasionally made some of his dorks look bad, which he absolutely had to point out to them in his role as conductor, don't you know?

Educational purposes.

Grins.

"Slava, stay tight on his ass," Lukyan ordered as both ships got too close and were forced into real space again.

There was a radius to the field. Smart boy over there would try running. In a ship with the maneuverability of a small planetoid.

"Oskar, warning shot, just because," Lukyan said.

Had a Samuur on the bridge and they did that sort of thing. And hell, it might even work. Weirder shit had happened.

So one turret went bonk. Single 8dm racing downrange, from four tubes forward and four more aft and slewed around as Slava turned to cut that freighter into a broadside.

"He forgot to raise shields," Tiny announced.

Shit, really?

"Oskar, let it track close, then detonate it early," Lukyan ordered, "Tiny, put me on his frequency for a pep talk."

"Blue button," she replied.

He found it on his board and clicked it.

"Attention enemy vessel," he recorded. "You will heave to for boarding or we will pound you into scrap for making me get off my ass. Am I clear?"

He replayed it, liked the tone, and hit send.

Welcome to the war, buddy.

Oskar did his thing and a pretty Roman candle lit the deep night between stars. Ship over there was still aggressively waddling, but that was a penguin on ice, trying to escape a leopard seal.

Ain't gonna happen.

"Slava?"

"Ten seconds to full broadside, then I'm sailing circles around him."

Lukyan nodded. Literally, knowing Slava. All turrets rotated port and locked onto a ship that on paper was massively huge and in reality had barely enough crew to cook and clean filters for the rest.

"We surrender!" a voice replied.

Lukyan was even feeling nice, so he allowed a video link to the fool.

Thogin.

Huh.

Lukyan wondered if the fellow was related to the Cousins in anything less than eighth degree. Probably safer if he wasn't, all things considered.

"Shut everything down but life support and APRs," Lukyan growled at the man. "No engines. No drives. No weapons. Only your auxiliary power reactors. Your crew will be dropped someplace safe later. I'll be boarding you shortly, and if anyone gives us any grief, you better hope you can swim to the nearest planet from here."

Pirate talk. Kinda came natural. Or came back. Muscle memory. Not like him and the boys hadn't used to make a living doing this to the Khet and Zuath, back in the day.

Adding the woman just meant that they might be respectable this time around, but he was careful not to say that around Tiny. She might get offended.

Thogin gulped and nodded.

"Cutting engines now," he said.

"Keep it that way," Lukyan ordered, then cut the line.

"Slava."

"Already circling in to take a bite," Slava laughed. "We docking or sending teams on backpacks first?"

"If he shuts down, maneuver to an airlock and line us up," Lukyan decided. "Tiny, watch everybody. Oskar, rotate three turrets out to cover our asses if someone happens along while we're working."

Assents. Professionals. Easy prey, but overwhelming force tended to work that way, as long as folks over there saw an out for themselves and didn't decide that they had to die fighting.

Auga ships on the frontiers got a little twitchy about that, but folks in other places generally marked it down as the cost of business.

As long as no patrol ships happened along...

"Sydykov."

"It's Lukyan. You're on, Kairat."

FORTY-ONE

Kairat Sydykov still remembered boarding a freighter at Bastion. Lucky for him, they'd been carrying stun wands and pistols, with only a couple of bigger tools to open bulkheads if they'd needed.

And he'd come from *Moonlight*, under Chief Sulaymanov, instead of one of the ones that Uly and Huff had crushed.

Dumbasses. Isann teenagers out joyriding in stolen flitters.

Lucky for him, Aibek had charmed Uly into not killing them all. Man had been utterly pissed. Making-examples-of-folk kinds of angry.

Kairat had seen the light. Or joined the winning side. Lots of folks saw it that way, even before *Nubia*. Today, he was Lead Trooper for Lukyan Chayka on a deep raid behind Auga lines to gather intelligence.

Still mentally looking over his shoulder for a shark to suddenly emerge. Like Uly had done to them that first time.

"Assault deck, stand by for docking," the bridge called. "Talking to locals across the way and they claim to be behaving."

Kairat nodded inside his boarding armor and leaned enough weight into the ax in one hand to make sure it would hold.

Meter and a half of carbon-fibre thicker than his thumb. Ax head backed by a hammer, with a spike on the end. Lever. Basher. Killer.

Not as elegant as an icemace or a shadowwhip sword, but it would get the job done and he wasn't supposed to be shooting anyone.

Just intimidating the shit out of them.

"First team, in," he ordered, watching a group of his killers slide into the airlock and draw weapons.

Standard-sized hatch at the far end, but double wide from there back, so a lot of bodies could flood through in a hurry.

Piracy was as much science as engineering, after all.

They'd closed up this whole bay behind him but not depressurized it. Wouldn't lose much air if the airlocks got blown, and nothing had to slam shut if it did.

By the book. Worse, by a book that Uly and Solomon had dramatically revised and updated when they got their hands on it.

Like, scary. But Humans, you know?

Kairat felt and heard the two ships dock, his air louvers still open for now. They'd slam shut as soon as pressure changed, but the extra sound was usually helpful.

"Locking in," Team One called. "Positive pressure far side. Standing by to open."

"Everybody armed?" Kairat asked on the general line. He waited a beat. "Open it."

Beeps as the big doors did their thing. Then bodies moving like someone had pulled a plug in a bathtub, draining his people into the other ship. Kairat flowed with them.

Professional pirates. Teams marked off to do things. First Team had the folks in the other room. Next six teams didn't slow down as they flashflooded the rest of the ship. Then a bunch more behind that to handle technical things.

Thogin conductor and crewmate. Center of whirlwind.

Kairat had met the Legal Department, so he knew the species. Doubted that this one was nearly as sneaky, and he only had one side-kick, so a lot harder to take an adult Isann down by themselves. Could still do it, though.

Team One stayed close.

"Any issues with being taken prisoner temporarily?" Kairat asked the small humanoid.

"Really?" the man asked. "Dropping us off somewhere?"

"Only want your ship," Kairat said. "The Corsac Fox is moving into this region of space and decided to teach the Auga some lessons."

Bullshit, as far as Kairat knew, but Lukyan had instructed him to feed the prisoners that set of lies, knowing it would get back to the authorities at some point. After they got released somewhere, which wouldn't be any system around here where they might warn anyone what was coming.

The little Thogin gulped, but nodded. Helped, being outnumbered and outmassed and outgunned. Centered the mind.

Kairat remembered being stuck in a big auditorium with the other survivors of Bastion, wondering what his fate would be.

Lucky that Aibek had managed to charm the right folks. And that the Chief of Chiefs recognized how bad that could have gone.

"Team Four, Engineering secured."

"Team Two, bridge under control."

"Team Three, forward barracks empty."

"Team Seven, aft barracks empty."

"Team Six, collecting strays for everyone."

Kairat nodded. Mostly Ononguli folks, but a fair leavening of others. Plenty of training. And eating in teams, sleeping in teams, and friendly competitions. By team.

Build the camaraderie. Useful now.

He locked in hard on the Thogin.

"We're going to your bridge now," Kairat ordered. "Then rounding up your people and putting them in safe places out of our way. You'll get home for the Dark Solstice, if we don't have any problems."

Or whatever the Auga celebrated as holidays. Probably somebody's birthday. Some important Auga.

Only two Isann demigod heroes of that stature, and Uly was still alive.

Whatever.

"Team One, move out," Kairat ordered, nodding the Thogin into motion.

FORTY-TWO

Lukyan liked it. Not quite textbook, but damn, it was nice to inflict a *Tuesday* on somebody else for once.

"Slava?"

"Got folks already on their bridge, confirming everything and getting ready to move," Slava replied.

"Detach and back away," Lukyan ordered. "Sooner we get them gone, the sooner we can follow."

Nice part about this crew was that Slava could handle things. Same with Oskar.

Space developed between the two ships.

Dmytro was on the hulk, pretending to be in charge. Looked good on the resume. Look at Maks, for instance.

The two ships separated and *Warhammer Rose* slid off. Got some range, so that the prisoner could fire up their generators and go.

"CONTACT!" Tiny yelled abruptly, utterly harshing his mellow in the worst possible way. "Possible warship on intercept vector."

Crap. Patrol ship had been shadowing the freighter. Or coming the other way and stumbled over them. Wasn't like this wasn't happening exactly in the middle of the highway, for everyone to see.

"All hands in motion," he ordered. "Tiny, tell Dmytro to get gone as soon as he can. We'll catch up later. And what are we facing?"

"Striker of some sort," she replied. "Heavy patrol class, from the read I'm getting. Maybe our scale for displacement."

"Locking on," Oskar barked. "Slava, which broadside do you want?"

"Stay inwards," Slava replied. "I'll cut up and over Dmytro from here and bring you to bear."

Lukyan nodded.

Sailing circles, and it was easier to keep doing that right now, because whoever it was had come up behind them, so coming from Izabh instead of Shingi.

Which made sense, as Auga started assembling one of those punitive missions to go pound on Uly and folks at Avocur.

At least that was his read from the kinds of ships in port and the fact that a lot of cargo was being hauled. More than a place like that needed for anything else.

And Maks was a pretty smart fellow.

"Oh, hey, that's weird," Tiny offered, making Lukyan's horns itch. "Enemy warship has a mixed loadout. Dual 8dm tubes in a single turret forward, with triple sixes in two others, fore and aft. Hang on while I look this one up."

Uly had stolen *Vauquelin* from the Auga. That had included a complete Auga database of ships. And they did things slowly.

I mean, they built fast, but only one new design every decade or two, depending. Maybe four such designs in service at any time, with old ones retiring for scrap as new designs were built to replace them, with a small expansion baked in.

"Warship identifies as HES875D74," Tiny continued. "Confirm an older model Light Patrol Striker. Think we outmatch him."

"Agreed," Lukyan said, studying the records she brought up.

Lots of small wavebolts, but most of those were defensive in nature. Same number of heavier tubes, but six of theirs were 6dm, instead of *Warhammer*'s 8s.

Still, gonna be messy, but all he had to do was drive them off, because Dmytro was sharp enough to corkscrew his horns getting away. Maybe that Auga could track them, maybe not.

Especially if someone bashed skulls with him.

Ononguli were good at that.

"Let him get close to range for his 6s, then let him have all of our 8s and see what he does," Lukyan ordered. "Hold out of range if you can, but our job is to distract him right now."

Conductor over there was aggressive. Charging. Feeling his oats today or something.

Or did he think that Lukyan hadn't already taken possession? Was he driving off the pirates, instead of recovering the ship?

Anything lighter, and Lukyan could see letting the Auga ship dock to help, then pulling a Dan move and swarming him in reverse.

"Tiny, get me Dmytro on a secured line," Lukyan ordered sharply. "Laser single-beam if you can. Nobody listening."

Her whiskers flickered when she concentrated. He'd learned that early on.

Same as Ononguli ears tended to straighten or curl with some folks.

"Your two," she replied.

"What's up?" Dmytro asked.

"Wanna Trojan Horse him?" Lukyan asked.

"Shit, it's Tuesday and we're back at Lacium, aren't we?" Dmytro grumbled.

Lukyan laughed.

"Something like that, yes," he agreed. "We're going to joust. You hang out here and hopefully we can either punch him hard enough, or maybe let him chase us off enough that he tries to come over and help you. Cut your engines or something and broadcast a distress beacon."

"I'll come up with something," Dmytro replied. "You better come back for me. If I have to share a cell with Adrian, you're never hearing the end of it."

Lukyan shuddered.

Adrian Sobol had always had a reputation as a hardass, but usually a successful one. Until he met Uly and got all his luck stolen by a group of Humans.

Plus his crew.

And his ship.

And his rep.

Maks was the Sobol everybody wanted to grow up to be, these days.

Possibly Lukyan's fault. At least a little.

"You play wounded orkac," Lukyan said. "He falls for it, and we'll go all furlo on him. Deal?"

"See you on the far side." And Dmytro cut the line.

"Slava?" Lukyan asked. "You get that?"

"Sure, turning away now and putting some space between us for the fight," he replied. "Oskar, a little earlier on your first salvo might be useful."

"And make it ragged," Lukyan ordered. "Amateur hour in the turrets. Junior varsity crews. That sort of thing."

"Coming up," Oskar said. "Firing two at random."

And two bolts went, followed by a ragged stream of five more.

One tube remained perfectly silent, like maybe it had suffered some sort of permanent malfunction that kept it out of action.

Rude. Lukyan liked it.

"Tiny?"

"We're selling rope," she replied. "He's buying. Enemy has changed his course. New vector will put him between us and the freighter on an escort heading. Dmytro just sent out a distress call, saying that they were able to break out and capture their invaders, but needed reinforcements to hold them."

"Perfect," Lukyan pronounced. "Nobody is dumb enough to send shuttles out in this mess."

Well, Dan had done it. He'd watched. Costs had been ugly, too.

But she'd won.

And if that Auga thought that the freighter's crew had fought back, then there couldn't be that many people aboard. Maybe few enough to manage.

A dozen or so, instead of a hundred.

Bit of a difference, there.

If *Warhammer Rose* could swindle them.

"Slava?"

"He's letting us go for now, it looks," Slava replied. "Dumbass never fought a pirate before?"

"Never fought Uly and Sterling," Lukyan corrected him. "Have your teams reload and stand by to Tuesday somebody."

Hard laughs. It had become a verb. He could live with that.

Today was gonna get messy.

FORTY-THREE

Tiny had heard about Lacium.

That *Tuesday*.

The one where the galaxy changed for so many people, even if they didn't hear about it for years. Like her kin.

Still, she'd looked it up. Studied what Uly had done, during a weird case of mistaken identity that had involved a stolen Ononguli raider in Human hands. And other races.

It had kind of started there. Everything.

"Lukyan, I think he's letting us go," she announced, watching the other ship slow down and fire a barrage of lighter wavebolts at them as *Warhammer Rose* accelerated away.

"Good," he replied. "Slava, all ahead crazy."

"All ahead crazy, coming up."

Tiny studied the layout of the system, then echoed boards from what the pilot was doing. And the gunner. She dialed down all of her jamming signals, like maybe power to the engines had to come from somewhere and Lukyan was cutting everything but life support in order to run.

Silly, but it appeared to be working.

"Tiny, they're following the manual," Lukyan said, apparently watching her ears and whiskers and correctly reading her confusion.

Uly had done it. And it had worked.

Shouldn't the Auga have heard about it?

She glanced back to make eye contact, then went to her boards.

"Yes, manual," he continued. "The one that says to rescue the ship and capture all those silly pirates that are trapped aboard, when you chase off their ship. Manual even says to chase us in a bit, so maybe they do something silly like plan to dock exactly long enough to put all their own boarding crews onto the freighter before racing madly after us."

"Except that it won't work that way," she completed the thought.

"A-yup," Lukyan laughed. "Slava, you handle things."

"Oskar, stay guns to port forward," Slava called. "Everyone else, stand by for crazy."

Tiny rotated all her own systems forward, then offset to port some, expecting things on her left side shortly.

Warhammer Rose jumped to warp. Barely.

On a planetary surface, they'd be leaving tire marks in a driveway, and smoke in the air, as Slava slewed the ass end of the ship around, turning to port at high speed and describing a hard arc.

"Dropping now," Slava said. "About a light-hour out, off both vertical and horizontal planes from previous engagement."

"Excellent," Lukyan announced. "Everyone that needs it take a quick potty break. Fifteen minutes for folks over there to get disorganized."

Tiny studied her scans of the patrol ship. Defensive firepower, but not as much on offense. Neither had hit the other during the exchanges of wavebolts so far, but that had been staying back at a distance.

Still, she marked everything she could and highlighted interesting bits. Like a tendency to keep their bow down when sailing at *Warhammer Rose*. Kept the turrets centered, but caused maneuverability issues.

Plus anything else she could think of, but fifteen minutes went by pretty quickly.

"All hands, this is Lukyan," he announced behind her. "Time's up. Slava, CHARGE!"

FORTY-FOUR

Lukyan had taken lessons from Sterling's Starfare School.

Shit, but that kid was dangerous.

Worse, Solomon Wyndham was just as scary at ground operations, and had added several chapters to the curriculum for armies.

And raiding teams.

Dan had refined it.

Kairat had hopefully stayed up to date on it all, because the proof was about to be in the pudding.

All ahead crazy.

Variable Pulse Spatial Generators meant a bubble that kept ships from being too close. Or from getting away, if you had them inside your bubble.

And that knife had two edges.

Warhammer Rose dropped out of jump at stupid fast, with Slava already reversing everything he had to slow them down.

Wouldn't matter for a couple of minutes.

Might bring them to rest more or less on top of the other two ships.

Which would be interesting.

"Got them docked," Tiny called. "Hearing radio distress calls on several frequencies. Not sure they've seen us yet."

"Oskar, I want the cop banged, but not the freighter if you can manage."

"There's a reason I'm on this vector," Slava sassed. "He's a shield in front of the bigger ship."

And he was.

This time, eight big bolts went out in a single, crisp salvo. And, because Oskar was being a punk today, he threw both 2dm and all four 1dm turrets into that mix.

Impressive as hell, coming at you, Lukyan had to guess.

As long as it was the other guy.

"Defensive fire, but somebody caught him on the wrong engagement plane," Tiny called.

"Again, not my first rodeo," Slava laughed harshly.

They were low. HES875D74 had moved to dock with Kairat and Dmytro. His bow was pointed the right direction, but *Warhammer Rose* was below him, and he had to detach and roll to bring his own turrets directly into line.

Wavebolts were seeker weapons. You could fire them in any direction, then let them turn and maneuver as they needed to hit.

But distance was inversely proportional to damage. The farther it had to run, the weaker it got.

Oskar's 1dm bolts were just insults thrown at someone in a dance battle. The 2dms weren't much better. Bucko's defensive fire over there still had to go out, turn around, then race back inwards to stop his 8dms from slamming into shields and hull.

That took time. And cost power.

"Second volley in flight," Oskar said unnecessarily.

And the silly git hadn't thrown the defensive bolts into this one, rightly presuming that someone over there might start shooting finally.

Sure as hell wasn't getting away.

"Enemy has detached and is trying to back away," Tiny called. "Currently suffering fighting in his own corridors."

Because he'd fallen for it, and lined up to march combat troops over and retake the vessel from amateur-hour pirates.

Knowing Kairat, someone had fired Painspheres into and through the airlock as soon as it opened.

Even Lukyan didn't think that Firespheres were immediately warranted.

Probably.

Kairat was Isann, so less bad blood with Auga uniforms thans say, an Ononguli might have.

Probably.

"We're gonna slam this salvo home," Tiny yelled loud enough that everyone would hear.

Lukyan studied her board and saw what she saw.

Yeah, probably.

"Oskar, defensive only," he ordered.

"Defensive fire, comin' up."

Boom.

Damn, that was pretty.

Two Ononguli bucks, trying to impress the same woman, bashing skulls together until they both saw stars.

Not that Lukyan had done that more than a few times.

Lots of stars over there.

"How's Dmytro?" he asked, mostly because that guy was too close to the Striker right now.

"Laughing," Tiny replied.

Lukyan nodded. Sounded like that pirate. Painspheres and charge. Like Humans took enemy ships.

He studied the boards. HES875D74 had suffered collapsed shields all down this flank. It might be possible to actually kill the ship, if he poured everything he had into them right this moment.

Bash and rend and torch and gnaw.

He had a better idea.

"Tiny, where's Kairat?"

FORTY-FIVE

Kairat hadn't been first through the airlock. Commanding officers weren't supposed to LEAD assaults like that.

Just be close enough to yell at the men and women on point.

Nobody over there had been expecting Painspheres. Certainly not three of them, detonating in a small space and inducing nausea and vertigo.

And boarding armor only shielded you some.

Pretty troops in pretty lines, currently puking inside their pretty helmets.

Making them less pretty.

Kairat was Isann. He'd had his people lead with stun weapons.

Uly hadn't killed them afterwards because of that.

Useful lesson.

"Team Two and Three, secure the prisoners," he yelled as bodies flooded the enemy ship. "Beware of vacuum warnings at any moment."

Get EVERYONE on the enemy ship as quickly as possible, because Dmytro had locked up all the Auga prisoners in an aft storage room, with his own folks flying and managing engines right now.

Either this worked, or it didn't, so time to leave it all on the ice, a term he'd picked up from some of his Samuur troopers, who were all jocks when they weren't also nerds.

Charge. Dodge. Shoot anything that moved and wasn't in blue armor.

Anything.

Better safe than sorry and he was using stun weapons so he could apologize later.

If he needed to.

Auga corridors. He'd toured *Vauquelin* in the yard to learn how the Auga did things. And they'd built training facilities to similar scales, to get you used to doors, stairs, and lifts.

Bodies in motion.

"Warning. Vacuum detected," a voice announced, right as a wind came up.

Briefly.

Hatches and firebreaks started tripping, slamming shut to hold things in.

Hopefully, all of his people had gotten across the gangway before it happened, but he was committed.

And stunned folks weren't going to be a problem for a half hour or so.

"Push," he ordered. "All teams, get me forward to the bridge. Failing that, general havoc."

"Team Nine, we got aft a ways before things locked."

"Take out engineering if you can," Kairat ordered. "Don't break anything."

You had to remind the juvenile delinquents not to use Firespheres. Natural inclination to destroy things.

Counter-productive today.

"Team One, counterattack underway in main corridor. Could use some help here."

"Team Four, vector down," Kairat called. "Five and Six, find his corners and push his flanks in."

Most of the security personnel on this ship were probably behind him right now, being taken prisoner. The rest were reacting to an invasion warning and rushing to trouble.

Admirable, but he had surprise.

Hopefully, he had numbers, too.

Kairat moved with his command squad, then turned left when he got to a corridor.

Yes. There.

"Get that hatch open," he ordered, stepping back as bodies went to work.

You could override things from the bridge on an Auga ship.

And most pirates that had any sense.

There were still things you could do locally.

Like blasting the front panel off with a door buster, then manually connecting the right wires.

The door opened. Kairat fired into the opening as soon as it moved, but there wasn't anybody there.

Just in case. Then he moved.

Noise behind him was Team Eight.

"You lead," he waved them forward. "Up a deck and that way."

Maybe, just maybe, he could get to the bridge from an odd angle, popping out into the main corridor not far from the conductor's office.

That was how *Vauquelin* had been built.

Time to find out if it held true here.

FORTY-SIX

Kairat stalked up to where one of his troopers was poking an optical sensor around a corner, while the rest of Team Eight watched the other direction.

"Think that's it, sir," the woman said quietly, pointing at an image on her screen.

Two Emro defensive in gold and red boarding armor.

Big'uns. Not as scary as the Sabre Scholars he'd met.

"Any explosives?" he asked.

"Negative. Just sidearms."

The book had specific thoughts on a situation like this. Solomon Wyndham had amended it in a number of places, inserting the words audacity and ferocity.

"Team Eight, on my mark, around the corner and firing," he said quietly. "Command squad to hold the rear flank while you charge. Stand by. Three. Two. One. MOVE!"

And he was the calm eye of a storm of bodies.

And beam fire.

Kairat listened, pointing his pistol the other direction with his people, but it was empty over there.

"Secured, Commander."

"Moving up," he said. "Rotate responsibilities."

Bodies flowed back and forth. He found himself standing at that main hatch to the bridge.

Audacity and Ferocity.

Kairat leaned over and pushed the comm button that an Emro body had been concealing.

"You can open it and be taken prisoner, or I can blow it open and come in firing," Kairat said. "Your choice."

About that moment, the deck beneath his feet whiplashed with a metal earthquake and half the lights in the hallway shorted or went dark as some explosion rattled through the entire hull.

Glancing back, sparks continued from something burning inside a bulkhead.

Not his ship. Not his problem.

Yet.

Gravity was twisted. Hell, felt like *Warhammer Rose* had surprised the hell out of them, from the way everything had a pronounced tilt under his feet.

WEIRD feeling on a starship.

"Okay," he continued. "You had your chance."

"WAIT!"

And the hatch opened.

Kairat REALLY wanted to throw himself to the deck, but he was the commander around here, and that would be unseemly in front of his killers, so he held his ground as his asshole puckered hard.

He pointed a pistol at the bodies over there, but nobody was shooting.

That was good.

"We surrender!" an Emro woman called.

Big woman. Big and green and mean. Made his Samuur ladies look small and cuddly by comparison. Not that he'd ever mention that out loud.

Kairat walked onto the bridge and scowled at everyone, even as Team Eight got sorted and joined him.

Commander. Gotta lead. And hopefully not get shot in the process.

"Stand down and order everyone on your side to do the same," Kairat announced.

"We already have," she said. "The ship has suffered significant damage and requires repair immediately."

"Walk over to that wall, all of you," he waved. "Quietly and polite. Team Eight, take charge. Team One, what is your status?"

"Folks surrendering here, sir."

"Engineering?"

"Team Nine. Same."

Kairat nodded.

Audacity and Ferocity.

He switched channels on his comm.

"*Warhammer Rose*, this is Kairat Sydykov," he said. "Enemy vessel appears to have surrendered on terms."

FORTY-SEVEN

Tuesdays.

Cuts both ways.

HES875D74 had smoke trailing out in places, which was better than plasma venting. Circuit breakers needing to be reset, instead of rescue operations to get sailors off the hulk before it detonated.

"Do we leave the freighter here?" Oskar asked. "Or just blow it in place?"

"Negative," Lukyan replied. "Might stash it somewhere. Or pull a *Wren* and put a small crew aboard to get it home whenever. Keeping HES875D74."

"Duh."

Lukyan smiled.

The good old days really hadn't ever been that good, but rose-colored glasses made everything prettier in retrospect. Especially *Compass Rose*-colored.

A Patrol Striker might and might not have the information he needed, but they sure as hell weakened this frontier with it off-line.

If he hadn't brought this many extra crew with him, he might have to blow it. Or autopilot it into a nearby star to destroy it entirely.

The freighter had most of the data he really needed, considering where they'd come from. The Striker might have the rest.

"Kairat, how quickly can that beast move?" he asked.

A pause at that end. No doubt asking the crew.

"We need an hour to confirm a few things is what I'm being told," Kairat replied.

"Slava, transmit them a course and destination, then get us over to Dmytro so we can move bodies around," Lukyan ordered. "Tiny, I seem to remember you have command training?"

Whiskers and ears going like mad over there when he smiled at her.

"Yes, sir…"

"Take command of the Striker," he ordered. "We'll get most of their crew off and figure out where to put them, but I need it in motion and I need Dmytro sailing the tub as soon as he can dock and handle that. We'll be close, but you'll have a warship at your fingertips."

She nodded, eyes HUGE. But she could handle it.

Lukyan sat back and started working out crew rosters and rotations. Kairat already had a lot of folks with secondary crew skills, so he only needed a few experts off the freighter, plus security bodies to get all the new prisoners onto *Warhammer Rose*.

Any bodies that could lift or hold a gun. All hands on deck.

Shit had gotten weird.

At least it was somebody else's *Tuesday*.

FORTY-EIGHT

Tiny walked aboard the enemy vessel that was now her prize command and tried to act like she belonged.

Even worked until she got to the bridge and saw the command station and remembered that the conductor had been Emro. Big. Way big. Bigger than even a Samuur woman of normal size, to say nothing of Tiny.

Her scowl could probably etch hull.

She sat down and let her feet swing like a six-year-old sitting at the adult table.

It did not improve her humor.

Still, she had trained for this sort of thing. *Vauquelin* used Auga technology, and Governor Maks had absorbed all that architecture when making *Warhammer Rose*. She found the right button and pressed it.

"Engineering."

"Time to flight?" she asked simply, grinding her jaw shut and keeping her whiskers centered.

As much as possible.

"We could limp now, sir," the woman replied. "Don't want to stress anything, so we shouldn't go fast until we trust these systems better, but

I think we're in good shape. Got a lot of bodies back here to fix shit when it breaks."

"Stand by for power," Tiny said.

She didn't know the boarding teams that well, and Dmytro had stayed on the freighter, sending her some of his people, along with bodies from *Warhammer Rose*.

Tiny figured that she'd learn everyone's names over the next couple of days, but time was short and tea ceremonies could wait.

"Pilot, you ready?" she asked.

Isann man, pretty recently joined *Warhammer Rose* from their fleet as hulls got built and people could transfer to Uly.

Like her.

"Aye, Chief," he replied.

Chief, because Isann habits, rather than *Conductor*. Or whatever her rank should be.

She had technically joined the pirates, hadn't she? Except that they wore Uly's blue uniforms and she was a Lieutenant. Or something.

Sort it all out later.

"Ahead slow until you're sure," Tiny ordered. "Then warp slow as well, working with engineering to bring things up to speed. Shut it down without waiting for orders if something breaks, am I clear?"

"Aye, Chief," he replied.

Tiny leaned back, then grumbled when she couldn't touch the back of her chair without nearly laying down.

"Engineering."

"I need someone to come up to the bridge in a little bit," Tiny said. "A team to rip out the conductor's station and replace it with something my size. Probably everyone else later, or not, depending, but I will be comfortable when we sail into harbor."

Because if the galaxy doesn't fit, make it.

Even tiny Samuur women.

PART SEVEN

IMPERIAL SECTOR SEVENTEEN

FORTY-NINE

Suka Kuri had had, in the end, to be goaded into asking Dan.

A bit hilarious, for an old woman like her to suddenly develop nerves at this stage, but she understood. Masym was Dan's mission, in ways that Stradosha had belonged to Suka Kuri.

Not the center of attention, but the anchor upon which all the other plans hinged.

They had a mission. Fifty-eight percent female by pure biology, with those in various expressions of their general sexuality understanding that there would be societal expectations to produce offspring at some point, purely for the mathematics of a new colony. And all had been okay with test tubes and medical assistance, if it came to that.

They could still present however they saw fit, and Humans, like the amazing range of skin colors, had an entire spectrum of sexualities they might feel comfortable in.

But Suka Kuri had withheld asking, until nearly the end. Dan's mission, with so many knives being juggled that nobody knew when one more might break a camel's back.

And then Ciah had dragged Dan into her dojo and confronted the old woman with an impossible situation.

Troublesome Warrior Children could be like that.

Thus, Suka Kuri found herself on the surface of Masym, walking the streets of Brahyrst and ignoring the surprised stares of Humans who should have known that aliens existed. Emro were present. Mazhin, perhaps less so. Khet and Ononguli, not at all.

But one old Emro woman, with two daughters—three including Nasrin—only stood out a little.

And Suka Kuri was walking on the surface of a Human world. It was a thing she hadn't imagined that she would ever do. Formerly, because they were so far away. Presently, because Uly was home attempting to hold the Auga back for an entire year, while all of his wives were with Suka Kuri, attempting to build his future.

Even for an Exemplar of the Arts, it was a heavy load.

"Are you well?" Yanouk asked, watching her.

Yanouk, who had once been a promising child prodigy, now grown into a dangerously interesting young woman. Just as Anari and Nasrin had as well.

"Tea, I think," Suka Kuri answered.

It was not a physical discomfort. Perhaps emotional.

How many paths for the future of the galaxy diverged from this exact moment, with four alien women inside a Human bubble of space and time?

Surrounded by strangers.

Not an outraged space. Surprised. Humans knew that there were aliens out there, but even on Masym they were few.

Until today, when three green titans walked among them.

Yanouk used her height to peer over the crowd. She saw something, because Yanouk waved once, pointed at someone, and began to walk that way. The crowd parted around them.

Suka Kuri found herself at the entrance to a sidewalk cafe. And a Human woman who had gone a great deal paler around the gill slits and eyes at her approach.

"Mistress," the woman said in a tightly-bound voice. "Four? My apologies that we are unlikely to have seating that can easily accommodate you."

"One chair for my sister," Yanouk said, pointing to Nasrin. "We three have towels that can be unrolled on the floor, where kneeling will put the table at an acceptable height."

Because nothing ever fit an Emro woman unless specifically designed that way. And they had not made the sorts of plans that would see everything set up ahead of time. Nor did she wish to balance precariously on a tiny stool that might crack under her weight.

Tables were moved with a synchronization that Suka Kuri found impressive. They found themselves on the patio of the cafe, a mere rope separating them from passersby on the sidewalk. One somewhat young woman as a server, marshaling the rest of the staff like a wizened general. Even the manager at the door took her orders without hesitation.

Suka Kuri smiled at her. At all of them.

At Masym and the galaxy.

She had come this far. Dan was doing this thing. Alien women had only chased off a few prospective recruits, which was for the best for everyone, anyway.

They still had no idea what was coming.

Tea. In what she understood were the largest coffee mugs available, but Suka Kuri was not offended. Human tea. With Human ingredients.

An alien thing.

And, just because, she ordered a plate of rolls, so she could butter them with something yellow, blue generally being the default in much of the galaxy beyond Human ken. Jams and jellies were only exotic by ingredient, though the apple butter was something she very obviously needed to make sure Dan took home.

"Won't work," Anari said quietly, nose pointed at the apple butter.

"No?"

"Apples are extreme heterozygotes," Anari nodded. "Fruit from any given cultivar won't necessarily resemble the parent tree. I'm given to understand that almost all apples these days are either wild-grown, or grafted onto a hardy rootstock. Makes transport interesting, but means that some enterprising soul back home can plant a whole bunch of seeds, wait a few years, then start determining which flavors they like."

"Uly will appreciate that," Nasrin noted. "Something for everyone, if they have patience to seek it out."

Suka Kuri laughed with delight, as that thought so exquisitely summed up the man and his approach. And all the things they were doing to help him.

Here she was, complaining about kneeling on cold concrete, and Nasrin had boiled it all down.

Laughing tentacles.

Others around them relaxed and smiled back tentatively. The day was coolish, but clear and calm. Rather lovely, and the tea hit the spot, melting a knot that had worried itself into the space between her shoulder blades.

"Have we done enough to gather the seeds of what Uly needs?" she asked the table, watching faces turn serious and scholarly.

Dan had come for bodies, intent on ensuring that Humans continued to be part of the *Spinward Reaches*. Colonists had brought ideas and certain equipment, but there was almost nothing of a technological base that couldn't be made easier and cheaper on a more advanced world.

That left culture.

And she had acquired five lovely physical copies of the Odyssey, as well as electronic versions she intended to translate into galactic on the flight home.

The Chief of Chiefs would appreciate getting his own personal copy, as well as one for their planetary library, to sit next to the *Karaŋgılıkka*.

Other books and videos of Human origin had been acquired. They would remind these Humans of who they had once been, until it finally came time to initiate *Danumash* and *Batyr* into the wider galaxy, though she hoped that Uly was still around on that day.

"Is there anything like Moss School?" Nasrin asked quietly, tentacles seemingly tasting the faint breeze for clues.

Suka Kuri considered all that she had learned from her few Human friends, both back home and the ones that Dan had specifically asked her to interview before allowing them to join this mission.

"No," she decided after a long pause. "They have musicians and artists, but nothing so formal as Moss. There have been, from the records I have consulted, those few who might have been Exemplars, had they the opportunities."

Human history was almost as deep as Emro, once you found the right sources, and she had acquired a number of histories and biographies for her research library.

But no, nothing like Moss had ever taken root. Possibly because Humans so loudly embraced Sabre.

"We have farmers and ranchers," Yanouk offered. "Scholars and shopkeepers. Even a few warriors, though not many. We do not have pure artists as Moss might understand them."

Suka Kuri nodded. That had been the missing element, however unconscious it had been to her.

Worse, Masym might be the wrong world upon which to seek such things. *Danumash* would have such scholars, but they might be as stuffy as Elias had been when he first joined the mission. The man had loosened up since, but had spent most of his time in scholarly pursuits as befit the Historian to the Court of Traiffe.

And a man intent on tracking down the Lost Tribe, but even then, the clues he needed were probably found at the two capitals, Gralbo and Bolton.

But he would miss the musician. The actor. The painter.

Suka Kuri put down her coffee mug and located her comm.

"Dan."

"I may have a need," Suka Kuri explained. "Might I reserve as many as ten of the remaining spaces before we finish?"

"Who am I missing?" Dan asked, because she was smart enough to leap to that valid conclusion instantly.

It was who Dan was.

"Moss School," Suka Kuri replied. "As your kind might have stumbled onto a thing, rather than formalizing it in one of those stuffy institutions that Elias has been haunting since we got here."

Dan laughed, seeing the man, as brilliant as he was, in that same light.

Only Dionysia had truly leaned into becoming Human, as the Yarikh might have seen them.

"Ten is easy," Dan replied. "I can stop now and let you have that last allotment, as I have folks that haven't gotten around to making up their mind."

"The ones I need might not have understood the nature of that call," Suka Kuri replied. "Thank you."

"Chat soon."

And Dan left it up to her.

Her three friends and fellow students watched her expectantly. As did the waitress supervising things.

Suka Kuri locked eyes with the Human woman. Nodded, when she saw the question unasked in those expressive eyes.

"What is Moss?" Suka Kuri asked their waitress.

The woman nodded silently.

Suka Kuri turned to Nasrin, surprising her.

"You are the outsider here," Suka Kuri reminded her, reading the profanity and eye roll in those tentacles and laughing some more.

It felt lovely to laugh with friends.

"Moss is an Emro School, primarily," Nasrin explained, pointing to the three of them. "It travels the galaxy learning about art. Not to maintain it into permanent stasis, but to learn new ways of looking at it. New means of expressing ancient ideas more in tune with adapting civilization. Preserving the best parts, and allowing the dross to wither."

The woman watched the four of them with narrowed eyes.

"How big is the galaxy?" she asked.

"Immense," Suka Kuri replied first. "Humans are generally safe in this corner as long as they stay put. Trouble is unlikely to come looking for them. We came because we had a need."

"Human colonists," the waitress said, with a hint of emphasis on the first word.

"Human colony," Nasrin replied, nodding with the same intensity. "It needs Human art."

And again, Suka Kuri was struck by how well Nasrin Monfared could distill things down to the fewest possible syllables, without losing anything in the process.

The Human woman was jarred onto her heels, nonetheless.

"Which kinds?" she finally asked.

"Yes," Nasrin smiled.

Perfect.

Perhaps she needed to turn the Mazhin woman into a Moss Adept at some point. Possibly when she wasn't looking. It was only fair, after all.

Human eyes get large in surprise, presumably to take in the most light in dangerous situations. The waitress did that now, then withdrew for more tea, probably to give herself space to think.

And breathe.

Suka Kuri nodded at Masym and enjoyed her tea.

FIFTY

Nasrin studied their waitress as the woman returned from whatever had taken her out of sight for several minutes. Wasn't a trap, because her body language and smell were wrong for that, though Nasrin and the others were armed and dangerous.

It was a Human world, after all.

The woman came to rest and studied them with hard eyes.

"I know an artist," she announced simply, focusing on Nasrin, as though mesmerized by tentacles. "In about twenty minutes, he'll be busking at the park down the street."

Then she nodded that way, deposited a fresh mug of tea, and vanished inside the cafe.

Nasrin turned to the other three.

"Busking?" she asked, a Humanism she'd never encountered.

"A musician, playing for the public in a public place, collecting tips as people walk by," Anari replied. "Lousy way to make a living. Good way to practice and get better."

Nasrin nodded, reminded yet again of what a sheltered childhood she had had. Then her teenage years in *Danumash* slavery.

Then Uly.

She could see it, but you didn't have such things on a ship. Open mic nights might be a close companion, if she was reading the language correctly. Or not.

They enjoyed their tea in a subdued atmosphere, something having been drained out of the conversation by the waitress. A new person checked on them. Male. Slightly befuddled, by being put on the spot.

The first one wasn't in the cafe anymore, her smell having evaporated.

Odd.

They paid, using thalers that Dan had gotten from a local bank, departing to smiles and *bonhomie* all around.

The crowd wasn't a crowd so much as a group of folks roughly following them, four alien women being utterly mundane otherwise, but Nasrin led them in the direction of the park.

And smelled their waitress before she saw her.

Heard her before she came into sight.

Singing.

Nasrin was still occasionally teased as *The Songbird* for the performances she had put on early in Uly's legend, recruiting and cementing things in a way that few people truly understood. She had a good voice and a better understanding of tone than most, though the three Moss women with her were all expert quality or better.

Nature of Moss School.

But the waitress was singing with power, rather than control. Emotional resonance that warbled some, not as an exercise in diaphragm contraction, but in heart overfilling and bleeding into the words.

Then she came into sight. The woman, with a Human male beside and a bit behind her, playing a guitar with a small amp plugged in, but turned well down. Or maybe not even on, and he could wrest that much sound out of it.

Chords, for the most part, but sharply clean in execution, fingers moving like her tentacles as she watched. Impressive mastery of his instrument.

But the woman...

Songbird. And Nasrin could say that. The crowd had been drawn into her gravity well and held by her tones. Love and loss. Pain and hope. Freedom on the verge.

Not a song she knew, but Nasrin hadn't been exposed to much Human music, and Mazhin stuff tended to have less emotionally ragged edges. Less fingers reaching into your chest and grabbing hold.

Power. Raw and absolute, as the woman's unamplified voice took possession of the park, heads turning from a distance, bodies coming to stillness from whatever they had been doing before. The guitar was simply a sonic stage upon which she strode, the two Humans deep into something that Nasrin didn't think she was emotionally mature enough to understand, being still young as her kind measured things.

Suka Kuri's smile spoke the volumes Nasrin needed. Anari's head nodding to the beat. Yanouk absorbing the words to the point she might repeat it tomorrow.

Moss School.

One song ended and the duo went straight into the second with a nod and a quiet word. A third. A fourth.

Change was beginning to pile up in front of the pair, filling the guitar case as strangers offered whatever prayers might be granted by a goddess of song.

Time passed in a blink, but also an entire afternoon crammed into perhaps twenty minutes.

It only felt timeless and over too soon.

"Thank you," the waitress said at the end of a song. "You've been most kind."

She turned away from the audience and squatted down next to the man, breaking the spell she had been casting.

The audience awoke as from a dream and began to wander off, even the aliens in their midst largely forgotten. Quickly, it was only the six of them, the man having collected all the change into a pocket and putting his instrument away.

He was lost, but handling things in a way that reminded her of Kit. Relaxed and agreeable. Aware of the deep waters all around him but not at all intimidated by it.

Simply stood there and waited for whatever he was supposed to do next.

The waitress stood and took a deep breath, then stepped right up to Suka Kuri and looked up.

FIFTY-ONE

Suka Kuri could not help the smile. The day might have been utterly perfect. At the very least as completely charming as any she'd enjoyed in a while.

"I am Suka Kuri," she introduced herself to the young woman. "Exemplar of the Moss School."

Not that it would mean anything to a Human on Masym, but it framed everything.

"Delphine Zahra," the woman nodded back. "My husband, Marten."

"I am unfamiliar with that music," Suka Kuri offered, leading the woman in a certain direction, mostly to see where they arrived to.

"All of it was original," Delphine replied. "I write lyrics, he writes music."

"All of it?" she challenged, treating the youngster like a bright Seeker.

"No music is completely original, Elder," Delphine shrugged. "Nor are chord progressions, because mathematics has already explained everything, merely providing the mosaic pieces which we can thus assemble into new forms."

As perfect an explanation of Moss School as you might ever encounter, too. Suka Kuri was impressed.

She studied the male. He studied her, eyes wide with expectation but no body language of any hostile or negative emotion.

He had been, perhaps, at home, or just possibly at work. A call from his spouse. A rush to the park to perform, possibly sight unseen and no questions asked at all.

A bit protective of her, from the way he stood, but not shadowing her. Sheltering.

Then to simply play with everything he had while she sang, an unplanned performance, busking in the park on a crisp afternoon.

It had been decades since Suka Kuri had done the same. She almost felt the need to fix that, but Masym was perhaps not the correct planet upon which to do such a thing.

It was Dan's mission, and they yet needed some level of obscurity once they had departed.

Still, she would. Perhaps Bastion. Maybe Rayzian.

Probably Saari, if she was feeling a touch rude.

"Marten?" she confirmed.

"Indeed, Exemplar," he said in a quiet tenor voice.

"Suka Kuri. Nasrin. Yanouk. Anari."

"Ladies," he nodded to all of them, then did a thing where he managed to somehow fade into the background without ever moving.

Impressive. Especially considering that he was a guitarist, and they weren't usually so quiet.

"How may I assist, Delphine?" Suka Kuri asked the woman, putting her in the position to grab agency and do what she would with it.

"Does the Moss School have Humans?" Delphine asked quietly.

"Not yet," Suka Kuri acknowledged. "That could change."

Because Suka Kuri and her friends had been talking about the need for Human art.

"They say you are leaving forever," Delphine said.

"Off on a grand adventure is probably more accurate," Suka Kuri replied. "But yes, we are unlikely to return to Masym in the near future. Or even medium."

Delphine turned to her husband and some unspoken conversation occurred. And they didn't even have tentacles.

"Gonna need a real job of some sort," Marten finally said quietly.

"No," Suka Kuri said bluntly. "Moss works a different way."

And it did. Emro towns often competed to host senior adepts. Funds existed to support any Exemplar that passed.

Moss and Sabre had to be free, or they were nothing.

Marten was surprised. Delphine had all the anguish of something enormous in her eyes.

Possibly both of them in crappy jobs, trying to make enough to support themselves so they could do art in stolen moments.

The worst possible way to treat artists.

"What could we do?" Marten asked.

Perhaps the more emotionally resilient half of the pair. And they were a pair, though Suka Kuri didn't know what Marten did, save that he had dropped everything when Delphine asked.

"Absorb Moss School," Suka Kuri said. "Then transmit it."

The fact that Anari and Yanouk gasped almost as loudly as Nasrin told her that they hadn't seen it.

But none were Exemplars. Merely young Adepts, all having learned enough to take those first long strides of what would be a lifetime journey.

Exemplar was a thing in the hazy distance. It always was. Even for old women like her.

Then Marten endeared himself to Suka Kuri forever by merely turning to Delphine and nodding. Once. Sharp.

Yes.

Delphine's eyes were filled with unshed tears. Her breath was almost nonexistent.

Dreams, approaching.

Suka Kuri remembered those days, as well.

"How?" Delphine asked, her voice breaking harshly.

"Come with me," Suka Kuri instructed her. "We need to get you signed up, then packed."

"And then?"

"And then I need to find a handful more like you, for the adventure of a lifetime."

FIFTY-TWO

Dan stood between Elias the Yarikh and Rabiu the Khet as *Free Trader Polat* broke contact with the station and backed slowly away.

Part of her already missed Masym, but three months here had simply reminded her that it wasn't home. That Aurtan might not be home, if and when she made it there one of these days.

Uly was at Bastion, and she missed him immensely.

Solomon was handling security as usual, but was talking to the station like he was captain of this tub.

She turned to Elias.

"Thoughts?" Dan asked the man.

"I know hardly more today than I did before," he nodded. "Having delved, however, I have eliminated many possibilities, leaving only nearly an infinite number of alternatives."

"Wasn't like we were going somewhere important," she reminded him. "Ass end of anywhere, at least from *Danumash* or *Batyr*. Way the hell out to the edge of the map and then some. Only central because there are hinterlands from here with even less to speak for themselves."

"How soon until we tell everyone?" he asked her, leaning out to include a Khet in the conversation.

"About the time we go to warp," Dan replied. "Want them to have a little time to settle in and be looking forward instead of backwards."

"Like you," Rabiu pointed out.

She stepped back to form a triangle and smiled at the man.

"Like me," she smiled. "Still got a long haul to get there, but this is a major step in the right direction, when it comes to building out the *Spinward Reaches*."

"We still going sideways first?" Rabiu asked.

"I lied to everybody about where Bastion was," Dan laughed. "Might as well make it extra hard for anyone to track us."

"Think they will?" Elias asked.

Dan shrugged.

"I brought my full force, just in case," she reminded them. "We're not a warship, but I dare any pirates to try something. Solomon was using all that storage space forward as a series of training spaces before we started loading people and gear. They're hungry, and they knew the calendar just as well as everyone else."

Rabiu nodded soberly.

"Well, we're in motion, so technically I am supposed to be acting like a conductor around here," he said with a grin that went all the way to his headcrest. "You can always introduce me later, but you two should clear off my bridge and let Yalwa do his job."

"Gosh, that would be lovely," Yalwa called from his station.

Dan laughed and moved to the hatch, Elias close behind as they got out into the hallway and started forward.

"Nothing?" she asked. "Dionysia shared bits, but not much."

"Not much to learn," he replied, falling into step with her. "Nothing more than about two thousand years ago is anything but fairy tales and founding myths invented from whole cloth."

"Not surprising," Dan agreed. "I honestly don't think that anybody knows that truth."

"I got the impression that all of current Human space in Seventeen might have been colonized outward from one of about ten worlds, none of them that far from the current demarcation separating the *Seven Crowns* from the *Institutional Republic*. But short of walking there, I have nothing."

"Ask Uly," she grinned. "Maybe he'll authorize a clandestine mission one of these days. That would let you train up a group of Yarikh to run over there in the fastest ship you can build, slip in, ask annoying questions, then escape later."

"The thought had crossed my mind," he grinned back. "Nomiki will have to approve it, as well, though."

"We'll see them both soon enough," Dan said.

They were at the hatch, so she went ahead and opened it.

Solomon rose from his station and nodded.

"We've just transitioned to warp," he said. "Rabiu has formally relieved me of command."

That got a laugh as well. Rabiu the pirate accountant hadn't really wanted it, but had volunteered, then had little to do while Solomon pretended to be in charge so she could walk on the ground with the rest of the Humans.

And the Yarikh.

"You ready for the next step?" Dan asked.

Solomon got sober and quiet, then nodded.

"Aye, sir."

FIFTY-THREE

Solomon Wyndham had been too young to be *eligible* in the time before Uly. More than one woman at Masym had seen him with adult eyes, which had taken a lot of getting used to.

Tall, sure. Big. Sabre School Adept, sort of, depending on who you asked and how they were keeping score. He was still figuring out what to do with his life.

Fourth son of a Duke. Never going to inherit the title.

Supposedly useful for political purposes, but his family had gotten him into the navy early, so that he would accrue seniority later.

When it might matter.

If he cared.

Yesterday's news.

He fell in with Dan and Elias Ioannidis as they continued forward.

Emil and Gennadi were guarding a door when they got close.

"Status?" Solomon asked them.

"Everyone accounted for among the travelers," Emil replied. "Teams are on standby, but well out of sight for now. Waiting for you to give the word."

He turned to Dan, but she waved him forward instead.

"Fall in," he ordered the two, an extra level of weird because they'd been his mortal enemies on that day he met them. Same as Dan was his captor.

And Uly still technically held his ransom.

Not going back to *Danumash*.

Ever.

Solomon opened the hatch and strode through, four in his wake.

Big auditorium. Four hundred and eight people, plus a few pregnancies at various stages.

He turned and walked up onto the big stage as the noise below him slowly died down to stillness.

Uly made this look effortless. Natural.

Solomon had written a speech, memorized it, and thrown it away half a dozen times. Always too stilted. Too something.

He'd handle this like meeting new people. Even four hundred of them.

Stage. Lectern. Crowd.

"For those of you who don't know me, I am Solomon Wyndham," he said, a hidden microphone somewhere picking up his words and boosting them. "I have been pretending to be the captain of this vessel, the *Free Trader Polat*, while we were in Human space."

He let that hang. Saw a few folks dawn with a hit of recognition and maybe a little dread.

"This is Dan Chastain, who is actually in charge," he gestured. "Elias Ioannidis is a historian. Gennadi and Emil are exactly what they appear to be."

A moment to focus himself. Letting the words find him, which was Uly's suggestion for public speaking.

Come from the heart and the gut, and let everything else roll with it.

"All of you have signed up to join us at the colony on Bastion," Solomon said. "And no few of you have discovered that there are many aliens out there, including some who are part of this crew. The truth is even better than you imagined. Dan?"

FIFTY-FOUR

Dan stepped up next to Solomon and studied the crowd. She had interviewed every one of those people at some point, letting her color, gender, or class background weed out a bunch that might have caused her trouble later.

And she'd been able to be selective, when three times as many people wanted to sign up as could be taken. Doctors. Vets. Scholar. Shopkeepers. Farmers. Workers. Dreamers. Artists.

She'd like to say the best of Humanity. Or at least close.

"I might have misled you, at least a bit," Dan said simply, letting everyone come to a perfect stillness. "Bastion is not four hundred light-years galactic west of Masym, like we told folks. It is close to eleven thousand light-years away, around the curve and well inwards towards the core. Subterfuge was necessary because Humans are a tiny fraction of a much, much larger galaxy that is far more dangerous than any of you probably imagine."

Barks of negation. A few growls of indignancy. Mounting hostility.

She turned to her left and nodded.

Nasrin was generally out of sight from the audience. She nodded back, and the entire Congress emerged, walking out onto the stage.

Assembled.

Dan was at the center. All of her Combat Team. All of the Congress plus Suka Kuri.

The audience slowly fell to silence.

"This is the Congress," she announced, leaving off a few bits. "I *Speak* for it, but we are all equals, and represent seven of the known species, with several more not currently part of this organization. You will meet them all, eventually, because my husband is a former naval officer from *Batyr* who is now the *Warlord of the Spinward Reaches*, centered at Bastion. We are half of his advisory council."

The auditorium was lit. She saw a body stand, as if to ask a question.

Duchess-in-Waiting Jacquel Pery. *Danumash* noble of the highest crust.

"Are we safe?" Pery asked simply.

"I needed more women than men because the original team out there includes exactly one Human female and nine men, including my husband, Emil and Gennadi, Solomon here, and a few others," Dan told her. "But I couldn't tell you the truth then, because Bastion already has a population of over one hundred thousand citizens, heavy on Ononguli like these two ladies and Khet like Ciah here."

Dead, dread silence. The best kind of surprise.

The ex-Duchess at least had the mental and emotional fortitude to sustain herself in the face of such a shock. Others weren't so certain.

"And because this is also a transport vessel intending to make an incredibly long voyage to get home, I brought my security forces to protect us, in case some dumbass pirate decides to get frisky," Dan said to the room. "I used to be a *Batyr* privateer operating on the frontier with *Danumash*, so I am familiar with how those things work. And because I wanted you to feel safe. Solomon?"

She turned to the man and suddenly saw who he'd be when he was forty. When that light brown hair started to fade down as the grays came in and the lines she could see on his face today were age instead of stress.

Some woman would be thrilled with the man. Perhaps several, because she didn't intend to limit people unless they wanted it. Linked clusters of folks might even be better, because children could come from many sources and clans could include many species.

Solomon had seemingly stepped over some boundary that had

been separating him from maturity. Dan could see it in how he compared to that pudgy kid she'd first met when they boarded *King Hewitt II*.

Back at the beginning.

Solomon took a breath and faced the room.

"Combat Teams, assemble in formation," he barked.

The audience had to turn and look, because folks were coming up from the rear of the space, through a couple of service doors that weren't obvious.

Two hundred of the toughest, meanest, most dangerous killers she'd been able to locate, then train up to the sorts of standards that would have gotten them employed on a ship like her old Forward Cruiser *Marshall Castillon*.

Human levels of dangerous.

One hundred up each side. Full armor and weapons, though slung instead of threatening.

Every size. Every shape. Almost every species she knew at present, missing only the Ancyn and a couple of others. And she would expand to three hundred when she found enough bodies to fill those slots, rather than cutting away these men and women. Discovering the Samuur had allowed her to add a bunch of big, nerdy jocks to the Ononguli and Khet she'd already had.

Silence, still and ugly.

"These are the men and women who enlisted to protect you from any danger," Solomon informed the group. "There are no humans in that group today, but their commanders include myself and Dan. You will be welcome if you wish, but you are also here because we hope you'll help the ten of us show the rest of the galaxy the best parts of what it means to be Human."

Lovely. Dan deeply approved.

Solomon had presence. He could hold everyone's attention. Being young and handsome helped with the women. Being a warrior conveyed things to the men.

Sabre School Adept, in all the best ways.

The ex-Duchess was certainly eyeballing him with new vision.

Dan separated herself from the Congress and walked over to his side, making this a Human thing. Nervous eyes watched the guards, then eventually settled on her.

"It will be a longer sail than you expected," she told them. "But we selected this vessel to provide everyone extra space and as many comforts as possible. Later, these men and women will be out of uniform and available to help you learn more about your new home. They are all friendly, but Samuur make better wrestlers than you while Khet can still breathe water, before you challenge them to any sorts of sports competitions. Past that..."

"Dan, this is Rabiu," a voice interrupted with a jolt of sound. "We've just been knocked out of warp and someone is pointing wave-bolts at us."

Huh. Early. She'd figured that they would wait for a few more hours before attacking, if only because that got *Free Trader Polat* farther away from Masym.

At the same time, nobody knew how fast the ship could go, so they might have worried that she could get away if they didn't move.

Like she'd told Solomon, everyone could read a calendar.

"Rabiu, I'll be along shortly," Dan replied. "Bring us to alert, but don't provoke them."

"Trojan Horse time?" he asked.

"As we planned it," Dan answered.

She turned back to the room.

"We will protect you," Dan announced in a grave voice that carried off the far walls. "Combat team, deploy to operations stations now."

Solomon broke into a run and trailed the group. Emil and Gennady went the other direction, but she and the Congress kept their arms in a separate vault.

"For the rest of you, I think everyone would be best served if you stayed in here," Dan told her colonists. "This is the central part of the ship, armored and insulated the best and I doubt that pirates want to blow us up. More likely, they are looking for agricultural slaves and the like. Since some of my people have personal experience with that sort of thing, we'll be annihilating them in the process."

"Annihilating?" Pery called from the audience.

"You people signed up to be free," Dan replied. "My job right now is to make that happen."

She moved.

Suka Kuri nodded once, then stayed put. The woman had no business in a boarding action, and understood that. Plus, she could keep these people calm against whatever happened.

Dan had known the risks, going in. A very public affair, with firm dates and a big freighter that wasn't armed.

On the outside.

Trojan Horse, indeed.

Now she just had to make it work.

FIFTY-FIVE

Rabiu won the bet. Yalwa had insisted that they'd be six hours out of Masym when the dipshits attacked. Rabiu had taken the under and points.

They might still call him the Pirate Accountant for a reason.

"What do we know?" Rabiu asked Yalwa.

The man was Khet, like Rabiu, so they shared a vast cultural experience that had helped on the sail out.

"Interceptor," Yalwa replied. "Overgunned, but they look small. Maybe a single 4dm forward and twin 2s aft?"

"We're in Human space," he reminded the guy. "They're about as primitive as the Isann or the Samuur were. Maybe a half-step up, but most of that's engines that can go reasonably fast. Uly thinks they are all using fifth-hand tech out here. Crap sold to them by Zuath merchants or maybe a Mazhin clanship that wandered a bit afield. The bodies will all be Human, though. That's the risk."

None of the non-Humans—and Yarikh really were close enough for this—had gotten off the ship, save for Dan's Congress. But they all knew Solomon. He'd be the basis of comparison, though Uly and Dan had both impressed upon Rabiu how special that man was.

Most of the pirates out this way would be like lazy Ononguli. Piratical, but only because having a real job involved making sure the mistergates actually worked and were maintained properly.

Slobs, with pistols.

Against Dan, with six months to think about how it might go down and some really smart people consulting.

Which was why he'd taken the under and would be collecting later.

Assuming they didn't screw this up and turn into specimens in a Human zoo somewhere. Piruz had stories about his time with *Danumash*.

"Ordering us to heave to or be destroyed," Yalwa commented. "Did we sound that stupid when we were pirates?"

Rabiu chuckled.

He'd been corporate. On his way to a Directorship somewhere on that day that Uly came along. He'd only run off to be a pirate later.

"Yes," he agreed. "Think teenage punks burning their names into desks. Add alcohol. Then make them Human."

Yalwa shuddered, but he was right.

Humans.

Solomon came through the hatch.

"Do you need a Human face for negotiations?" he asked immediately.

Rabiu looked over.

"Been replying with text and voice-only so far," Yalwa said. "They don't seem to care, as long as we don't do anything stupid."

"That's coming," Solomon nodded. "Rabiu, you have command. I'll be working defense with my people while Dan does her thing, so make sure you lock the hatch behind me, then arm yourselves. Am I clear?"

Rabiu gulped and nodded.

Human, but that also meant people like Solomon Wyndham. No longer a snot-nosed kid, but instead a Sabre School killer.

Man had that gleam in his eyes today.

Shit was about to get ugly.

Solomon nodded back and vanished. Rabiu reached down under his command station and keyed the combination that opened a drawer. Space suit. Helmet. Gun.

Everything a fellow needed for a party in Human space.

FIFTY-SIX

Dan got to the armory just as Emil had the door open and Gennadi went in, handing out weapons unasked and without looking. Everyone had theirs stored and ready, so it went quickly. Boarding armor. Her Icemace. Nasrin's Omnibow and bandoleer. Yanouk's Squad Exostunner.

Time for battle.

"Any change here?" Emil asked as he and his sidekick got themselves geared up.

"Negative," Dan replied. "You support Solomon and the flight crew as trained. We'll be disrupting."

Emil had a harsh laugh. Losing his leg hadn't slowed the man down one notch. Getting an Ononguli replacement had made him occasionally suggest adding horns to his helmet.

"Dumbass pirates are in for a surprise," Emil noted, then he and Gennadi were off.

Yes, she supposed so. Four hundred colonists. Mostly civilians, with a few retired and demobilized veterans that might decide they wanted an adventure later.

Two hundred of her killers.

And the main crew of the *Free Trader Polat,* all drawn from extra bodies carried aboard *Vauquelin* on the Stradosha raid. Like aboard *Nubia,* every one of them trained to put down their apron or welding goggles and strap on combat armor.

Moreso, because she'd been expecting something.

Rabiu had sailed out to the rendezvous with the absolute minimum number of bodies to run a ship that had been as automated as they could make it. All the extra people were because she'd been expecting to cook and entertain an extra four hundred strangers on the way home, and that took bodies.

And because she used to be a pirate in the region of Masym, back when she'd been younger.

Dan checked everybody. They checked each other.

It was good.

"Rabiu, what is our status?" she asked, keying the main line.

"There is much wailing and gnashing of teeth here," he replied with a chuckle. "We might be up to rending our clothing and offering pigeons as sacrifices to gods that have turned their faces away if this goes on much longer."

The man was a dork with a literary bent. And had obviously spent way too much time around Suka Kuri.

"Past that, they ordered us to shut down so they could board, under the usual threat of mayhem," Rabiu continued. "My scan shows that thing to be smaller than the old Corsac Fox that is now *Batyr* these days. Single Four and a pair of Twos."

"Normal for this region," she assured him. "My concern had been a big *Danumash* warship that might shoot first and go for a crippling hit."

"I think the weeping and terror overall up here sold it," he replied. "Though Yalwa might have overdone things a bit."

"I'm a fragile flower," Yalwa yelled in the background. "Somebody hold me!"

Dan shared Nasrin's eye roll.

"Keep up the good work," she said. "Out. Team One, what is your status?"

"Someone had us armed and armored already," the man replied.

"Don't figure we get to count this against a new record for deployment?"

"And you would be correct," Dan agreed.

But his words told her that they were in position. And not just lined up outside the airlock.

Dan had something evil in mind today.

FIFTY-SEVEN

Lawry Tinett studied his prey.

Free Trader Polat, supposedly out of someplace called Bastion, off west somewhere, though nobody had been able to locate it on a map and none of the outsiders had talked.

Aliens, he knew. A few of them. All women, from the reports he'd paid good money for. Bunch of black folks in charge. At least they thought so.

Lawry had been raised in the *Seven Crowns,* so he understood that the dark-skinned ones weren't really good for much, unless they were good looking.

Same with aliens. Fetch a pretty good price, where he was hauling them.

After he and the boys had their fun.

He glanced over at Rankev Campbell. Boarding Lead. Man responsible for going over and explaining to those folks that they were prisoners now and could either go along with it or get themselves killed.

There were always some dead-enders that took the violent way out. Sometimes themselves. Sometimes forcing someone else to pull the trigger.

Bunch of colonists might think they were tough. Pirates would show them a thing or two.

Especially the brown ones.

"Thoughts?" Lawry asked.

"Big ship," Rankev grunted. "Lots of folks milling around."

"Figure you'll need everybody, just to keep them in line," Lawry said. "I can run a skeleton crew here for a while. You won't need more than a few hours to get them rerouted to where we can offload everyone and sort them into strong backs and valuable commodities."

"They giving you any grief?"

"Usual bitching and hollow bullshit about the authorities," Lawry laughed cruelly. "Like the law matters this far from Bolton. They got an unarmed ship, filled with all sorts of useful cargo, some of it product and most of it bodies. We got the guns. Not a lot they can do about anything at that point."

Rankev matched his laugh.

"In that case, lemme go round up all the extra bodies," he said. "Four hundred colonists, heavy on women folk?"

"Yup."

"Ship that size probably has a crew of twenty or thirty?" Rankev continued. "Or do they have fifty or sixty, because they didn't figure that the colonists knew jack shit about flying?"

"I'd go with the latter," Lawry replied. "Reports say the woman in charge seems to know her shit, so assume you gotta put a hundred bodies aboard with a lot of guns, in order to overawe them and control things. Shit, we can always just back off and pound the damned thing into scrap if they give us a reason. Or blow a couple of places to open space and claim the wreck and the material goods without the slaves. That's on them."

Rankev nodded and rose. Big guy. Burly. Bully.

Exactly what Lawry wanted in a situation like this, where violence was about the only language those silly gits would understand.

Nothing ever changed in this game.

FIFTY-EIGHT

Solomon studied his teams.

Dan had her two hundred. He had his two hundred. If not as elite, still trained up to his standards of combat infantry, after Solomon had spent that long voyage to Stradosha thinking about ground and corridor tactics with a new eye.

From Rabiu's reports, he'd called it an Interceptor. Except that they were in Human space briefly, so it was likely more of a Corvette. Escort platform, because the larger Destroyer was intended to go after the smaller Frigate Cutter hulls and hold the forward line in action, while Cruisers and Battleships sailed behind that and lobbed heavier wave-bolts at each other.

Nobody around here would even understand Striker and Devasta-tor, which just made him smile. Suka Kuri had charged him with trans-lating Human infantry tactics for Uly's armies.

He had a small battalion right here, about to put it all to the test.

"Solomon, this is Dan, what is your status?"

"Elias and Dionysia are in position," he replied. "I've got my people pulled back enough to entice the bad guys into charging forward. You ready with yours?"

"Affirmative. Rabiu, how long until they dock?"

"The usual threats and bluster are taking a bit longer than we expected, but I think that's laziness on their part and not sneakiness," Rabiu replied. "They have finally started to slide in on us and we are drifting. Matching and lock in roughly six minutes, but that's just a wild-ass guess at this point."

"Understood," Dan said. "All teams, five minutes to trouble, if you have anything that needs a last-minute something."

Solomon looked around. He'd pulled most of engineering and just about everybody else. Suka Kuri had the passengers, but the pirates had to get through him to get to them anyway. And Dan.

Five minutes let him open a nearby hatch and slip through.

Elias Ioannidis and Dionysia Stavrou stood there nervously. They'd been public faces on the planet and station. And had volunteered to mislead the pirates today.

There was considerable risk, but the Yarikh had all struck him for their willingness to step into the breach.

"Five minutes until they start docking," he said as they turned to look at him.

"Will they really fall for it?" Dionysia asked.

"Our butts are on the line if they don't," he replied. "At the same time, we specifically brought a lot of people with us on this mission for precisely this purpose. Exactly this expected outcome. Too much value in one place, and not enough guns to scare off pirates."

"Practically an invitation?" Elias asked.

"Uly doesn't like pirates," Solomon reminded him simply. "Nor do I. They could have ignored us entirely, and chose not to. They do not get to complain later that I brought a really big fucking hammer."

Solomon paused and took a breath. Emotions were acceptable. As long as they were controlled.

He needed control. It was a Sabre thing that Suka Kuri continued to teach him. Control the violence, so you could loose it as needed.

He would be unleashing havoc shortly enough.

Elias and Dionysia both blanched at his tone, but they only looked Human and he understood that they had been born in a paradise that never saw war. Never tasted hunger.

Never knew evil.

"And they will fall for it?" Dionysia asked him.

She'd spent the most time with Dan, Elias being in libraries and universities as much as he could, doing research.

"They will see the charade, as long as you sell it well," Solomon told her. "I will be behind you when they decide to push. Dan will be ready when we get them trapped. I can't promise that you will be entirely safe, but I intend to hammer them down hard and fast so that they can't hurt anyone."

She nodded. Not Human, but close enough, perhaps.

Solomon had spent enough years among aliens now to place her on a scale, especially now that he had so many more Humans to deal with.

Close. But only close.

"You'll be fine," he told them. "Just stay low when trouble hits."

They both nodded now and he withdrew.

Down the main corridor towards the auditorium, because Elias would tell the pirates that all the colonists had been assembled for a pep talk when trouble happened.

It was even accurate.

All the rest would be the ugly bits.

FIFTY-NINE

Rabiu studied the scans of the ship. Hunk of junk, really. Pirate slobs.

Insulting, really.

This was the best you got?

Still, they thought they were all that and a bag of jelly beans, so he let them have their moment in the sun.

"Yalwa?"

"Probably would have been easier for them to park and me to dock with their ship," he groused, equally offended at how sloppy this pirate ship, this *Tripoli Blackbird*, was handling things.

"As long as they're coming to dinner and not shooting at us," Rabiu reminded him. "And can't get far if they do manage a breakaway."

"Oh, *Polat*'s got way more power than she looks," Yalwa reminded him back. "Coulda outrun those goobers, but they got bolts and we don't. And Dan wanted to make a statement."

"As long as it's Dan making it," Rabiu said. "Promise I'll get you something better next time."

"Shit, right now, I'm probably the best qualified here to fly that tub," Yalwa said. "You can handle most of *Polat*'s needs."

"Gift fish," Rabiu said. "Don't count them until they hatch."

"I'd still like some guns, next time."

"See what I can do," Rabiu assured him. "All teams, docking is imminent. Repeat: docking is imminent. Stand by."

SIXTY

Solomon watched a screen. Camera set up on the main mud room, this side of the airlock.

Elias and Dionysia standing in the middle of the room. Unarmed. Not dangerous.

Not a threat that would provoke trouble, he hoped.

You never knew.

The hull rattled as the pirate ship made contact and locked on.

Human ship, like he and Dan had both been trained on, so folks had been taught how to disable those circuits. Keep two ships docked, unless you wanted to significantly damage yours by twisting away and possibly colliding.

All he needed were a couple of minutes of confusion.

On the screen, the airlock lights began blinking. Warning everyone they were opening, but he didn't have sound.

It opened. Nothing happened for a long moment. Probably the pirates making sure there weren't surprises on this side of the airlock.

Some of the scenarios he and Dan had worked out involved an artillery barrage and a mad charge at this moment, but Dan wanted the pirate taken.

If they got free, they could shoot, and *Free Trader Polat* couldn't.

Bodies came through the airlock. Humans. Lots of them, which Solomon found weird to look at. Ononguli tended to be smaller. Samuur bigger. Khet wider.

All Humans here.

Guns pointed at Elias and Dionysia. Exorippers, rather than things with stun settings.

Pantomime. Big, bad pirates in cheap boarding armor. Piecemeal stuff, really. Whatever someone might manage to tack or strap together. Same with the weapons.

Solomon had been navy from the beginning. *Danumash*, then an Ononguli ship with all their stolen equipment, so well maintained. Quality stuff today, because Uly had the budget for it and understood giving everyone the same pistol or carbine.

These people had crap.

Solomon watched a dozen folks enter the mud room. Language must have been pretty ugly, from the way Elias and Dionysia cringed. One of the pirates walked right up to her and palmed her breast, then pointed a gun in her face when she tried to resist.

Other guns at Elias.

Solomon memorized the face. They'd have a chat later.

Arms, pointing at the hatch behind them. Deeper into the ship.

Towards him. And his teams.

One of the bigger pirates seemed to be in charge. Not the handsy one, but hadn't stopped that one, either. Big guy gestured Elias and Dionysia to lead. Followed closely, guns pointed at them.

Solomon counted more bodies coming through the airlock. Lots of them. Not enough.

Dionysia was leading, walking with a sharp step that opened up just a little space to the pirates, like a woman trying to escape what she knew was coming.

Only if he failed.

Elias stayed midway, but got a gap as well. The pirates seemed to be laughing.

Then a hatch opened down the long corridor and he actually heard them coming.

New camera watching, so he swapped views. Listened to coarse men casually discussing rape as a hobby. All the things they thought they would get to do with the new prisoners.

To the new prisoners.

Solomon was down a side corridor, watching part of his team across the way. Dionysia stepped into view and kept going without a stutter. Elias was a moment behind her.

Solomon nodded to the trooper directly across from him as he hit the switch to close the bulkhead hatch that Elias had just walked through.

"NOW!"

SIXTY-ONE

Solomon had already closed up his louvers and was running on bottled air. Wouldn't do much to attenuate the blow, but every little bit helped. That and distance.

The trooper across the way was holding an Omnibow with a Painsphere on the tip. As were the two with him.

Nasrin had taught him the usefulness of the weapon.

If you didn't mind a touch of collateral damage.

Solomon leaned around the corridor, already firing at anything and everything. Mostly to stop the pirates in their tracks.

Somebody hit the lead guy dead center with a Painsphere anyway. The jolt hit Solomon in the face like opening the fridge door to a fish that had gone rancid three days ago.

He kept firing anyway, forcing his stomach to remain down.

More explosions down the hallway. More screams of pain, surprise, and agony as folks discovered what uncontrolled vomiting tasted like. Especially in a suit, if they'd closed their faceplates.

Because nobody over there had the control to open them right now. Most folks were going down like the Reaper himself was threshing them.

Then the other teams opened side hatches and began flooding them from both ends.

Solomon forced his body to behave and led the charge.

SIXTY-TWO

Dan heard Solomon's team launch their attack on the radio. That was her cue, as well.

Concealed hatched slid sideways along the starboard wall of the mud room. Her people were already firing at the men suddenly caught flatfooted.

All men.

She was not that surprised. The Ononguli and Khet were fine with women in the piratical occupation. Humans—at least *Danumash* who was closer—tended to be sexist pigs in the modern age.

Bastion would have none of that shit.

Anari and Yanouk were first into the room. Nasrin paused exactly long enough to fire a Painsphere through the airlock itself, then the Congress was charging after it.

"Team Two, you have bodies down here," she said, leading Team One though and onto the pirate.

Somewhere behind her, hatches would be slamming shut, dividing the invaders into smaller boxes, even as they got hit from all sides.

She wanted the asshole on the bridge.

"Team One, disabling the airlock controls," a man called on the radio. "Team Three, go."

Most of her people would be through quickly, but they were already behind her and losing ground, because Yanouk and Anari had long legs. Teams One and Two would hold the intersection point between ships. At least as long as possible.

The pirates could always try to flee.

Try.

The Assembled Congress was aboard their ship.

Speed was the key. Audacity. Ferocity. Energy.

RAGE.

Move faster than he can react, whoever he is. Get into his face, then his mind, then his back pocket.

Smaller ship than she was used to. Almost tiny, compared to even *Batyr*. Yanouk was making excellent time, occasionally firing her Squad Exostunner from the hip without breaking stride.

Bodies to hop over as they kept moving.

Finally, someone woke up and slammed a firebreak shut in front of them.

"Stand clear!" Nasrin called, so bodies dropped to the sides of the corridor, looking for whatever cover they could find in doorways and architecture.

Dan watched Nasrin pull a breaching charge sphere and attach it to her omnibow.

Something Dan had thought up, then had her people invent and build.

Nasrin fired and it hit, detonating a shaped charge that destroyed the door controls with an earthquake that probably rattled all the way through the ship. Bodies stepped up quickly and started playing with wires.

Thirty seconds and the hatch opened again. Everyone fired into the gap as soon as it appeared, surprising two men who went down looking the wrong way.

Charge.

Light Interceptor. Corvette, by displacement, maybe. Small.

Bridge wasn't far away.

This time Nasrin simply put her breaching charge into the hatch itself. Not designed to resist that sort of thing, so it exploded inward across the space.

Dan was third through. Men were still in shock at the smoke, noise, and destruction that had erupted into their lives.

"Who's in charge?" she demanded, twenty guns pointed at three pirates.

Hands found sky.

Older man. Maybe forty. Bad, long years. Like he knew what a jail cell smelled like.

He locked eyes with her, but wasn't really there mentally. Shock. Made the brain do strange things before you came back to yourself.

Dan had a stunner today. She shot him.

Everyone else opened up at her signal. Three bodies crumpled over.

"Team Four, what do we have?" she asked as bodies filled stations and started typing.

"Team Nine. We own Engineering."

"Team Six. Think we found their armory. Under control."

"Team Four. Bridge intact and controlled."

Dan nodded. Idiots must have thought that she hadn't spent six months preparing for today. With Uly's resources and her Congress to shape it.

Dumbasses.

"Team Five, I have what appear to be cells here. And maybe prisoners. Not letting them out."

"Keep them isolated from our new friends as we round them up," Dan ordered, turning to Ciah.

"Got it," the Khet woman said. "Katya?"

"With you."

Bodies in motion.

"I'll start gathering pirates," Yanouk said.

Anari left with her. Others filed out quickly, leaving Dan and Nasrin on the bridge.

"Rabiu?"

"I counted ninety-six invaders on my deck," Rabiu replied quickly. "Solomon has them either out or surrendered at this point. What's the crew on a ship like that?"

"Likely no more than another forty or fifty at most," Dan replied. "Team Four, get me a roster and count."

"Coming up, sir."

"Solomon, how are you doing?"

"Threat neutralized, Commander."

Ouch, that boy sounded angry.

Dan wondered what he had seen or heard that put that level of contained rage in his voice. Honed down like a razor, then left out in the rain for a few days to rust some.

"Solomon, you take charge of cleanup," she ordered. "All bodies stripped of gear and transported to this ship. Team Five has cells."

"They'll fit right in."

She let that one go.

"All hands, this is Dan. Report any troubles with locals and check in regularly until we account for our pirates entirely. That is all."

Now, what should she do with these assholes?

SIXTY-THREE

Solomon had kept four of his pet pirates separated from the others when he helped Dan's people put them in cells on the other ship.

The one that called itself *Tripoli Blackbird*.

He wondered if that was chance, naming it on their part, or if they knew what a blackbirder was.

Slave-taker. Usually via con job, convincing people to sign up for a new life on another world, then trapping them there. Sometimes raids with guns.

He thought of his new friends as the Chief of Security and top lieutenants. They'd been leading the invaders. One of them had laid hands on Dionysia.

Solomon had even let them all wake up again afterwards.

They were awake now. Hatch with gaps in it that let you see inside without having to open the thing. Slide a meal tray underneath without enough space for someone to slide out.

Angry Human guarding them.

They didn't seem pleased.

Solomon didn't care.

"Who are you?" the biggest one demanded.

He'd been in charge.

Dan was in charge now. Solomon was merely her sword. Or her hammer.

"The ones that took your ship," Solomon replied with a growl. "And your troops. And your crew. If I'm really lucky, commander will let me take your life. Executing people like you certainly makes the galaxy a better place."

That got through to them. They probably saw him as a kid, instead of a ten-year veteran naval officer of the *Spinward Reaches*.

And Sabre School Adept.

He refrained from ordering the hatch sealed and life support turned off, but Solomon could taste that. Crave it.

But justice must be by the books, else it is merely another form of piracy.

And it wasn't like they wanted to take this particular breed of man —and ALL of them were men—back to Bastion.

At the same time, he really didn't want to just turn them loose. Stranding them on a world like Gorge might be fun. Might not be safe. Back to Masym, probably.

"What next, boyo?" the leader asked.

Not the captain. Dan had him separated off in another wing of the ship. *Tripoli Blackbird* had an amazing number of places to store prisoners for a pirate ship.

Not that Solomon had any doubts as to why.

"Now, I turn your asses over to Masym," Dan said loudly, coming around the corner.

Accompanied by Dionysia and Nasrin. Fool might be better off choosing a firing squad than facing those three, just looking at the anger carved into their faces.

Solomon found a smile, after all.

"What?"

"They have laws on the books for men like you," Dan told him cruelly. "Especially when I turn over all your records and they charge all of you with slaving. This ain't *Danumash*, punk. Shit's illegal here, and they like us because they think I work for *Danumash* Intelligence Services. Governor there might shoot you himself."

Solomon thought it unlikely. At the same time, he found the

thought cooling that raging fire in his belly. He'd been able to protect most of the passengers.

But only most.

They'd still laid hands on Dionysia. That man probably deserved something slow and painful to die by. Probably just as well that Dan was in charge.

Something on his face must have shown, because the four men shut up. Slammed jaws shut and stopped even muttering.

Solomon nodded and turned to his superior officer. His boss.

The Boss.

"What are your orders, sir?" he asked politely, in front of these punks, because he'd also heard the sorts of racism out of their mouths that reminded him of that shit Thorley Eldridge.

"Take half your teams and maintain security on this ship," she ordered. "Yalwa will fly it, but you'll execute command, like you were doing at Masym. We'll reverse course shortly and deliver our friends, then keep this ship with us for as much of the flight home as it can manage."

"You'll never escape us," one of the dipshits in the cell barked, then cringed when Solomon turned to face him.

"You want to come with us?" he asked simply. "Her husband is the Warlord of the entire *Spinward Reaches*. I'd love to drag you before a court where he's picked the prosecutor. And the jury are all aliens like these two ladies."

"Aliens?"

"I'm Yarikh," Dionysia was suddenly standing next to him, sneering at them. "I only look Human. Close enough for fools like you."

Cruel. And word would get out, but that would be the mass of alien soldiers pouring out of side corridors and ambushing these punks.

LOTS of aliens. Scary ones, but only if you didn't know any better.

Humans like him were still worse.

Dionysia cowed them herself, which was good. She deserved it.

SIXTY-FOUR

Suka Kuri had, as she saw it, watched Solomon Wyndham grow up. Helped. Dan might be his Sensei, in all the ways that mattered, but Suka Kuri had provided him with the emotional and cultural anchors that had let him turn into Sabre School.

Not one like Yanouk or Anari, who were both mixing Sabre and Moss. And both on their way to Exemplar, one of these decades.

Sabre, nonetheless. Student of close combat. One who learned. And then taught.

He seemed well off-center this afternoon, but better than he had been since the pirate attack that he had helped disrupt, then crush.

And she had moved herself aboard *Tripoli Blackbird*, cramped into a small officer's cabin, because she'd seen his need for someone. And not someone Human, because he had seen the worst of his kind, from the stories that had gotten back to her, though he had never once spoken on the topic.

They were in deep space, having left Masym for a second time, after depositing the prisoners. Running hard on an oblique course designed to confuse, with both ships stopping regularly to check in with one another.

Solomon was conductor, in the same ways that Rabiu had been. Making decisions, while technical experts like Yalwa executed them.

But Solomon was off-center.

She had brought him to a training gym aft where they could talk. The ship was loaded with supplies, intended for masses of prisoners being transported, but the ship was running lean.

They had the space to themselves.

She knelt. He joined her. A candle on a low table nearby kept the tea warm. Suka Kuri served him in her role as tea master, watching the young man alternate between cogitating and fulminating.

"I know I am not," he finally said, "but I still feel like a failure."

"Dionysia?" she asked, having spoken with the woman and several others as part of the debrief and lessons learned.

Solomon nodded.

She studied him.

"Do you have feelings for the woman?" she probed.

He jolted for a moment, then turned deep inward for a long breath of silence.

"No," Solomon finally replied. "It could have been any of the women, and I think I would have reacted the same."

Suka Kuri smiled. He relaxed.

"That is the mark of Sabre," she told him, watching surprise unfold in his eyes.

Suka Kuri nodded.

"Sabre, to the outsider, teaches violence," she continued. "They see the open hand forms. The weapons. The dance-like kata. What they do not see is the purpose. You are not training in these things to become a better pirate, Solomon."

"No, to protect people from them," he said grimly. "And I fell short, but not so far short as to be a failure."

"Only because you have set yourself to pursue the highest possible standards," she reminded him.

He blinked, then internalized her words. She watched him reframe himself.

It was almost like watching a new person being born, and it brought her immense delight.

Adept was merely the statement that someone had learned how to learn. Had memorized a certain chunk of curriculum as a Student. Had begun to understand how those pieces went together as a Seeker. And then had learned how much there was yet to discover.

Thus, an Adept.

Many made those first steps. Few turned it entirely into a lifestyle. Or a lifetime.

Those were eventually the Exemplars. Dan, someday.

And, quite possibly, Solomon Wyndham, who had just stepped outside of himself long enough to turn around and look in.

The highest possible standards of Sabre School, which were high, indeed.

And she had two Humans now that might achieve that dream in her lifetime, to go with two young Emro women merging the two Schools into a new thing.

Because both Sabre and Moss sought to learn new things, rather than ossify old ones.

Truly, that might be the single greatest mark she could make on the galaxy, to bequeath it that many more like her.

"Thank you," he said solemnly. "I needed that."

"I thought so," she replied in teaching mode. "Sometimes, we forget to credit all the things we have accomplished, when encountering some small shortcoming."

"It does not have to be perfect today," he quoted back to her. "Merely better than it was yesterday."

"Indeed," Suka Kuri beamed.

Because if you walked far enough, those tiny, incremental changes would add up into something amazingly impressive.

"We have Moss among the Humans," he continued. "Sabre is represented by Dan, and I suppose myself. Now that we have more Humans, should we look for Sabre among them? Or should we put out the word on a wider format to draw Emro Scholars of the Sabre School to help teach?"

"They will come, eventually," Suka Kuri pronounced. "But not to teach you and your new kin things of Sabre."

"No?" he asked, confused again, but that was being newly born.

"No," Suka Kuri shook her head and smiled. "You will be teaching them."

PART EIGHT

SUMMONED

SIXTY-FIVE

Uly happened to be in a meeting with Maks, planning another aspect of what he figured would be coming when he got the actionable intelligence he needed. They were on the station itself, but *Nubia* was docked and he could board in less than five minutes from this seat.

Avocur was peaceful. For now.

Auga ships had stopped arriving to be taken by *Wardog Charlie* and his friends. Freighters were running in from Saari, Bastion, and Krilic, hauling supplies and bodies.

And adding firepower to the station and the squadron of Yarikh ships that had been assembled.

Uly didn't know how much firepower he was looking at, but the notes from that commander suggested confidence on their part to handle most tasks.

He doubted that they could hold off a Devastator line, but didn't ask, fearful that he might be wrong on that topic and that was one thing he really didn't need to explore too deeply just yet.

He had pointedly not asked Mel how advanced they really were as a civilization. Nothing good would come of such knowledge.

Then the hatch opened and Piruz walked in, tentacles telling stories that Uly could read. Possibly Maks, too.

"Lukyan and the *Warhammer* just emerged at the outer boundary marker," Piruz said simply, just in case. "Has a second ship with him that has the lines of an Auga Striker."

He was looking directly at Maks for that latter bit. Maks shrugged.

"You sent a pirate off to do piratical things to the Auga," Maks reminded them. "You do not get to complain later when he's successful."

Uly snorted. All of it was true.

"Any emergency on their part?" Uly asked.

"Haydar didn't think so from talking to them," Piruz noted.

"Round up the Legal Department and Sterling," Uly said. "Have them join us here as soon as Lukyan and whoever else he wants can board the station. And make sure you have a courier ready to run as soon as I have an update."

"Got three in harbor, Uly," Piruz replied, reminding him. "Krilic, Saari, and Bastion runs all kinda held a little over. Maybe they knew?"

"He's early, but maybe not for Lukyan," Uly said. "Still, this might be it. Keep things less rumorful for now, while we determine how badly the Auga Emperor wants Avocur, okay?"

"On it," and Piruz departed.

Uly turned back to Maks.

"Can we hold Avocur?" Uly asked his friend.

Maks had seen it first. That need for warships. Which had necessitated shipyards in which to build them. Which required banks to finance them. Which flowed from people.

Maks had assembled the people. Uly had watched and helped.

"Not if the Emperor really intends to take it from us," Maks replied. "Nothing can stop the Auga, if they throw enough ships at it."

"Except themselves," Uly smiled.

"Fellow's got to eat," Maks nodded. "Without that, kinda hard to conquer the galaxy, isn't it?"

"Can we really starve him out?" Uly pressed.

He'd seen the studies. Approved the logic and the findings. Even watched and participated in war games where folks had tried out the tactics.

Starfare had taken this problem and torn it apart under Maks's guidance.

It would work, or it wouldn't.

"Again, he could stop us," Maks shrugged. "Convoy everything in massive formations, guarded by teams of Devastators and dozens of Strikers that could hold us off. They still have to feed **that** mob."

"And we've convinced enough people that this tactic might work," Uly agreed. "Someone will have told them, because Rayzian still has leaks at the palace level though we haven't told Anna enough."

"Merely that an Ononguli Swarm might succeed under new management," Maks said. "Why, do you have a better idea?"

"Maybe," Uly replied. "It goes back to me remembering some of the ancient history I learned when I worked for someone else. Things that can be done to defeat a larger formation like this."

"Do tell?"

"When the others arrive," Uly assured him. "Rather not have to explain it twice."

"Gotcha."

They sat and finished up on the little details that had gotten disrupted. Mostly reviews and approvals of things that were already happening, because Uly needed to know at a high level what was being done in his name.

And by whom.

Sterling arrived first, getting coffee and taking a spot in a corner, with Maikki Hudaibirdi joining him in addition to Aibek. And looking more comfortable, but Sterling had sent a note that he was expecting the woman to rise to command soon enough.

Perhaps now, depending on this meeting.

The Legal Department all wandered in quickly.

Lukyan brought a Samuur woman named Lahja Arifullen, who got introduced as *Tiny*. She had apparently taken command of that Auga Light Patrol Striker after it had been captured.

"Captured?" Maks asked.

"Took a lesson from Dan's book," Lukyan grinned. "Let them board the freighter as if rescuing it from us, then swarmed them like proper Ononguli."

Swarm. It was the Ononguli signature. Lots and lots of small ships, hitting you from all sides, to the point that something got through.

Downside risk was that big ships might swat wasps in the process. Wasps that had crews.

"What did you do with the freighter?" Uly pressed, once the details of the ambush had been laid out cleanly.

"Stowed it," Lukyan nodded. "Flies too slow to get back here in any sort of reasonable time, and I figured that I should bring everybody with me, instead of leaving twenty or so behind to haul it in later. They'd be at least another two weeks behind me if I'd done that."

"Good choice," Uly said. "Time's more important than another hull right now. Give me the rundown."

He sat back and listened with his tentacles as well as his ears. At least that was how Haydar and Nasrin occasionally described it.

"Auga's both pissed beyond hope and stunned almost stupid that we took Avocur away from them," Lukyan began, getting serious. "I have read logs of messages from the captured Striker that talk about it. They still don't get you, by the way."

"Bureaucracy rarely understands jazz," Sterling pointed out to much grim laughter.

"Agreed. From there, they have ordered the assembly of a fleet, intended to force you to withdraw under fire from Avocur, after which they will capture or destroy the station."

"Why destroy it?" Ethir asked. "If they can drive us out, presumably they can starve the station into surrender eventually. And them folks is nothing if not patient."

"Thumb in the third eye," Uly said. "We stole it and insulted their honor, so they must own it or end it. Sound. Stupid, but sound. Tell me about the fleet."

"They're bringing up a Diamond, Uly," Lukyan said. "Four Devastators and escorts. Presumably a freaking mob of Interceptors like they do. Several Patrol Squadrons are also ranging around, mostly to try to locate your fleet if you sail out to meet them, so they can either stop you themselves, or vector the big force down and catch you without the station's guns."

"Again, sound," Uly said. "Logical. Bureaucratic. I'm sure there is a page in a manual that tells them exactly what to do in this situation. Sterling, how would you resist?"

"Four Devastators are enough to kill *Nubia*," Sterling said. "Even with *Vauquelin* and the others assisting, because they will be so much heavier. Generally quad mounts, with four 12dm each in three turrets, two forward and one aft. They do have a Fleet Flag design with five turrets, where the aft two are offset on the corners for bombardment and three forward. They might send one here."

"They might," Lukyan said. "Notes were a bit ambivalent, but that's one interpretation of what I read that actually makes sense. How do we stop it?"

"We can't," Uly said simply, then had to wait for almost a minute for the noise to calm down before he could speak again.

He waited. Looked around. It wasn't so much cowing everyone into submission, as waiting for them to let him talk.

Patience.

"Even with Anna sending help, we can't stop them," he repeated. "Not if they send that much force against us. It is, quite possibly, irresistible. Even with Maks's ideas on swarms and convoys, which we will do, one way or the other."

"You seem utterly calm in ways that should probably frighten me," Haydar noted from his quiet corner of the table.

Uly smiled at him. At everyone.

He turned to Maks.

"I need several old, large freighters that you don't mind being badly used up and scrapped," Uly said. "They will be irrecoverable from this operation."

"I can get you hulls," Maks said. "Less here, but I can send a note to Anna and buy some ships that are currently on the beach somewhere with trade down and crews off doing things because warships are more important. Where?"

"Send them to Krilic," Uly said. "They can start from there and meet us midway, deep inside Auga space, where we will pick up the one Lukyan and Tiny here captured and left behind."

"What are we doing with them?" Lukyan asked.

"Attacking Izabh before the Auga can launch their irresistible force after me," Uly smiled. "If they can't get out of harbor, they can't attack Avocur."

"Another Zhoralong raid?" Haydar asked.

"No," Uly said. "Something much worse."

The grim shudders around the table let him know that they were all envisioning a worst-case scenario.

Pity, he thought, locking knowing eyes with Sterling, because they were all going be dreaming far too small on this one.

Then Uly told them.

SIXTY-SIX

Sterling had asked Uly for a private meeting. Those were the best to yell at one another. You could do that when you had people who respected one another.

And trust, because whatever decision was finalized behind those doors would be accepted, and nobody would ever hear how you'd gotten there.

"Coffee?" Uly asked as the hatch closed and they were alone.

Dan should have been here, but she wasn't, and Haydar wasn't right for the situation.

"I'm good," Sterling replied evenly.

"What can I help you with for this mission?" Uly asked, eyes already glittering with the expectation of a good howl back and forth.

"I have heard your plans for Izabh," Sterling said. "The logic is entirely sound. And I doubt that anyone else will really appreciate what you intend, but I've studied enough naval history to get it. That's not my problem."

"You don't think I should command this attack," Uly nodded, eyes never leaving his.

"Correct," Sterling said, taking a deep breath as he marshaled all this logic. "As with Stradosha, this should be a thing that the Corsac Fox orders, but then sends a force off, such as *Vauquelin*."

"You are correct, Sterling," Uly said. "And you are wrong."

"Sir?" Sterling asked, a touch confused.

He'd been prepared for an argument. Like last time, when Dan stepped in. She wasn't here.

"The future of the *Spinward Reaches* probably hinges on the outcome of this battle, Sterling," Uly told him. "In that, I have to be there, because the final results are as much political as military, and I will have to shape them in real time. I will be accompanying the fleet. You, however, will be commanding it."

Sterling blinked.

It wasn't so much a punch in the stomach as an emptiness taking up residence where his belly was supposed to be.

"Sir?" he repeated himself, with far less conviction.

At least Uly was smiling.

"We knew this day was coming, Sterling," Uly told him. "The Warlord would have to retire to Bastion and do bureaucratic, warlordy things to shape an entire nation, and shouldn't be on the deck of a warship, except as its flag officer in the middle of a fleet. Like this. I will promote myself to Fleet Marshal shortly. You will promote to Echelon and command fleets. Dan will join you at that rank, but she will mostly be an Ambassador, not commanding ships except *in extremis*."

"Oh."

Sterling poked, and there was simply nothing there but hollowness.

"*Nubia*?" Sterling asked.

"You will command that ship in this battle," Uly nodded. "I've seen the reports from you and Aibek and I think Hudaibirdi is ready for *Vauquelin*. We'll have several other Strikers of various sizes, including the new one Tiny is commanding. She'll need a full crew as quickly as you can put bodies aboard, by the way, *Echelon Huff*. *Lindberg*. *Warhammer Rose*. Everything Anna can send. Whatever ships the Z'Goszan directors have in port or close enough to matter. Frankly, everyone we can spare. I'll ask Anna if she'll send DJ Gross to command one of your wings, but he'll answer to you. Fortunately, DJ would do that, while a lot of Ononguli commanders wouldn't."

"That's why she keeps him stationed at Krilic," Sterling said absently.

"It is," Uly agreed. "This is possibly the battle that founds the *Spinward Reaches*, at least as far as the history books are concerned. Everything else was small, but this is us launching a full attack intended to permanently damage the *Auga Empire* and force them to give way, rather than the raids we've thrown at them to date for purposes of keeping them off balance."

"It was always leading up to this," Sterling mused, finding his feet under himself again. "Everyone expected it farther east. On the current frontier separating the Sphere from the Empire."

"Where Auga keeps most of their warfleet," Uly said. "Defending against me—us—pulling exactly this sort of stunt."

"They'll never see this coming," Sterling said, waving a hand as Uly started to speak. "Oh, sure, they'll know that we took two ships. And probably understand that we'll try to get in their way to stop them from sailing over to Avocur and conquering it. Won't work, though, because they're two-dimensional tacticians. *Vauquelin* got away because of that, every time."

"And I expect you to bring to the table everything you know," Uly said, turning deadly serious. "Every trick. Every idea. Everything. We stop them here and we might buy ten or even twenty years of peace between the two nations, because they will need that long to recover mentally."

"Can we stop them?" Sterling asked his commander.

His mentor.

His friend.

"No," Uly said with a sad shrug. "They have to stop themselves. They'll do that, if we provide a strong enough case."

"And this is the courtroom," Sterling mused.

"It is," Uly replied. "You ready for this, Echelon Huff?"

"Sir, yes, sir."

SIXTY-SEVEN

Uly had hemmed and hawed on the topic, but had reached a point where his logic had crystallized.

As had his need.

And he'd gone to her, mostly because that framed the conversation in his head. Melpomeni looked at him across the desk as if they weren't the same species, which was probably more right than wrong at the moment, even as she presented as Human.

Wasn't, but it required medical scanners to know that.

He was the one that didn't feel Human today. But then, he was the Warlord of the *Spinward Reaches*. And that had a gravity field all its own.

"You're preparing for the attack on Izabh?" she asked as they settled.

Her office was austere, but had touches of color. A small bush in a pot that might be growing blueberries. A series of five cubes in descending size from indigo to lavender in shade.

Herself, in green. Him in traditional blue.

"We are," Uly replied. "Messages have gone out to all my allies. Summoning the Clans is how the Ononguli would classify it, and they are not wrong. Others will come. They will have many ships, but not large ones. Not yet. Maks is working on that."

"The Yarikh will be present," she said, tone measured and quiet and firm and confident and evasive in all the ways they could get when he started asking her pointed questions.

"How dangerous are the Yarikh, as a technological civilization?" he asked bluntly.

She still recoiled a shade under the tone, but then nodded and even grinned.

"*Invincible* was a spot in our history," she said, referring to the very ship they were sailing on right now, renamed *Nubia* in honor of Dan and her ancestors. "A specific time and place."

"When you had decided to withdraw from the galaxy and were deep into abandoning worlds you had previously inhabited," Uly acknowledged.

"At the end of that, yes," Melpomeni agreed. "The enchanted Black Sword that Zamir Aytiev saw in that unreachable harbor, though that was much later."

"About four thousand years?" Uly asked.

"Roughly, as I understand it, yes," she agreed. "We decided to withdraw. And built a perfect civilization on Traiffe, which was as perfect a world as we'd been able to find."

"Chasing off or destroying pirates that wandered along, until Kit," Uly completed the thought.

"Until Kit, yes."

Uly watched her eyes light up some. True emotions there. And she liked the young man that Uly had first met as a simple engine wiper on *King Hewitt II*.

How far they had come.

But she did care for Kit. That much was obvious, though Uly supposed that Haydar and Nasrin might accuse him of having hidden tentacles to see such a thing.

They were like that.

"Now, the galaxy intrudes, and I am, in many ways, merely the herald," Uly continued. "The Auga would have come to Traiffe in another thousand years or so. Or fallen themselves before then and not been a threat to you."

"Agreed, to both," Melpomeni said.

"I need to sail to Izabh and commit mass murder," Uly told her, watching those eyes grow cold and dark again. "To blow up ships and kill sailors for no other reason than my arrogance that Auga civilization is not the greatest possible thing that could be inflicted on the galaxy."

"And you are correct in that," she confirmed. "Nomiki and others have taken your measure, even at a remove such as this, and framed you within the logic of a national founding demigod."

"Assuming I survive," he corrected.

"Assuming, yes," she nodded. "At the same time, you have identified the dark elements of the Empire and consciously attempted to build a complete negation of those, while retaining the better parts."

"All beings created equal, instead of everyone equally second class behind the Auga themselves," Uly said.

"Thus, your Congress of Wives, instantiated by Dan," she agreed. "And your Legal Department, equally expansive and inclusive of ideas, legacies, histories, and personalities."

"Without them, I am no better than the Auga," he offered, suppressing the growl that usually wanted to accompany such words.

"And people have rallied," Melpomeni said. "Even the Yarikh, who have looked deep in their souls and found that we are close enough to you and yours in the ways that matter."

He shrugged. They had helped. Perhaps not as much as they could have, but more than he had been expecting, when they had volunteered to guard Bastion. Then Saari. And now Avocur.

At the same time, if they were that powerful, he risked the Yarikh turning into a Praetorian Guard. The ones that really controlled any political structure.

If they had irresistible force at all his major ports, they could control him, any time they wanted.

"You concern me as a people, Melpomeni Michelakos," Uly said.

"Because we could conquer you, if the right ideologue arose among our kind," she agreed quietly, already seeing it. "If a Young Hothead rabblerouser decided to sweep aside millennia of history and learning, setting himself up as a god to rule all the lesser species."

"You've just described the Emperor of Auga," Uly noted, watching her blink as the two statements aligned in her mind and left a sour taste in her mouth.

Melpomeni was an exceptionally brilliant woman, but she was an engineer.

Uly had been raised by an Assistant Deputy Secretary of the Party itself. And Anselm Fortier's equally capable wife, Tamsin Simon.

He understood politics at a visceral level. And had really amazing advisors looking out for him.

"I need to impact the Auga in such a way that they stop invading other worlds," Uly said. "That they choose to withdraw to current lines and honor them, instead of chopping off bits of the Ononguli Sphere. Of the *Spinward Reaches*. Or Imperial Sector Fifteen. Or Twenty-Four. Or any of the others. To hold what they have and be satisfied."

"Empires fail eventually," she said. "And I have seen your team's estimates that fewer and fewer Auga are being born with each generation, to the point that they will have a greater and greater problem holding their realm as time proceeds."

"That does not help me today," Uly countered. "Those problems are perhaps a millennium from now. Perhaps when they might have reached your space, plus or minus a Yarikh lifetime. If the Yarikh are intending to join the wider galaxy, I need you to do it today. Not to continue to act as a separate command with your own fleet of ships. Yarikh serve on my vessels. Have accompanied Dan on her mission. I need to know if you intend to build warships that will be crewed by the same mix of species as everything else in my service. That you will become part of the *Spinward Reaches*. Otherwise, I probably have to send you back to Traiffe and add instructions to all of my ships not to ever visit you again, but to instead keep you as isolated as you will have chosen to be. You'll get to deal with my successors. Or the Auga."

He watched her teeth come together. Lips compress and purse. Lines on her forehead as she digested his words. His implications.

His threats, too, if he was being honest.

Uly let the moment stretch. Let the woman stew.

"Those current ships might be a problem, then," she finally offered.

"Because they are far more powerful and dangerous than anybody else in the galaxy understands them to be," Uly smiled, watching her react in surprise. "Because they probably could, by themselves, destroy that Devastator force currently being slowly assembled at Izabh for an attack on Avocur, but you wanted that to not become obvious if you didn't have to unleash such havoc in front of so many witnesses, who might then grow to fear you as much as they fear and hate the Auga today."

Even a brilliant scholar like Melpomeni Michelakos could be caught off guard.

She nodded, licking her lips once in a most Human gesture.

And she was Human enough.

Just so much more advanced than she let on from a technological standpoint.

But Kit had shared his own suspicions after spending time on Traiffe.

"I need you to build me something more advanced than *Nubia*," he told her. "Barely, but not so much that we destabilize everything by letting my successors conquer Auga and everyone else if they chose. I need technology to move a single step forward, because Auga walks slower than the rest of us, and that edge probably lets us balance out the raw mass of numbers of fleets they could bring to bear if they panicked."

"Panicked?"

Good. Confusion was there, rather than concern. Or in addition.

"If we annihilated that force without working up a sweat, what do you think the Auga would do?" he asked her.

Then waited.

"They would realize that you were the single most dangerous creature in the entire galaxy, and that they needed to do everything they possibly could to assassinate you, either in person or via warship fleets," she finally said.

"How many worlds would they bomb into submission to accomplish that?" he fired back at her. "Excepting Traiffe, how many worlds could mount a sufficient defense to stop them? We'd be laying waste to a significant portion of the known galaxy at that point, either way. What does that accomplish? If I really wanted to kill that many people, you should stop me right now. If I wanted to live out the rest of my life in luxury, all I have to do is ignore the Auga while they continue their incrementalism. I'll be dead before they ever got to Bastion. You'll be dead before they ever found Traiffe. Then someone else would have to clean up the mess I left."

Uly stopped and took a breath, aware that he was growing agitated. Hot. Angry.

She watched him, but Uly got the impression that she was seeing something new. Or had never really seen him as a person. More like a symbol, however useful that had been in their planning.

Not Ulysses Fortier, the man.

"Building better ships for a wider crew component will require time," she breathed. "And upgrading the technology base of the *Spinward Reaches*."

"If that means Isann and Saari can build better economies, I'm all for it," he told her. "Better ships. More trade. Better factories producing goods. There are any number of other worlds back in your corner of things and beyond that are either fully abandoned or still so primitive that they cannot have the stars today. I'd like the Isann to start visiting them. They'll appreciate that, and will handle it as explorers and diplomats. Bastion can become a center of intellectual things. And that means that any technology you introduce will eventually spread far wider. Z'Gosza and Rayzian become lily pads sharing it outward. Eventually, even Auga, but they will not move as quickly. Especially not if such things are from the barbarians on the steppes."

Her grin was fleeting, but there.

"I would ask if you understood how rare your mindset is, Uly, but I have spoken extensively on the topic with Suka Kuri, and she agrees."

"I was raised in a world where the goal was feeding everyone," he said simply. "Housing them. Educating them. *Freeing* them. Letting people rise as far as they could on their own merits, instead of inheriting wealth or power that let them oppress others. Whoever that *other* might be. If *Batyr* falls short of that at times, Auga falls much further and most of the rest of the galaxy cannot see beyond their own species first and foremost."

"And even the Yarikh fall into that trap," she admitted ruefully.

"But for Kit," he nodded, watching even a woman with skin as dark as hers blush some.

Mostly, it was in the eyes. Having tentacles helped, even if he didn't. You couldn't convince the Mazhin of that, so he'd given up trying.

"But for Kit," she agreed. Then locked eyes with him. "How do we thread this needle today?"

"Give me some experimental something that has lots of flash and noise that can distract from what I'm really doing," he told her. "A superweapon, maybe, but make it more of a bomb that is not something we could build lots of or fast. Extremely rare and delicate ingredients. Or a jammer that shuts down every frequency. Something big and rude that cause the Auga to react, but not to completely panic. I want them to ask me for peace when we're done, not determine that the galaxy isn't big enough for both of us to survive."

"I am an engineer," she reminded him in a knowing tone.

"Swear Kit to secrecy, even from me, then ask him how fine you two can cut that line," he told her. "Grab Haydar and Roshan and maybe give them a few hints, so you can blame them later for whatever deviltry they get up to. Something that works for today, but won't work tomorrow. Or won't upset whatever balance we can attempt."

She shook her head, smiling, like she could not believe him, then nodded.

He could almost hear the thought bubbles over her head.

"Uly gets shit done."

Lukyan had suggested printing that on T-shirts or the outsides of hulls, just to remind people.

He did, but that was only half the secret.

He had friends who would help.

Like now.

SIXTY-EIGHT

Maks liked his cabin on *Warhammer Rose*. He'd specifically made sure that the design had ambassadorial space, and had claimed it for this hard, fast run to Rayzian.

They were summoning the clans. Nearly five years later than Anna's original predictions for the next war with the Empire, but that was Uly.

Nyri. Zhoralong. Stradosha. A dozen other places, leading up to Avocur.

And then one big monster of an event, if Uly could pull it off.

With the help of the Ononguli who had been expecting him to be there for them.

All his Ononguli kin had been dreading that next hammer blow landing on their horns. One of their worlds. Taken. Another one. Another bite. Flattening the Sphere.

Before eventually ending it.

"You're looking amazingly pensive," Chervonya noted.

He turned and studied her on the bed, a tablet in her lap and such perfection that he wished someone would paint her in oils right now to capture her essence.

If that was possible.

"Keep coming back to those big events that we've been part of," he told her, moving to sit in his favorite chair so he was watching her.

Appreciating her everything. Beauty. Brains. Drive. Smile.

"History books conclude with you making this run?" she asked, watching him.

"Or start the next volume right about now," he agreed. "This is the one that everybody had been waiting for. Now the Horde has to put up or shut up."

"Think they will hold out?" she asked, turning to face him squarely.

Maks considered his words. She knew him better than just about anybody. Save maybe Lukyan.

"We're about to stand before the *Vatazhko* with a lit match," he said. "Most will probably find a way to join us, but there will be a few hard-headed punks that hold out."

"And at least one spy she's never managed to catch," Chervonya reminded him. "I've occasionally wondered if we should bring in some Mazhin and tell people they are mind readers. They aren't, but that might be enough to make someone panic and flee or something. Out themselves as the crook."

He paused and considered it. Woman was significantly smarter than she let on. Ever.

It would probably work.

He rose and keyed the intercom.

"Bridge, Tkachenko."

"Slava, is Lukyan on duty?"

"Stand by. Nope, looks like about to sit down to lunch in the forward wardroom galley. Problems?"

"Negative," Maks replied. "I'll go to him. Thanks."

He rose and Chervonya was already sliding off the bed to join him with a serious face.

He still took her hand like they were teenagers on a date as they exited the cabin and went looking for trouble.

Lukyan marked him as soon he entered and Maks could see the man checking a calendar in his head.

Not Tuesday. Even he wasn't that mean.

Usually.

Still, he and Chervonya took up a spot directly across the table from the man, watching Lukyan's skin turn almost pink as he got nervous.

"You are entirely up to no good," Lukyan said, then immediately dug into his noodles, shoveling like he expected an alert siren at any moment.

"I was talking to my wiser and deadlier half," Maks offered, mostly to watch Chervonya go the other direction and blush so hard he could feel the heat coming off of her skin. "She had a really great idea for finding our spy on Rayzian."

Lukyan chewed and swallowed, then slowed down.

"Oh?"

"Long term, invite some of Haydar's folks to visit," Maks said. "Or Nasrin. Maybe the whole Congress, but Mazhin folks are the key."

"Because everyone thinks they read minds?" Lukyan apparently guessed.

"Something like that, yes," Maks agreed. "Have Anna make a point of having them investigate people."

"Folks will shit bricks if she did that," Lukyan noted.

"And that might not be the worst thing," Chervonya offered, just short of a snarl. "She needs to rattle some cages here. This might only be the opening salvo to cleaning up the Council and the palace."

"And I take it you want me to sell her on it when we get there?" Lukyan asked.

"No, that's later," Maks countered. "Some quiet moment when it's just the two of you or something. I want surprise coming."

"Gotcha. What's short term?"

"We're going to summon the clans," Maks said, watching Lukyan pale again. "You'll be aboard *Warhammer Rose*. She might join us in *Storm Crow*. Whoever else might be coming. Right now, nobody knows much beyond a run from Rayzian to Krilic to the rendezvous point with Uly. Right?"

"Correct," Lukyan agreed. "Operational security, plus timing because Uly will have a ship there that we send to him when we leave, because we've got a longer sail to get there."

"So I need you to take complete command, right now, Conductor Chayka," Maks turned deadly serious. "Do not tell anyone anything. Keep it to yourself and me and Chervonya. Not even Anna. Not because I don't trust her, but because I want her to honestly shrug when our spy asks her to override you."

"You think they will?"

"I think it will come up," Maks offered. "That several folks will demand answers from the *Vatazhko*. That you are acting on Uly's orders means that they get nothing."

"What's that gain us?" Lukyan asked.

"We gather everybody up at Krilic," Maks said. "Then give them a wrong destination and only share the real one at the first rendezvous point, two days out from there. Close enough to the right path to shift, but not directly on."

"Because somebody will either have engine troubles and have to drop out of formation, or will have sent a message to the ground at Krilic and it will result in a mass of Auga ships consolidating at the wrong place to stop Uly," Lukyan said.

Maks watched the anger in his friend's eyes.

"When we find them, I want horns ground off," Lukyan growled quietly.

"I'll hold them down myself," Chervonya nodded. "Anna expects me to replace her on the Council, one of these days, so I want a clean house when I get there."

Someone had tried to kill them at Zhoralong, only failing because Uly was lucky and good, and whoever had done it hadn't sold Auga the complete sailing information to park a big enough force in place to win.

Maks watched his two favorite Ononguli initiate a conspiracy of their own, then stretch it out to include him.

"What if the spy doesn't tell anyone in time?" Lukyan asked.

"Then we bring in Nasrin or Haydar and tell them to get mean," Maks answered. "Like Chervonya said, this has gone too long and needs to be crushed so utterly that the responsible clan disowns whoever did it and maybe changes their names afterwards. Just so you understand where I'm coming from."

Lukyan nodded. Maks held out a hand and his best friend and former commander shook it.

Uly might be saving the galaxy, but they needed to save the Horde first.

From itself, if they had to.

SIXTY-NINE

Anna got the midnight alert as soon as folks identified *Warhammer Rose* arriving in orbit. Lukyan was already in a shuttle, headed to the ground, having not even parked his ship before leaving. And the note said that Maks and Chervonya were with him, and nobody else save pilot and a few bodyguards that traveled with important players.

What did it say that those three felt the need for such protection on Rayzian? Coming to her palace, yet?

That trouble was finally here.

She went ahead and woke Harald up, watching him groggily answer the comm and run a hand over his hair to smooth it some.

"*Vatazhko*?" he gasped when his brain caught up to his eyes.

"I think this is it," she told him, one of her oldest allies on the Council. "*Warhammer Rose* is here."

The Ononguli Council. The Lords of the Endless Plains themselves.

Harald nodded once and turned into some terrible demon from legend, like a scarecrow possessed by a demonic spectre.

"Roust the rest?" he asked.

"No," Anna told him. "I wanted you to have a few hours to prepare, if this is the thing that requires a Council summons in the morning."

"Understood," Harald replied. "I'll put a pot of coffee on, then make a few calls anyway. Everything quiet enough for now, though."

"Talk in a while," and she cut the line.

She and Uly maintained a regular correspondence, though his mail sometimes piled up and arrived in strange sequences. Especially as he moved around from Saari to Bastion to this new place at Avocur that had become central to so many of his plans.

And possibly the future of the galaxy.

She looked around her space, but didn't care to have anyone else here. Not if those three were coming to her and not saying hardly anything over the comm.

That could not be good news, but it might be the thing she had spent so many years dreading.

That Next Auga Invasion.

A beep on her personal comm turned out to be from Klyment Gavrilyuk, aboard *Storm Crow*. Nothing obvious, unless you knew the man as well as she had to when he commanded her flagship.

"Maintenance cycles complete," he wrote. "Laying in supplies shortly."

Because he understood what it meant that *Warhammer Rose* had arrived. That the fleets would be setting out, ships cycling forward to some rendezvous where they would join Uly and the *Spinward Reaches* in some terrible battle to the death with the *Auga Empire*.

Anna knew that there was no way to keep a lid on this, when it finally happened, so she could only hope that everyone and everything moved quickly enough that the Auga could not react in time.

Zhoralong had nearly cost her Lukyan. Someone was going to die slowly and painfully for that, over and above being a traitor in her Court.

She went ahead and showered, then dressed comfortably formal for what was coming. Lukyan hadn't spared the zeonx getting to the ground, so she had a pot of tea almost perfectly timed when her bodyguard opened the door and admitted those three, then closed it behind them.

The palace library was probably the best spot for such a meeting, with all the books and data at hand if someone needed it, while not being her office. Lukyan stepped close, hugged her, and kissed her on the cheek.

"It is not my fault," he murmured.

Meaning Maks had done it, whatever it was. He had that look in his eyes, so she hugged those two as well.

They sat. Tea got poured. The room stilled.

"It is time to Raise the Horde," Maks said simply, face gone deadly serious.

She still flinched, despite having had an hour and more to presume such a thing.

Still, this was the groundquake itself. Sending out the call for every ship that could load up supplies and sail into danger.

And, for the first time in centuries, the Ononguli Sphere was launching a formal attack on the *Auga Empire* instead of responding to one. Not an invasion, but even they merely conquered orbital space over their next target, then held it like a tick in heavy fur until the Ononguli had to withdraw.

Could she make the Empire stop?

No. But Uly might, and that had been her entire purpose in drawing the man into her politics, once she understood that. Why she had sacrificed a woman she thought of as a niece, though even that hadn't been as onerous as a political marriage could have been, from what she had seen and heard.

It was still the game of empires.

"Lukyan blames you for something." She studied Maks.

"I ordered him to assume command of the Ononguli Fleet," Maks replied evenly.

Anna had to bite back the profanity before she slung it across the room at the man.

She was the *Vatazhko*.

The *Lord of the Endless Plains*, herself.

Maks nodded, so he understood how dangerous the ground was under his feet. That mollified her.

"Why?"

"Because we still haven't killed our spy," Chervonya answered grimly instead.

"Because there is no way to keep quiet a mess of ships this big," Maks added. "We will sail to Krilic and assemble. At that point, Lukyan will transmit to the conductors present what their course will be. And only then."

Anna paused, and saw the logic.

Uly trusted these two men. The two women present as well, but these two had been there on that *Tuesday*. Had been with Uly the longest, excepting only one of his Ononguli wives, who had been in prison with them earlier.

"Somebody leaks at Krilic?" she asked, already confirmed by the way nobody immediately spoke, so she nodded. "And they might not be smart enough to see the trap coming, if nobody says anything and I go meekly along with it."

"Not that I have ever seen you be meek, Anna," Lukyan muttered.

She grinned at him.

"Maybe I should try?" she teased, mostly to watch him turn crimson with blush.

And she could do that in this company, which was nice. The Council, with a few exceptions, was a pain in her tail most days. A necessary evil that usually involved herding a mob of antsy orkac about to stampede at any moment.

"Uly will be there, but he has already promoted Sterling Huff to overall fleet commander," Maks said. "The expectation was that DJ and Lukyan command wings, with you and *Storm Crow* forming part of a center, supported by his other allies and a couple of new surprises they apparently have been planning."

"New allies?" she asked, then it registered. "The Lost Tribe. How dangerous are they?"

"Uly is confident that he can confront a Devastator Diamond and escorts, Anna," Chervonya said. "Not just drive them off, but beat them. Badly enough that the Emperor asks him for peace afterwards."

She turned to her real niece and parsed that into...something.

The Yarikh had built *Nubia*, which was thousands of years old and everyone still agreed could probably defeat *Storm Crow*, nose to nose.

What could they do if they really wanted?

One of these days, she presumed some sort of reckoning, but it might stay contained among the Humans. If possible.

"What do I need to do at this point, besides sound the call?" she asked.

"I need your permission to buy a set of old freighters," Maks replied. "Stuff on the beach. Old. Crap you won't mind permanently losing to the war. Uly has given me a budget, but I'm not planning to pay top dollar. Folks will show a tidy profit, if they have what I need."

"Because Uly's up to something?" she asked the man.

"He is," Maks agreed. "And, like Lukyan commanding, knowledge of the truth will be limited, mostly so you can tell the old farts later that I refused to tell you, when they demand answers. Send them to me. I might even reply."

Anna could still remember that nervous punk, that first day on *Scavenger Angel*, when he'd stepped up to play in the big leagues. The light-years he had come since then, to sit here and functionally threaten to snap his fingers under the snouts of some of the rowdier Council members.

And he would. The smile on his face promised that.

"You worried about making enemies?" she asked him.

"Not really," Maks shrugged. "I'll be worth more than any of the clans in another three years. Give me ten and I might put Uly in a position that the Auga Emperor is jealous. Then they can decide if they still want to be mad at me. Worst possible thing they could do would be deciding to take it out on Chervonya."

Yeah, Anna could see that. Her niece had spent too much time around these two pirates. And Uly. And Dan and her Congress.

Chervonya Borisov would be too much of a handful for about anybody on the Council today, let alone in a few years.

Anna found herself looking forward to putting Chervonya's name forward for a seat, mostly to see what the fire-breathers did. They'd lose that battle, too.

Anna took a breath and commended her soul to the Endless Plains.

"Do you have a message prepared for transmission to the clans?" she asked.

"Uly wrote most of it," Chervonya grinned. "We tweaked a few things, but honestly, that man's at least half-Ononguli."

"He's half-everything," Lukyan announced. "*Karaŋgılıkka. Tiikeri. Z'Gosza. Tuesdays.* That's why he's so damned dangerous."

Anna paused to parse that, but it was obvious her lover was seeing something that had eluded her. She asked with her eyes.

"He stops to understand you and your culture," Lukyan nodded. "Then uses that to get inside your head. Did it to me. To the Khet. The Isann. The Samuur. The Yarikh. Doing it to the Horde next."

"And then the Auga," Anna breathed, finally seeing the shape of the thing Uly had spent these last few years building.

Frightening, really.

And it might even work.

SEVENTY

Lukyan was back aboard his *Warhammer*, missing Tiny but she had a better gig going on right now, though he didn't know if Uly would keep her there long term.

Or if that man had something even sneakier planned.

And Dmytro was constantly bitching about having to do her job, but that was because he'd gotten spoiled with her doing it instead of him. Lukyan turned an indulgent scowl on the man and got him to shut up.

Briefly.

"*Storm Crow* calling," Dmytro said quieter. Possibly chastened. "Gavrilyuk."

"I'll take it in my office," Lukyan replied. "Slava, don't let Dmytro fly us into anything while I'm gone."

"No promises, boss."

Lukyan rolled his eyes at all of them and got to his space. His desk. His volume.

His air.

Deep breath. Key the comm.

Gavrilyuk hadn't changed one iota in the last decade. Man had been born old and crotchety, then grown into it from the legends floating around the Horde.

Commanded Anna's flagship. Not the biggest, baddest ship in the fleet. Like *Nubia*, a Fast Devastator. Meaner than any Striker. Faster than any Devastator beyond Uly's.

"Anna won't tell me anything," Gavrilyuk growled.

Lukyan checked the border of the screen. Haydar had sent home another update to his latest security code for encrypting communications.

By now, everybody else understood what *compulsion* meant and didn't argue with the Mazhin.

"That's because I'm under orders not to tell her," Lukyan replied.

And *Technically Correct* was always the best kind. Everyone would assume that Uly or Dan had given him those orders, instead of Maks and Chervonya.

Gavrilyuk's face soured another ten degrees.

"What am I allowed to know?" he asked in a dark, dour voice.

"That you and I will be at the center of the shit when it happens," Lukyan replied. "Flanking *Nubia*, I have no doubts, unless Huff puts us on opposite wings instead, but DJ will be there, so I got no clues."

"And the parts the two of you keep dancing around without saying anything?" Conductor Gavrilyuk, Commander of *Storm Crow* itself demanded.

"If you have to ask me that, you already know that answer," Lukyan growled back.

Gavrilyuk nodded. Grimaced. Flexed his shoulders down and his ears out, like a man who had seen it all.

And Klyment Gavrilyuk probably had.

"Krilic?" he asked obliquely, like he'd already figured out the what and just wanted the when.

Smart man.

"Krilic," Lukyan agreed.

"Better be good."

"Pal, I'm gambling with the future of the Sphere itself," Lukyan replied grumpily.

"That's why I'm glad Anna picked you, Chayka."

Then the son of a bitch cut the line with a grin while Lukyan's mouth was still hanging open.

How the hell do you top that?

Except that Klyment Gavrilyuk had just put his blessing on things, in a way uniquely his while probably obscure to everyone else.

If DJ Gross was also that easy to convince, they might yet manage it.

SEVENTY-ONE

Haydar was willing to admit to being a control freak. Helped that he was both surrounded by others and by folks who *got* that about him.

Data Nerd, First Class, Expert Tier.

Roshan had long since won the old competition to invent better control systems. It had been something to keep the two of them sane while slaves of the Humans at *Danumash*.

Until Uly had come along. Even then, it had taken a while. Or Haydar had been too committed to both trying to help his friend keep them alive and still competing with Roshan.

Solar winds long since past.

The two of them had joined Engineer Michelakos in the lab/studio that Kit Simonson had been allocated, after his promotion to Speaker to the Yarikh. Or something. Kit was sitting to one side, so it was two Mazhin and two Humans in here.

More or less.

"Why me?" Roshan asked as the woman finished her explanation.

"I'm given to understand that you two have a decade and more experience designing control systems for things," Michelakos replied. "This is merely a larger version. More robust. Capable of some level of automated decision making, if programmed ahead of time. Which these will be."

"You want to fly a freighter entirely on remote control?" Roshan was asking.

It was probably good that the Yarikh woman wasn't fluent in tentacles. She might be offended at some of the subtext involved.

Things you didn't say to a lady, as it were.

"Entirely," Kit stepped in. "Bring it to a point. Drop it out of warp. Move it around like a remote-control car. Won't work in warp, so they have to handle all that automatically on a timer. Then we need enough noise flying around so that nobody can hack the signal to take control of them away from us. That's you. I seem to remember Haydar mentioning ON MORE THAN ONE OCCA-SION that he had forgotten more about information security than the Auga had ever learned. Time to prove it. You're here, Roshan, because I didn't figure you'd *ever let me hear the end of it* if you weren't."

The snort was entirely semaphorical. Also probably for the better.

Wasn't like the kid was wrong. And he **had** made that claim.

Haydar was ninety-nine percent certain he could back it up.

It was that other percent.

"What if it goes wrong?" Haydar asked.

Michelakos did a thing with her Human eyes to suddenly appear not-Human anymore. Chilling.

Uly did that, occasionally. When you pissed him far enough off.

"Then there are contingency plans we will have to fall back on," she announced in one of those dark, quiet, cold, scary voices that mothers used to get their cubs to obey.

Be good, or the Auga will get you. Or the Danumash.

And she was close enough to Human in that moment, but not Uly. Not on a good day, anyway.

Danumash slave overseer, maybe. They had that same level of implicit violence that they could convey on scent alone.

Haydar studied Kit. Remembered the kid he'd known, even before Uly, but only in passing. Down in engineering, learning a new trade, while slaves got hauled between two facilities.

A Human hand came up. One index finger in the air, instead of in Haydar's face.

"You have been sworn to secrecy," Kit intoned. "Remember that."

Shit, Kit had been around Melpomeni too much. He'd learned that same tone from her.

Or it was a thing all Humans could tap when they got serious enough.

Dan did it, too.

Haydar nodded.

"Her people could win this battle by themselves," Kit said in a kind of off-hand, throwaway tone that was all the more chilling for how casually he said it. "Uly doesn't want that. He wants everybody there, acting as a team, because that's how the *Spinward Reaches* doesn't turn into another empire later. Everyone. Together. Your job is to sell the swindle."

Haydar blinked. And ignored the profanities Roshan was throwing around. Kit might be able to read them. Melpomeni would, if this kept up.

"Swindle?" he asked.

"Uly's idea," Kit reminded him. "How we do it is a different thing, and this should work. And work the way Uly needs it."

"Why?" Roshan growled, which was impressive, as introverted as he usually was.

But this was Uly. And he *Spoke* for the Mazhin.

"Uly understands that the Yarikh are more than they seem," Melpomeni said, then had to pause while the Mazhin laughed in her face. She even smiled, but Haydar and his people had long since figured that part out.

"Go on," he said, when they got control of themselves again. "Sorry."

"No, you are correct," she nodded. "The squadron was designed and built as if we had to take on an equal force of ships at least as powerful as *Nubia*."

"Which is more dangerous than a Devastator, save for they have more wavebolt launchers," Haydar noted. "Smaller, but one hell of a throw-weight anyway."

"Indeed," she said. "Working with Kit, I have a design for a greatly improved Neutron Omnipulsar, that apparently being a design that has not changed appreciably in millennia, and thus could be invented without disrupting everything else."

Haydar turned cold eyes and tentacles on the kid.

"If you can't hit me, you can't hurt me," Kit said simply. "I only have to hit you occasionally at that point to win."

Shit, that logic held water, too.

Most ships added more small wavebolts. 1dm and 2dm. Fired defensively to intercept bigger things incoming and disrupt them. Risked getting overloaded and having to fall back on the short-range Omnipulsar.

Because the Omnipulsar had become standardized an awful long time ago.

"*Nubia*, or the next one?" Haydar asked.

"The next one," Melpomeni said. "The ship we will build for Uly and Sterling that is better than what they have today, and thus will give him an edge that offsets the greater mass that Auga can throw at him. Like the Devastators. Tomorrow's problem, but Uly's ships will have the design first, and probably not sell it on as quickly, to keep pirates from mounting them before the authorities can."

All of which made sense. And probably foreshadowed something really interesting in about five or maybe ten years, as that technology did expand.

What was the future going to be like, with Uly to shape it?

Haydar sighed. Roshan offered support and obscenities in equal amounts, leaving it for him to organize.

As normal.

"Remote control systems for cargo freighters?" he asked, circling long ways back to the start of the conversation. "And jamming systems, both ECM and ECCM, that will have to be installed. Where?"

"Just *Nubia*," Kit said. "You'll control things from the bridge. We don't trust anybody else to manage it. Or to know the tech."

A nod to Melpomeni Michelakos, reciprocated.

Again, not wrong. It could be made to work. And Uly was relying on him to do it.

Wouldn't necessarily win the battle. Might lose it.

Best not to fuck it up, then.

"Okay," Haydar said hunching forward. "Let's talk system redundancy first…"

SEVENTY-TWO

Uly had a view out his porthole that showed Avocur station nearby. Always nearby, except when Sterling took the ship out for quick flights to test things and train his people.

Maikki Hudaibirdi was settling in nicely on *Vauquelin*, having had a year-long mission in two directions to learn everything and impress both Sterling and Aibek, which was all the more difficult because of the differences in temperaments involved.

She had it.

And Sterling could trust her on his wing. Similarly, both of them could rely on Eskil and the ships of the Samuur and Isann, both the older vessels that were more at risk and the newer ones specifically designed and built to take on Auga warships in direct combat.

Piracy was a completely different way to sail and fight, which was why the Ononguli so often put their bigger warships on the beach and sailed the small raiders when peace broke out.

Anna had brought the Horde up to a war footing, but held them for a while.

Wouldn't have to after this, because even those that went off and raided other Auga worlds would be helping the overall cause by tying down squadrons and fleets defensively.

That was another Auga point to exploit. A tendency to build solid walls and fortifications before expanding. That also caused them to not take forward risks, though they had tried several tactics against him over the last few years, most of which had blown up in third eyes so spectacularly that they would probably not try again in his lifetime.

A chime caused him to nod and turn back from the view of the stars. He stepped to the desk and keyed the hatch open. Eskil entered.

"You wanted to see me?" the Samuur man asked as he entered.

"Sit," Uly gestured. "Get you some coffee?"

"Please."

Uly fiddled with the device, then sat in another chair, instead of putting a desk between them.

Eskil Haldur. First Commander of the Samuur fleet, save that that entire force had largely joined the larger *Spinward Reaches* these days.

"Because time was pressing and we have too much to do, I have not gone ahead and reorganized all of my naval forces to the degree that I will need to," Uly began, watching ears and whiskers flicker.

Eskil remained silent. Watching.

"I have promoted myself to Fleet Marshal, mostly to open space below me for others to fit in," Uly continued. "Sterling is now an Echelon, which is the lowest of four flag ranks."

"Flag?" Eskil asked.

"Traditionally, allowed to raise a personal flag when commanding a squadron or fleet," Uly nodded. "When those are permanent formations, instead of task forces thrown together for a specific mission."

"Like *Virta*, *Niemi*, and *Koski*, sent to Bastion to see what those furless weirdos were up to," Eskil grinned.

Uly matched it. Eskil was one of his favorite people, but he knew that the furless left the Samuur confused on a variety of topics.

One simply had to start from honor and find the most ethical solution, then the Samuur made perfect sense.

"Exactly that," Uly agreed. "I wanted to confirm your interest and willingness before I offered you a similar promotion. Echelon of the *Spinward Reaches*."

Ears back. Whiskers a blur. Eyes big with surprise. Possibly a little butt wiggle before pouncing.

"Sir?"

"Sterling will have seniority on you, from being promoted sooner," Uly continued. "But you will be his peer. In this battle, that would put you in a position to command a wing or a fleet."

"I would ask why me, Uly, but I already understand it," Eskil nodded. "Do you think it wise?"

"Assuming Anna allows it, Lukyan will join you when he arrives," Uly replied. "The Samuur, having learned about the broader galaxy, immediately set out to meet their neighbors and challenge their honor. All of their neighbors. You impressed Maks so much that he decided to build his first yard for warships at Saari, with Bastion only getting the second and Isann the third. That is how much both of us esteem you and your people, Eskil. And with what is coming, I want to make sure that the Samuur see themselves as equals. Mine. Anna's. Chief of Chiefs Usupov. Everyone. Having you commanding a force made up of all species does that. Is this something I can tempt you with?"

"Tempt me?" Eskil laughed. "I might have to tackle you and hold you hostage until you signed the forms, Uly. Of course, I would be honored."

"You are the First Commander of the Samuur," Uly reminded him. "Already a commodore, as *Batyr* might see it, first among the various equals that are all those commanders. Nothing much changes here, save that Ononguli ships will be sailing under your command. Khet. Isann. Bastion."

"Do the Mazhin build warships?" Eskil asked, eyes narrowing. "I seem to remember Haydar offering hints."

"Pirates," Uly clarified. "Clanships will occasionally send off all the crazy youngsters to get it out of their systems for a few years, before they mature and calm down. Haydar did that. Several of the Mazhin men in my original team were captured off such pirate ships, with others being on clanships captured by *Danumash* raiders in turn. Did we need such a thing?"

"Most likely," Eskil stated. "Recruit enough of them to matter on your other ships. That might provide the outlet the matriarchs needed instead."

"Since there are clanships currently trading between Bastion and

Rayzian, I will rely on you sending a message to the Paramount and asking him to get involved in such recruiting," Uly said.

Eskil blinked, then nodded.

"Aye."

"So, Echelon Haldur, I wanted to talk tactics with you," Uly continued.

"How are Auga going to handle this?" the man asked. "At Zhoralong, they were waiting for us, but hadn't brought sufficient force, though the experts tell me that it was close, and that without you, we might have lost."

"Sterling would have won faster and easier," Uly shrugged. "But there is a Human element to naval warfare that involves a greater aggression than most species generally exhibit. Including the Auga. I expect them to either be caught in harbor by surprise when we arrive, or to have sailed out to meet us somewhere, in which case maneuver warfare becomes critical."

"Us hunting them at that point, or them hunting us?"

"Maks and I have discussed the need to keep operational security as tight as possible around fleet movements, because Zhoralong confirmed an Ononguli spy," Uly said. "It is possible that the Auga try to intercept us, but it is also possible that they simply wait for us to arrive at Izabh and have concluded that the force they have in place is sufficient."

"Is it?"

"No," Uly replied. "But the action will be terrible and mistakes can cost us greatly. I need *Lindberg* and a few other ships out looking for trouble. Patrolling, but not engaging, because intelligence is more important than victory right now."

"Like you had Lukyan doing?" Eskil asked.

"Yes, but there I had a set of systems I expected, and he got lucky with the second one," Uly agreed. "Here, it could be anyone, anywhere."

"What's Tiny doing right now?" Eskil pressed. "Can I have her as a Trojan Horse?"

"She's training crew and preparing," Uly replied. "And I'm getting good reports."

"She's also flying what is very obviously an Auga warship, so she might be able to do something like *Vauquelin* did at Stradosha, if she was careful."

"Is she?" Uly asked.

"Everyone calls her Tiny because she is," Eskil grinned. "At least compared to us. Shortest Samuur woman I know in military service, where even most of the men are taller. Humans are smaller than Samuur, so you don't see it, but she's had to fight every day of her career and overcome impossible odds to get where she is. Reminds me of Dan that way."

"I'll reach out and see if she's ready," Uly said. "Are you?"

"The Auga have no honor," Eskil growled fiercely.

"No, you have that wrong," Uly replied. "They have honor. What they have not learned is to extend that to other species. You and I are going to chastise them on that topic."

"You can count on me, Uly."

"That, my friend, is why you are here."

SEVENTY-THREE

Uly got Tiny seated in his office. Unlike talking to Eskil, he sat behind the desk, making this more formal.

He'd read all the reports on the woman. Interviewed folks who knew her.

And there'd been a reason he'd assigned her to Lukyan's crew in the first place, not overriding that Ononguli pirate, but convincing him she would work.

Tiny had.

"Sir?" she asked as they sat.

"Are you enjoying commanding the former HES875D74, Tiny?" he asked.

Technically, Lieutenant Lahja Arifullen, but everyone called her Tiny, and he was given to understand that she might not answer to anything else.

"Aye, sir," she replied. "Not as nice as *Lindberg* or *Warhammer Rose*, but a well-built ship. Well-founded, as well. Odd mix of firepower, but useful, as it is heavier than combat interceptors, so better able to engage them and pirates. Not stout enough to take on enemy Strikers, though."

"Escort duties are what I want it doing," Uly told her. "Using all those Sixes to interrupt enemy firepower before it threatens us. I wanted to confirm your willingness to sail that kind of battle."

"All in, sir," Tiny said simply. "Probably too much time with Lukyan and that mob, but I understand how a ship like that could be fought."

"Good," he agreed. "Given a Samuur commander, you should give it a Samuur name. And yes, I appreciate that your crew is a diverse mix of people. I have a purpose here."

She paused, studying him closely.

"There is a Samuur demigoddess," she said in a sideways kind of voice. "A great sailor from our own Iron Age, perhaps on a par with Zamir Aytiev of the Isann, though with wind instead of stardrives. Her name was Sivi Salavat. Probably a good name for a patrol craft."

"Excellent," Uly said. "Keep that in your pocket, because for now, I want you to continue calling the ship HES875D74 on this next mission."

"Sir?"

"I spoke with Eskil, and he wants you to go on a wide, forward patrol, Tiny," Uly said. "Looking for those Auga warships that we are convinced will be looking for us as we move."

"Pretend to be one of them?" she asked. "False flag and all that?"

"Only as a cover," Uly nodded. "Don't engage them any more than you have to. Run, once you confirm something. We'll be moving forward as soon as I have confirmation from Lukyan and Anna that they are coming up on my left to rendezvous. At this moment, Avocur is the distraction to keep Auga's third eye centered on us. You're my shield wall."

She brightened. They might be Star Age, but the Samuur still held on to a weird mix of primitive ideals. The good ones, anyway.

"The hound, leading the hunters to the fox?" she asked.

"Exactly that," Uly smiled. "How quickly can you load up supplies and be gone?"

"Day. Maybe a day and a half."

"Take priority over other vessels and do that," he ordered. "Eskil will provide you all the secondary details you need, as well as the timing. Questions?"

She paused, indecisive, which was out of character for the woman. "Ask, Tiny."

"What happens if Commander Chastain does bring back a bunch of Humans, sir?"

Not what he'd been expecting from her. At the same time, Uly hadn't really told many people, and Tiny had only recently moved to a closer circle of commanders that he dealt with on a regular basis.

Part of the reason he had finally needed more flag officers to handle things. The *Spinward Reaches* were finally turning into a place, with a fleet, and needed structure.

"I expect that most of them will settle on Bastion, at least initially," he replied. "But they'll be Human, so some will join the fleet, while others will move into trade, given Bastion's central location to a great many other places. You might get some Human crew at some point."

"Are they all as aggressive as everyone says?" she pressed.

"They can be," he nodded. "We can be. We can also not be. It's mostly that our ability and willingness to resort to excessive violence is probably greater than most species. You can still take three-quarters of the Humans you meet and pin their shoulders to the mat."

"Only three-quarters?" She seemed insulted.

Uly smiled.

"I knew a fellow in school, before I was commissioned," he told her. "Two hundred and ten centimeters tall. One hundred and fifty kilograms. Jock, like you. Athlete in several sports, though not wrestling. Probably at least as strong as Eskil."

She blinked, trying to process a Human that size.

"We come in as many sizes as colors, Tiny," Uly smiled at her. "That's another odd element of Humans you will become accustomed to."

"If you say so, sir."

"They'll be people, same as everyone else," he said. "A bit more primitive than Isann or Samuur, but not terribly so. The ones Dan will recruit will be the ones willing to walk blind into some grand adventure. It will be the next generation where the homebodies will emerge. And they will. For now, I needed Humans to exist in the broader galaxy, so that a generation from now, we're part of the *Spinward Reaches*."

"And nobody knows who the Lost Tribe really is?" she pressed.

Uly studied her. Weighed her soul, as his mother Tamsin would have called it.

"We both are," Uly told her, watching whiskers fly. "Neither group, Yarikh or Sector Seventeen, has the original homeworld of Humanity, Tiny, but do not tell anyone that. At some future point, I know a place that might be our original home and would like to send a ship or three there looking."

"Zamir Aytiev," she nodded quietly.

"Or Sivi Salavat," he smiled, watching her jolt with understanding. "Yes, all of the *Spinward Reaches* as a place. As a people. As my Mazhin friends call it, the rainbow gumbo, filled with all colors. All flavors. All possibilities. But that's after we handle this task."

"I'm up for that, too, sir," she brightened.

"Then make sure you stay alive to see it, Tiny," he reminded her. "I'll need you on the far side of all this."

"Ye can count on us, sir."

"Good, because here's what your next mission will involve..."

SEVENTY-FOUR

Lukyan had always respected DJ Gross. Hardass of the first order, but you needed something like that—*someone* like that—to anchor the corner at Krilic. And keep the leash on people like *Wardog Charlie*, though that ship was still at Avocur, guarding Uly.

At the same time, Lukyan had never really been friendly with the guy. Mostly waved at him in passing, maybe coming as far back as Krilic once every year and a half or so, back when he'd been making a living out on the fringes of Khet space.

Nothing had changed about the man in at least a decade.

"Bunch of yahoos already pouring in," DJ said as soon as the line secured.

Lukyan looked around his office and nodded.

"Mostly my doing," he told the man.

Anna was in port, aboard *Storm Crow*. Couple of other big Devastators accompanying her, but she'd let Maks put him in command of the force.

At least until Uly and Sterling got involved.

"And nobody will tell me what's going on," DJ groused.

"Also, my doing," Lukyan sighed. "We have a leak somewhere. High up at the palace on Rayzian, to have gotten enough details to Zhoralong to matter, last time. This time, I'm under orders to handle things differently."

Again, that vague innuendo that Uly was pulling his strings, when it was really Maks, but he'd known the kid for nearly two decades. First Officer on *that* Tuesday.

Best friend before and since.

DJ scowled. It was an impressive scowl. Man was used to cowing Ononguli pirates into behaving with nothing but the force of his personality.

That, and they'd retired the old *Tanis Dragon* and put him in a brand-new Heavy Striker remarkably similar to *Vauquelin*. Also named *Tanis Dragon*, so they might have retired the old Light Striker version permanently or something to upgrade DJ. Gonna need the extra fire-power, with what was coming, because the stations at Krilic would have to stand on their own while this fleet was elsewhere.

And *Tanis Dragon* would be on Uly's wing.

"So what will you tell me, Chayka?" DJ finally asked.

"Anna has Summoned the Clans," Lukyan replied, using the formal term.

The call to war, when the Auga invaded. Everyone drop everything and grab ships. Sail into danger, blowing shit up in a lethal, hostile swarm that hadn't ever worked to actually drive the *Auga Empire* back.

This time, Uly was counting on winning.

Lukyan would have to consult the history books to find the last time that had happened.

And even DJ could blink in surprise. It was good to know.

"And put you in command?" DJ asked.

"Left me in command, but only for now," Lukyan corrected him. "Uly and Sterling Huff will command. All of us. Including you."

"I'm okay with that," DJ said, remarkably even smiling as he did. "How does it play out?"

"Between you and me, we'll assemble all the yahoos here," Lukyan said. "Locked and loaded. Then I will provide a vector for our first rendezvous, while sending a messenger to Uly and Sterling letting them know we're in motion. Two or more big forces will gather up along the way, then we'll avalanche Izabh."

And there were lots of details being left out, but DJ Gross was smart enough to see them. Probably even fill them all in with extremely accurate guesses, but that was why Anna had him guarding her flank.

Not many conductors she trusted with that sort of thing.

Not many Ononguli conductors he'd trust with a job that serious.

"How soon?" DJ asked, as if it was a done deal.

"Six days," Lukyan said. "Time to resupply in place and repair anything that comes up, then we don't stop moving until we return to either here or Avocur, depending."

DJ nodded, lips pursed.

"I'll be second in line behind you," DJ promised, then started when Lukyan laughed.

"Third, behind *Storm Crow*, most likely," he countered. "But even then, I expect Sterling to have you commanding a whole wing."

"You think?"

"*Wardog Charlie* appointed themselves harbor lifeguard at Avocur," Lukyan reminded him. "Every ship coming or going got inspected at gunpoint by those yahoos. Sterling has a much better appreciation of what you had to handle. And how good you are at it."

"Oh."

Lukyan smiled.

"And Anna wants a planning meeting, day after tomorrow," Lukyan said. "You, me, Maks, Chervonya, her. Maybe a couple of others, but I'm not hearing anything from her suggesting it at the moment."

"We'll be ready," DJ said. "Been standing ready since the first lunatic sailed into harbor and announced that the war had begun."

"And it has, DJ," Lukyan reminded him. "Shortly, we're going to be attacking an Auga imperial world with as many ships as can be brought to bear. It's going to be ugly."

"Kid, it always is," DJ laughed. "We'll have you covered."

Lukyan nodded.

Because Anna had sounded the horn to call all the fighting ships, and sent a big chunk of them here, while others were going to be turned loose with orders to raid and harry other Auga worlds, all along the frontier.

The war had begun.

SEVENTY-FIVE

Solomon had enough experience now to understand that he could command starships. He simply didn't have any interest in it.

Still, it had been necessary for this mission. He glanced over at Yalwa.

"About ten more seconds," the Ononguli gentleman nodded.

Solomon's job was to supervise, as most of the crew were his people from off *Free Trader Polat* anyway. Yalwa had done the flying. And most of the commanding, but he'd also explained to Solomon how he had trained Rabiu on the flight out.

They were almost home.

Solomon settled in and counted heartbeats. It was a good way to meditate without meditating. Keeping your focus in place while drifting it backwards and seeing the whole battlefield as an entity.

"And dropping. Oh, shit!"

Solomon studied the boards and agreed.

"Get me IDs immediately," he said. "And stand ready to reverse and flee."

"Looks like they're friendly," Yalwa said. "Seeing *Tanis Dragon* and *Storm Crow* in the middle of that mess. Plus *Warhammer Rose*."

All of these fleets were friendly? Solomon gave up counting hulls and started estimating small squadrons. These were Ononguli ships. They would fight like fire teams, instead of marching lines.

Light infantry, sliding along the enemy's weak spots instead of hammering them in the center to break through. That one force centered on *Storm Crow* could do that, too.

Both tactics worked. It frequently came down to the quality of the troops involved, both from what he'd read and who he had commanded.

"Hail from *Warhammer Rose*, Lukyan Chayka commanding," Yalwa said. "Four seconds lag."

"Main screen," Solomon replied automatically.

He couldn't imagine anything Lukyan had to say that this crew didn't need to find out immediately anyway.

Lukyan Chayka had not changed, though Solomon thought of himself as having grown up from a kid to an adult since he'd met the man that first time at Lacium.

The lag held, until the light-speed wave carried the image to *Warhammer Rose*.

"You are absolutely the last person I was expecting to see," Chayka said with wonder. "What's your situation and how do I need to adjust my schedule?"

Yes, that was the man Uly had known. Sharp. Precise. Compact.

"We captured a pirate vessel on our return flight, Conductor," Solomon said. "*Free Trader Polat* is sitting out in the darkness while we scouted the moorage, having been gone so long. What have I missed?"

"Uly has declared war on the *Auga Empire*," Chayka replied. "The Ononguli Horde has gathered and we're two days from sailing out to assist, but he'll be glad to see you. Should we send a messenger out to Dan, or is that you?"

"That's me, sir," Solomon said. "I'll rendezvous with them and be back in a couple of hours."

"I'll let my folks know and Anna will no doubt have a big meeting on *Storm Crow*."

Solomon was shocked to hear that. The *Vatazhko* herself was here? Leading the Ononguli into battle?

But then, Uly probably was, too. Hopefully, Sterling could keep him safe. And Dan. And everyone else.

"See you shortly," Solomon said, then cut the line and nodded to the real conductor here.

"Stand by to reverse course," Yalwa said simply. "And gone."

Which was good, because apparently much had happened, and Dan had gotten them home soon enough to participate in what was coming.

Whatever was coming.

SEVENTY-SIX

Dan had grabbed a semi-random sample of her new Humans and brought them to the bridge. The ex-Duchess was among them, along with Freda and Ellen, mostly because those three women honestly had about the entire spectrum of Human experience to draw on between them.

They were not part of the Assembled Congress, but had taken to advising her informally. Providing a conduit back to the other four hundred folks.

They were on the bridge of *Polat*. Pery was standing next to Rabiu's station, without the least flinch when his gill slits and headcrest moved. But she'd also possibly come the furthest mentally and emotionally, of all the newcomers.

Polat dropped into real space. *Tripoli Blackbird* was already there, on a forward flank like Sterling would have done it, but he'd trained Solomon as much as she had.

Ellen gasped.

"That's the Ononguli Horde?" she asked quietly.

"More Ononguli ships than I've ever seen in one place, yes," Dan answered carefully. "Not all of them by any stretch, but probably half of this force will be moving on, based on what Solomon tells me. *Free Trader Polat* has no business in that sort of thing, so most of you will continue on to Bastion and we'll catch up later."

Pery turned to face her.

"You're about to sail into Götterdämmerung?" the woman asked. "And expect us to just keep walking? What if you lose?"

"Then the Auga eventually win," Dan said. "You've learned enough now to know what that means. At the same time, the *Spinward Reaches* are building up to the thing that might resist them in another generation or two."

"Are we allowed to accompany you?" Freda asked quietly.

She was the youngest here, but still smart.

"Some of you might, yes," Dan offered.

"I'd like to meet the man so impressive that he has all of the Congress as wives," Pery said.

Dan wasn't worried about the woman. If anything, the former duchess had seemed more interested in Solomon, though that young man had kept a studied distance.

Might be shy. Might not like women. Might not want to interfere with the mission.

Dan hadn't asked, because Solomon was a grown man. Sabre School Adept.

He could decide. Or ask her for help as his teacher.

Dan turned to Ellen and got a nod from her as well, so she got Rabiu's attention.

"Sure, I can get the ship home without adult supervision," her favorite pirate accountant grinned. "I assume you and Solomon will want to take as many troops as possible with you to Uly?"

"That's my guess," Dan said. "We might also simply leave you the majority of forces and just take the Congress and a few others. Let me talk to Anna."

"I'll operate as if resupply and then on to maybe Saari from here, before a run lateral to Bastion," Rabiu nodded.

She'd let him plan that. Her job had been to recruit a block of Humans that was big enough for breeding and maintaining a colony in the *Spinward Reaches*, because at the end of the day the Yarikh were only Human in shape. They were indeed a new species, with everything they had done to modify themselves.

She would find out everything else she needed shortly.

SEVENTY-SEVEN

Anna had, of course, foolishly asked the gods if things could get weirder, sitting here in Krilic as they got organized for whatever shenanigans Lukyan and Maks had planned next.

Those same gods had, obviously, decided to laugh in her face and up the stakes.

At least it had been Dan and her mission, returning with success.

And she had brought three new Humans from Sector Seventeen with her aboard *Storm Crow*, in addition to the Congress of Wives and all of her original Humans that had accompanied her to that semi-mythical place called Masym.

The newcomers had been around aliens enough to be calm, right up to the point that Dan introduced her as THE *Vatazhko*, at which point two of the new women panicked a little and the third simply nodded.

But that one was *Danumash* royalty, if Anna had understood the explanation correctly.

Humans had some very weird ideas on how to make civilizations work, and Anna knew that she'd been spoiled by Uly.

Lukyan was just finishing up an explanation of the last year, supplemented with details from Maks and Chervonya. Dan grimaced, then turned to the Mazhin woman known as Nasrin.

"Any chance they are on this ship?" Dan asked.

Anna had considered it. She'd left Harald back on Rayzian with Stefaniya Baran to supervise things, then brought her two worst fire-breathers with her: Bakhtiar Teke and Nihal Pasternak.

Anna didn't think those two had leaked, but someone on their staffs might have.

"I can find out," Nasrin said simply, then turned to look Anna dead in the eye. "How rude do you want to get?"

She understood that the offer wasn't physical torture.

Emotional, maybe.

But then, if someone was guilty, they might die a thousand deaths around a nosy Mazhin, and that would at least offer ideas about things that maybe Anna should have investigated at some point.

Everyone had been cleared, but someone had still leaked.

Somewhere.

And Uly was putting himself on the line right next to the Ononguli Sphere, so maybe the stakes had finally reached a level where things should get a little rough.

"What did you have in mind?" she asked the Mazhin woman diplomatically.

"Bad Cop."

"Can you find them?" Anna asked.

"Dunno," Nasrin replied. "Can make people uncomfortable enough for Suka Kuri to identify them, even if I can't."

Anna turned to the Emro woman. Looked up at her. Elderly, but not slowed down. Spry and deadly, if you knew what to look for.

Moss School, but only because Sabre School had been harder on the knees. She was still training at least four Sabre Adepts right now.

Suka Kuri simply nodded, eyes sober and deadly in ways that sent a shiver up Anna's spine.

Exemplar of the Moss School. About as dangerous as anyone in the galaxy might strive to achieve.

And it would probably work.

"How do we proceed?" she asked.

"Have a larger staff meeting," Dan said. "Invite all of your senior people and their aides. The Congress will be there to update them and plan for what comes after this coming campaign."

"I've already outraged a few folks by not telling anyone anything," Lukyan offered with a chuckle. "DJ Gross and Klyment Gavrilyuk both accepted that I'd been ordered not to tell Anna or anyone else a few things."

"Eventually, they'll find out that I issued those orders," Maks interjected. "Instead of Uly or you, Dan. It was necessary then and remains so, now."

Anna did appreciate that those two were willing to fall on their swords, if she or Uly really had to come down on them, but they were doing what they thought was right, and Anna didn't have any reason to doubt them.

"So folks understand that you're looking for an intelligence leak?" Dan asked. "A mole of some sort?"

"Or simply a spy," Anna replied. "Could be any of a number of things, because usually the Ononguli and the Auga as a people are mortal enemies. One of my people might be dealing with someone under the table who wasn't actually Auga, but part of the Empire."

"I'll find them," Nasrin said casually. "Gonna be rude, but I will."

"I have your back," Halyna said simply.

"Same," Katya added.

The two Ononguli Wives.

All three Emro women nodded as well.

Then every one of them.

Anna almost felt sorry for whoever it was, but that person had almost cost her Lukyan, as well as Uly.

She might have to dig up and dust off some of the really ancient methods of torture and execution, when she had a certainty.

There were still a lot of them on the books.

"Before we leave, or after?" Anna asked.

"Let's start as soon as possible," Dan said. "Something like this might require peeling several layers back, so we should start immediately, expecting that we'll still maintain what Lukyan and Maks have planned."

Yes, she was afraid that Dan might say that.

SEVENTY-EIGHT

Nasrin usually grumbled that so many people saw the tentacles and squelched sideways. Panicked at what a Mazhin might learn about them.

Most folks did only have five senses, after all.

Mazhin lived in a realm an order of magnitude more interesting and detailed.

The room was gumbo. The good kind, rather than that brown shit *Ahmadi* had served originally. Heavy on Ononguli, but that was Anna and her people, including two other Lords of the Endless Plains and staff.

The Congress Assembled still intimidated the shit out of people, but that was usually because they saw it as Uly and his harem, rather than Dan and her sisters. Not sister *wives*. A combat team, composed of many species representatives who could be ambassadors for Uly or Dan as needed.

Speed and brains.

And she was, among the current Congress, the youngest by lifespan. And that mostly because Mazhin tended to live half again as long as everyone else, so they were slower in the teen years, too.

Not as long-lived as the Yarikh, but perhaps closer to them than others. She nodded at Dionysia as that woman settled along the outer edge of the large conference room with the other aides to the main players.

Among the Congress, only Dan, Suka Kuri, and Halyna sat at the big table today. Katya had threatened to bite or butt anyone putting her up there, but that was mostly for show, as she would have done it had it been necessary.

Any of them would. That was the power of the Congress.

Nasrin had specifically located the chair the greatest distance from the coffee machine. Opposite corner, so she could circumnavigate the big table in the middle of the room while going and returning.

And maybe her tentacles were a little louder and more excited today. Showing off. Drawing attention to her, because most of the trouble she wanted to cause would start in the other person's mind.

Mazhin had no telepathic abilities, as the other species might have defined such a thing. What they had was a much greater sensitivity to scent. And the ability to talk to one another with semaphore, but there weren't any cousins in the room.

Only her sisters.

"If we could bring this meeting to order?" Anna announced, causing the room to settle some and focus on the *Vatazhko*.

Nasrin waited for folks to come to rest, then immediately rose and started around the table, silent as a hunter and smelling bodies as she went by.

Ononguli had a rich, earthy taste. Those Endless Plains they endlessly worshiped, even the ones who lived on starships. Part of their diet. Each had a different flavor, but within a range she had already identified.

Heads turned and bodies tracked her, but Anna was talking. And Nasrin didn't need to make eye contact with anyone to study them in great detail.

Learning about the Human need to be looking at someone had been one of the weirdest things as a kid. Before that, she'd only been around her kind.

Still, her presence stirred still waters. Churned up the muck at the bottom of the pond, as it were.

Bakhtiar Teke and Nihal Pasternak had brought six people into the chamber with them. Aides, ranging from Chief of Staff to runner. Anna had similar folks, plus all of her senior external advisors, including Lukyan and Maks in that group. Chervonya fell in the middle somewhere, as Nasrin could smell the other Ononguli weighing that young woman for a seat on the high council one day soon.

She'd do well, but even Chervonya wasn't certain what she wanted, mostly because Maks would be off doing things, rather than staying still at Rayzian. Pity.

But maybe Anna needed her own kind of Congress like Uly had? Nasrin made a note to mention that to Anna in private circumstances. Maks and Lukyan were three-quarters there already. Chervonya could use them, though Maks would be as stuck separate as Anari and Sterling tended to be.

Maybe peace would break out and everyone could have a few years to live quieter lives.

Nasrin got to the coffee machine with a thorough map of the room. Not something she could explain to anyone but a Mazhin. Well, Uly would immediately grasp it. And probably Sterling, too.

But they were special cases.

The coffee robot was an efficient beast. Punch a few buttons, wait, and it would customize to your needs. Spoil you, really.

Some days, it was nice to be spoiled.

Nasrin turned back to the room as the machine growled and whined. About half the people in here could see her, but most were listening to Anna talk. Then Lukyan as he filled in details, with Maks adding tidbits.

One man stood out. Ononguli. Took her a moment to place him. Hryhoriy Kovalenko. Chief of Staff to Bakhtiar Teke.

One of the fire-breathers, per Anna.

He was locked on her from across the way, but not like a guy watching a woman. More like a rabbit that had suddenly spotted the hawk overhead.

Interesting.

Nasrin wondered if someone had quietly hinted that Anna was getting serious about hunting for spies. Or maybe the man was just a specist. An Ononguli minority still ran hard on that tendency, even after having had to rely on Uly and the *Spinward Reaches* for the last several years.

Still, locked on her.

Nasrin heard the machine beep and turned her face to it, keeping her tentacles watching Kovalenko as she worked.

His smell was wrong. That also stood out to her, though she supposed that none of the other species in this room would detect it.

Nasrin picked up her warm mug and turned back to the room, locking herself hard on Kovalenko before nodding and turning to finish circling.

That man flinched.

If he was a specist, he'd be giving off hatred of some flavor. Disdain. Something. Occasionally, a twisted lust, but Nasrin had never sorted out the kinds of crosswiring failures that triggered that response. Presumably, power games, and Omid wasn't the woman to ask.

Maybe Suka Kuri could explain.

For now, she walked, tentacles pointed at Kovalenko, even as her face betrayed nothing. Watched him watch her, possibly unaware that her tentacles were almost eyes that way.

His smell got a little rancid with the most petite terror. Weird, but detectable, though she had no idea what was triggering the response.

Still, everyone else here either liked her or hated her, and Nasrin had mapped the room for those folks on either side of the divide that Anna had intentionally opened in the Horde by marrying one of their daughters off to a Human. Even if it was Uly.

Most in here understood the future and looked forward to it. Teke and Pasternak were going to be dragged by the horns, but were putting up less fuss than they had in the early days. Both men saw the future. And their two options.

Cooperate with Uly and maybe win. Maintain biological purity and certainly lose.

Stark, but Uly had laid it out for them. And been proven right.

Dan raised an eyebrow as Nasrin came around the table. Mazhin didn't have body hair, so that bit of Human structure had to do a lot of communications work, but Nasrin had learned that language. She nodded meaningfully, glanced at Kovalenko, and watched him flinch hard.

Worth investigating, though she wasn't about to spook him just yet.

SEVENTY-NINE

Dan knew what Nasrin was up to. They'd discussed it as a Congress initially, then the two of them later.

Bloodhound, but that was a rude way to frame it. Probably accurate enough for an outsider.

She followed the line of the woman's gaze and watched the impact on one of Teke's people.

Hryhoriy Kovalenko. Possibly a bigger asshole than his boss, though Teke tended to simply be a punk. Specist, but casual about it, rather than virulent.

Mostly pissed at the galaxy that the Ononguli needed outsiders to help them survive, when their entire culture went a little too deep into the old cowboy mythos of rugged individualism.

Buddy, won't work in this day and age.

Still, his reaction to Nasrin was telling. Spooked. Like, bad.

Dan wondered what Anna had said. Or to whom.

Mole hunting was always an ugly business. And to suggest bringing in Mazhin with their secret powers was just rude, because the goal was to cause the other guy to flinch badly and reveal himself.

What had Kovalenko done? Why was he reacting this way?

Dan stared openly at the man for a moment, until he saw her, then she turned back to Anna, feeling his gaze on her ear.

Even more distraction, because now he had two women to worry about.

Around her, the conversation was ranging into a variety of details. Technical stuff for the various commanders to convey to their squadrons, because this size of a fleet had to move delicately, when the Variable Pulse Spatial Generator wake of this many ships moving disrupted things to the point that folks would be kicked out of flight and have to wait hours to recover.

Better to fly on various vectors, then come together regularly to check in and maintain an overall coherence.

Since she wasn't commanding anything, Dan could just listen. Halyna was handling most of the questions that got sent their way, with Suka Kuri offering occasional commentary.

Letting Dan listen. And watch. And haunt.

Poor Ononguli fellow was sweating. Like, way more than the situation called for.

Unless Nasrin had gotten into his head.

Dan turned back to stare at the man. Smiled enigmatically, because he worked for someone who was often a pain in her ass and she owed them a ration of retribution for it one of these days.

He flinched. Hard. Raw terror filled the man's face for a second. Dan smiled more.

And was not prepared for Kovalenko to suddenly jump up and start running for the hatch.

What the hell?

"Somebody stop him," Nasrin barked hard.

Zamira Ismailov was a Second Dan black belt in a form of wrestling/grappling called Karmap. Isann woman. Isann open-handed combat form that the Congress had added to their overall curriculum.

She rose smoothly and bounced Kovalenko off the back of a chair with a shoulder check, Isann being about the same mass as Ononguli, but usually shorter.

Then, she got rude, even as the rest of the Combat Team flowed into motion.

Terrible Gaff was a Khet form. Intended to go after gill slits and big eyeballs with a hooking motion that would grab neck or ear on other species.

Worked really well if someone got hold of your horns, too. Zamira caught one and twisted inward. Ononguli were designed to butt horns like a pair of unruly moose. Straight on. Didn't have a lot of rotational strength to resist.

Especially not when Zamira dropped to one knee as she shifted around a common center. Kovalenko slammed into the deck face first with the sort of resounding bong that usually meant a bad concussion on a human.

Ononguli were literally designed to take it. Still, didn't help the man when Zamira landed on his back. Or Katya caught an arm and twisted it in tight. Any farther, and things would be tearing. Kovalenko stopped moving at all.

Dan knelt down in front of him, where Zamira had his head turned the opposite direction from where his arm would go if these two women pulled.

Drawn and quartered, as it were.

Several guards had started to move.

"We have the situation under control," Halyna ordered the room in a voice too big for the space.

LOUD.

Nasrin moved close. Studied the punk. Nobody Dan knew as a person, so much as a spot on an org chart and an advisor to someone she really didn't like all that much.

Dan turned to Teke and let him feel the measure of her scowl. He had half risen, then stopped because Yanouk had an enormous green hand on his shoulder, ready to slam him back down.

"What's going on?" Teke asked, but it was the voice of bewilderment, rather than rage.

Either a good actor or as confused as Dan was.

Except that Kovalenko here was acting awfully guilty.

Of what, she would find out shortly.

Dan rose and met Anna's gaze.

"You'll handle it?" Anna asked.

Dan heard the gasps around the room, and understood that the Congress would be gaining some terrible element of mythology and legend when this story got around.

And folks would think twice about crossing her or Uly in the future.

"We'll handle it," Dan agreed, then turned to Yanouk. "Bring him, too, but politely. At least until we discover what this one is all about."

Zamira had Kovalenko on his feet. Guards around the outside of the room had stepped forward, then stepped back when the Congress scowled at them as a unit.

A Combat Team, first and foremost. Congress of Wives only later. Best you remember that.

Bodies were in motion.

"This meeting is adjourned," Anna was announcing as Dan followed Zamira and her prisoner into the corridor.

EIGHTY

Anna knew better than to get directly involved. She might have been pretty good at the rough and tumble pirate life a generation ago. And was still in pretty good shape these days.

Those women moved as a single entity with lots of arms and legs.

And one mind.

So, she followed. Politely.

"Lukyan, you supervise with Maks," she said as she got close to the hatch. "Chervonya, with me. Everyone else, you will be updated."

After I figure out what's going on. And decide what to tell you.

If then.

Isann were denser than Ononguli. Zamira moved Hryhoriy Kovalenko with hardly any effort, his arm folded back and up in a way that looked painful. Dan and her people were in a combat mode that wasn't asking questions.

And probably not taking prisoners, if anyone gave them any grief.

Anna followed, sticking with Chervonya inside a bubble of hostile women. And two men.

One of the training gyms ended up being their destination. Anna assumed psychological torture, as Dan's Congress had claimed it for themselves for now, a private space for their training, where Solomon Wyndham might be the only male normally allowed in.

He met them at the door, a fighting sword held negligently in one hand like he had been training and paused.

"Oh, found him already?" Solomon asked as he stepped to one side.

Anna was frequently jealous that men like Solomon would automatically take orders from Dan. Or any of her women.

She had the Ononguli Horde. Obstreperous only began to describe those men. Maks and Lukyan still surprised her.

"Solomon, you have the door," Nasrin ordered.

Anna watched him move to where he could hit anyone entering with that sword in a single slash, then come to perfect stillness, a male caryatid only lacking a twin on the other side.

Hryhoriy Kovalenko got put on a bench. Bakhtiar was allowed to stand to one side, but had already figured out that he should keep his mouth shut unless he wanted to sit as well, because Yanouk and Anari bracketed him like a child standing between his aunties.

The look on his face was not excited. Anna didn't really care, assuming that Nasrin and Dan had the right person.

Or the start of some network that needed to be rolled up and smashed.

Percussively.

Nasrin walked right up to Hryhoriy, then moved around behind him and between Zamira and Katya Zehlennko, those two holding him in place on the bench. Anna watched Nasrin lean in until her tentacles caressed the man's head in a way that was somewhere between horror-filled and pornographic.

Depending on where you were standing.

Hryhoriy managed to not quite scream, but still made a noise that would haunt Anna for a while.

A wet mewling that escaped his lips before he could compress them far enough.

Terror, given voice.

But Anna had told Nasrin that Bad Cop was acceptable, so Anna needed to get involved at this point.

She looked at Bakhtiar once to cow him into silence, then went to talk to the man's Chief of Staff.

"What have you done?" Anna demanded in a hard, cold voice.

Hryhoriy latched his eyes onto her like the only sane spot in his galaxy. She wondered if Nasrin had already broken his mind.

Anna wasn't aware of any sort of overt specism on his part. Nor worse than most, anyway, and even Bakhtiar had mostly been stubborn because he didn't think that anyone else could help.

Not that he saw them as a lesser species. Mostly, he was in it for power and wealth, both of which the Lords of the Endless Plains accumulated.

"*Vatazhko*?" Hryhoriy asked in a sad, broken voice.

"Why did the Mazhin woman pick you out of a crowd, Kovalenko?" Anna pressed, moving close enough to dominate his vision and obscuring all the other alien women in the room.

It seemed to help. Some.

His mouth opened and closed, but nothing came out except ragged breathing.

She decided to play a hunch, since she had already spread rumors about why Nasrin was present.

"What did you tell the Auga, Kovalenko?" she asked in a more conversational voice.

Good Cop, she supposed, which said a lot considering how angry she was.

And probably still the least rageful woman in here.

But someone had warned the Auga that Zhoralong was a target. And Lukyan had been there, protecting Uly.

Along with the entire Congress.

Something got through to the man. His crazed eyes stabilized some. Breathing improved. Mind still kind of broken.

"We don't need their KIND!" he roared, voice going from a whisper to a shout but the body was anchored tightly in place. "Let all the aliens be destroyed. They will poison the Ononguli Sphere!"

Anna blinked. Surprised. Shocked.

She wondered if Nasrin really had broken the man. Or Dan.

Good Cop wasn't good enough. She squatted down in front of him, about two meters away. It put her below him, but let him center on her and see the rest as legs.

"You warned the Auga that we were coming?" she asked quietly.

"The Corsac Fox will be the doom of the Sphere, Anna!" he pleaded. "They needed to destroy that man, and all his aliens. The Empire will spend an entire generation moving west and taking the Khet and the *Spinward Reaches*! We'll be saved!"

She closed her mouth rather than answer that.

Anna Shevchenko had access to the journals of every *Vatazhko* for the last six hundred years. And all of them had impressed on their successors the importance of recording all those little details, uncertain what might prove critical a century later.

The *Auga Empire* moved slowly. The Auga as a species had perfected themselves, as they saw it, then invented the goal to make the galaxy perfect by ruling it. Regardless of the opinions of barbarians they encountered along the way.

Killing Uly might gain them a generation. Maybe. Not even a lifetime. A few decades, at most. And the Empire would continue biting off chunks of the Sphere, inheriting worlds that emptied of populations because the Ononguli would not live under imperial control.

But Uly might actually stop the Empire. Entirely.

Anna was still shocked that he didn't want to destroy the Empire. Merely force it to acknowledge that it did evil to everyone else and find a more ethical solution.

Coexistence, where all were equal. All were welcome.

She stood up and rotated in place to look at all the women in here, most of whom were Uly's wives, because Dan had decided that to be the best way to ensure that every species would have a representative at that highest level. Equal to the Legal Department, and their superior in many ways, because Uly was committed to Dan and the rest of them. Even the two Emro women who weren't married but were still part of the Congress.

She and Chervonya were the outsiders in this room.

Well, Bakhtiar had gone pink, but that was shock and shame on his part when she met his eyes.

"Anna, I had no idea," he gasped.

And, because Anna Shevchenko had to embrace a little bit of evil today, she turned back to Nasrin.

"Is he lying?" she asked.

Bad Cop walked over to stand next to her. Close enough that Bakhtiar was literally shivering with fear as Anna watched.

"No," Nasrin said.

"He fears us," Suka Kuri suddenly spoke up. "Resents us to a certain degree, but hates the Auga worse for all the things they have done going back generations."

Bakhtiar nearly fell over, suddenly spinning to look up at the towering Exemplar of the Moss School.

Suka Kuri had a prim smile. Not warm, but not frigid either.

"Is that true?" Anna asked Bakhtiar bluntly, drawing his eyes back down to her.

He turned scarlet instead. Nodded, keeping his head bowed.

"She is not wrong," he offered quietly.

"But you have not betrayed me?" she asked, glancing over and getting a shake from Nasrin.

"I have not," Bakhtiar Teke pronounced, looking up like a man still expecting Solomon to run him through with that sword from behind .

Three steps and that was all it would take.

Another glance over and a nod from Nasrin.

So, a man possessed of great arrogance and stubborn will, but not a traitor. Good to know.

She dug in a pocket and located a comm.

"I'm here," Lukyan replied instantly.

"Where are you?" Anna asked.

"Outside the hatch," he said. "Maks and I figured it was safer to keep guard than let some yahoo in to bother you."

And he was not wrong, either.

She nodded to Solomon, who palmed the door control and slid to one side. Lukyan looked in, noting the Sabre Adept, but didn't enter unbidden.

Like he could taste the flow of emotions in here.

Anna walked right up to Bakhtiar, shivering as the man was, and put an arm around his shoulders.

"This one is safe," she said, watching as Maks and Lukyan finally entered. Carefully. "That man is a traitor to the Horde."

Kovalenko was up now, lifted bodily to his feet and being escorted out by Halyna and Katya, the non-Ononguli in the room standing back.

Because this was a thing for the Lord of the Endless Plains to handle, and they all apparently recognized it as such.

Anna nodded to Dan and moved Bakhtiar ahead of her as Chervonya led the other four and escorted their prisoner out of the room.

Lukyan paused, then looked back at everyone.

"This is still only the beginning," he promised them.

Anna nodded and followed him out.

There would be others. Some of them might even try to run.

None would escape her wrath.

EIGHTY-ONE

Dan released a breath as the hatch closed.

"Should I wait outside?" Solomon asked.

Because he was that smart.

She considered it.

"Yes," and he left.

Only the Congress remained behind. Dan turned to Suka Kuri.

"Now what?" she asked, more ignorance than anything.

"That man will be executed according to the ancient laws," Suka Kuri replied grimly. "The look on Anna's face had no mercy for him. And because she had previously summoned the clans, treason takes on an extra level. His immediate clan will disown him. They may have to change their names to escape association with his crimes."

Dan grimaced. Ugly. But traitors had to be taught a brutal lesson, lest others think to follow in their tracks later with only a slap on the wrists.

Only the most committed specists would follow through, watching that. And she knew there were a few left, possibly still in positions of power, though again, Anna was going to get brutal before this was done.

Her scowl had promised as much.

"What did Lukyan mean, there at the end?" Ciah asked.

"I presume that there are still some Ononguli ships out there in the harbor, all set to race off to meet secretly with some Auga representative," Anari spoke up. "As soon as they know where we're headed, so they can sell that information to the Empire. Like last time."

Dan nodded. Zhoralong cast a long shadow over the last decade.

"Anything we can do to stop them?" Ciah pressed.

"I'm pretty sure that Lukyan and Maks are going to sell people a dinner of poisoned meat," Suka Kuri chuckled harshly. "Let them feast on it and not tell everyone that the fleet is changing course until we're in motion. That is how I would do it. Especially if they lay out detailed steps from Krilic. Ships will accidentally get lost, racing ahead to warn the Auga, then maybe not catch back up the fleet later. Anna will have names."

"Maks will grind horns off," Yeong-Suk noted. "That man's pissed beyond all measure."

"Sees himself responsible for not stopping it last time," Yanouk agreed. "For not tracking all the comings and goings that let whoever get away with it. Don't think anyone who suffers a mechanical breakdown of any kind recovers socially after this, unless they can convince Anna. Gonna be messy."

"And this is what we've been building towards since Halyna joined us," Dan reminded them. "That was Anna's way to make sure that Uly stayed engaged with the Sphere. That all of us did. And we have managed to distract the *Auga Empire* so much that they've pretty much stopped attacking Ononguli worlds, instead going after us plus places in Sector Fifteen for the last several years."

"So she has to come ride to our rescue?" Yeong-Suk asked.

"Something like that, yeah," Anari laughed. "Good turnabout. Dan, how seriously should we take what's coming?"

"What did you have in mind?" Dan asked the tall woman.

Anari had the most experience as an imperial citizen, before she'd kidnapped herself to join them.

"We are the Congress," Anari said, glancing around. "Should we appoint ourselves as Uly's Ambassadors and field agents, with one of us each on Anna's big ships that we trust? Not the ones we expect to turn traitor, but showing the flag on *Warhammer Rose, Storm Crow,* and whoever else?"

"Anybody know anything about Tiny?" Ciah asked. "Lukyan put her in command of a captured Auga Patrol Striker, then he and Uly left her there for what's coming. We know Maikki and Taija, among the Samuur. Should we be looking at Tiny, too?"

"I'll handle that," Suka Kuri announced.

Dan met the older woman's eyes, then nodded.

Suka Kuri knew what Dan wanted in a future member of the Congress. And there were any number of Samuur women that the Paramount could suggest, but whoever she was would need that special something to stand out. Especially as impressive as Samuur could get when they fixed their eyes on something and wiggled their butts before pouncing.

"Yes," Dan agreed. "And remember, we're going to be meeting up with Uly and the other half of the fleet at some point, so we'll need to spread out there as well. Lukyan has a rough estimate of ships. *Nubia. Vauquelin.* A few others. But we don't need to solve it today."

"What's necessary from this point?" Anari asked.

"Probably a hanging," Yanouk replied.

And she was not likely wrong.

EIGHTY-TWO

Lukyan kept his growls inside.

Anna was being THE *Vatazhko*. Teke looked like a man who would spook at a loud sound. Pasternak had rediscovered his manners in the last hour.

On this side of the room, Klyment and DJ had decided to flank him, like Lukyan was supreme naval commander or something, while they were only Lukyan's right and left hands.

Maks was never going to hear the end of this.

Chervonya was close to Anna, but not standing as part of the Council. Maks was behind her, protecting everyone's shield side, even if from behind.

Halyna Bondarenko and Katya Zehlennko had the prisoner in a double arm bar that didn't allow him to move much more than his head unless he wanted a lesson in pain.

Man was hardly on his feet, but that was because something had happened in that room to let all the steam out of Hryhoriy Kovalenko.

Like, permanently.

There wasn't anybody in this chamber who wasn't Ononguli. Nobody else was welcome, because this was Horde politics. And about to get really, really ugly.

And Maks had ordered him to assume supreme command of the Ononguli Fleet, at a time when Anna had Summoned the Clans to war.

A deep breath, and Lukyan found his rage. Incandescent, but usually banked somewhat. A pirate from distant Sector Fifteen for the longest time. Preying on Khet and folks way o'er yonder.

Until that *Tuesday*, when he had sealed his fate.

And Klyment and DJ were flanking him today. Punks.

Lukyan Chayka took a step forward, thinking about Zhoralong.

Specifically, about a pair of Samuur ships that had had no business being in the middle of that mass. About how that one Auga Striker had decided to score a soft kill when he realized he was about to be over-whelmed by someone with a better sense of tactics.

They would have killed Eskil and all the others. Folks who had come because Uly had asked them to help his new friends, and that had been the most honorable solution.

Because honor defined the Samuur like exploration did the Isann.

And stubbornness was probably the Ononguli metric.

"Hryhoriy Kovalenko, you are charged with high treason by the *Vatazhko* and the Lords of the Endless Plains," Lukyan announced in a slow, ugly voice, watching all the minor players around the edges of the room flinch at his tone.

Eskil would understand his rage. So would Uly.

"Moreover, the *Vatazhko* has called the Horde to war, so your crimes are capital in nature," Lukyan continued, tapping deep into that well of angry fire that threatened to erupt out of his mouth like dragon's breath if he wasn't careful.

Or stopped caring.

"Will any speak for this man?" Lukyan announced to the room, walls reverberating because he was close to not caring anymore.

Faces turned to Teke and Pasternak, expecting them to stick their hands in that wasp nest. Even Lukyan didn't think those two were that stupid.

Anna stepped forward instead.

"The accused has confessed his guilt in the presence of two members of the Endless Plains," she told the room. "He has not sought mercy, nor been granted any. However, it is possible that he could buy his life with the information that he has already volunteered, as well as other things that we might learn from him at a later date."

Silence. Oppressive and heavy, like rusty iron chains around the neck and shoulders.

"Kovalenko, do you acknowledge these charges?" Lukyan demanded of the traitor scum in the center of the room.

"I do," that punk murmured, just loud enough to be heard.

"Do you acknowledge your guilt?" he pursued relentlessly.

"I do," Kovalenko called.

Still quiet, but louder.

Lukyan knew that Anna hadn't promised the traitor anything prior to this, so she was the one offering him any hope at all. Lukyan had been at Zhoralong with Eskil.

But, because these men and women had decided that he should command the Horde itself today, he turned in place slowly, making eye contact with everyone, from guards to Lords.

And a lot of naval officers in the room that had been at Zhoralong with him. Or might have gone, had they been close enough to hear the invitation.

All of them were here to answer Uly's request for help.

He came back to rest. Managed to contain his snarl down to merely a scowl that still caused Anna and the others facing him to flinch a little. Maybe that bit of hiccup that brought bile up from the stomach for a moment and made you taste that sourness a second time.

He really wanted to kill this man. And take his time doing it.

Zhoralong.

But Eskil would demand a clean death. Quick. Painless.

Honorable.

So be it.

"Hryhoriy Kovalenko, you are found guilty by a court of your peers of treason in a time of war," Lukyan announced in a voice like nine kilometers of bad gravel road. "The sentence is death. Make your peace with the Endless Plains, for you will never see them again."

"I would ask for mercy," Anna replied, in a voice without any.

Because Maks had put him in command of the entire, freaking Horde today. At least his best friend in the universe had a sober, angry face, too.

"Hryhoriy Kovalenko, the *Vatazhko* requests that your sentence be delayed," Lukyan announced, mostly following a script in his head.

And a few older cases that had gone down like this, though without the stay. Horns ground off then heads removed. Lukyan could taste it.

Or maybe that was the scent of utter rage all around him.

"So be it," Lukyan pronounced. "You will be conveyed to a place of imprisonment where you will live out your days until it is determined to complete your sentence. Guards, remove this traitor from my presence and strike his name from the clan records."

The gasps around him were honest. Kovalenko Clan would be tarred with his guilt. Teke might be removed from the Council itself, for having employed such a man for so long and not catching him at his treason. His own clan might remove him from the Council to see if that would be enough to placate the rest of the Horde. Certainly Teke would be up shit creek with Anna.

And a lot of conductors around them.

Disappearing to his estates, never to be seen again in public, might be the smartest thing Bakhtiar Teke could do. The terror in his eyes suggested an appreciation that his own guards might decide not to stop the next assassination attempt.

And Lukyan had no doubts that there were a few folks out there that would try.

Halyna and Katya dragged the dipshit out of the room, not that he was resisting.

They were making a statement, because they spanned a bridge between the Sphere and the *Spinward Reaches*.

And everyone here knew it.

Lukyan blew out an angry breath and sucked one back in, trying to extinguish that blowtorch in his stomach.

Maks stepped forward, surprising damned near everyone in the room.

"That was one," Maks announced in a voice like planets colliding. "There will be others. And I will be watching."

Lukyan nodded, when heads turned to him, because most of these yahoos still thought of Maks Sobol as Lukyan's First Officer from *Compass Rose*. Instead of one of Uly's people.

Like he was.

"That was the first," Lukyan promised. "Conductors, to your ships. The Horde will sail in four hours."

PART NINE
ASSEMBLED

EIGHTY-THREE

Uly had done everything he could think of. Messages back and forth to Krilic and everywhere else, bringing in supplies and more ships to defend Avocur. And more to go to Izabh with him.

Haydar appeared on the screen in his office.

"There's news," Haydar offered in that bland, newscaster voice he did when he was pulling a fast one.

"Second Law of Thermodynamics," Uly retorted with a grin. "No news is good."

"You might like this one, though," Haydar grinned back. "One of your wives just arrived in-system."

Uly nearly exploded out of his chair.

"WHAT?"

"Zamira, and she says that she has good news, so I get to prove you wrong," Haydar laughed uproariously.

And he could. Only Dan was really closer than his old friend.

"How soon?" Uly asked.

"They just hit the edge of the system with an update packet from Lukyan and Anna that I'll start digesting," Haydar sobered. "She'll be aboard the station in about an hour."

"You have command," Uly told him.

"Figured that," and Haydar cut the line.

Sterling was aboard *Nubia*, handling all those last-minute things. Everyone else sat poised, waiting for the words that Zamira was probably about to deliver.

Uly knew that he wasn't about to get any more work done, so he went and took a shower, mostly to break his day in half. Then settled in at the airlock connected to the main shuttle bay on pins and needles as the craft came alongside then entered.

A tunnel extended and connected, then bodies started coming through.

Uly was right there when she appeared. Theirs had been a political marriage, as many of them were, but Zamira threw herself into his arms, nearly staggering Uly backwards with her weight as they kissed.

It had been more than a year. Eventually, they paused, noses touching.

"I won the draw," she grinned. "Everyone else is jealous."

"It's nice to see you, too, wife," he teased.

More kissing. He hadn't expected anything like it, but had found joy with all of them, even as he was the symbol and the outsider to Dan's Team, rather than the driving force.

But how many people got to have that many interesting spouses, all at once?

"I should probably update everyone," Zamira finally said, still locked on tight, but slightly embarrassed at their display.

"It would be nice," Haydar replied from somewhere behind them.

Zamira turned nearly silver.

"Quick meeting first," Uly told her, untangling themselves enough to stand while holding hands.

He led her to the nearby conference room and got them settled.

Sterling and Eskil were both on a screen from their shipborne offices. Haydar represented the Legal Department and most of the station at present. Zamira brought news.

"At that point," she concluded after forty-five minutes, "Lukyan ordered the fleet into motion. I came ahead on the fastest courier Maks had, with all the details you'll need to make rendezvous with the Horde and with Tiny when she returns, then we'll parse ourselves out among the fleet."

"And Lukyan has set a trap?" Sterling confirmed.

"Yes, but he and Anna aren't sure that anyone falls into it at this point, after what they did to the traitor," Zamira nodded. "More likely, that message doesn't get to Izabh in time for them to sail, so he wasn't sure what the Auga commanders would do."

"That's Tiny's job to ascertain," Eskil said. "I've instructed her to get close and Sterling has estimated where the Auga will station their forward patrols to intercept us when we sail out."

"Are we expecting a massed battle in the middle somewhere?" Haydar asked. "I've seen all the plans, but there was no certainty to anything, and I'm not really detecting any now, either."

Uly considered it, then turned to Sterling's image.

"I need a patrol out right now, running hard to see if they can find Tiny and learn what she knows," he said. "Failing that, if the Auga have sailed. I assume they will know the rough timing of the Horde, but they'd be an utter fool to let us meet up without harassment."

Sterling nodded.

"If I was in command over there, I might just run lateral, with the expectation of hitting Lukyan's force head-on first," the young man said. "That will cause them grief, since he's turning away to set his trap."

"Can we load up immediately anyway?" Uly asked. "Take a run at the Auga fleet and try to catch them in a flank? Send someone to Lukyan and either meet early or get them in as fast as we can? Do we trust the Auga?"

"Not even remotely," Eskil laughed. "I vote for a forward patrol with all of the attacking force. But that's me."

"And I agree," Sterling added. "The time has come. We pull everybody together and hit them before they can hit us. That will give us the advantage, because they won't be mentally as prepared as we are in that moment. Especially if we can kick them out of warp instead of the other way around."

All eyes turned to him. Uly nodded.

How many years had he been building to this moment? Stealing *Iron Wasp*? Capturing *King Hewitt II*? Receiving orders to transfer from *Vanguard Lesauvage* to *Marshall Castillon* when the former was put into drydock for a massive rebuild after a battle?

A lifetime, it seemed. And a charmed one, to have met Dan. And the Mazhin. And the Ononguli. And everyone else, including his wife that was holding his hand on the table.

If the *Spinward Reaches* were to become a thing, he had to hold the line against the *Auga Empire*. Stop them here. Repulse them.

Force them to change, when the only language the Auga spoke as a people seemed to be strength.

Power.

"Echelon Huff, make the fleet ready to sail," Uly ordered. "Echelon Haldur, you will depart immediately to locate *Sivi Salavat* and rendezvous with the best intelligence we have, so we can plan this battle. Questions?"

None. He nodded.

"Then I intend to spend the rest of the day with my wife, gentlemen," he grinned. "Don't bother me until after the fire is out."

EIGHTY-FOUR

Eskil was still getting used to blue. And the single wide gold band around each cuff. Uly's regular officers wore thinner black rings, but he was Echelon now. Bigshot.

Perhaps even more important than First Commander of the *Samuur*, because he was Sterling Huff's peer in the *Spinward Reaches*. And would be Lukyan's at some point, though that man might remain as some sort of Fleet Marshal equivalent over the Ononguli instead. Or in addition.

As long as Maks and Anna had enough to blackmail him into staying. Eskil wasn't fooled. Lukyan would have returned to *Compass Rose*, though he might build himself a much nicer version next time.

Assuming there was ever enough peace to put down the sword.

They would see.

"How much trouble are you expecting?" Eskil asked his First Officer as they jumped up into warp and started a run outwards to find Tiny.

Hemmo had been studying everything Haydar had been able to piece together from various sources, which had turned out to be a great deal more than Eskil might have imagined, save that both Humans and Mazhin saw eye-to-tentacle on military intelligence.

Throw in some whiskers, and he was learning.

"The Ononguli have been fighting the *Auga Empire* for centuries," Hemmo replied gravely. "Haydar got as much of that information as the *Vatazhko* was willing to share, which was frankly more than I imagined possible, and has been synthesizing it down into useful analyses of strategies and tactics at the military, social, economic, and political level."

Eskil looked over, tearing his eyes away from warpspace.

"Too much?" he asked.

"Do the Auga hide anything?" Hemmo asked.

Eskil chewed on that.

"They believe that their pantheon is destined to rule everyone," Eskil finally replied. "And that nothing in the galaxy can stop them."

"Almost nothing," Aava offered tartly from her Gunnery station.

Eskil nodded.

"Almost," he agreed. "We're going to."

"Given that, Haydar and Sterling plotted several points in space where they expected Auga squadrons to be stationed, patrolling laterally on a plane to find anyone trying to sneak through," Hemmo noted.

"Do we assume Tiny went through, or around?" Eskil asked.

"Didn't she find a barber or something that they were going to use as a stand in?" Saku Korhonen asked from his research station. "A Zuath, I think?"

"That was the rumor," Hemmo said. "If it worked, we will find out when we find them, I would presume."

"But we know where to look for trouble?" Eskil asked, waiting a beat for ears to rotate back. "What? I plan on being sneaky."

He could almost smell the eye rolls.

Too much time around Ononguli pirates.

"We do," Hemmo said. "I've laid out a course for Osman that should keep us clear, but that's all estimated at this point."

"We can take anything less than a Heavy Striker," Eskil reminded them. "Not that I want to, but we will be prepared. Osman, you have the deck. I'll be in my office. The Auga might have people watching Avocur and dumb enough to jump us, but more likely they are waiting for everyone to move out in a few hours, so they'll ignore us. Do not hesitate to fight anyone small."

"Aye."

Eskil nodded and rose.

Tiny was out there, doing her job to find the Auga fleet when it decided to move.

Uly was counting on both of them.

EIGHTY-FIVE

Captain Maikki Hudaibirdi sat in what she still thought of as Sterling's station, though the rest of the room had changed radically. All the crew stations faced inward now, letting people see around the screen in front of them to what others were doing.

Sterling and the Emro Moss Adept had planned it out, then staged all the parts, taking out half the bridge as soon as *Vauquelin* had come to rest at Avocur, then swapping the other half as soon as that task was completed.

Never once had this ship not been ready to immediately fight.

And it was her ship now, with Sterling aboard *Nubia* permanently and Aibek on Uly's staff as part ambassador and part Legal Department.

An old friend being rewarded, even though Uly hadn't known the Isann that long, nor met him under the best circumstances, but Aibek had become one of them.

Like she had.

Maikki opened a line aft to where her new First Officer was seated, separate, in case something happened to the bridge.

Commander Meder Orozaliev was another Isann. An ex-pirate who had come highly recommended for experience on long voyages and a happy willingness to serve second to a female. And an alien.

Not yet a given with many Isann men, but Uly would win them all over eventually. You only had to mention the words *Black Sword* and their eyes took on a peculiar, distant reverence.

Maikki was almost jealous that the Samuur didn't have something as unifying as the *Karaŋgılıkka*. She made a mental note to ask.

Meder was smiling at her.

"Captain?" he asked.

"Confirming your status," Maikki said.

"Last-minute potty breaks completed on time and snacks packed," he laughed.

It was good.

"Stand by."

She cut the line.

Jatau Kaita the Khet was still piloting today, while Andrii Dovzhenko had moved from Gunnery to Sensors, with the Zuath woman Pallabi Chaudhuri taking Andrii's old station.

"Andrii, anybody in front of us?"

"All of Auga and eventually the rest of the Humans," he replied, glancing up at her and winking.

Maikki had learned early on that a loose, smiling command crew that could tighten it down and go bobcat on someone was far better than always being serious. Her cousin Eskil had personally broken her first commander out of service for being a prissy martinet that had chewed up officers regularly because nobody could ever read his mind and do it the way he demanded.

Lessons that had stuck with her for more than a decade.

"Jatau, do we have the signal from the flag?" she asked.

"Affirmative, Captain," he replied. "Sterling's got us pushed out ahead of the rest of the force as a tripwire. Just a handful of scouts running interference ahead of us."

"And hopefully they turn and run back to the den to tell everyone we're coming," Maikki reminded them. "Andrii, set a fifteen-minutes reminder for when we're going to turn to intersect Lukyan's force, so I have time for coffee."

"Timer set, sir," Andrii replied, sobering.

The war was about to start. All of the everything that had happened up until now was merely the opening music. The prologue.

"Jatau, take us out," she ordered.

Vauquelin vanished into warp space.

EIGHTY-SIX

Sterling had always known that one of these days Uly intended him to sit in the big chair.

Command station, *Nubia*.

Commanding Officer, Nubia.

It was still a rush to actually do it, looking down at his old friends, including two he had known longer than he had known Uly.

Well, three, with Haydar, but the Mazhin had all been slaves until that day, and he hadn't really known any better. And they didn't hold it against him today. Nor did Uly.

You could be redeemed in Uly's mind. You had to want to become a better person, then actually do the work, but Uly would draw a line separating you from the dumb stuff you'd done.

The idiot you'd been.

And it was possible to work your way into something like this.

Echelon Huff. Senior Fleet Commander of the *Spinward Reaches*, because Uly shouldn't even be with this fleet, but Sterling understood the need.

At least he would be exercising a flag this time, instead of commanding, currently seated down along one side with Zamira in the place where Dan and the rest of Combat Team would be if they were here.

Would be when they got here.

Except that they wouldn't. Zamira might swap out. Dan would probably come over, except that she might stay aboard *Storm Crow*.

The Combat Team would be on other ships.

Safe ones, because Lukyan still expected betrayal at some point, ships and names as yet unknown.

Speaking of which...

"Oh mighty and terrible data nerd, I have a question," Sterling said as they watched other ships transitioning to warp ahead of them.

The scouts. *Vauquelin*. Half of the Yarikh, with the other half to trail *Nubia* in case trouble happened.

Haydar's tentacles did a thing that Sterling was pretty sure was a visual profanity, but didn't ask.

"Sir?" Haydar asked innocently, even turning to look over his shoulder and up.

"Lukyan and Anna presume traitors as yet undetected," Sterling said. "And I've heard Zamira's reports on what Nasrin did. Without doing that to other Ononguli conductors, is there a way to stack rank our possible enemies inside the fleet?"

Uly had turned to look, as had Zamira. Both had gone deadly still.

Del looked up, but Yaqub was locked in on his controls and Drew was in the zone.

Haydar's tentacles stilled, then locked on.

"What did you have in mind?" the older Mazhin asked in a deadly voice.

"I know that some half-dozen or so conductors knew about the Zhoralong raid but didn't go," Sterling replied. "I'm willing to presume for now that the folks who did go with us are less likely to have sold us out, because they expected the Empire to win that battle. Throw in a mass of folks along the way that knew from the shadow that our logistics train cast in the process. Is there a way to filter the Ononguli structure to find conductors that might have been talking to our known traitor? Might have carried the message at least partway to Auga? Wouldn't be that hard. Sail to a spot and leave a message, if the other side knew to check regularly or you could send a signal of some sort."

"The term you are looking for is a dead-drop, Sterling," Haydar replied quietly. "I can think of a few colonies near the current Ononguli-*Auga Empire* border where it might be possible to swing in and deliver a message, possibly as part of a cargo run."

"Would it be a freighter or a raider?" Sterling pressed.

"Not a warship like *Fire Diamond*," Uly spoke up. "Likely still an Interceptor of some sort, but one that stayed active. Especially if you are running to the border and might run into Auga ships or other Ononguli pirates."

"So how do we narrow it down?" Sterling asked.

"I ask Anna or Lukyan if they have a list of every vessel that sailed out of Rayzian from the moment the wedding ended until the fleet departed three weeks later," Uly said. "I'm sure they've already looked at it, but that's a huge list of ships, most of whom would be on honest business."

"And we have now confirmed a link to this Kovalenko punk and Teke," Haydar nodded. "That narrows it down tremendously, if you look at it that way. Still likely to get too many false positives."

"No, you eliminate most of them pretty quickly for size, owner-ship, and sailing mission," Sterling corrected him. "Anyone who made it to Zhoralong can be eliminated as well. Then you have a much shorter list to dig in on. Maybe have Nasrin board and inspect with the Team. I'd personally like to surprise the Auga as much as possible with what's coming. They'll know something. I'd like that to be as little as possible, assuming that our traitor has transmitted to them the complete order of battle for Lukyan's force. What they know of it, anyway."

Sterling turned to Uly.

"Does anyone outside this ship and your inner circle suspect the Yarikh?" he asked.

Uly jolted in surprise.

"I didn't think you did," Uly replied.

Sterling grinned.

"They put their folks at Saari, when the Samuur, for all their right-eous intent, could not have driven off a committed invasion force," Ster-ling replied. "Either they didn't really like those people that much, or they knew the Yarikh on site were perfectly safe from the barbarians. I presumed the same when they moved a force to Avocur. Do we know how deadly they are?"

"Extremely, but they would prefer not revealing that to the galaxy, Huff." Uly turned all formal. "If that secret can be kept, they promise to help us build some new ships that are better than *Nubia*, by allowing our technology to take a full step forward in the shorter term than generational scales."

Sterling whistled. Anari had talked about Traiffe and the folks she had met. And he had spent enough time around Melpomeni Michelakos to understand how smart she was. And Uly had mentioned the new Neutron Omnipulsar design, but they had to build those first, then retrofit ships to carry them.

Or build new fleets.

Tomorrow's problem. Today, he had a war to wage.

"Hey," Drew said. "We're up next."

"As you bear, Mr. Roscoe," Sterling replied.

Because he didn't ever need to give that man orders.

Just point him at a problem, then let him solve it.

Kinda like the rest of them.

EIGHTY-SEVEN

Tiny had come to really appreciate *Sivi Salavat*. The Auga built quality ships. Not as good as *Lindberg* or *Warhammer Rose*, but not a slouch.

And they'd even chased off a pirate accidentally, dropping out of warp yesterday at one of the designated rendezvous points and catching someone literally in the act of what she presumed was a stolen cargo swap, because both ships took one look at her, then ran like hell.

She and her crew were still grinning at that.

"CONTACT!" Fedir Ponomarenko called from his Gunnery station. "Inbound vessel, just dropped out of warp. Stand by for sensors."

"Pilot, get us in motion," Tiny barked, switching screens on her panel to see who had decided to join them. "Up and out, in case we need to run them down."

She already knew that Fedir's teams would be scrambling for their stations.

A light appeared on her screen. She opened a small vid feed aft to a Zuath male in an Auga command uniform, already removing his apron.

Nasir Sharma was a barber. Even Samuur needed such a thing, though why someone from a hairless species like the Zuath would choose that as a career, she had never really grasped.

"Need command presence?" he asked, the background in his barber shop having been adjusted to look like her bridge.

There were no Ononguli, Isann, or Samuur citizens of the *Auga Empire*, so she'd found someone who could pretend to be the conductor of this vessel. And he'd done a pretty good job of it so far.

"Stand by, Nasir," she nodded, then muted him and went to her other screens.

"Oh, hey, that's *Lindberg*," Fedir followed up. "Incoming message from Echelon Haldur. Echelon?"

Tiny couldn't resist.

"Nasir, you're on," she said, switching comm channels like they'd practiced, then listening in.

Eskil's ears could have been pinned together behind his head as he saw a Zuath Auga naval conductor scowling at him on a screen.

"Attention, pirate vessel, this is an Auga-claimed system," Nasir announced, really getting under some of those deeper tones and pushing. "State your business."

Tiny giggled, but she'd muted herself first. Still, it took Eskil a long moment to catch on.

"Very funny, HES875D74," he said. "Change flags. I have an updated mission assignment for you."

"Thank you, Nasir," Tiny said, swapping signals. "*Sivi Salavat* here."

"Good," Eskil scowled. "That was nice. Rude, but nice. I need to have you do that to the Paramount sometime, just to watch him freak out."

"We aim to please," Tiny told him, still grinning. Ears, whiskers, and chin. "Everybody stand down."

"The fleets are in motion," Eskil told her. "I have a full packet for you to read, but time is extremely short, so send me over your logs as well, then stand by to come about. I need you to cross over and meet up with Lukyan's force, while I return to Uly and update him with everything."

"Manas, belay the stand down," she said, turning to her pilot. "Get *Lindberg*'s course transmission and execute it soonest. Eskil, do we need to pick up any passengers here?"

"Negative, Tiny," the man said. "My packet contains everything you needed to know, and you'll pick someone up at the far end. You read the executive summary I've transmitted, then either ask questions or go to warp directly. Cutting the signal now."

And he was gone. Just like that. Just like Eskil, though she'd never served directly under the man. He was still something of a legend in Saari, and that had been *before* they met the Humans and everyone else.

Now they all wore blue uniforms.

Tiny opened the ship-wide.

"All hands, stand by for high-speed warp," she announced. "*Lindberg* has arrived with orders and I will update you as I know."

She cut the line.

"Manas, plot your course, then hold," she continued. "I'll be reading."

She opened the file and gasped.

EIGHTY-EIGHT

Tiny completed the Executive Summary a second time, then nodded to herself.

It would work, but Eskil and Uly were relying on her to handle several things. Fortunately, they had spoofed the one freighter they had stumbled across a week ago, confiscating all of their recent logs files under the Auga logic of superior firepower.

Those people could be assholes, at least when nobody was willing to push back. And she'd been under orders to act like them. Or Nasir had, and had done so.

"Manas, no change here," she said. "All ahead full and stand by to transition to warp."

She located the button and connected with Eskil.

"In motion now, sir," she said. "We'll find the *Warhammer* and see you on the far side."

He merely nodded and cut the line from his end, but she'd been expecting that.

Sivi Salavat was on her own. And none of Uly's people trusted any other courier to make the run across to find the Ononguli fleet that was slowly headed this direction.

That was her job.

Warp surrounded them.

"Okay, people," she said as they settled in. "Uly has us running a message to the Ononguli fleet. We know where they are supposed to be headed, so we'll update them. Eskil and his crew will be driving inward to Izabh to determine what those Auga folks are up to, and if they are coming out to launch their attack yet. We know the Auga like to move slowly and deliberately, so we can outrun them if we are careful. Biggest risk right now is that Uly thinks they will attempt to attack the Ononguli force before the two sides can come together, and we might run into one of their patrols or even their main force. I'll have Nasir off-duty for the next several days, so we will be relaxing personal grooming standards, but only a little, and none of you can grow a beard like a Samuur in less than a decade anyway."

Chuckles. Eskil had always said that you wanted a team who could joke in the face of danger and terror. Tiny understood that today, but it had been weird getting there.

"I will break down this message pack and make sections and summaries available for departments," she continued. "Plus, Uly sent along a message for everyone, laying out the stakes and the intent. That will get posted in the wardroom for everyone to read while eating. This is what you've trained for. Prepared for. Why you put on the blue uniform in the first place. We're here to stop the *Auga Empire* and make the galaxy a better place, and it starts here. Manas, you have the conn."

She had a lot to read.

<h1 style="text-align:center">EIGHTY-NINE</h1>

Eskil nodded as *Sivi Salavat* vanished. Tiny had transmitted her full log for the last three weeks, so he knew where she'd been. And who she'd swindled.

He added a note about the two vessels that had been here when she had arrived. Nobody he knew, but Maks or Haydar would want them taken care of at a later date.

Recruited or destroyed, one of the two.

"Osman, what do you need?" he asked his pilot.

"Digesting their sailing logs now, Chief," Osman replied without looking up. "Know where we're going. Know where I would go if I wanted to hit Lukyan on the track he told everyone he was following. Wondering, based on this data, if they have sailed already and that freighter Tiny hassled knew something that they didn't mention."

"What would that imply?" Eskil asked.

"If we run hard forward, I have an estimate of where I might find them," Osman replied. "We could turn inward at that part, darting over occasionally to look for wakes, because that fleet's gonna leave a mess behind them as they sail. Probably detectable for more than a day, then I have them nailed in place for everyone else to kitty pile."

"Show me," Eskil ordered.

He reviewed the data. Sterling's map updates, which really weren't fair to the bad guys because he was with maps like Haydar was withencryption systems. Tiny's data added a layer. Lukyan's two plots in blue and purple. A yellow bullseye in the center.

"Why here?" Eskil asked, wanting to know Osman's logic.

They had all served together for a while, and hadn't had time to cycle in non-Samuur officers, though Eskil wanted that when this mission was done. Tiny had a completely mixed crew. As did Maikki.

"They need to hit Lukyan before they can meet up with Uly," Osman said. "Maks sent a note that since they knew where to find him, they are most likely to try that first, then probably turn and come at Avocur from an oblique angle immediately afterwards, intending to slide around our forward patrols so they could drop in for tea without any warning. That's the best estimate I got, based on someone running from Krilic and dropping a data packet with our friends."

Eskil nodded.

Risky, but Uly and Sterling had specifically put him here and had him send Tiny over to escort Lukyan in, because they trusted his judgment on these sorts of things.

He'd been there at Zhoralong.

"Do it," he decided. "If we run into a patrol, assume we're right and run like hell without confirming anything or looking back. If we don't, we'll make a zig-zag pattern back towards Izabh until we find them or don't. Osman, you have conn. Take us out."

NINETY

Lukyan had drawn Maks into his office and closed the door. Coffee with brandy, because he needed it. Stress was grinding his horns, but honestly nobody else could have done it better. Nobody but him and Maks knew all the moving parts. Even Anna and Chervonya were at a single remove.

"Chances it happens on a Tuesday?" Maks asked as they settled.

"Already assumed that," Lukyan replied grimly. "Shit works that way, and we *Tuesdayed* someone else last time, so it's our turn. Why aren't you aboard *Storm Crow*?"

"Because you and Uly and a handful of others will be deciding the future of the galaxy," Maks replied quietly. "Anna is awesome, but this is bigger than merely the Ononguli Sphere."

"You are not getting a birthday card from me for this, you know," Lukyan offered.

"Big surprise there," Maks grinned, then went dark. "This is also why I ordered you to assume command. Yes, in Uly's name, but Klyment and DJ won't immediately think of the broader repercussions of anything they do. They'll just be bashing horns in bigger ships. I needed you outthinking the Auga commander in charge over there."

"And we haven't so far?"

"*So far* is the key," Maks nodded. "Kovalenko's misinformation will hurt the Auga, but several ships have dropped out of formation. I will be reviewing their maintenance logs, with Marlowe and Sadeq along, when this is done. You might yet be sentencing more people to death for being dumbasses. They were warned, several times."

"Are the Auga going to get fancy?" Lukyan asked. "They've got a Devastator Diamond. We don't have anything that can resist that."

"And we don't have to, but try to convince the Horde that." Maks shook his head. "They'll go horns first. I need you thinking like a Samuur to slip sideways and pounce. Or a Human getting behind them and slamming a shiv home. Remember, they are only as good as their logistics, and a fleet like that eats a LOT of food on a daily basis. They cannot stay out for that long without starving or putting into port somewhere to eat. At that point, we can tie them down hard."

"Blockade an Auga world?" Lukyan asked. "We can't hold that kind of discipline."

"We can't," Maks agreed. "Uly can. And will. And you will have a really fucking big hammer in your hand for Horde hotheads who want to argue."

Lukyan shook his head, but didn't argue. Like him, Maks had returned to Rayzian that one time and everything had changed. They'd both grown up. Which said a lot about the Ononguli as a culture.

"We won't know their full force until we meet it," he said. "How do we plan for it?"

"They're Auga, Luk," Maks grinned fiercely. "They'll see Ononguli ships and sail up like they have a hammer and we're an anvil that needs to be pounded on. Four Devastators have an impossible number of 12dm tubes to use. Something like twelve each. Twenty if they bring a flagship, which they might, given the risks and campaign."

"And I'm supposed to stop that?" Lukyan asked sourly.

"No, you fix them in place," Maks said. "Then we go pirate."

"Okay, that I can do," Lukyan nodded. "Been thinking in Horde terms. Forgot that we're Human now."

That got a grin out of the guy. Neither of them were Ononguli anymore, except in biology, and he supposed that was the key here.

Horde tactics had never worked. Merely delayed the inevitable.

They needed something new.

He paused, eyes narrowing as he studied his best friend.

"Where are they staging food?" Lukyan asked. "Can we catch them loading from a warehouse somewhere? How do they warehouse?"

Maks leaned back and thought. It was all his fault, anyway, thinking about defeating the Auga by starving them out. Lukyan was willing to let the kid's logic drive things now.

"I need Sterling's maps," Maks announced.

Lukyan powered up a screen and turned it halfway.

Maks typed. Doodled. Cursed under his breath. Doodled some more.

"They were expecting us along a given line, assuming their spies sold us out and haven't since," he said. "Here are a couple of places that they might put a bunch of cargo. We're talking twenty thousand sailors, with this many ships. It becomes a mathematics exercise to feed them."

Lukyan nodded.

"As soon as we find Uly, I'm happy to send some scouts lateral, look-ing," he said.

"Do it now anyway," Maks challenged. "In and out. All we need are scan logs showing what's there, because it will be supplies for a fleet or nothing."

"How'd you get so smart at this shit, anyway?" Lukyan teased.

Wasn't prepared for Maks to suddenly turn into a war god on him.

"Uly sold me a ship cheap," Maks said quietly. "Then took me aside and told me that what he was doing would change the entire galaxy, core to fringe, **forever**, if he could make it work. At the time, I thought he was only talking about those yahoos in Z'Gosza and maybe the Sphere, but nothing stops him from expanding that to the *Auga Empire*. Once I realized that, I started putting pieces together."

"Including an investment bank, then shipyards, *et cetera*."

"Money makes the galaxy go round," Maks told him. "A lot of people see it as leisure. To me, it became power to change the Horde. And everyone else, because then we met the Isann and the Samuur."

"Do you need to buy an Auga bank at some point?" Lukyan asked, only half teasing because he'd known the kid for twenty years at this point.

"If I thought there was any way in hell they'd sell me one, I would,"

Maks shrugged. "Or even let me start one. Import/export financing, because trade with the *Spinward Reaches* and maybe the Sphere blunts some of the need of the Empire to conquer us. And draws folks into our orbit."

Lukyan nodded. A lot of things would change after this.

Hopefully for the better.

NINETY-ONE

Dan had set up regular meetings with Anna, and brought Nasrin with her frequently, both for a radically different point of view as well as because the youngest of the Team really was her second-in-command, if they had to slice things that finely.

Any would step up and do in any pinch.

They were in Anna's larger office on *Storm Crow*. Sailing at fleet speeds, where many ships had to follow precise paths because of wake issues and limited to the speed of the slowest ship, which was usually the heaviest.

Anna had a concerned look as they settled around the room, Nasrin on a couch, Anna on the end, and Dan across from her.

"What can we help with?" Dan asked.

"I think you've set most of it in motion," Anna laughed darkly. "Or Nasrin has. Rumors of mind control powers among her kind are rippling about. A few folks will react very negatively, but they were already too specist to join us in the future. This just drives them further away."

"Anything we need to worry about?" Nasrin asked.

"Not today, but your kind need to be warned that some punks will want to get ugly in the future," Anna said. "For now, I'm hoping that guilty consciences do the most damage to folks. Maks has sent notes that he's watching. Between those two elements, I suspect that most of my troublemakers will be toeing the line for now."

"What about Teke?" Dan asked.

He'd been called a fire-breather by Harald first, then several others. Hard-headed, even for an Ononguli. Generally honorable, just stubborn.

"He might be collateral damage," Anna stated, shrugging eloquently. "Kovalenko will possibly buy his life by telling me everything, but Teke should have known better. Should have had structures in place to catch such things. That he didn't makes him look at best like a fool. Pasternak is quietly working on him to simply resign his spot on the Council and take an early retirement. I've remained quiet because I want their side to talk themselves into it."

"Like normal," Dan said. "They still think Zhoralong was their idea."

"And that would have likely turned out differently had Lukyan not decided to take *Fire Diamond* at the last minute, where he could protect two Samuur ships, who were protecting Uly. One little thing that had so many ramifications. I'm just glad I have the Samuur on that flank and not somebody else. I can literally trust the Paramount when he gives me his word on something, because that one will fall on his sword rather than break it."

"Eskil and the others are the same," Dan acknowledged. "That's why Uly was able to recruit them. Honor defines their civilization. At least for today. Like you, they have some specists to overcome, but their legends were explorers, so they had mentally prepared themselves for what they might find out there."

"Do we know who's behind us?" Nasrin asked. "Coreward from Fourteen and Twenty-One?"

"I have started asking any Mazhin clanship that comes along, but I get the impression that there is another wide gap, uninhabited at present, like Dan has mentioned runs through the middle of Seventeen. Might be nothing but space."

"I'll leave myself a note to send a message to Traiffe," Dan offered. "They might have information."

"I'm willing to bet that they gave it to Sterling," Nasrin interjected. "He might not have done much with it yet, but they probably knew and we should consult his records."

"Too much going on," Anna shrugged. "Will it stop, after this?"

"If we win," Dan said. "Simple as that, really. A win here forces them to rethink. We'll send messengers to talk. Hopefully, the Auga imperial bosses will listen. If we can stretch that wider, maybe the next Ononguli war doesn't start."

"Are they a balloon, though?" Nasrin asked. "If we push in here, do they swell somewhere else, going after folks that might have had a quiet frontier instead?"

"Only if they cannot admit that they are anything but conquerors," Dan replied. "That they must attack all of their neighbors, all the time, merely pausing from time to time to absorb worlds before moving on."

"That adequately describes their history since the first Ononguli ship encountered the first imperial patrol," Anna noted. "And all the centuries in between."

"You have Uly now," Dan told the woman. "And all of the *Spinward Reaches*. That's a lot of friends. More importantly, we're not rivals challenging your borders. Even if we filled every world between the two, which will take millennia, we're building on trade and equality, in ways the Auga are not emotionally equipped to handle."

"Hopefully, we can win," Anna muttered darkly.

"My faith is in Uly," Nasrin announced. "Look at what he has managed, starting on the day that he and Dan boarded, bringing along Kolya, Gennadi, and Emil to free me from slavery."

Dan smiled.

They could do it, because Uly knew how to make people his friends.

Even his enemies.

NINETY-TWO

Uly looked up as the hatch opened and Sterling nodded.

"Eskil's back," he said.

Uly exploded into motion, then paused and took a breath, understanding that he was wound a little too tight these days.

He joined the others on the bridge, Zamira also appearing quickly. The squadron was at rest. Waiting. It had paid off.

"Confirmation, Uly," Eskil said as soon as he came into view. "The Auga fleet has moved. And is currently going after Lukyan and the Ononguli. Tiny will be there by now, so we're ready to intercept."

Uly settled in his new station, no longer at the top of the bridge, and considered.

Haydar entered behind Zamira. Drew behind that.

The top team was present. At least everybody he had.

Still, there was one other he needed right now.

"Engineering Research, Kit."

"Is Mel close?" Uly asked.

"Standing behind me, hold on."

And Engineer Melpomeni Michelakos appeared on the screen.

"How can I help, Uly?" she asked, concern showing in her eyes.

"I need one of your ships to make a highest-speed-possible run to where Lukyan is," he said, watching her frown but not reply. "The Auga have moved out and are going after Lukyan's fleet first. We need to coordinate, and the sooner all of these forces can be in one place, the better it will be for us, as slow as everyone has to move."

"He's right," Kit murmured in the background.

She turned and studied the much-younger man, but Kit was off-camera, so Uly didn't know what she saw. Something, because she nodded a moment later and turned back to look at him.

"I'll contact them with orders," she said simply.

"Sterling will send you the information they need," Uly said, then cut the line.

Sterling and Haydar were already typing furiously, so Uly nodded. Squeezed Zamira's hand, because she understood that he needed some comfort right now.

Deep breath.

"Eskil, you know where they are?" he asked, looking up.

"And where they're going," the Samuur Echelon confirmed. "They are sailing reciprocal to Lukyan's original course, so he would have slammed right into them if he hadn't diverged after Krilic. Thus, we know the spy chain appears to have been broken at present."

Uly turned to Sterling.

"How soon until the next fleet rendezvous?" he asked.

Sterling or Haydar would know to the minute.

"Eighteen hours," Sterling said. "I'll have orders organized for everyone to come about at that point. Do we split things up and have people run lateral as fast as they can, to get to Lukyan and Anna, or sail as a force?"

Uly had forgotten that he left the line open.

"Uly," Melpomeni said abruptly. "The Yarikh ships can all get there faster than everybody else. That includes *Nubia*. As Lukyan Chayka is bringing up the bulk of forces, and your surprise, do we get there first and then prepare to harry them from the rear as ships and squadrons can converge?"

Tempting. Oh, so bloody tempting.

"Hold that thought," he told her, then looked up at the one person he had assigned to handle that very question.

Dan had pointed out more than once that while Uly had a variety of special skills, the ability to identify the best person to delegate a task to had served him almost as well as the ability to understand and charm entire cultures.

"I put you in command for a reason," Uly told Sterling, watching that young man seemingly swell in size.

"Aye, sir," Sterling said. "Stand by."

Uly nodded. Then rose again and began to pace while he watched Sterling flicker rapidly through all of Eskil's data. Others remained silent, though Haydar offered tidbits, apparently watching the same screens and noting details.

Two minutes, and Echelon Huff had become a new person. It was there in the face. In the eyes that locked on Uly for a moment, then looked up.

"Echelon Haldur, at the next rendezvous, we will form into two task forces, by speed," Sterling said. "You will assume command of the slower contingent and make best speed forward as a fleet to three designated points where we will either be waiting for you, or have left a messenger. The Yarikh vessels will proceed at maximum speed ahead of the rest of the fleet, where we will meet the Ononguli force and begin harrying the imperial invasion. Questions?"

"I need resupply," Eskil said immediately.

"The cargo ships will be present at that laager," Sterling said. "You take precedence and handle maintenance as needed when you assume command. We'll see you there."

"Aye, sir," Eskil said.

Uly watched the main screen go dark and a sigh ran around the room.

Sterling opened a line.

"Command squadron, this is Huff aboard *Nubia*," he said. "Stand by to return to warp. *Lindberg* was our reason for waiting here, and we will drop out again at the next coordinates, where we will reorganize for the final run at our foes. There will be updated orders at that time. See you on the far side."

Uly nodded and turned back to Mel.

"Thank you," he said, leaving many details unspoken.

Not for long, though. Word would get out that those Yarikh ships were fast. Faster than even *Nubia*, who could run down tiny ships specifically built for speed.

Thus, the galaxy had fallen so far from whatever glory days had existed so many millennia ago, before the Yarikh withdrew and opened space for all the other species to rise.

Including the Auga.

More importantly, for everyone else to come together to resist them.

It started now.

NINETY-THREE

Sterling missed Anari. The thought that he'd see her again shortly kept him going.

Like Uly, he understood that what was coming was a campaign—a small war, really—that would be an entire section of some future *Karaŋgılıkka*.

Uly was like that. And, he supposed, Sterling Huff would qualify as one of his knights when all this was transmitted to eternity by Moss School.

And he knew who would do thatt.

The various squadrons from Avocur had come together, seemingly for the last time until the war itself. Many ships had remained behind to protect that place, but Uly had chosen to meet the Auga forward. In their space, rather than his.

It was a statement of principle, as much as anything.

"Everyone accounted for," Haydar announced as they waited. "All ships within the sound of your voice, Sterling."

Sterling nodded. Uly had put him in command.

This was command itself.

"Transmit the packet," Sterling said, then counted to ten before he opened the line to talk to the entire moorage.

Some fifty ships around him, with another block back at Avocur protecting the station then Lukyan and Maks bringing seventy-some more up on his left.

One of the largest fleet movements since the Auga had declared victory after capturing Semeonis nearly thirty years ago, when the last Auga/Ononguli war had ended in yet another defeat for the Sphere.

Sterling drew a breath and envisioned how Uly would do it. More charismatic, because he had that gift of finding exactly the right words. Instinctively, but didn't that describe how a battlefield suddenly rearranged itself when Sterling was watching?

This was no different. He brought the line live.

"This is Echelon Huff," he began simply. "Tiny and Eskil found them for us. Lukyan and Maks are coming up to stop them from invading. The Isann have provided us with the Black Sword. The Khet mapped the future of trade. The Yarikh stepped up to help. All of you are one with us today, as we go to stop the Auga and protect our homes. From invasion. Occupation. Conquest. Uly and I are running ahead of the rest of you to make sure that we have the imperial fleet stopped where we want them, so you can come in behind us and deliver the crushing blow. All of you. All of us. One people, represented by the flag of the *Spinward Reaches*, because we are all equal there. And that is the dream that causes us to stand up today and hold out a hand to the Auga. Today, it is a fist, because they only understand fists. Maybe tomorrow, it can be open in friendship. I rely on you to help get us there. To get them there. Echelon Haldur, you will assume fleet command. Task Force Huff, come about and prepare for maximum warp. Yarikh *Hoplite Tyche*, all ahead full and we will be coming up behind you. Yarikh *Hoplite Hyperion*, form up on *Nubia* and stand by for our run. I will see the rest of you soon, my friends."

He cut the line and blinked when he heard sniffles around him, but Sterling supposed that he had put it all out there for everyone to see. Distilled down as well as he could.

Uly's smile and nod meant everything, because Sterling still woke up from nightmares, back aboard *King Hewitt II* and subject to a stupid, incompetent, angry drunk of a captain named Tevin Winter. Second son of a baron who should have never been allowed to rise to command, save that his social rank and wealth demanded it.

The Auga were no different.

That was the type of galaxy that was going to have to change.

NINETY-FOUR

Lukyan had happened to be on the bridge, doing command things, when the alert sounded. Another one of those breaks where the fleet came together, organized, then hopped again, meeting with scouts and getting shit more or less organized.

Maybe less than more, but everyone was headed the right way, and Maks was very publicly keeping score.

Tiny appeared on the screen. Only the Samuur would call a woman that big *Tiny*. She outmassed him. And he looked her in the nose.

Still, she had her shit together.

"Transmitting you a message pack from Sterling and Uly now," she said immediately. "They are in motion and looking for the Auga fleet."

"We've found them," Lukyan replied. "Or rather, where they will be, hopping like lily pads lateral across what might charitably be called their current frontier. Worlds they own, where a lot of food has been stationed forward to feed them. They are coming after us."

"Where do you need me?" she asked.

And that, right there, was why he liked the Samuur so much. They might all be jocks, but that just meant he had to see himself as a coach and them as players on a pitch.

Never any complaints from them, save not getting enough playing time.

There would be plenty here, because he wasn't holding back any subs for the second half. That would be Uly and the rest coming up fresh.

"Tighthead Lock," Lukyan replied, literally pulling up his notes on game rules on his screen to make sure he had it right. "Your job will be sliding escort behind my forwards as Scrum-half and Fly-half make their run around the right flank on contact."

The look of surprise on her face was probably equal to the dorks on his bridge. As many mouths had fallen open.

Like he hadn't studied Samuur ground sports as a way to talk to his neighbors. Nerds, the lot of them. Sports nerds.

Ononguli teams wouldn't be worth shit against the kitties, except to run their furry asses into the ground in the first half. Maybe mixed-species teams would be balanced?

"Roger that," she said after a breathless moment. "We're going shield-side?"

"I want them pinned in place and forced to rotate to engage me, Tiny," Lukyan replied. "They have a castle made up of four monstrous centers with a lot of firepower, but not much maneuverability. And normally, Ononguli would go at them and peel off. I want to immediately pivot them in place and force their commanders to either break and reverse, or turn the whole damned thing around to face us. Either way, they buckle under the load."

"Who do you have holding Loosehead Lock?" she asked.

Lukyan could hear his bridge people suddenly typing furiously as they tried to figure out what the hell he was talking about with the alien woman.

You bozos put me in command for a reason, ya know.

He smiled evilly at his people, then grinned up at her.

"That's me," he told her. "*Storm Crow* and that squadron will hold their attention with a feint to Loosehead Prop and Blind-side Flanker, where their mass will force the enemy commander into an ugly choice. I'm gambling that he ignores you to his detriment. Or worse, lets you throw intercepting shots across his own flank and bow to break up attacks on me and *Storm Crow*. We only need a little chaos to ruin their day."

"Mark me down for six," she said simply, cutting the line.

Dmytro looked like he was having problems counting his toes with his boots on.

"Exactly as I laid it down before, you idiots," he told them. "Our allies don't speak the same language as a Horde Swarm Right with Hammer Back Left, so they wouldn't know what to expect. I've just translated it into Samuur. She'll be there on our bow."

"If you say so," Slava offered unconvincingly.

"She's offering a point spread," Lukyan said. "That's how confident she is that it will work. Rest of you pound it into your horns that the Samuur are there to save our butts, because Anna asked nicely and Uly promised to protect them. We're gonna do the same. Plus, at Zhoralong, Eskil and Ursula would have died, but for us and Uly. This is them paying us back. All of them. All of the Samuur, coming to our aid today, with a shit-ton more people coming behind her. Our job is to nail them down."

"What about Haydar's surprise?" Oskar asked.

"We're holding that back until he's here to handle it," Lukyan replied. "Maks got it set up, but that's a move for after we backfoot those yahoos and they have to make stupid choices on the fly, because if there's one thing the Auga don't do, it's get crazy in the face of crazy. They'll stick to their playbook as long as they possibly can."

"And then?" Oskar asked.

"Then Uly and Sterling will be along to see them to rights."

NINETY-FIVE

Suka Kuri had looked forward to her time with Tiny and the crew of *Sivi Salavat*.

She saw Uly's dream described in the crew around her, though she would never mention that to them. All of the species of the *Spinward Reaches*, gathered together to do a thing. Looking around the bridge, smiles greeted her, though most of them were a shade intimidated to have an Exemplar of the Arts sailing with them.

She smiled back.

Tiny—Commander Lahja Arifullen on paper—was a most interesting person, but Suka Kuri had already determined that she would not be correct for Dan. Nor Uly. Not that she wasn't extremely capable and intelligent, but she lacked that subtle something that would put her into the rarefied realm of the Congress itself.

Not that she would ever tell the woman that her voice would be the veto, when it came time to discuss.

Like many others, Tiny was a starship commander. That was a different set of skills and intentions than what Dan needed in an ambassador and Combat Team member.

A woman of the Congress.

Still, Suka Kuri had helped shape Starfare, once Uly had expressed it as a thing. He had built it, with Sterling and Haydar adding elements of their vast expertise, as well as chunks Solomon had brought along that Sabre simply didn't contemplate.

Organized warfare, because Sabre was a single student, learning from a teacher, then passing it along later.

Humans had something that so few others even contemplated. And Suka Kuri didn't like to have to consider the need to stop Humans from becoming a threat at some later date, if they leaned into violence on a scale and degree that other cultures and species did not.

Not even the Auga and their Empire.

Tiny would be excellent at Starfare as a student. The Samuur had only recently broken out of a small sphere and a few colonized worlds. Not turned themselves into pirates like so many others had, especially in the face of the Auga reach.

They had met Uly and been captured by his charisma, like so many others. Including her, but he was far too young for her.

Safer that way, as she could look at what he needed in a wife, companion, confidant, advisor, ambassador, and guardian.

It was a heavy load for any woman to carry.

Looking around the bridge in flight, she contemplated Human children. Dan and Uly. Sterling adopting. Same with the other men who might find partners, which would be different than spouses, because Uly and Maks had created a legal structure that didn't favor immediate blood relations first and foremost.

Would the next generation ruler be a woman, and perhaps need men as husbands, at least symbolically? Suka Kuri understood the need to make Uly at least a demigod while he was still alive. He wasn't even holding it against her, but she could see when he wanted to roll his eyes at her from time to time.

Uly understood the need. And was willing to let her, Dan, and Nasrin shape it. That was why it would work.

Anari, but more likely Yanouk, would need to deal with the possibility of the Congress adding husbands at some point, becoming a large polyamorous cluster perhaps, where who you loved and who you had children with overlapped, lacking exclusivity. It had largely begun with Anari and Sterling anyway.

Freedom to love, without limits. It was a new thing, as far as she could tell, but Suka Kuri understood that most worlds were dominated by a single species. Most governments, as well. The Ononguli Sphere was no better than the Khet of Z'Gosza that way. Nor the Auga.

Nor *Batyr* and *Danumash*, but at least they had the benefit of ignorance for the most part. Unknowing of the wider galaxy, protected by a band of empty stars that were probably why a Yarikh ship fleeing Traiffe had felt safe.

She wondered if she would ever learn that truth, or would have to settle for the lies and legends that had accumulated.

Tiny looked up and Suka Kuri felt the weight of the young woman's gaze.

"We're expecting combat with the next drop, Elder," Tiny said, quiet but firm.

"And I have sat through many more space battles than you have, mostly watching," Suka Kuri reminded the youngster.

Old did not mean frail. It occasionally meant smart enough to keep her mouth shut. And sometimes to inject a comment or question when it might be necessary to shape diamonds.

And only mostly, because some of the things she'd done in her youth made Haydar's tales seem a bit tame, but the average person didn't need to know that.

Not even the exceptional ones like Tiny.

Tiny took that with a grain of sand and nodded.

"You'll need an emergency suit," Tiny noted.

Suka Kuri reached out a hand and touched the drawer below and beside her where one had been put, specifically fitted to her size and shape already.

Tiny nodded again.

"Countdown to expected interception?" she asked the room.

"Eighteen minutes," the pilot Manas Umarov replied.

"All hands, this is Tiny. Eighteen minutes to contact. Get everything done you need to in the next ten, then be locked in because we're escorting the Ononguli flag into battle today."

Suka Kuri nodded.

Lukyan had commanded his forces frankly better than she'd been expecting, but that man kept revealing uncommon talents. She could see why Anna wasn't about to let him get away.

And Maks had transformed himself into a thing without analog in any of the cultures she'd ever known.

More than a Khet Trade Factor. More than an Ononguli Banker.

In many ways, she supposed that Suka Kuri and Moss needed to transform him into a demigod as well. Messenger to Uly and part of his eventual pantheon, when the *Flight of the Corsac Fox* took its place next to the *Karaŋgılıkka*.

And she would need to shape that one herself. It would need the touch of an Exemplar of Moss to give it heft, because Uly and Dan would need it conveyed and transmitted far and wide so that other species wishing to resist imperial subjugation understood that they had friends out there.

Options.

Hope.

NINETY-SIX

Maks had a spot on the bridge of *Warhammer Rose*, off to one side like *Nubia* and able to participate without being in the way. Like *Nubia*, Chervonya could sit next to him and they held hands as the timer counted down, snug in suits against emergencies and trouble because Lukyan understood that Uly was the only irreplaceable player on the field. Nasrin was on his far side, but she'd made it clear that she intended to merely be present as a representative, rather than taking an active part in anything whatsoever.

Able to speak in Dan's voice. Or Uly's. But only if the situation required it.

Warhammer Rose would be sailing into danger. Squadrons of other ships around them. *Storm Crow* would draw a lot of attention. *Sivi Salavat* would be causing her own flavor of grief.

But Maks and Lukyan went back a long time together. It was entirely appropriate that he be here with Lukyan for this cataclysmic battle. Hopefully, a final battle, because Uly and Sterling—and everyone else—had come up with something that stopped the Auga permanently.

At least as permanently as could be done. The *Auga Empire* was a thing that had never had to deal with someone mean enough to stop them. Nor powerful enough.

But then *Tyche* had come out of warp at the most recent stop. That final one where everyone tightened everything down one last time.

He'd been tempted to order Lukyan to wait an extra couple of days for Uly and the rest of the Yarikh. Hell, the man might have even listened.

But then Maks had looked at his best friend in the galaxy and seen all the new lines in Lukyan's face. Dealing with yahoos. Herding goldfish, because orkac don't move in three dimensions.

And, talking to Anna and Chervonya, Maks had come to understand how much a purely Ononguli attack would mean. Uly and the others could deliver a killing blow, but the Sphere—the Horde itself—needed to start this.

To push the *Auga Empire* back, however little they actually managed.

A first.

So they had come to Aeris.

And, because Lukyan had a sense of humor as black as the nights above the Endless Plains, it was a *Tuesday*.

Maks felt Lukyan's eyes on him. They shared a grim smile, because after this many years as friends, words weren't even necessary.

Simply a nod.

"Slava," Lukyan said simply. "Count us down."

NINETY-SEVEN

Tuesdays, you miserable shits. Deal with it. I had to.

Lukyan kept his inside voice inside. For now.

Kept the snarls and profanities in his belly, rather than howling them to eternity.

Lacium. *Iron Wasp*. Uly. *Tuesday*.

It had started there.

It didn't end here, but he couldn't think of a better bookmark to set things off. End a section. Start one.

Idly, he wondered what had ever happened to *Legend of Ymnan* or Conductor Kyauta Bukar. *Spirit of Iniquity* and Conductor Zorion Erlantz Aldana. That argosy he'd been sailing with on THAT Tuesday.

When the galaxy changed.

Hopefully, for the better.

And then stars appeared. Aeris. And the first salvos in the next war.

Uly's War.

The Corsac Fox.

"All ships check in and confirm your sailing vectors," Lukyan broadcast.

Ononguli fleets didn't do flag officers. Hell, they barely qualified as formations, with every punk and yahoo going off on his own to do things.

Lukyan still smiled at the memory of Sterling Huff breaking everyone else to the bit at Nyri.

And the kid would be here in a couple of days.

Then, you will be doomed.

Inside voice.

Lukyan figured that he had four other ships that he could truly count on. Out of nearly eighty, once everyone had come together.

Storm Crow. Tanis Dragon. Sivi Salavat. Tyche.

And the *Warhammer Rose.*

Everyone else was just here to make noise and frighten the Auga fleet into making what was hopefully the first of a whole raft of dumb mistakes.

Until Sterling got here.

Tyche was the one that frightened him. Captain Diamantina Vlahou, conducting. Uly's notes suggested that a dozen Yarikh *Hoplites* thought they could take a Devastator diamond.

He didn't have a dozen. But he did have one.

"*Tyche*, take the Fly-half position to our stern and trail our course as we run," he ordered, receiving a green blink back, but they didn't talk much.

Hopefully, they could prove themselves on the battlefield.

Dmytro had gone pale. Gulped once. Nodded.

Lukyan missed having Maks as 2IC. Man had been better at just about everything, while Dmytro was just pretty damned good.

"Status of enemy fleet?" Lukyan asked his bridge.

"Not surprised by anything but the direction of our arrival," Oskar replied. "They are sailing out and forming up. Both sides are out of range of 12s as they come together."

"*Storm Crow*, begin your rotation now, taking your squadron to his strong side," Lukyan said simply. "*Tanis Dragon*, you have low vector to exploit gaps as they develop, but do not come off the bench just yet."

After a couple of weeks, he was even starting to talk like a coach. Eskil was never hearing the end of this, either.

Deep breath.

FOUR FREAKING **HUGE** AUGA DEVASTATORS over there. And, sure as shit, one of them was a flagship.

The small three had quad 12dm turrets. Four barrels each turret. Two forward and one aft. That punk at the rear of the formation had three forward, then two more on the rear corners, letting him throw twenty wavebolts at a salvo if he wanted.

Nothing else on the field could match it. Not even *Nubia* when Sterling got here, but he was willing to grant that the kid would do a better job than anybody else.

But those yahoos were facing the Ononguli Horde today. In a battle of Lukyan's choosing. The Auga defending one of *their* worlds, instead of taking another one away from the Sphere.

This, then, was the line Uly wanted drawn.

"*Sivi Salavat*, start your attack run," he ordered calmly.

Whole bunch of smaller ships flying around, but nothing in the Striker class at all over there. Porcupines of Interceptors, racing hither and yon and starting to get close enough to his own escorts that they could fight their own, localized duels, none of which would likely matter one damned bit, unless and until someone made a mistake.

Hopefully, the other guy.

"Here they come," Oskar announced quietly, as a wall of 12dm bolts started to climb out of the gravity well.

"Ononguli Fleet, hold your fire," he ordered, then waited a beat. "Tiny, honor must be served."

Because Samuur. Jocks and nerds.

Samurai.

Sivi Salavat fired a single 8dm back.

Neither side was in range, unless they wanted to start picking on escorts, which wasn't on the menu yet. All those 12s weakened, then faded, torn up by omnipulsars anyway as they went by.

A single 8 outbound looked like a raised middle finger.

Because it was.

"Ononguli fleet, ENGAGE!"

NINETY-EIGHT

Captain Diamantina Vlahou had been given specific orders from Melpomeni Michelakos, Engineer to the Court at Traiffe, and one of the few people who could override other things.

Like getting *Tyche* across the gap between friendly forces faster than any modern ship by one of the other civilizations could manage. Fast enough to let Chayka and the *Vatazhko* know that help was coming, even before the rest of Uly's force arrived.

Yarikh-built vessels, even an old antique like *Nubia* who had once been *Invincible*, were better. Faster. Tougher.

Deadlier.

And she had been specifically ordered to put that capability in the hands of the Ononguli fleet commander.

"Pilot, how fares our course?" she asked.

Stylianos Galanis didn't look up from his screens, washed by their light. Other ships kept bright, bright lights at all times, but Diamantina believed that lowering them in times of battle helped frame the mind better.

"*Salavat* is in motion," he replied. "*Warhammer Rose* follows. I will be describing a sliding arc to port before reversing to starboard to follow *Warhammer*'s path."

Diamantina nodded, then turned to her Second-in-Command, Effrosyni Katsarou.

"Weapon priorities?" she asked, confirming.

"Our weapons have better range and coherence, while maintaining similar diameters," she replied. "At the peak of left-hand movement, we can put a spread of wavebolts into action that will be extremely effective at overloading an enemy vessel's defenses. Primitive cultures still use the turret as an aiming system. Since we launch vertically from the hull, then let the bolt reverse course, we have far more launchers than would be obvious from our displacement."

"And I wish to retain certain surprises," Diamantina said, pushing back some against her subordinate who wanted to charge in and cripple one of those so-called Devastators.

Tyche could survive. Possibly even escape harm, since other escorts would move to protect them and the heavier ships would be distracting the others.

The Engineer had also laid down specific limitations on what was revealed, at least today, understanding that the battle when the rest of her *Hoplite* sister ships arrived might be legendary.

Effie nodded grimly, ceding superiority.

"Eight bolts of 8dm will be adequate for a ship of this tonnage," she reminded her 2IC. "Similarly, the 4dm bolts. Use them as such until I authorize more."

"What would be necessary for that?" Effie asked.

"I will let you know when I see it," Diamantina told her sternly. "For now, we are just another warship in the Ononguli formation. Chayka counts on us and *Salavat* to protect him and cause various havoc with Auga command decisions. I will remind you that the entire point of this battle is to merely place our enemy and hold him here, while more firepower comes up. It is not necessary for us to win the battle by taking drastic and potentially suicidal actions today."

Grumbles, but to be expected. The Scholar herself had selected these ships and crews for service beyond the system limits of Traiffe. A willingness to let the Lost Tribe drive certain actions. And negotiate the future of the galaxy with all of the alien neighbors.

Tyche was here as a statement of purpose. Of principle. Just as *Sivi*

Salavat had fired the first wavebolt in anger, because the current Samuur civilization defined itself by honorable actions above and beyond all other things.

The Yarikh had been scholars for millennia, but had not forgotten how to fight, if only because pirates and fools occasionally challenged Traiffe orbit, not understanding that they were bearding the dragon in its lair.

But the Auga had to be stopped. And the sooner the better, because eventually they would come to Traiffe otherwise, and the Scholar would have to destroy them. And the next several fleets they sent.

At some point, every other civilization in the galaxy would come to understand that they had not yet made it almost as far back, technologically, as the Yarikh had been when they retired to live quiet lives of contemplation and technological research.

Seven thousand years ago.

"Coming into my turn," Stylianos announced.

"Standing by to fire," Effie replied.

Diamantina nodded.

"First salvo downrange," she ordered.

For the first time in millennia, the Yarikh had gone to war.

NINETY-NINE

Lukyan watched it work. He'd studied Starfare, but was an old dog and didn't necessarily pick up new tricks all that fast.

Sterling had still made it easy to read. And the fleet tactics stuff had been polished by several other crazy, warlike Humans and Mazhin.

Plus, he was intentionally doing something weird here, and relying on the non-Ononguli to make it work. One on his bridge, watching him with her tentacles, but Nasrin hadn't spoken aloud in something like twenty minutes.

Giving him all the glory, Lukyan supposed. Something.

He watched a shield wall on the Auga left falter. Near match for numbers at the escort scale, offset by three Strikers in good, old-fashioned line astern, sliding around them like water beading on a football. Or a puck racing across the ice, which made a better image, since he was about to go into the corner after it.

"*Salavat,* slow down five percent from current speed and maintain heading," he ordered, uncertain why, save that it felt entirely right. "*Tyche,* accelerate and pass under *Warhammer* to shift the enemy plane of engagement as you move ahead of the formation."

Drew had pulled that shit at Zhoralong. Everybody built turrets on tops of hulls, rotating and elevating to shoot.

No reason you couldn't have them underneath, save that folks had gotten into bad habits at some point.

Something. Except that he was watching *Tyche* fire another salvo of 4s. Straight up, over, then engage. And hitting harder than they should have. No bigger, but not degrading with range like he expected.

"Maks, I'd like a study on whatever the hell *Tyche* is doing," he told his friend. "Maybe the next generation of ships don't need turrets?"

"I'm having discussions with folks," man replied cryptically.

Like he'd already cornered the market and hadn't mousetrapped everyone else yet.

Good thing Lukyan had a percentage in a couple of banks and shipyards. He was getting too old to command warships, though he'd never admit that in public.

Maybe time to retire when Uly did? Go live on Rayzian as Anna's Plus-One and call it good?

No, he'd be her ambassador, like Maks, forever running around, putting out fires.

Tuesdays, ya know?

Didn't have to win today. Had to not lose. Had to emulate a pack of hungry furlou, circling a herd of orkac and picking off strays while forcing them to stay perfectly still instead of hitting Krilic or Avocur.

The Horde was really good at that, if they could hold any sort of discipline for long enough.

Which was usually impossible.

"Oskar, hold offensive fire," Lukyan decided. "*Salavat*, keep up the 6s but hold the 8s. *Tyche*, defensive only for the next four minutes. *Tanis Dragon*, I need some heavy artillery right now."

Again, instinct, but a lifetime of piracy, and this wasn't much more. Patterns of ships moving around. Starfare logic, with horns attached.

The Diamond had been mildly disrupted. Commander over there had largely ignored Lukyan and his wing of trouble because DJ had a group of heavy hitters suddenly throwing a lot of shit at his bow and Klyment had started walking slower around his far side, firing broadsides that had to be dealt with.

Not a lot of damage back and forth, mostly because Lukyan hadn't tried to press home anything. He'd get his horns ground off if he did.

And didn't need to.

Center of the battlefield was Auga. As expected. Tactically. Strategically. Temperamentally.

Play to their egos. Rude, but Starfare had a whole chapter on psychological warfare that included some amazingly vicious things Sterling and Uly had come up with. Or Solomon, studying ground armies.

Offensive fire tapered off this way as the other two groups got rowdy. Noisy.

Distracting.

"Oskar, come about zero-two-five and accelerate like mad," Lukyan announced. "*Tyche*, rotate your engagement forward and let us cover your butts as you charge. *Salavat*, you drop into Left Wing and Fullback as we pull away, but do not let anyone catch you. Time for the hit and run."

Outside, the Auga held the center, but the *Warhammer* had gotten around his flank. Didn't really matter, because the Diamond was solid on all four points and had a lot of escorts shifting and defending.

Except that there was another Auga presence on the table. Quiet, up until now.

Standard Auga station. Lots of defensive firepower. Not a lot of offensive. Unless crazy Humans came along and upgraded 2s to 6s and 8s to 12s. Like at Avocur. And Saari. And Bastion.

Not Aeris.

Standard. Cookie cutter standard. Trained against because they owned several exactly like it.

And *Tyche* wasn't remotely like anything else on the battlefield.

Today.

Took them folks about ninety seconds to wake up from their rummy games and soap operas and realize that one-third of the Ononguli force had broken away from the battle and was charging right at them.

"Radio traffic just went off the scale," Dmytro said in a bored voice.

"Who called it?" Maks asked.

"Looks like Nasrin won the pool," Dmytro replied.

Lukyan caught her grin. Mostly in the tentacles. She'd guessed best how long they would miss what he was about to do.

"Diamond is attempting a wide, port turn as a unit," Dmytro continued.

"The whole formation?" Lukyan confirmed.

"Affirmative. Everybody, rotating around an arc instead of rotating in place and going full engines to come to rest and start back at us. Dumbasses."

Worse, they might have just given him another fifteen minutes freedom of movement. Lukyan had honestly been expecting them to flip, stop, then charge.

Could they even maneuver that many ships and not come apart?

"*Tanis Dragon*, you heard?" he asked.

"Affirmative, *Rose*," DJ replied. "What do you need?"

"Harry them, but not too close," Lukyan said. "I wanna see if they can pull off a turn under fire. Dumbest thing I've ever heard."

"Glad I'm not the only one," DJ laughed.

"*Storm Crow*, a couple of nips in his ass as he goes would be nice," Lukyan continued. "Pause forward movement and chivy him along instead."

"Understood, Chayka," Klyment acknowledged.

Shit, could they really pull this stunt off?

ONE HUNDRED

Diamantina studied the overall plot, listening to Chayka's chatter with the other Ononguli commanders and the Samuur woman.

All highly competent. Simply too relaxed and informal for her tastes, but she did understand that the Yarikh were an entirely different form of civilization than everyone else, regardless of similarity of shape.

On Traiffe, things were done with purpose. Orderly. Organized.

Stodgy had been the word the Scholar had used, when briefing her and commanders of this force. Diamantina supposed that she was seeing it in action here.

The Auga flew predictable patterns that could be analyzed, understood, and defeated.

The Ononguli didn't care. Or were incapable of matching them.

Instead, Chayka had laid out a plan relying on an insane number of mistakes by the Auga commander, compounding themselves slowly over time until the results would boggle the mind.

She was rather happy that she had not taken the bet with Stylianos after the briefing, as she would have lost.

And Diamantina still didn't understand what Stylianos and Chayka had seen, save that they had. And it had worked.

Tyche was currently the single closest vessel to the station, all civilian traffic having run as soon as possible when battle arrived. While the Auga had formed up and sailed out to fight.

Leaving the station unguarded.

"Effie, status of the station?" she asked.

"Standard, exactly following the designs as laid out in Huff's records," Effie replied.

Having spent time at Bastion, Saari, and Avocur, Diamantina shook her head in disbelief. Uly had upgraded all three of those significantly, even with Yarikh defending squadrons in place.

The Auga were counting on their legend more than anything here. Save that the *Vatazhko* of the Ononguli had mentioned that this was the first offensive invasion of Auga space in centuries. And that they would not have risked it without Uly and his allies.

Which included *Tyche* today, and *Hyperion* shortly.

And Huff.

Diamantina turned to Effie.

"Now, you may unveil our next surprise," she told her 2IC to great grins. "We'll pretend that we're specially configured to pull this stunt one time, and only one time, so return to the previous rules of engagement afterwards."

"How many?" Effie asked.

"Twenty and twenty," Diamantina decided. "Lead with the 4dm wavebolts, then the salvo of 8dm, once he commits defensively. Spread your fire out as much as possible, because Chayka wants the station damaged, but not destroyed. If we annihilate it, the enemy fleet may simply turn and sail to the next station before we are ready for them."

"Twenty and twenty, standing by," Effie acknowledged. "Stylianos, take him down our port side and let Tiny and Lukyan know. They'll arrange these escorts as needed, but we'll be subject to panicked fire at some point and the captain is correct that we shouldn't wipe out that fire as well."

"Coming around," Stylianos replied. "Maintain speed?"

"Yes," Diamantina said. "We are not coming back for a second pass, so the others will swing through with us and out. Other ships will be tasked with scouting this force later."

Diamantina leaned back and watched. Chayka had been right. Insane, but correct.

Would it be enough?

ONE HUNDRED ONE

Maks watched the screen between him and Chervonya, specifically focused on *Tyche* because they had quietly warned Lukyan they were about to upset starship technology in this sector of the galaxy.

He wanted to understand both how they did it and how to counter it.

Uly would need new ships. Turrets might be a thing of the past, if the Yarikh were dispensing with them entirely. You lost power when the bolt had to turn instead of racing straight at a target, so they had something to make their bolts better. Much better.

Then *Tyche* did it.

"Holy shit," somebody muttered, but he didn't look up to see who. Might have been Lukyan.

Might have been himself.

Tyche had just fired a mass of torpedoes, all at once, like a pufferfish taking a deep breath. The station had been firing at *Tyche*, but escorts had specifically been tasked with mass interception and interdiction at this point to let them act. And *Warhammer*, coming up behind. Maybe even Tiny, though she didn't have 8s beyond the one pair.

Maks counted twenty 4dm wavebolts. Tiny had sixteen launchers of all sizes on her Patrol Striker, including six 1dm tubes when that ship class normally only had four.

Then twenty 8dm joined them as a second wave, about the time the station started targeting the lighter ones and engaging.

Shit.

And they were playing possum, because they'd said they would, even at this point.

How many wavebolts could that ship charge and fire at one time?

Worse, *Tyche* only displaced like a heavy Interceptor. *Fire Diamond*, for scale.

What could a Heavy Striker version do, if the Yarikh got angry? Or a Devastator?

"And now you knuckleheads see why we did it this way," Lukyan muttered loudly in a matter-of-fact voice.

Maks agreed.

"Ononguli squadron, break off all offensive operations and begin pulling away from Auga vessels," Lukyan ordered. "Let the diamond come about, but don't necessarily make it easy on them. *Storm Crow*, off on your vector, then withdraw when you are ready. *Tanis Dragon*, do not get ambitious, as they'll be right jolly pissed and looking for someone to savage. You're the only one close at present."

"Not for long," DJ replied.

"Oskar, it will be an afterthought on our part, but put everything you can into the station, holding light for defense. Tiny, stay mostly defensive but feel free to toss your 8s this direction as well. Honor will be served."

Maks watched the station on a split screen, but it was mostly a foregone conclusion. Still, *Tyche* had made sure that all of the bolts impacting were fists instead of lances. That many explosions, knocking down shields and kicking in bulkheads, might have been enough to cut the station into pieces if *Tyche* had intended otherwise.

Uly had sent notes about a revolution in Neutron Omnipulsar technology, as yet unknown.

Maks wondered if he would have to send spies to Traiffe to learn how they were building wavebolt systems.

He knew a few more Humans these days.

And it felt like the Auga might study this battle and panic themselves.

For them, it might pull them back from invading.

And it might convince them to roll the dice and send as big a fleet as they had after Uly. Or Traiffe.

Rayzian needed to step up its game as well.

ONE HUNDRED TWO

Tiny had been commissioned in the before time. When all that the Samuur knew about were a few Zuath and Ugothan merchants that fed them advanced technology, but not enough to really matter.

Kalev Karjalainen had gone to Bastion. Uly had come to Saari. She was commanding a stolen Auga Patrol Striker with a crew less than one-third Samuur, fighting a pitched fleet action against the Auga invasion force intent on taking control of the *Spinward Reaches*.

And Saari.

No.

Behind her, the Auga fleet was slowly coming about. It was a mess, too, because they'd apparently never trained those big ships to maneuver in a formation like that.

No, merely step up in your face and punch you. Club you over the head repeatedly.

They'd never learned to dance.

Something the Elder had previously mentioned drew Tiny's head up and over to the big Emro woman suddenly watching her in return.

"They don't know how to dance," Tiny repeated quietly.

Suka Kuri studied her with hooded eyes. Inscrutable. Penetrating.

The crew whispered about the woman, but Lukyan had quietly told her that most of those legends were based on shit he'd been in the room to see, so Tiny always approached the woman like she could give the Paramount orders.

Probably could.

"What does that tell you?" Suka Kuri asked quietly.

Because she almost always answered you with a volleying question, usually designed to lead you either to some point obvious in retrospect, or a place you might have never gotten to on your own.

"They fight in lines. Move in lines. Think in lines," Tiny replied. "There is nothing whatsoever of the individual to their culture. They are almost exactly the opposite of the Ononguli that way. And perhaps the Samuur to a certain degree, though we are deeper into individual sports, I suspect."

"And you would be correct, Tiny," Suka Kuri replied. "They do team sports. Team things. Even their transportation tends towards the mass, so that no one will ride alone and possibly think revolutionary thoughts."

"Like how civilization might be better for everyone, instead of just the Auga?" Tiny asked, one part of her mind tracking Manas flying and Fedir taking defensive potshots with the 6s and throwing 8s at the station as fast as his crews could reload.

"To them, the Auga are destined to lead, so what is good for the Auga eventually trickles down to the other species," Suka Kuri noted.

Tiny started to say something. Stopped herself. Chewed on it, ears and whiskers going different directions.

Suka Kuri watched enigmatically.

"It is inefficient," Tiny finally said, not making it a question, but a statement. And not a hostile one.

Merely fact, repeated aloud, as a starting point for thought.

"Their logic, as *they* would see it, is sound," Tiny continued. "However, they cannot absorb Uly within that pattern. Their entire structure would repel such a thing, and thus either collapse, or at least stumble badly."

"Uly intends the latter," Suka Kuri noted.

"But does not preclude the former, because his intent is to provide the greatest good for the greatest number of people, while not actively harming anyone more than absolutely necessary to maintain—*achieve*—equality," Tiny spoke, discovering the words as they came out of her mouth, rather than digging into something she had thought long and hard about. "We are all equal, or we are not. At the most fundamental, this is the starting point where he differs from them—from almost everyone, really—and thus comes to radically different conclusions."

"Where does that lead you?" the Elder asked, eyes sharp and focused now.

"That I had seen this in terms too stark," Tiny replied. "Good and evil, without allowing shadings of gray. But even that is wrong, because that is Auga thinking. Uly sees it in ethical terms. A flexible Utilitarianism, but I have not delved deeply enough to slice it finer than that."

"Nor has he," the Exemplar replied, taking Tiny's breath away. "In his case, it is not a defined philosophy as such, but a series of decisions, where each branching is weighed, often instinctively because he does, for the outcome that provides a better result. Moving everyone closer to a thing that lesser minds might qualify as Utopia."

"Lesser?" Tiny asked quietly as Fedir launched his last two big bolts back over a shoulder, then locked the turret in place with a nod.

"What is Utopia?" Suka Kuri asked simply.

Tiny was rocked back onto her heels. Even seated and strapped in.

Felt almost like the Elder had booped her right on the snoot.

Tiny blinked. Breathed. Realized that she had gotten into a major philosophical discussion with an Exemplar of the Moss School in the middle of a cataclysmic naval battle.

But the woman had asked a question. And noted earlier that she'd seen more fighting in her time than anyone else on this vessel.

What was Utopia?

"Freedom," Tiny replied, voice as small as she was, it seemed. "Freedom to act. To think. To live."

Suka Kuri watched her with predator eyes now.

Tiny found the words, even as they sucked all the breath out of her chest in speaking them.

"Freedom from fear," she enunciated, revelatory. "Everything flows forward from that. If you do not fear, you can try new things. If failure is merely a starting over cleanly, you can take risks without worrying that you will lose everything, which would thus preclude most from even attempting, happier to eke out the tiniest incremental improvements, against the random chance of black swan events that take everything away from you. Uly would free us from the Auga. Not their political control, but their threat itself. He would force the Auga to change enough that even those they control have the chance to live without fear, and thus explore how much better their lives might be."

"At what cost?" Suka Kuri turned dark now.

The bridge around them had fallen nearly to silence, all heads and ears tilted in to listen, as if they could taste how important this conversation might have become.

In the middle of a battle.

But battle, like all competitions, only showed who you were. Revealed the truth of the inner being.

"At the cost of control, Elder," Tiny said, finding a new firmness in her voice that hadn't been there before. "That others might be better suited to rule. Not by biology, but by temperament and education. Where **species** was not the defining characteristic of who should control the galaxy. The Empire simply cannot absorb such a concept, from what I have studied, and would have to fall."

"Uly does not wish to destroy it," the woman said.

"Failure will take many forms," Tiny breathed. "A loosening of control if they are smart enough to allow it, that the whole might shake once and settle into a new form. Otherwise, the shocks might bring the entire edifice down, causing far more pain and suffering than is necessary. Uly would prefer not to do that, so he is striking at the force they sent to strike at him, rather than bombarding any of their worlds in the manner that imperial forces have been known to exercise. Those who have chosen violence, rather than the innocent."

"Are they innocent?" the woman asked.

Tiny felt like she was falling. That dream again.

But the woman had asked another question. A series of questions, leading her and this whole crew someplace.

Where?

Revelation. And, perhaps, revolution.

"They are innocent until they learn that there is another option available that is more ethical. Less evil. More *Utilitarian*," Tiny said. "Until then, they must be protected from the outcome of their ignorance. The others can be fought on their terms, which have been brutal and will continue to be, because Uly loathes bullies above and beyond all other things."

"Exceptional, Tiny," Suka Kuri smiled at her finally. "Truly exceptional. Thank you."

Me? She gasped, but had no more words.

Well, a few, but nothing at all to do with this.

Tiny blinked and tried to breathe as she found Manas, watching her with a finger poised to take them to warp, Aeris Station badly mauled in their wake and with an Auga fleet losing ground as *Sivi Salavat* accelerated up and away.

Success. And she had been deep in a philosophical discussion with an Exemplar of the Moss School while it happened.

"Engage," she ordered, watching Manas push his button.

And then warp.

ONE HUNDRED THREE

Lukyan had reviewed all the logs. Records from *Storm Crow* and *Tanis Dragon*, as well as what *Tyche* had been willing to send over.

Tiny had been a bit terse, but it wasn't aimed at him, so he ignored it. She'd had to deal with Suka Kuri. That would challenge anybody.

The squadron had withdrawn. Blasted its silly ass back into space, then corkscrewed a few times to throw off any Auga getting stupid enough to chase, before all three forces came back together at the next rendezvous. Cargo freighters were being emptied of food and spare parts as fast as shuttles could carry things around. He'd hopped a ride over to *Storm Crow*, because Anna was the *Vatazhko*.

He was just the dork that Maks had ordered to take command in Uly's name. Possibly the greatest swindle in Horde history, but Lukyan still didn't know if he was *doing* the swindle, or *being* swindled.

Maks, of course, refused to answer certain questions on advice of counsel. Smart boy.

He kissed Anna on the cheek, them moved to a spot around the table. DJ and Klyment were here. Dan and all of the Team present. Him, Maks, and Chervonya.

Tyche had smiled and nodded at the invitation, then ignored him entirely.

About what he'd been expecting.

Lukyan rapped his knuckles on his coffee mug and sighed.

"It could have gone much worse," he announced, but Maks laughing stopped him right there.

"It couldn't have gone much better, you fraud," Maks said with a wide grin. "That station will be at least a year being repaired, and I'm literally your expert on the topic because I've built three of them now."

"And the Devastators didn't take much damage, but their escorts got pounded pretty mercilessly," DJ added from his corner. "Nobody warned them that we were going to aim heavy wavebolts at Interceptors, which forced them to pull all the way back until their own heavies could protect them."

"They spent far too much time focused on *Storm Crow* and worried about *Tanis Dragon*," Klyment added. "Let you get past them to pound the snot out of their base. So shut up and accept congratulations on a battle fought pretty damned well, Chayka."

He felt his ears go painfully straight, even as he got so hot he figured he might have turned tomato colored.

Lukyan shrugged. Maybe he was just too sour for shit like this. Too many years of piracy in and around Lacium and Z'Gosza.

"Do they move this fleet somewhere else?" he asked the room, looking around.

The man he figured would know wasn't here yet. Anna was politically as sharp as they got, but Lukyan had still done this as a career, instead of an enlistment like she had. And DJ and Klyment had both gotten too important to fly dangerous stunts for at least a decade, if not longer.

Suka Kuri stirred. He should have known that woman was even more dangerous than legends might lead you to believe.

"They will hold briefly," she stated in a firm voice, eyes locked on his. "Repairs on escorts sufficient to keep them intact, or decisions to hold them back and send them to the nearest shipyard for repairs."

Lukyan ignored everyone else in the room and focused on the Exemplar.

"Do they come after us, slide sideways to hit Krilic eventually, double back to Izabh, or turn and go after Avocur and Uly?" he asked.

Might as well lay it all on the table.

Exemplar of Moss School, because Sabre was too hard on the knees.

Uh huh.

Lukyan had long since stopped believing that part. Woman was just like Anari and Yanouk.

Both, at the same time, without giving too many details away.

Look at what she'd turned Solomon Wyndham into. Dan might get most of the credit, but Lukyan wasn't the least bit fooled.

"They will double back one station," she said simply. "Resupply and send orders back to Izabh for all of their supply ships to be brought forward for rendezvous in the middle."

"Piracy?" Maks asked, the second most recent pirate in here.

"They will expect you to harry such a force," she noted. "Some portion of their escort force will be withdrawn to protect them. Not enough to stop you. Enough to entice you perhaps."

"Because going after them instead of the battle fleet leaves them an opening to go crush Avocur," Lukyan completed the thought.

"That is my read," Suka Kuri nodded.

Lukyan leaned back and thought about it.

"Uly's here tomorrow," he told them. "And Haydar. I'll run it past Sterling, but I have an idea for how to deal with that. Partly, it involves a swindle on our part."

"Oh?" Dan asked, surrounded by her killers, all fresh back from a recruiting trip and probably a little hungry, from the tidbits he'd gotten.

"If we sent a chunk of our own fire-breathers off after them, they might believe their plan worked," he said. "Maybe half the Horde present. The half that I'm always worried will bite me if I turn my back on them anyway. Anna, I'll have you order them detached for piracy duties, without them knowing any better."

"Send a messenger to Eskil Haldur," Anna said. "Have him intercept as well. Maybe split his force in half. Yes, do that. I like the thought of those punks competing with Samuur and Isann and Khet sailors in a free-for-all over Auga shipping."

"Eskil brings his main force here," Maks said. "Or rather, halfway, once we know their vector."

"Maks, I need you detached and supervising Haydar's surprise, since it moves so slowly," Lukyan said. "Get them over where they don't have to travel far for their own interception. Suka Kuri, which world will the fleet retreat to?"

"I'll check a map after this and work with Maks," the Exemplar said. "One of three, and they'll need to move first so I can identify their vector."

"That's you two," Lukyan said. "DJ, you want to lead a strike patrol with the hotheads?"

"I can already name most of the folks you'd want to send," DJ replied with a grin. "Let me round them up after this and we'll get a head start. You mind if we raid Izabh itself?"

"Exercise judgment on your part," Lukyan temporized. "If the Devastators suddenly realize that they can't eat, they might turn back and we lose our chance to nail them in place."

"Gotcha," DJ nodded. "Hit and runs instead of anything serious."

Lukyan nodded back and looked around.

"Repair. Resupply. Movement. What am I missing?" he asked the table.

"Nothing, near as I can tell," Dan replied. "You've stopped their motion towards Krilic and the Sphere. If Suka Kuri's right, they'll turn and go back at Avocur next, which was their original plan. Since you've nailed down their spy for now, they have nothing special to go on except overwhelming force to crush Avocur."

"DJ, you take your bozos and get moving soonest," Lukyan decided. "One *Tyche* is frightening. The rest of that squadron might convince the Auga to run like hell for home and we never get a chance like this again?"

"Is that the worst outcome?" Suka Kuri asked, but he wasn't one damned bit fooled.

Never trust a philosopher.

"Yes," Lukyan told her simply. "Uly wants them broken hard in such a way that they'll talk afterwards. Defeating them in battle on their terms—even with the bullshit surprises we've dug out of the closet for this stunt—does that. If they go defensive, they still have the chance to attack again later, somewhere else. Krilic or an Ononguli world might be made an example out of. I want this controlled."

"How do we beat them next time?" Klyment asked.

Lukyan's cheeks hurt from the grin.

"I don't have to," he told the man. "Next time around, they'll be facing Sterling Huff. Fuckers are doomed at that point."

And they were.

He'd seen the kid work.

PART TEN
COMMITTED

ONE HUNDRED FOUR

Uly had the team in place when *Nubia* came out of warp. Sterling commanding. His officers across that row. Zamira holding his hand in public like she'd gotten comfortable doing.

Everything.

"That is a thing of beauty," Sterling said as the main screen showed the Horde at rest.

"Lukyan calling," Haydar announced. "General news."

"Main screen," Sterling replied.

Uly still had a hard time not sitting up in the big chair, but it was getting easier. Zamira squeezed his hand. She understood.

Lukyan appeared.

"Things are in motion already," he said simply. "We fought a battle two days ago and stopped our friends dead cold in place. They appear to be ready to reverse course in the next few hours, based on what my scouts have been monitoring nearby at Aeris. Sterling, you ready to take over?"

"Not yet," Sterling teased in a light voice. "Uly's up to something first. We should do it aboard *Nubia* instead of *Warhammer Rose* or *Storm Crow*, though."

Uly grinned when Lukyan's eyes shifted.

"It will be good," Uly assured him, but Lukyan didn't seem certain.

"If you say so," the man replied. "Bring everybody over for dinner?"

"I'll let the Spatula know to go a little crazy," Uly grinned. "How many?"

"Me, Maks, Chervonya, Anna," Lukyan said. "All your wives. Maybe the woman commanding *Tyche*, but she's a bit prickly, except when fighting."

"I have her commanding officer with me," Uly said. "Mel can make that call for us. Four hours good, or do we have a fuse burning?"

"I'd like to start pulling back from here," Lukyan said. "Put this entire force into motion, splitting certain elements off for other tasks. Can we run an hour backwards on a certain course then laager?"

"Send me the coordinates," Uly said.

"Transmitting now," Lukyan said.

Uly looked back and got nods from Haydar and Del both.

"See you there," he said.

Lukyan cut the feed from his end.

Uly looked at the others.

"He sent a full packet, Uly," Del offered. "Decrypting it now and will have the executive summary shortly."

"Route it to my office and I'll read it there," Uly decided. "Sterling, you're in charge."

He rose and Zamira moved with him, but she'd become far more affectionate than before her long trip. Uly supposed that all of them might have missed him, and while he was looking forward to seeing Dan, all of them were wonderful women and fun to talk to.

He supposed that he might be spoiled, but the costs to get to this point always brought him up short.

Zamira kissed him as soon as the hatch closed.

"You've gotten serious again," she said, grinning and sitting on this side of the desk.

He shrugged and moved to the other.

"Occupational hazard."

He pulled up his computer and started to read. Must have made a sound, because she was suddenly reading over his shoulder.

"That's why we're already backing up," she muttered.

"Smart move," Uly agreed. "Frees them up to make choices, at a point when he has already screwed up their plans and now they don't have spies feeding them tidbits."

"Can the Auga even operate in the dark like that?" she asked, but all of his wives had studied the Ononguli/Auga wars closely.

Anna's people had been fighting the Auga for centuries, and it had fallen into something of a pattern.

"I like that Suka Kuri is driving this," he told her. "And her logic is sound. They have to make a choice. As soon as they do, that commitment will become locked into stone, as far as they are concerned, and we can take advantage of it."

"Haydar," she nodded.

"And *Hyperion*," he agreed. "We have a couple of good surprises that have been assembled for this mission. If they take long enough, we'll have the other half of Eskil's force as well. The extra firepower would be nice, but I more like that it will become everybody, where this first battle was Ononguli."

"With Tiny," Zamira noted. "Her crew is broadly mixed, so we'll have stories they can tell as people move around."

"Yes," he agreed. "And we are very close to doing it. To pulling it off."

"What happens after we succeed?" she asked, ever the optimist.

"Hopefully, they'll listen to ambassadors and negotiate," he said. "Not sending any of you until they decide to behave, but that will be on them, and I'm willing to unleash Sterling and tell him to show them the full measure of Human rage if they can't act like civilized beings."

Her shudder was eloquent. He kissed her, just because.

All of his wives were close, and he'd get to see them shortly.

He was looking forward to that almost more than stopping the Auga.

ONE HUNDRED FIVE

Dan had planned to use her seniority to claim place, but the others all grinned and stood off to one side as the airlock hatch opened.

And Zamira had taken a full step to one side, so she didn't get bowled over when Dan practically tackled Uly. She did outweigh him. And might have missed him.

Some.

Lots of kissing.

"Glad to be home?" Uly finally asked.

"Maybe," she considered.

Then all the others were there, too, and she relinquished her hold on the man so he could greet the rest of his wives. This was entirely her fault, after all, so she probably did have to share. Zamira had won the draw last time.

Eventually, they ended up in the big wardroom, already configured for dinner and planning.

She sat to one side of Uly, with Nasrin on his other. Suka Kuri was on her other side. Dan ignored the larger conversation where the four Ononguli brought Uly and Sterling and Haydar up to speed on everything they had missed.

Suka Kuri tapped her arm and leaned way down so they could have a quiet conversation.

Dangerous woman.

"I went aboard *Sivi Salavat*, as you know," Suka Kuri began.

Dan nodded. The Paramount had made it clear that he had any number of women that might be good enough for a spot on the Combat Team. And in the Congress of Wives, which was an even higher bar, except that it wasn't.

The one presupposed the other, because Dan's standards really were that high.

"Initially, after spending time around the woman everyone knows as Tiny, I was not impressed," Suka Kuri continued. "Yes, smart. And extremely capable. Lukyan saw that and put her in command of the stolen Auga ship they had taken, and she has thrived."

"But?" Dan asked.

"But she lacked that certain something I was looking for," Suka Kuri described.

"Pity," Dan replied.

Maikki and Taija were also both interesting, but hadn't really made the cut as far as she was concerned, either. Inari Johansson might, but she tended to be a little too quiet and reserved, though she might come out of that. There hadn't been time to investigate more fully.

"However," Suka Kuri said, drawing Dan's eyes back to the present. "Tiny saw something towards the end of the battle with the Auga."

"Oh?"

"Dan, it was like watching a flower open in the first sunlight, as she took that idea and expounded it in three dimensions," Suka Kuri said, grinning. "Mind you, we're still under fire at that point, though the station was largely neutralized, but she utterly transformed from a mere warrior into a philosopher. I'll blame your Human Socrates, but she did most of the work, while I watched."

"Interesting," Dan said. "So you would keep her on the short list?"

"Having not gotten to know Inari as well as I might, I'd have Tiny first, Dan," Suka Kuri said. "And I didn't want her here, because she needs time to digest that. And to focus on what's coming in this next battle, where her ship and *Nubia* are the only two that truly represent the *Spinward Reaches*."

"Because the rest are almost exclusively Ononguli ships, save for our dozen that are purely Yarikh," Dan agreed. "What did Tiny see?"

"That the Auga could not dance," Suka Kuri said. "Her words, not mine. Her conceptualization of them as limited in ways that dance as a thing was foreign, but a way for her to express a most cogent and concise Utilitarianism that I've not really heard anyone except Moss School Adepts ever discuss."

Dan nodded. All of the Combat Team mixed Moss and Sabre, though really only Yanouk and Anari expressed it publicly. They were all warrior-scholars. Such a thing was necessary to belong, because they had to fight, and were all ambassadors for the *Spinward Reaches*.

Not even for Uly, though he represented the whole. What she was building would outlive him. Outlive her. Outlive all of them if she did it right, providing a core of advisors married directly to the head of government in ways that they watched him and one another and kept both honest.

"Are you returning to *Sivi Salavat*?" Dan asked.

"Actually, I was hoping to trade with you," Suka Kuri grinned. "While Yanouk and Anari are both brilliant students, I suspect that what happens here will need to be the capstone of Uly's *Karaŋgılıkka*. At least Volume One. Perhaps your Homer, flipped inside out where Uly wanders lost in the wilderness for years, before coming to the place where he can gather up all the Hellenes and go make war on poor Priam."

"At least Helen didn't start this," Dan grinned back, then sobered. "But we will need one of Priam's daughters for what comes."

Suka Kuri sobered as well.

"We will need to create an intelligence service that can learn about the inner circles of the *Auga Empire*, then," the woman said. "Things that are not common knowledge, even there. If such a thing happens, it will be the very definition of a political marriage, and not one given as much thought as Anna put into finding Halyna."

"Agreed," Dan muttered. "Possibly a threat. Possibly an opportunity. And yes, we will need to find a way to look inside the Empire in greater detail. Zuath, Ugotha, Emro, Thogin. Several others. Maks talks about opening a trade bank, but doubts that they would let him."

"We need to make it to tomorrow, when all of this is settled as much as it can in the short term, to be sure," Suka Kuri nodded, then leaned back and listened to Lukyan finish his talk.

"At that point, you arrived and we moved to this new base," Lukyan concluded after several minutes. "I've taken it about as far as I can, with the help of some really smart people, but that's it."

"There's a reason I listen to those ladies, Lukyan," Uly said, to general chuckles. "You've done an excellent job, and I look forward to what Anna does to the rest of Kovalenko's network when she gets home. Like you, I was at Zhoralong and have a bone to pick with some people."

"So we're ready?" Lukyan asked.

"One last thing," Uly said, rising.

The rest of the room was slower up, but Dan knew it was coming. She turned and nodded as Omid entered from the kitchen, where she had been watching and waiting.

Lukyan was slowest to rise. Anna had to drag him to his feet.

"I've talked to Anna about this, without you in the room," Uly said, stepping close to the Ononguli man. Others did the same, until he was ringed by friends.

"Sterling has been promoted to Echelon, which is a new flag rank in the *Spinward Reaches* mimicking something similar in *Batyr*," Uly continued. "Eskil joined him, representing the Samuur at that highest rank among naval officers. I would like to take this opportunity to promote you to Echelon as well, Lukyan Chayka. One of three, and senior to everyone else in the *Reaches* by virtue of that. I understand that Maks promoted you to commander of the Horde when nobody was looking. And that Anna allowed it. This does not detract from that, but does add to your authority with everyone else. Everyone who belongs to the *Spinward Reaches*."

Dan grinned when Lukyan turned to Anna and got her nod. Her smile. Maks might have stolen a march on everyone, but she had taken advantage of it to bash horns in the Horde and set the man up to be seen as her mate.

Dan heartily approved of that, too. They made a good pairing, same as Maks and Chervonya.

Idly, she turned to Haydar, wondering if he needed a girlfriend.

"Don't you dare," he hissed so quietly that she was the only one who heard it.

They shared a grin anyway, then turned back to see Lukyan put on the new blue jacket that Omid had hand-sewn, because fabric was her love language.

Lukyan seemed bigger when it was done. More sure of himself, but that was the vote of confidence of everyone in this room for all the things he'd done thus far, when she'd just listened to him talk about making it all up as he went.

Lukyan Chayka made good choices, and that was what mattered.

Eventually, after all the hugs, everyone settled again. Then Uly rose, waving them to remain in place.

"My friends, we have done it," he said simply. "Brought together all the moving parts. Caught the Auga in a bad situation, where they cannot extricate themselves without loss. Without us allowing it. My hope is that becomes leverage we can use to create a true peace. Lasting peace is probably impossible, but every day we can force it upon our enemies is another day where it might take root anyway. Where they might change into something better."

He paused, slowly scanning the room. Dan felt the power of those eyes and remembered again the first time she'd fallen in love with him. And why.

"First, as I have noted previously, we have to go kill a lot of people," Uly explained as he turned serious. "They don't understand any other language yet, which is unfortunate but a fact of the day. You have moved mountains getting us here, and there are a few more left, but I have confidence that we can prevail, because all of you believe in me as much as I believe in you."

He had to stop there because folks were applauding and whistling. Her included.

Uly let it run for a time, then waved them to silence.

"I'm sorry that Eskil isn't here yet to take part in this, but Echelon

Huff and Echelon Chayka, I will turn over planning to you at this point," Uly said, sitting.

Dan took his hand and felt the mad power flowing through his frame. He would need a lot of cuddles later, which was a sword she was willing to throw herself on.

Dan leaned over and kissed him anyway.

Battle, then the Congress of Wives would come into its own as the **Voice** of the *Spinward Reaches*.

And the future of the galaxy, if she could pull it off.

ONE HUNDRED SIX

Sterling had a planning chamber he had specifically created by knocking out several bulkheads and creating a three-dimensional projection space where he could walk into the middle of a battle, freeze it, and look in all directions.

It changed the perception of time and space to do this.

Anari sat to one side and grinned at him, every time he looked her way, but they were both more shy than Uly and Dan about public displays of affection. Especially as he had Haydar and Lukyan in here with him.

Melpomeni and Kit didn't count, sitting next to Anari and leaning on one another in a casual, comfortable way Sterling looked forward to relaxing into, one of these days.

Lots of ships projected, but he only cared about a few blocks as he moved around.

"Devastators at the center," he noted. "One of them a flag. From your notes, they sail professionally well, but nothing exceptional."

Lukyan nodded.

"They've never tried a stunt like that, but didn't do too bad," the man replied, looking dapper in his matching uniform today.

"I'll have a fast wing with *Warhammer Rose*," Sterling continued.

"A heavy wing with *Storm Crow*. *Tanis Dragon* will be fine, off bothering people elsewhere and keeping the Empire on its toes and off my back. That leaves the Yarikh wing."

Melpomeni nodded at him.

"How dangerous would it be if I took *Nubia* in, with a double ring of *Hoplites* in front of me?" he asked the Engineer.

"We could overwhelm them on launchers," Melpomeni replied evenly. "What *Tyche* did to the station, except that we have a great many launchers on each ship, and faster generators to recharge them for the next shot."

Sterling nodded. Nobody had provided him technical specs, but he'd reviewed the logs Lukyan and Maks had recorded of what they'd done to the station.

"They'll have fifty-six 12dm launchers," he noted. "Plus all the escorts that will no doubt panic and flood in when they figure out what we're doing."

"Mass matters," Haydar offered simply. "Remotely controlled ships can be battered into rubble, but that takes time. But since there are no crews involved, nobody cares about any damage until control systems and power generation are impacted, both of which are well to the rear."

"Shields, both physical and psychological," Sterling agreed. "With the sword stabbing in from behind them. And a shield wall around us in the scrum, but the Auga will be like peeling an onion. With all the tears involved."

"So peel them," Anari noted. "In the *Karaŋgılıkka*, Zamir Aytiev did a thing. I will dig up the story and share it later, as it is only tangential to this. The Devastators are a threat, yes, but only so long as they can maintain formation to attack. What happens if you eliminate all of their escorts on one wing? The Yarikh can do that just as easily as destroying the bigger vessels, with as many wavebolts as they can bring to bear."

Sterling turned and studied her, then saw it.

"We can outrun them, anywhere they go," he said. "Including back to whatever system they take refuge in."

"And then you have both Eskil and DJ Gross available as reserves to bring up later," Anari nodded. "Enough to do to them what they intended for Avocur."

"Viciously rude," Haydar noted. "And my portion is slow, but that only matters while they are in motion, so yes, we could do that. Do we hold it back as a surprise for a potential third battle?"

Sterling paused. Walked to a different corner of the round projection and looked back. Did that two more times, seeing the battle from all sides, which he couldn't do when it was joined, but could set up here.

"Haydar, roll this projection back to where the Imperial Fleet set itself at the beginning," he ordered. "Then forward at one hundred times speed."

Fast enough that he could see the whole move organically.

Yes. There. And there.

"Pause there," he said, slipping into the middle, until he was standing exactly at the center of the Devastator Diamond, as it began to react to what Lukyan and Tiny had done.

Sterling smiled at the Ononguli who was his peer today. And his friend.

"You got an idea," Lukyan said simply.

"Yup."

ONE HUNDRED SEVEN

Uly occasionally had moments where he simply stopped and looked back at all the years that had passed since he boarded *King Hewitt II*. Suka Kuri had suggested to Dan that he was writing his own *Karaŋgılıkka*. Or rather, she would, where he would no doubt become a demigod like Zamir.

It did not generally fill him with joy.

Dan was seated on the couch next to him, touching. They were in his quarters on *Nubia*, Dan having no doubt claimed precedence as First Wife, Zamira having gotten him to herself for the last month.

"You've gone dark," she said simply, a mug of real hot chocolate in her hands because they had brought home several tons of cocoa and a small orchard that would be transplanted from that ship at some point.

Uly nodded.

"Killing people does not fill me with excitement," he said.

He could do that with her. Here. Private.

Not be a Human, who frightened others because most species simply didn't reach as deep into violence as a tool of diplomacy.

He could be vulnerable around her. It was nice.

She waited. That was the nice part.

"And yes," he continued, "it will be necessary. Hopefully only this one last campaign, and then we can do something more productive."

"What would you do, if the Auga became civilized?" she asked.

Uly considered it.

"Hire Aibek as Odysseus, but make sure he took his wife with him," he grinned.

"Send Zhyrgal instead," Dan replied evenly.

"Oh?"

Uly had met Aibek's daughter a few times. She had struck him as smart and inquisitive. Young. Barely an adult these days, as the Isann measured it.

"You captured her mind, that first time," Dan told him. "More than I did. Or Suka Kuri. The Black Sword."

"Because that is the core dream of the Isann, even though you rescued it," he reminded her.

"We all work for you, Uly," she nodded. "Your dream. We are all tools of it."

"And I am a tool of history itself," he agreed. "There are days I feel like I have almost no agency left, save to take this thing I have created and continue it to whatever logical end might be on the far side."

"It will be good," she reminded him.

He needed that occasionally, too.

"Where would you send her?" Dan asked.

"Imperial Sector Forty-One," he said, mostly to watch her eyes bug out a little.

She mouthed the words, but no sound came out.

"I think we came from there," he continued. "Us and the Yarikh. A long time ago."

"I've heard suggestions of twenty thousand years ago," she offered.

It was his turn to nod.

"Any Humans over there might have died out," he said. "Or transformed. Or not changed one iota. I don't know. And don't care today, because the Auga sit in the center of the map and threaten everyone on all sides, at least until we can convince them to behave."

"Would they go after *Danumash*?" she countered. "*Batyr*?"

"If they did, there is nothing either of them could do to counter it,"

Uly replied. "Even their biggest, best fleets couldn't stop what we're talking about crushing here shortly. My hope is that the Auga react in shock to this, and focus their attention on us and Anna, building up this frontier in such a way that maybe it becomes a permanent border in their minds. We can always break that down later with trade, but getting them to stop is the first step. And the best present I can offer to the next three generations behind us."

He watched her nod solemnly.

"I brought home four hundred Human colonists," she reminded him. "Humans will become a permanent part of the *Spinward Reaches* now. It will be a while before they challenge anyone on numbers, but they will be present."

"A place where all species can be equals," he stated simply. "*Danumash* keeps slaves. Aliens when they have them, darker-skinned Humans when not. *Batyr* does not, but has other issues they will need to overcome, as their racism is simply less virulent than *Danumash*."

"How did you turn out as you?" she asked, dark eyes glittering at him.

Uly considered an evasion. A deflection. But this was his First Wife. His partner. His closest friend.

"My father, Anselm, rose as far as he wanted," Uly began. "Assistant Deputy Secretary. Only a few steps below the Secretariat itself. He specifically chose to rise no higher in my time, and I do not see his logic changing later."

"Why is that?" she asked.

"There are things that get decided at those top levels," he told her. "When I was old enough to hear him and Tamsin discuss it over the dinner table, I wasn't mature enough to understand. That only came later."

"What kinds of decisions?"

"What courses the Institutional Party itself will take," Uly said. "Who will be punished. Who will be rewarded. What mistakes are merely minor and which end careers and possibly lives. Anselm was at the level to execute such decisions, but not for the deciding. I have finally reached a point where I could understand the difference, which eluded me then."

"How?"

"Less blood on his hands, for one," Uly said. "The system was good, but needed correction from time to time. Punishments deployed. Victims identified and ostracized. Resignations, voluntary or not, forced. His job included fulfilling the will of the Secretariat, rather than picking out individuals himself. Less guilt."

"Do you have guilt, husband?"

"I intend to wade into battle in a few days," Uly replied. "And blow up a great many ships, killing thousands and more sailors, mine and theirs both, for what future historians might mark down to mere ego. The suggestion that I have a better solution to history than anyone else does. If that isn't the very definition of arrogance, I challenge you to find me a better one."

"Suka Kuri and I discussed this over dinner, the other night," she smiled. "We might have found you a Samuur wife, but I need to meet her and see."

"Tiny?" Uly guessed. Suka Kuri had been aboard *Sivi Salavat*.

"Yes, but she is not to know until later," Dan instructed him, so he nodded. "According to Suka Kuri, Tiny reached deep inside and found a most interesting expression of Utilitarianism. On her own. In the middle of that battle. While talking to the Exemplar."

"The Samuur have a saying," Uly said. "*Battle, like all sports, shows who you are. It reveals the truth of the inner being.*"

"Just so," Dan agreed. "According to one dangerous old woman, Tiny put herself at the top of the short list with that conversation. And for the same reason your arrogance is worth listening to. Worth following."

"How so?"

"You seek out the best result for the largest number of people," Dan explained to him. "While protecting the weakest and the innocent, even to the detriment of the larger."

"Very few sacrifices are worth the cost in the long run," Uly said.

"Exactly," Dan said. "You have a better idea of how to establish and construct an entire civilization. One that even those stodgy old farts at Traiffe don't have, because they are mono-species like so many others."

"Can we make a multi-polar culture work?" he asked her.

"The Congress of Wives," she replied simply. "All of us, equal. All of us, part of your household, and not bimbos in silk dancing costumes for your entertainment."

"Oh?" he grinned at her. "Was that an option?"

"Maybe," she grinned back. "If you're a good boy."

Uly laughed. She was good for him. They all were. Kept him grounded. And gave him that many more hands with which to do things. Sterling, Eskil, and Lukyan had their place, but Uly understood that the Congress was foremost. Should be predominant. Then the Legal Department. Then the fleets.

As it should be.

He held out a hand and she took it.

Now he just had to convince the Auga to listen.

And the rest of civilization.

ONE HUNDRED EIGHT

Uly sat off to one side of the bridge. It had become his place.

At some point, there would need to be a command space aft where he and Sterling would sit while organizing entire fleets, but for now, *Nubia* had the best command crew he had been able to assemble. And it would probably be on that next ship, when he convinced the Yarikh to build it for him.

For now, they would do this thing, or they would fail.

He had no doubts that he could do terrible things to the Auga invasion fleet.

This one.

They would send another. And another. Until he convinced them there was a better way.

Sterling caught his eye.

"We're almost ready, Speaker," Sterling said, turning formal.

This was a formal moment. A page-turning event.

An ending.

And, hopefully, a beginning.

"Haydar, put me on wide broadcast," Uly said.

All of the Ononguli ships were close. And the Yarikh. And Tiny.

Everyone had a sailing vector from this spot that would drop them directly in the path of the Auga fleet, indeed sailing out to attack Avocur, as had been their original mission.

Battle would erupt. It would be ugly.

And necessary.

Haydar's tentacles waved. Uly rose, knowing that a camera would stay focused on him. Nasrin was on one side. Suka Kuri the other. Dan was off on her mission.

Uly was not alone, but it felt like it.

How many billions of beings might watch this speech later? Trillions?

"The *Spinward Reaches* will work because of you," he began simply, looking at the camera. "All of you. The Ononguli Sphere has faced the *Auga Empire* for centuries, but they were alone in resisting. You are no longer alone. The *Spinward Reaches* has heard the call and ridden to your assistance. Together, we are much greater. Ononguli. Khet. Zuath. Ugothan. Emro. Thogin. Mazhin. Yarikh. Isann. Samuur. And, yes, Humans. All of us assembled in one place to resist. Committed to the task of protecting our homes and our friends. The Auga see us as barbarians that must be civilized, even at the point of a spear, but they are wrong. Their Empire recognizes nobody but themselves. We will have to change that. You will have to, when you stand up and demand that they behave. But that is tomorrow. Today, we ride into battle to stop them. To draw the line that we will hold. The edge of the *Spinward Reaches*, until such time as these worlds decide that perhaps they would rather trade with us than be victims of Auga. That is also tomorrow."

He paused and took a deep breath.

"We are unified," Uly continued. "Representative of all the species in the west and north. We will do this thing. Because it is the right thing. For the right reasons. To free the galaxy from tyranny. Tomorrow, you will defend them from bullies, but today, they are the bullies and must be resisted. We are that shield, and that sword. All ships, you have your sailing orders. Sterling will transmit a countdown, and we will ride. I will see you on the far side, in battle."

He turned and nodded to Sterling. Haydar waved back.

"Counting down from ten," Sterling said simply.

Uly considered standing there, but he had said his piece. It was up to Sterling and Lukyan now, with him and Anna reduced to spectators who might have opinions and nothing more.

Nubia leapt into warp.

ONE HUNDRED NINE

Sterling had timed it. And had sent scouts in to confirm the timing.

The Variable Pulse Spatial Generator put out a field. When merely on and not driving a ship, it created a bubble of static that prevented other ships from crossing.

Thus, piracy, when a bigger or faster ship could force someone else out of warp. And into battle.

All he was doing was piracy at a frightening scale, with the thirteen Yarikh ships maneuvered ahead and parked exactly on the vector that the Auga Devastator fleet was sailing. Combined, they created a massive wall in hyperspace.

It kicked out the Auga fleet, almost exactly on schedule. Worse, all the escorts and the Devastators came out in a mess with them, jumbled up on odd vectors as they had been adjusting minutely.

Everyone had hit that wall and bounced down.

If he wanted to be a first-class shit, Sterling could order his force to immediately withdraw, backing far enough to jump away themselves and forcing the enemy fleet to spend an hour or more reorganizing to do it again.

Next time, though, they might actually be prepared. Better to punish them now.

"Haydar, what is their status?" he asked.

Data Nerd and Map Nerd. It was an unhealthy combination. For the other guy.

A projection appeared. Messy. Nobody at risk of collisions, he didn't think, but that would require an hour to carefully get all their threads straightened out.

"Echelon Chayka, this is Echelon Huff," Sterling said over the command line. "You're on."

The Yarikh Wall across the front, already starting to slide to their right, moving in behind the cluster of escorts around *Warhammer Rose* and *Sivi Salavat*. On his left, *Storm Crow* and an anvil of Ononguli capital ships, pulling to the left and starting to open fire at extreme range.

Folks would have to engage them. Defend against them, when everybody was surprised, confused, and out of position.

By design.

Sterling watched ships erupt with defensive wavebolts, most of them so far out of range that they would fade from existence without impacting.

Panic.

The Yarikh Wall became a crescent, with *Nubia* in the center and off-line a little, because Mel had explained how much weaker his flagship was than the other twelve in everything except symbolism.

And the ability to throw 15dm bolts.

"Yaqub, what is your status?" Sterling asked.

"Drew, can you slide me in and down just a shade?" Yaqub replied. "Get this sphere to touch those three."

Sterling saw the engagement range his Gunner was seeking. Drew was already typing.

Uly had taught them that a good crew didn't require the commander acknowledging and repeating everything. That just slowed shit down.

The commander's job was to train everyone. To supervise them. To override if necessary.

Storm Crow and *Tanis Dragon* would hold a corner and then the wall itself. Anchor ships and minds in one place, already engaged. If the Auga commander was decisive, he might charge at them.

Sterling didn't think that was allowed in their navy. They would be deliberate, instead. Perhaps deciding to engage Anna and Klyment and ignoring the other wing.

He could only hope they would fall for it a second time. Uly could break them right here if they did.

"Broadside fire commencing," Del said in a voice better suited to a waiter explaining the lunch specials for the eighteenth time.

Sterling dialed his second screen in closer. It was a thing of beauty, from a purely technical standpoint.

Three Devastators and a Flagship. Fifty-six 12dm wavebolts headed down range. And timed such that the flagship fired first, then the others in a sequence that cause all of those monsters to fly almost perfectly in a row.

Pretty.

Dangerous as hell, but he'd told Klyment it was coming, and they had arranged all their escorts in two rows to intercept such things.

Storm Crow poured fire into the defensive as well, heavy bolts shattering one another at midfield.

"Sterling, this is Lukyan. We're in position."

Sterling checked the map again to be sure. Watched a second salvo go downrange at *Storm Crow*. Eventually, some would start getting through, except that his Heavy Wing wasn't doing anything offensive, so it might not. That was when mistakes got made, but everyone was still following his game plan.

Including that Auga commander.

Third salvo launched.

"Strike Wing, this is Huff. Unleash hell."

Everyone facing the wrong way. Looking at the flagship of the Ononguli Sphere, taunting them at the edge of range, and sliding away such that the two might slowly orbit a single point for an hour, shooting pointlessly at one another.

Except that they had forgotten about him.

Well, not forgotten. Light bolts fired his direction from the escorts.

A few 8dm, from ships like *Sivi Salavat*. A bunch of 6s that were tenuous at best.

Lukyan and Tiny and a few others opened up.

Then the Yarikh Wing hit them with an *impossible* number of 8dm wavebolts.

And *Nubia* spoke.

Better, nothing aimed at those Devastators. Just as Anari and Zamir Aytiev had suggested.

All of it aimed down at the escorts.

Sterling was almost certain he could hear that Auga Admiral screaming in disbelief, because that wasn't how battles were supposed to be fought.

You're fighting Humans now.

Fire at *Storm Crow* ended as every one of those monsters suddenly began rotating heavy turrets back the other direction, thinking that they had to defend themselves against their death in incoming wavebolts.

Except that they didn't. Not the big ships, anyway.

The wall of fire slammed into the escorts. Even Sterling grimaced at the savagery.

Interceptors didn't do well when impacted by two or more 8dm bolts. Even after degrading them partially with 1dm defensive fire and every Neutron Omnipulsar that could be brought to bear.

More than one ship simply went dark, something broken inside.

It was almost impossible to actually make a starship explode. You had to punch a lance-style bolt through Engineering laterally on the exactly correct vector. And still get lucky. Even *King Hewitt II* had survived, and he'd been at the safe end when that bolt punched starlight through the bridge instead of aft where he'd been.

But you could break shit. Cut power lines. Rupture coolant systems. Blow holes in life support.

"*Storm Crow*, full salvo now, please," he said, unnecessarily, as those ships had suddenly fired everything they had.

Not nearly as much or as heavy, but a useful jab on the blind side, after a cross to the jaw had someone seeing stars.

And, again, at the escorts on this flank exclusively. Not as much damage, physically.

Emotional brutality itself.

"Strike Wing, Phase Two," Sterling said.

Another wall of death, this time at the flagship exclusively.

He watched every single Auga vessel fire every damned thing they had at anything that moved.

Wasn't going to be enough, but he knew that. Uly had laid down careful rules for this battle, understanding that Sterling could have taken the Yarikh Wing right down the center of the Auga formation and overwhelmed them. Shattered them.

Ended them.

The Yarikh would need to explain themselves. Later. Fully. Or he would be making the case to Uly to cut all ties with those people and isolate them entirely.

They could conquer the galaxy if they wanted.

Sterling Huff only barely trusted them not to. Especially today.

Auga flagships were built tough. Durable. Endurant.

He still kicked them in the face hard enough to rock that ship. Possibly could have gotten a kill, but he'd warned everyone what he could do in swatting the escorts on this wing, so they didn't hold anything back in protecting their flagship.

For a long moment, all fire ceased.

By design on his part. Shock on theirs.

"Haydar?" he asked.

"It's ugly, Sterling," Haydar replied. "They saw *Tyche*, but didn't understand that ship. Now there are eleven more, and they are panicking over there as understanding dawns."

He looked over at Melpomeni Michelakos and got a stern nod back from the woman.

There would be a reckoning, but only after this fire was put out. After the *Spinward Reaches* where the Yarikh lived were safe.

Only fools fight in a burning building.

"All forces, begin your withdrawal," Sterling ordered. "Maintain defensive fire and formations while they decide what they want to do next."

For *Storm Crow*, that was risky because they would be sailing forward into the space where the Auga fleet needed to go if they wanted to continue on to Avocur.

If they could get clear of the disruption.

But the Strike Wing was starting a turn back as well, orbiting outward like the Diamond had tried to do at Aeris.

There was a path open to the Auga commander. If he was smart enough to withdraw.

Some of his ships might be days before they fixed enough systems to do that. Sterling wondered if they would be abandoned in place instead.

Uly's plan called for this fleet to move far enough back to let them.

Mercy, if they recognized it.

Futility, if they didn't. He could always charge right down their throats, especially as his boards showed only a couple of his ships too damaged to continue, compared to nearly half the Auga escorts.

Mismatch.

What would they do?

ONE HUNDRED TEN

Suka Kuri understood Humans better than any other person she had met did. The result of seeing Uly and Dan at their worst. And their best. Of watching Sterling Huff and Solomon Wyndham grow up before her eyes, just as Yanouk and Nasrin had done.

She supposed that she was the only alien in this star system not really surprised by this outcome. And that included the Yarikh, who were only once-Human.

Ononguli made excellent pirates, but not the most organized sailors. Khet understood business at a fundamental level. The Isann sailed. The Samuur competed.

Humans *fought*.

It made them experts.

The only thing that was saving the galaxy today was that Uly and Dan were the ones that had emerged from Imperial Sector Seventeen, rather than some *Danumash* conductor wandering well off course and running into a lost pirate of some sort.

Of course, most of them would have been killed along the way, like that one *Danumash* officer that Uly still hated, even dead.

Suka Kuri understood the panicked shock that would ripple badly through the *Auga Empire* after this. After the almost clinical way Sterling had shattered this supposedly invincible fleet.

Perhaps just as well that his Skyhawk had once born the name *Invincible*, before being renamed in honor of Dan's tribe, who might be closest to the Yarikh. And possibly the original Lost Tribe that had spawned both cultures.

Sterling had turned himself into a being that primitive cultures might worship as a war god, without any understanding of the young man himself.

And Uly?

Karaŋgılıkka. Odyssey. Iliad.

She turned and caught his eye with her movement.

"Do you *Speak* with them now?" she asked, mostly *pro forma*.

That part of the legend that she herself would be transmitting to future generations, with all of the other Wives save Nasrin on various friendly flagships, recording observations for her and ready to communicate Uly's needs instantly.

"No," Uly replied evenly. "This will break their minds, but not their will."

Even Suka Kuri could shudder, discovering that there was an entire next level of deadliness beyond Sterling Huff.

And that Ulysses Fortier had ascended to it.

That conversation with Tiny. The understanding that Uly could ripple a groundquake through the *Auga Empire*, with the intent of coercing it to settle into a new formation that could become a force for good in the galaxy.

Or fall, a half-buried statue that a random traveler discovered later in the desert.

Everything Uly had done to date was merely to get their attention. That was the part that even an old woman could shiver at.

She was Exemplar of Moss, and still didn't know if the language had a term to encompass that thing that Uly and Dan could achieve, because the pairing of the two added up to so much more.

"Do we warn them at all?" she asked, almost reading a script that existed nowhere but her mind.

Uly's Legacy. His *Karaŋgılıkka*.

"They could have chosen not to do this thing," Uly replied darkly. "Not left Izabh. Nor Aeris. They can choose to surrender now, asking for terms that will be lenient. I doubt that they can. Not yet. Not until confronted with the truth that the *Spinward Reaches* would prefer to be free."

And she was back to listening Tiny expound on freedom from fear. Yes, that one would make a good addition to the Congress, if she chose.

And it would be her choice. Even Halyna had chosen to accept the *Vatazhko*'s request. All the others had been happily all in as soon as Dan had propounded the concept of the Congress.

"Signals are changing," Haydar called over all the other voices. "They still don't know how to encrypt their communications, so I am listening in on the command channel linking the big four and two wing commanders. The arguments are getting rather heated and somewhat more profane than would normally be acceptable."

"They've never been defeated before, Haydar," Sterling said simply. "One must make allowances."

Sterling Huff. A child still when she'd first met him. An adult now. War God.

And something more. Something Uly brought to the table.

Withholding the blade, which was not the same thing as mercy.

Uly nodded and watched the screen, not ignoring an old woman but looking past her.

Past all of them.

"Can they surrender?" she asked the back of his head, just quiet enough that he could choose to ignore her.

"*Serene Naddoddur* suffered a catastrophic breakdown at the moment when everybody else was madly fleeing for their lives, at least in their minds," Uly replied. "Urs Edvin Székely demanded the right to honorably surrender his blade. We accepted it. He serves his parole because he assumes that he will be executed for cowardice and treason, were he ever to return to Auga space. I do not hold him. His honor does that."

She pursed her lips.

"Should we make him Samuur?" she asked.

Uly turned to face her, eyes utterly confused for the longest moment, until he started laughing and broke the spell of darkness than had cloaked this entire bridge.

"The Paramount might never forgive me," Uly said, grinning. "I can't think of anyone that might crack the whip on themselves harder than having him around as an example. Make a note to discuss it with Maks later, after all this is done. And thank you."

She nodded and watched him turn back to the battle, but he was smiling. Sterling was smiling, too.

She had done the thing that would keep this battle from stepping over into apocalyptic terms.

This battle.

There would be another one.

ONE HUNDRED ELEVEN

Uly watched three forces maneuver slowly.

Nearby, Haydar listened in to the arguments, filtering things down to important parts. Those in favor of charging. Those pointing out that doom would result.

Those not caring.

Suka Kuri remained silent at this point, no doubt memorizing every element for future retelling. That was why she was here and Dan was with Tiny.

Watching important details.

Sterling and Lukyan conferred, maneuvering the two forces around to pinch the Devastators emotionally. Hold them.

Force them back.

Again.

Because at that point, he would destroy them. Publicly.

A statement.

Hopefully, someone would finally listen.

"Their commanding officer is duly rattled," Haydar called. "The others have made their cases, but things rest on a thin edge of insubordination."

Uly turned and shared a nod with Sterling.

"Strike Wing, come about and begin acceleration," Sterling ordered. "Heavy Wing, they shouldn't threaten you, but be prepared to stand them off for a bit if they do. We'll be on top of them like a furlo if they commit to a charge."

Uly shrugged and went back to the main display.

Time.

They needed time to change themselves. And a reason.

He had provided the latter. They were about out of the former.

They could withdraw easily enough. Or attack *Storm Crow* right now and none of them would ever make it home again.

Their choice.

It had to be their choice.

"That's it," Haydar said. "Saner minds are looking at being pinched. Orders are for all ships to come to starboard and head out, with the escorts shifting to protect the capital vessels."

"Mind their course," Uly said, unnecessarily, but wanting no details overlooked at this point.

"Orders are reciprocal to Enner, where they started after retreating from Aeris," Haydar said. "Not hearing any arguments, so the commander has them in hand."

"Spooked, like orkac," Drew muttered loud enough that Uly grinned.

They had all spent so much time around the Ononguli that they had picked up their idioms.

Shared culture. Mixed and forming something new.

A thing called *The Spinward Reaches*.

More time. Uly had patience. He had won this round.

Now he was herding them into a stockade.

Where the final battle would take place over an Auga world.

And Auga citizens would know what happened.

As would the rest of the galaxy.

ONE HUNDRED TWELVE

Haydar understood that the old woman wanted him taking the credit, but they both knew she was full of shit.

Still, Melpomeni had done the thing, once he had explained how he wanted it working.

The Yarikh had herded the Auga ships, using Drew's imagery. They were back at Enner, a nothing world that merely happened to be on one of the lateral trade routes circling this orbital distance of the *Auga Empire* from the capital itself.

A measure of how far outward the Auga in command exercised it.

Beyond this point on their maps it read, 'Here there be dragons.'

And Samuur. And Isann. And Yarikh.

But more importantly, Mazhin and Humans.

He was twenty years old again and doing stupid pirate shit because the clanships understood that sometimes the best way to deal with crazy kids was to send them off to vent all that madness on somebody else.

And he'd been pretty good at it, before turning himself into a respectable scientist later.

Then a slave.

Then Uly's sword hand. Fools might think Sterling Huff was the dangerous one, because they'd be distracted by his lack of tentacles.

Haydar was back to his pirate days.

Hell of a midlife crisis, eh?

"Haydar, you call the count," Del—DEL!—told him, taking Haydar's role as...whatever he did. Sciences. Sensors. Data Nerdery. Communications.

Del would handle both roles. And do it well. Better than most, because Haydar understood that Del was quiet and precise and got the job done with a minimum of conversation.

Kinda like his pirate boss was going to have to do.

Hell of a midlife crisis.

Haydar studied his boards. Eight simplified electronic boards that were utterly intuitive because he designed control systems as a passion almost as great as encryption systems.

All showed green as the last shuttle departed from the eight freighters that Maks had bought for him out of petty cash, because Maks had understood a long time ago that money would be the deciding factor when this day came.

You had enough, or you didn't.

You could buy eight massive, old freighters destined for the breaker yard in the near future, with the goal of just destroying them in battle and calling it good. Because a crazy Mazhin had had an idea.

And a mid-life crisis.

Dan was probably right. He needed a girlfriend to keep him out of trouble. Nasrin was too intense. Omid too subdued.

He'd need someone in the middle. Hypersmart. Able to get his jokes. Willing to even laugh at some of them.

He smiled.

Comm line opened, because all of this shit came down to what he'd done with Mel and Kit and Roshan in a quiet planning office, when Uly had laid out his plans for how this campaign might break the Auga.

Back before ANYBODY understood just how freaking lethal those Yarikh *Hoplites* were.

Fellow could get an inferiority complex.

Except that Haydar had their secret.

They only *looked* Human.

Weren't.

Not where it mattered.

Brilliant. Pretty. Semi-immortal.

Clinical.

Unable to reach deep and rattle the cages that woke up an old mad dog Mazhin pirate from where he'd been sleeping quietly next to the fire on a cold day.

Maybe a step less dangerous than Humans, but only a step.

Haydar looked up and made eye contact with Uly, understanding that tentacles wouldn't convey it to everyone else in the bridge.

Uly could read him. Nasrin was watching and scowling. Suka Kuri might understand, but not know how.

Didn't matter.

Uly.

The *Speaker.*

The Warlord of the Spinward Reaches.

"All vessels, this is Fleet Marshal Fortier," Uly said, because it needed to come from his mouth for a whole tentacle ball's worth of reasons. "Counting down now. Haydar will transmit the signal to launch our final attack on Enner."

Haydar pressed a button and commended his soul to whatever dark gods might have pity on him for the dumbass stunt he was about to pull.

The Auga would never forget him, that was certain.

Eight massive hunks of old, tired steel leapt up into warp.

Nubia followed.

ONE HUNDRED THIRTEEN

Uly watched as the fleet emerged at Enner after a short jump.

Four Devastators had clustered, but weren't immediately under the defensive guns of the station. Not that it mattered much, as they far outmassed it for firepower anyway.

Enner was an inhabited world. Population largely Zuath, with Ugotha and Thogin as the next largest minorities. Likely no Auga present in any useful numbers. Merely lesser citizens of the *Auga Empire* itself, a long reach that he hoped had grown tenuous with distance.

A glance over at Haydar. A tentacle waved in acknowledgment. Haydar's surprise was intact. Running well enough.

"Sterling, we are not opening battle with a demand for their surrender," Uly said aloud, mostly for posterity to damn him for his arrogance. "However, honor must be served. Fire one wavebolt."

"Gunner, one round only, targeting the station, fist," Sterling ordered.

Uly watched Yaqub push a button without any adjustments, so they had all prepared ahead for this moment.

Uly smiled grimly at the thought of a crew well enough trained to do those things. And knowing what orders were coming.

On the screen, one 14.7dm bolt headed downrange. It might actually make it to the station with enough force to scorch paint from this distance, but it would have to traverse most of the Auga fleet to get there, and they were already opening up with everything they had.

At a single bolt.

Panic had indeed infected them. Gnawed on their ankles in the darkness over the last few days.

Frayed their nerves.

He doubted that they had intentionally fired a bolt back at him to establish their honor. Several had been wildly programmed and were not a threat at this range. Even if he let them hit unmolested.

Still, honor had been served, and Uly could think of no greater lesson that the Samuur as a people could transmit to eternity than that.

As the Isann *sailed*, so the Samuur fought with honor.

It was probably a pity that they weren't in command today. The Empire would have to deal with Humans.

"Echelon Huff, you have command," Uly said, then moved over and sat between Nasrin and Suka Kuri.

The youngest and oldest of his advisors. And, behind Dan, probably the most dangerous.

Which said everything worth mentioning.

ONE HUNDRED FOURTEEN

Dan had spent a week and change watching Tiny. Listening to her. Understanding her.

Tiny had suspicions about why Dan was here, but that topic had been avoided. Tiny, understanding that she had a job to do, both as a commander and leading the only other multi-species crew present besides *Nubia*.

Eskil was only a few days away, but Uly and Sterling had planned this part of the operation with a fine control over Auga psychology, courtesy of Suka Kuri, Anari, and Yeong-Suk, all former imperial citizens with a vast working knowledge of how the masters operated.

And they considered themselves the Masters. *Danumash* aristocrats would have recognized kin, but both were too specist to ever acknowledge one another.

"Manas, we're in the same position as the last two times," the Samuur woman reminded her Isann Pilot. Then turned to her Ononguli Gunner. "Fedir, keep everything defensive until I change your targeting priorities."

Both men nodded. Nothing had changed, but a good commander reminded people at that last moment before shit got serious.

Multi-species. All of them, working together on a single ship towards a single goal, which was not—yet—a thing the Ononguli had embraced. That would change after this. Dan had spoken to Anna about putting Horde ships directly into *Spinward Reaches* service with mixed crews.

And everything that implied.

Tiny glanced over, silent. Dan nodded back.

Woman had a battle to fight. And *Sivi Salavat* was leading escort on this wing, protecting *Warhammer Rose* and a few other ships.

Dan studied the Samuur woman. And smiled.

They would have that conversation when they got back to Avocur, because Dan was certain that Avocur would become the new frontier world. That trade station connecting the *Spinward Reaches* to the *Auga Empire*, with the potential for everyone to get rich.

If they could get over themselves.

She didn't know if Tiny would be thrilled or appalled at the thought of an alien husband, even if it was Uly. Not everyone could put their own species prejudices aside, and that was the very first step Dan required of anyone.

Tiny was most of the way there, but would need to take that last step.

For now, Dan sat back and watched her fight.

ONE HUNDRED FIFTEEN

Sterling sighed. Part of him was disappointed at how this campaign was ending.

He was using a trick, rather than defeating them in honorable combat. Several tricks, because they had been no more prepared for the Yarikh than anybody else.

Including him.

But Haydar had the ugly thing today. And it would only work on a Devastator, because everyone else was faster and more maneuverable.

Still, he had inherited a great deal from Suka Kuri and the Samuur, and tricks irritated him. It verged on the dishonorable.

Sterling studied his plot. Two lines of escorts in something of an arrowhead ahead of him. The Yarikh as a crescent with the horns forward around *Nubia* and *Storm Crow*. *Warhammer Rose* and *Sivi Salavat* on his right, because they'd done that during two battles already, and Sterling knew that the Auga would have their heads turned that way in spite of what was directly in front of them.

But then, they might not understand the eight signals just behind the escorts, sailing in four pairs clustered into a large diamond ahead of *Nubia* and *Storm Crow*.

Matching the other diamond over there.

"Enemy Devastators opening up with 12s," Del announced quietly. "Other ships adding in their lesser wavebolts, but most of their escorts appear to be defensive at present."

As expected.

Those folks knew he could throw a whole hell of a lot of wavebolts down that slope at them. An overwhelming number, honestly.

Idly, he wondered if, like Székely, they were planning to fall on their swords when this was done. Imperial naval officers above a certain rank were almost always Auga. The lesser species weren't trusted, even when they had proven themselves.

He was facing four big ships today. Probably around twenty Auga total, all of the senior ranks on those four vessels.

Honor had been served. Uly was satisfied. The Samuur would be satisfied.

Sterling was simply here to destroy things.

"All ships, ahead normal acceleration," Sterling ordered. "Fire as you bear, maintaining the normal rhythm."

The Yarikh could utterly shitstorm things, but if they didn't do it today, the native population on the planet below might not believe stories later. That would matter.

Uly was winning a war of public relations, having defeated them by force of arms already.

Sterling Huff was his sword.

Because heavy ships had rear turrets, usually you sailed two lines that passed one another, broadsiding. Sterling had come to understand that you could fire at an angle anyway and let the bolt curl in and track true, at a cost of power.

Which was why most people didn't do it. Sometimes, though, it was useful.

His fleet was sailing right into the teeth of the Auga formation, damning the waste of the rear turrets. They still fired. Still hit. Still hurt.

And he was a spear going for someone's guts instead of two swordsmen dueling.

"Haydar, what is your status?" he asked as ships got into motion.

"Tracking true and responding to control circuits," Haydar replied. "I'm ready whenever you are."

Sterling nodded. Up until now, Echelon Huff had been operating under Uly's direct orders.

Playing for the galleries and the history books.

Now, it was his battle to fight. His war to win.

"Del, what is your status?" he asked next.

"All systems primed and ready, Echelon," Del replied.

"Drew?"

Mad cackles were probably answer enough.

He flipped a comm switch.

"All vessels, this is Echelon Huff," he announced. "Charge on my signal."

He closed the line and drew a breath.

"Del, light 'em up."

Sterling still remembered first meeting Able Spacer Delbert Blakeslee, the serene communications technician he'd always considered mildly average with faraway eyes and brown hair in the days before Uly, when a punk named Huff had been Midshipman: Astronomer's Mate aboard *King Hewitt II*.

How far they'd both come.

Del pressed a button and a small tune began playing in the background. Quiet enough to ignore. Loud enough to hear. Simple enough to understand.

Outside *Nubia*'s hull, no ship was talking with anybody, because Haydar and Melpomeni had come up with a way to boost signals jamming to obscene levels.

It would be like standing next to an airhorn signaling shift change.

You could wave at your mates, but no words would be exchanged.

Even his ships were on their own, but they'd known it was coming, and had worked together for long enough to understand what to do.

That, and the order, "*Go kill things.*" didn't require a lot of subtlety.

"Drew, you're on," Sterling said. "Yaqub, unleash the hounds of hell."

ONE HUNDRED SIXTEEN

Yaqub still thought back to the day he'd decided that Gunner on *Nubia* was a better gig than trying for a command slot on one of the smaller ships. Might still go for it after this, but that was because there weren't going to be a lot of battles left after this.

Not for a long time.

Sterling had spotted the bad guys with the searchlight, and one crazy-ass purpled punk was about to nail them to a board.

NINE!!! 14.7dm bolts launched as one. Wasn't going to be very effective at this range, even as they closed.

Wasn't the point.

EVERYONE was looking this way.

At *Nubia*. At him.

At nine bolts charging right at the flagship, when they couldn't order anybody to do anything about it.

Not that there were a lot of options. Everyone over there cut loose with everything they had, which was why he kept the medium and light shit back to stop his own hull from getting scorched, because *Nubia* was going to be the center of attention today.

The *Hoplites* had gone normal. Or whatever you wanted to call it. Eight and eight, instead of shitshow. Enough to keep crap off *Nubia*, which was all Yaqub cared about, because Drew was doing that crazy-ass surfing shit he always talked about.

Man had found the perfect wave, and was riding it to shore.

That the Auga fleet happened to be in his way was just too bad for them.

Yaqub fired every tube as fast as they recharged, rather than waiting for pretty salvos.

Nothing pretty in this mess.

Uly wanted chaos.

Sterling had ordered it.

He and Drew were making it happen with Del's help.

And nobody over there could say anything about it.

ONE HUNDRED SEVENTEEN

Uly watched things unfold.

It came down to this. To now.

Wavebolts in waves and swarms so heavy that they looked like a bridge you could walk over. Ships would be damaged and maybe destroyed because they could not coordinate with their neighbors. Could not overlap fire.

Could not protect one another.

His side was doing the better job, but they'd had time to prepare mentally.

This was yet another jolt to the Auga psyche. The Empire itself.

You could defeat this jamming. Once you analyzed it and understood how it was working.

That might take them months.

They had minutes.

"Haydar?" Uly asked in a conversational tone, watching those tentacles writhe.

"All true," he replied without looking up.

Uly nodded.

The only communications right now were tight-beam lasers from the front of *Nubia* to the rear of those eight drones, adjusting things as they closed, though at some point Haydar could turn off all communications and let them maneuver themselves.

Control Systems. His other compulsion and expertise. Beyond encryption technology.

Because it had come to this.

"Oh, hey, somebody finally caught on," Del said in a bright voice. "I'm getting a lot of bolts targeted on Haydar's orkac."

That was what they'd been calling them. Herd animals, with that laughing Mazhin as the Ononguli cowboy on his zeonx.

"Maintain pace and targeting of fire," Sterling said loudly, reminding Yaqub to throw all his heavy bolts at the other flagship as a further distraction.

Around them, the *Hoplites* were like metronomes, ticking slowly. *Warhammer Rose* and *Sivi Salavat* held a flank and pinched in minds on that side, having already twice defeated them in battle. *Storm Crow* was behind them where Anna was safe.

He needed Anna in office for another decade if he could arrange it. And Chervonya on the council sooner rather than later, because the Sphere would have to change, too.

Everyone was facing the future.

"And red-shift starting," Del announced. "Ships are starting to climb away from us to gain distance."

Uly considered how badly their natural response to climb instead of diving was about to cripple them. Wavebolts had that much farther to go to intercept incoming fire. That much weaker when they got there.

That much more damage he could do to them.

"Haydar," he said simply, waiting for tentacles to give way to eyes, so he knew the man was actually paying attention. "How much finesse can you put into play?"

Blinks. Tentacles would have knotted and required fingers to separate, and Haydar needed his hands right now. The Mazhin grinned when he realized that.

"What did you have in mind?" Haydar asked.

"I want the commanding marshal over there to survive," Uly said. "I want him going home and telling the Emperor himself what happened."

"What about the other three?" Haydar asked.

"Defeated does not require annihilated," Uly pronounced, listening to the calmness in his voice and damning himself anyway for what was about to happen.

Haydar nodded.

And went to work.

ONE HUNDRED EIGHTEEN

Suka Kuri had entered a type of fugue state where all senses were heightened and everything was being recorded deep. She wouldn't remember it all, but she could meditate with a voice recorder and recover every bit of detail later. Possibly with headphones on, replaying the voices on the bridge as though offering running color commentary.

Only a Human would follow the conversation Uly and Haydar were having, but she had long since stopped wondering if they were one being. Or if Uly was Mazhin enough that he could communicate by smell to other Mazhin.

"Defeated does not require annihilated," she heard Uly say.

Mercy. Of a sort. Hard and brittle. Jagged sharp and rusty.

But mercy.

The Corsac Fox had it in his power to wipe the skies above Enner clear of enemy warships today.

And was still trying not to, if the Auga commanders could be jarred loose from whatever *-isms* they might have held before.

If the galaxy could be shaped by a ground shock, instead of burned to the ground and rebuilt later.

Haydar Ramezani went to work, typing furiously but with a crisp precision that normally eluded him.

Every little detail.

Suka Kuri nodded and brought up a screen next to her station, dialing scanner images in and adjusting things to the level she required, in order for Moss to transmit the Battle of Enner to future generations.

Because it had just reached that tipping point.

The escorts were doing what they could, and being overwhelmed because everyone was targeting them. The four Devastators had flown in a pretty diamond, like they did, with the flagship at the rear. The closest one had understood what eight big freighters waddling towards them actually implied, long before everyone else had, and had given the order to flee.

But he could not tell the other three.

And made the mistake of going straight up and over, where only a Yarikh vessel wasn't immediately in trouble.

The other three had paused, indecisive. Uncertain. A hole opened in their formation that Yaqub was continuing to exploit.

Trouble.

Then they saw it, and the other three tried to turn away. Something.

It was already too late, because Haydar had control of his stampeding orkac and flew one into the port side of the lead Devastator, literally ramming it.

The eight were all uncrewed drones, so all the casualties were imperial. The two ships merged for a moment, then inertia spalled the one off the other, both tumbling around a common center and entirely out of control.

Mercy meant that the second did not track with the first and finish off that Devastator, when it would have been an easy kill.

Flown through it like an arrow into an apple.

Dead.

Destroyed utterly.

Here, merely broken.

The second suffered the same fate, one strike but not two. Not *utter*.

Three did something wrong. Bad orders. Bad execution. Something.

It turned into the freighter instead of away and rammed it bow to bow, both collapsing inward like aluminum cans bleeding plasma, parts, and bodies out the sides.

The flagship had the most time to react. And the greatest space. He managed to get up and clear and started running, but *Sivi Salavat* and *Warhammer Rose* had their entire wing of escorts already pacing him like furlou after a calf.

"Haydar," Uly said. "Hold here."

Suka Kuri remembered to breathe.

ONE HUNDRED NINETEEN

"Haydar," Uly said. "Hold here."

He watched ten thousand sailors die, but Haydar flipped engines and the freighters slowed enough for that one Devastator to slip out of the trap.

"Del, cut the jamming," Uly continued, nodding with Sterling because the battle had just ended and now they were negotiating surrenders.

Or executions.

Del's music ended and the bridge was silent save for typing and blowers. The smell of adrenaline across this many species had an interesting funk when mixed. Almost roasted nuts covered with lemon frosting, which was weird and new, but he'd deal with that, too.

Uly turned to Del.

"Get me the officer in command over there, and order all ships to cease firing for now, save defensive operations," Uly continued.

He waited as Del talked.

Fitting that most of the people on the bridge driving the action today were Humans, when he stopped and counted heads. Him. Sterling. Drew. Del.

Haydar was close enough.

Del nodded and looked up again.

"Got him."

"Main screen and conference mode," Uly said, rising from his seat. "Broadcast it to both fleets, all stations, and the planet itself."

Nasrin and Suka Kuri joined him, standing in front of the others as an Auga in a rumpled uniform appeared, all three eyes about as wide as they could get.

"This is your opportunity to survive this battle and become my messenger back to the Court on Ajorn," Uly began.

"Who are you?" the Auga demanded.

"Fleet Marshal Ulysses Fortier," he said. "Warlord of the *Spinward Reaches*. **The Corsac Fox**."

That last name got his attention, but Uly had been an imperial prisoner at one point, taken when Adrian Sobol's *Iron Wasp* was captured, and about to be *processed* when Uly escaped, stole Adrian's ship, and started his war on the Empire itself.

Yes, this gentleman knew the Corsac Fox.

"What do you want?" the fellow asked nervously.

"Does your honor demand that I annihilate you and the rest of your fleet today?" Uly fired back. "Or can I convince you to surrender? To carry a message to your masters? Can we have peace between the Empire and their neighbors, or must I continue making my point?"

Beside him, Nasrin gasped at his tone, but she understood the implications.

The ramifications.

That Enner might just be the first of many. That he might start hunting Auga squadrons while he had an irresistible force.

A big, fucking hammer.

Suka Kuri was listening. Absorbing. Remembering.

Third eye blinked. The hunting eyes weren't as obvious. Or as big.

The pause stretched.

Uly was made of patience, but he knew that he would run out at some point and finish them off. Maybe go crush the station, just because.

Messages would be sent. This Auga officer got to decide how.

"What does surrender look like to you?" the man asked.

"Your survival," Uly replied. "Your ransom, which your comrade Conductor Urs Edvin Székely aboard *Serene Naddoddur* gave me when he surrendered."

"And what happened to him?"

"Currently, I believe someone in Bastion hired him to run a small shipping company for them, the man having extensive expertise in logistics and executive operations," Uly grinned. "He believes that you will execute him for treason if he ever returns home, so has chosen exile, which is a pity as far as I'm concerned. He is free to return home when he chooses. Your ransom will be a message carried to Ajorn for me. And peace between our nations that we will subsequently negotiate. I will not send an ambassador with you until I am convinced that Auga honor would protect them, having once been your prisoner."

Third eye blinked again. Voices of disbelief in the background. Negation.

But Uly really didn't care about their feelings.

They could behave. Or he would continue to punish them, because a great many other systems and peoples would hear about this battle and rally to his cause.

To the *Spinward Reaches*.

As insults went, Uly was pushing the margins. Especially when a barbarian accuses you of poor manners.

Which is what they still thought of him as.

"That's it?" the commander asked.

More disbelief.

"I suppose I could eliminate your force entirely, then locate the planetary governor below us and deal with them instead," Uly answered. "Would you find that preferable?"

Would you prefer to die? Right here. Right now. Decide.

Third eye blink.

Uly was beginning to wonder if it was a nervous tic of the man, or a species reaction to shock. He would ask Suka Kuri when all this was done.

"We will surrender on ransom, Corsac Fox," he said, turning away from the camera. "Inform the other ships."

Uly turned to Sterling and nodded.

"All ships, withdraw to these positions," Sterling said, no doubt pulling the force back far enough that local rescuers could do something about three dead Devastators and all of the broken and scattered escorts, lying like discarded toys on the living room floor.

Uly turned back. Watched.

"What now, Corsac Fox?"

"Now, we will withdraw to the edge of the system, Commander," Uly said. "Let me know when you have stabilized your situation and are ready to talk again."

He turned to Del and nodded.

"Line cut, Uly," Del said.

Uly blew out a heavy breath. Nasrin took his hand and squeezed. He pulled her into a hug.

"Thank you, everyone," he said, looking around at some of his closest friends. "Sterling, transmit a well done to the squadron, then roll into laager and send a messenger out to find Eskil and another one to DJ. The war might have ended, if they are willing to listen."

"And if not?" Suka Kuri asked.

He looked up at the tall woman. Studied her.

Exemplar of Moss. And everything that entailed.

"Then it will continue until they are," he told her.

PART ELEVEN
BASTION

ONE HUNDRED TWENTY

Uly had finally gotten to live on the ground at Bastion.

Lyra and Voldomir Bondarenko had indeed found the perfect spot to build a capital city.

Isaure. On Isaure Bay, where the Zelie River emerged, overlooked by Aigul Ridge and the Cholpon Mountains.

Something for everyone, with plains to the north for Ononguli and Humans. Hillsides for the Isann. Water for the Khet. Enough planetary tilt for seasons, but exceptionally mild here, with snow not far away in winter.

Paradise, because if he was never returning to Gralbo, he was damned certain that he was going to enjoy himself.

Looking out over the room, Uly wasn't certain that he would be enjoying himself today. But that couldn't be helped.

It was the Hall of Voices, an idea he had inherited from the Mazhin Convocation. The Conclave of Species met here, and he *Spoke* for them. At least for now.

Eventually, they would elect their own presiding officer, but that was also not today.

For now, every planet owing him fealty and paying taxes had sent a representative. Usually several, because the Legal Department as represented by Ethir and Piruz had made sure that all of the species were represented below Uly.

And eventually the Congress would become separate, but for now, all of his Wives sat out there as Members at Large, along with the entire Legal Department and a number of ambassadors to places that didn't want to be left out.

Like the Khet of Z'Gosza or the Ononguli of Rayzian.

Eventually, there would be enough technocrats below him to nominate a Presidium, like the Industrial Protectors Party did, back in *Batyr*. Somewhere around sixty experts. Technocrats and Trade Factors. From them, the Bastion Council would be drawn, again targeting roughly a dozen beings, with the Chair being the Head of Political Affairs.

And, eventually, the *Warlord of the Spinward Reaches*, when Uly could subordinate that role to civilian control and trust that the military would accept such a thing. And also not turn itself into a Praetorian Guard isolating and later selecting rulers themselves.

He could see Sterling growing into that role. Especially since Uly didn't think there existed enough blackmail in the galaxy to get Haydar to do it.

Similarly, the Governor of Bastion would be responsible for executive authority for the capital system.

Uly was, for now, all of those, though he retained excellent advisors there, with Lyra and Voldomir staying put, as well as Zoryana and Anton Bondarenko.

Today, he stood before the Hall of Voices and called them to order. Something less of a formal rubber stamp than the Party maintained on Gralbo, but everyone was present. Behaving. Polished and pressed and cleaned up.

Because they had a visitor.

Dan had escorted the shorter man into the chamber amidst all the pomp and ceremony an Auga Ambassador to the Court deserved, much of it drawn from *Batyr* but including elements of other cultures as the Legal Department added and rejected tidbits from here and there.

They were creating a new thing. A thing that had never existed, anywhere in the annals of Moss, and that told Uly everything he needed to know.

The Spinward Reaches. As good a name as any, though some called it Bastion, after the homeworld and the entire concept that such a word contained.

All were welcome, if they behaved. All were equal.

Many were willing, so Bastion had expanded.

As Uly looked around the chamber, he even noted some of his new Human subjects and friends, off to one side instead of down with the formal people. Solomon Wyndham, fourth son of a Duke and Sabre School Adept, sat next to the ex-Duchess Jacquel Pery, though they were not holding hands in public, a *Danumash* upbringing that taught how such things should be kept for the private quarters.

As long as both were happy. And they seemed to be.

Dan came to rest. She was a head taller than the Ambassador. He outweighed her. She wore green. He wore the red and gold of the *Auga Empire.*

Uly wore blue, because he was the *Warlord of the Spinward Reaches,* and this was a military thing today.

He looked forward to civilian clothing, but it had been more than a decade in his case, and he didn't expect it tomorrow.

"Corsac Fox, I present to the Hall of Voices Peter Simonis, Ambassador to the Court, representing the *Auga Empire,*" Dan called, her voice lifting the rafters in a place where Voldomir had located and hired the best architects to make it work.

Following extensive protocol that the Legal Department had invented then worked out with the *Auga Empire*, Ethir emerged from the left and stepped up to Simonis. An oversized envelope got extracted from a breast pocket, then handed to the smaller man.

Ethir turned and walked to the front of the room, up the first of two levels so he was above the crowd and below the crown, as it were. At least as Piruz and the others had explained.

There, Ethir turned to face the room as he opened the envelope and read it silently, then nodded.

"Peter Simonis, you are accredited by the Empire of the Auga to speak for the Imperial Court while representing the Emperor in his dealings with Bastion and the government of the *Spinward Reaches,*" Ethir called formally. "What say ye?"

"So it is written," Simonis replied in a deep, lush, lovely voice that should have been reading the evening news.

But the Auga had decided long ago to perfect themselves with genetic engineering, settling on this form and shape and adding beauty, intellect, and longevity, both male and female.

Uly glanced at Melpomeni Michelakos and Kit, way back in a corner because the Scholar herself was seated among the representatives on the floor. The perks of rank, because she could, as she'd told Uly, and intended to nominate Dionysia Stavrou later.

Once Dan decided whether or not he needed a Yarikh wife, then reviewed whichever candidates were nominated.

Below him, Ethir turned around to look up at Uly, grinning since his face was hidden from most of the chamber. And he winked, because it was Ethir.

"The Ambassador to Auga, Warlord," Ethir announced.

Still a dork. But he would always be one, likely.

Uly nodded.

Ethir placed the document on a pedestal, then returned to his seat with the other Thogin, on one edge of the Legal Department because even Ethir didn't want his cousins getting into trouble without him watching.

Uly waited for the room to fall to utter silence, then drew a breath. He studied Simonis carefully, but all of this was for show, worked out in the preceding months as the folks on Ajorn got over their shock and realized that they had to act like adults for once.

For now. Uly didn't expect it to last.

They had been stunned. Not knocked down. Hopefully, it wouldn't have to come to that, but there were twenty Yarikh *Hoplites* in orbit above them today, ready to go junkyard dog on someone if they had to.

Sterling had specifically remained in orbit on *Nubia*, sending Eskil and Lukyan to the surface in his place, uniforms to one side where the military answered to the civilian government.

"Ambassador, be welcome to Bastion and the Court of the *Spinward Reaches*," Uly said, following the script he had helped write. "What business brings you before us?"

"Where once there was darkness, the Empire of Auga finds a place occupied by many people," Simonis replied, pitched perfectly to resonate the room.

Just lovely to listen to. Even reading actuarial tables.

"And your purpose?" Uly asked.

"The Emperor would learn who lives in this place," Simonis replied. "He would have peace between us, that trade might flow outward from Ajorn and bring the light of the Empire to the dark corners."

Uly had been willing to let him have that in his public speech. Simonis was playing for galleries extremely remote from Bastion, because they would see footage of today and make their own decisions.

And the Congress of Wives had escorted him into the room in their full combat regalia, including Lahja Arifullen. Because Tiny had impressed the shit out of both Dan and Suka Kuri, then volunteered when they explained in sharper detail what the job entailed.

"The *Spinward Reaches* welcomes our distant neighbors in the spirit of trade and community, Ambassador," Uly replied.

He found the gavel to one side and rapped it solidly against the lectern where he stood.

"This audience is ended," Uly proclaimed. "Let us gather in the lesser hall for a celebration of our new neighbor."

He watched the Congress turn Simonis and escort him sideways into the room where Omid and Vahid had run a merciless kitchen, preparing a feast fit to impress even those yokels from Ajorn. The various representatives followed, then Uly's Legal Department escorted him.

He had come so far since that day when Captain Dimka Savatier on Marshall Castillon sent him to take possession of *King Hewitt II*.

They all had.

And it was only the beginning, but it had begun.

ONE HUNDRED TWENTY-ONE

Uly closed the door and got the Scholar seated. They were doing this in his quarters rather than his office, so that it would be a little less formal.

Less brittle.

Nomiki Marinos sat on one end of the couch, with him at the other and Dan across the way in a chair. The Yarikh were still Human enough to appreciate hot chocolate, but Uly had learned to drink something from Khet that wasn't chocolate. But he was a guy, and women had the right receptors in the brain for chocolate.

"Mel briefed you?" Dan asked as they settled.

"She did," Nomiki replied with a shallow, grave nod.

Uly could have done this in a larger setting. Added Suka Kuri and Anari. Maybe the rest plus the Legal Department.

He wanted it contained. Compact. Friendly, if possible.

"I have a problem," Uly told the woman who led the Yarikh. "And most of the *Spinward Reaches* are now familiar with it, though they will not understand the potential repercussions."

"The Yarikh are too powerful," Nomiki replied, locking eyes with him.

"That, too," he said, causing her to flinch a little in surprise. "What I have is the problem that right now you risk becoming the power behind the throne of the *Spinward Reaches*. I have squadrons of *Hoplites* protecting my most important ports, and thank you for that, because it allowed me to do a thing today that I might not have risked for another decade otherwise."

"To push back," Nomiki said, sitting up a little straighter. "We did the math and analyzed your place on a variety of historical patterns, Uly."

"And determined that you could put me in a position to impact the Empire today," he completed the thought. "To fight them at Avocur and Enner, instead of over Traiffe."

"Elias determined, after Stradosha and then the run to Masym, that the *Auga Empire* is too powerful to fall of its own accord," Nomiki continued. "That they would continue for perhaps another two to three thousand years before the problems baked into their underlying structure caused them to come apart."

"They would have found you long before that," Dan noted dryly. "Sterling has done that math."

"And thus, we had several choices to make," Nomiki nodded. "Giving you access to some of our power now let us dictate a number of things to eternity."

"I like the way you frame that," Dan offered. "People will fear the *Spinward Reaches*, but pirates and would-be conquerors will know to avoid Traiffe like a plague."

She matched his smile.

"We did what we found necessary at the time," Nomiki concluded.

"And that time will shortly pass," he said. "Having established the *Spinward Reaches* as a place, a thing located midway between the Khet of Sector Fifteen and the Ononguli Sphere, I will need you to find a way to politely and quietly withdraw your forces. That, or fully integrate them under my and Sterling's command. And Eskil and Lukyan when they are present."

Her flinch spoke volumes. As did her grimace.

"And we would learn too much about you," Dan spoke in his stead. "Learn that even now you have withheld certain elements of your capability, in case you needed to chastise the Warlord or protect yourselves from him."

Low blow, but Nomiki shrugged.

"I will not dispute your words," she offered quietly, then sipped her cocoa. "Auga must be held at bay."

"As must the various barbarians that surround you," Uly offered calmly. "Mel understood that. And understood that there would need to be changes made. I have no concerns with you protecting your last world with as much and as lethal a force as you find necessary. The navy of the *Spinward Reaches* has other needs."

"New ships," Nomiki agreed. "New technology that slowly advances you from where the galaxy is today, while not giving you the weapons of the gods."

"I am not Zamir Aytiev," he told her. "Regardless of what others might think. Or rather, I am, and neither of us are demigods, Nomiki. Merely men, trying to accomplish certain goals that we feel will advance civilization. *Nubia* is a thing, but it is one ship, and the Auga will be able to match it after studying those battles. I doubt they could match a *Hoplite* in any way."

"We have studied plans made available by Maks Sobol," she replied. "What the galaxy was building before. What changes he has instituted with the help of the Isann and Samuur. What things he would like to adapt from *Invincible*, but lacks the tooling necessary today to achieve."

"And what does that add up to?" Dan asked.

"We have two options," Nomiki replied, turning to her and letting Uly study her silhouette. "We can show him how to make better weapons. Or, as Kit noted, we can show him how to make better systems overall, understanding that the many minds you and Uly have assembled will be able to drive things forward in greater leaps if we did that."

"Only until the Auga and others bought or stole the technology," Dan replied. "Then everyone advances as one and retains a general parity."

"Which does not benefit us, as the Auga have so much mass," Nomiki said.

"And too much bureaucracy," Uly countered. "They can know a thing, but will be a decade in executing it in steel and systems, if not a generation. With any luck, we can gain an edge on them and maintain it for my lifetime. After that, I hope that my successors and advisors, as well as the Hall of Voices, will be enough to maintain it. If that border hardens today, we can melt it again with trade in half a century, like chocolate. That might be the single greatest gift I can offer the future. Peace and trade and an Auga that do not feel the need to conquer and enslave everyone else."

She watched him. He watched her do math in her head, knowing that they would likely both live about the same number of years from here, but she was in her third century now, and he, merely in his fourth decade.

"I prefer a dragon sleeping inside the mountain," he told her. "You are a threat that others must be aware of, and stories of Aeris and Enner will only grow with the retelling. Your people here will engage with others and form relationships. I want that. What I don't want is you being in a position to dictate terms. I find that unacceptable, and am willing to let this entire edifice collapse again and dump the whole lot in your lap if I have to."

"What?"

"I had four crew members and a handful of prisoners," he continued. "Plus rescued slaves. We were taken by a pirate. Then captured by the Auga. Then escaped. Do you honestly think I couldn't collect up another group of folks and sail them somewhere coreward from you, such that you became the front line with the *Auga Empire* instead and had to deal with them yourself? Try me."

Dan had gone perfectly still, but that wasn't fear. That was measuring Nomiki for a blow if the woman moved suddenly.

Uly didn't do hand-to-hand combat. He didn't need to, because he had a group of Wives who were the deadliest people he knew at that sort of thing.

Led by the First Wife, seated a meter away.

And primed for violence.

Nomiki understood that. She sat perfectly still, eyes wide with surprise.

Uly figured that he'd just done something that broke all of their careful calculations about nation-founding demigods.

Good.

If they could do that math, so could the Auga Emperor's people. And they could fail, just as easily as Nomiki had.

Finally, the woman smiled. Shrugged to herself. Muttered something he missed.

"Kit spoiled us," Nomiki said. "He is among the most agreeable people I have ever known."

"That was part of the reason I sent him," Uly nodded. "I needed that, when I had Anari to act as the official side of things."

"And Kit, while brilliant and nerdy, is not a killer," Nomiki agreed. "Not like you two."

It was Uly's turn to shrug.

"And you are not bluffing," Nomiki continued. "I know that. As you and the Auga Emperor have to walk a fine line, you and I will, as well."

"I want your help turning the *Spinward Reaches* into a place where all species are friendly," Uly said. "And all are equal. Anything else, and the Yarikh are just Auga in disguise."

Low blow. Her grimace returned, but she didn't dispute him.

"I need you holding them at bay," she finally said. "Traiffe can be your dragon, as long as you are at the cave mouth."

"Then I need your help doing that," he said. "But on my terms, Nomiki. Not yours. You, supporting the government and civilization of the *Spinward Reaches* as an equal member. Or nothing."

"Will Ambassador Simonis bring peace?" she asked, haring off on a tangent.

But an important one.

"That is his charge," Dan replied. "The Legal Department isn't reading his mail, but Haydar is working on that. For now, they want a line held so they can do what they do best, which is spend time analyzing what happened and how to react."

"They are still reacting to Ixtin, aren't they?" Nomiki asked.

"Yes," Uly said. "I intentionally kept booping them. Kept striking their systems and forcing them to react. Stradosha deeply impacted things, from what stories have made it back to us. They are uncertain, and that is anathema to the Auga mindset. If I can get a decade of peace out of them, I think I can build us up to the point that we can resist their next attack and perhaps force them back afterwards."

"Their next attack?" she pressed. "You see it as given?"

"I cannot imagine that they chose to suddenly live in peace with neighbors," he said. "They never have. Not once. Even now, the Emperor's wiser councilors might be telling him to wait until I die of old age, then start up again, because they are nothing if not patient."

"Or they assassinate you," Nomiki pointed out.

"Which is why I need to protect Bastion," he nodded. "And the *Spinward Reaches*. And I need you to provide me the tools to do it, instead of holding them yourself. I cannot imagine that you won't start pushing the envelope on what you already know, as soon as you return to Traiffe, so it's not like we'll catch you. But we need to move today."

He left it at that.

One part of Uly's mind saw a vast convoy of ships, sailing towards the galactic core with millions of colonists, heading off to find some new adventure, hiding behind the Yarikh and forcing them to either flee in turn or emerge from their cave.

And he was mean enough to do it.

Her eyes reflected that knowledge.

"Okay," Nomiki said simply. "We will help. We will become part of your...what would you call it?"

"It will be a republic before I'm dead," Uly replied. "For now, a tyranny, but I'm trying to keep it as benevolent as possible. The Hall of Voices and the Presidium need time to mature. That's my job."

"Our job," she corrected him, holding out a hand.

"Our job," he shook it.

ONE HUNDRED TWENTY-TWO

Dan was in the part of the new palace dedicated entirely to the Congress of Wives. An entire wing, as yet largely unfinished because Uly didn't have five hundred Wives.

She had prepared by making a list of all known species, then adding in an additional ten percent, because Anari was a member of the Congress and Uly's Household, even as she and Sterling had finally married and were looking into adoption, fostering, and all other options.

Any child would have that many mothers. And at least one demigod as a father. They were still working on Sterling's legacy. And Solomon's.

Today, she had invited Tiny and Suka Kuri to a quiet tea. After the morning workout and brunch. Everyone off on their own, making their various spaces their own, now that they had places where they could decorate it themselves.

Dan had made sure that this wing had a lot of such spaces. Both public for entertaining outsiders as well as private for them.

Tiny was still settling. Still relaxing. She was still finding herself, having moved beyond piracy and command and moving on to dance.

Suka Kuri poured tea. Vahid had made scones on request, using

Human ingredients because Dan could indulge herself a bit in exotic elements.

What did it say about her that things from a Human world were an exotic delicacy?

Dan indulged. The others enjoyed.

"What questions can either of us help you with?" Dan asked, understanding that Tiny was moving slower than she probably wanted, but still far in advance of what many probably expected.

Again, if Dan hadn't thought that she could handle herself and the tasks at hand, she would have never moved forward with the woman.

"Does it ever end?" Tiny asked, looking at both of them but perhaps focused a bit more on Suka Kuri.

"No," the Exemplar replied, grinning. "At least, I hope not. If it did, that would suggest that I had run out of new things to learn, and that will never do."

Tiny nodded.

"There is, however, a fixed curriculum at present," Dan added. "Various Human forms that I have learned over the years, compressed and distilled down to a set of kata exceptional at combat and training. Sunflower Fist. Terrible Gaff. Karmap. At some point, we will go to the Samuur specifically to locate those forms that have survived among your people and see what of them we wish to add, while also teaching what we know. It will not be as necessary to break down cultural boundaries as it was at Z'Gosza or Isann, but our existence as a team helps foster the thing Uly wants to build, using soft power to capture minds."

"Foster," Tiny mused. "Understanding that he is a demigod with dread and dangerous powers, how will the Congress be handling births, adoptions, and fosterage?"

"Traditionally, someone wishing to foster would already have a stable relationship," Suka Kuri said. "Often, children were traded equally, so both could be raised outside the immediate household and thus establish alliances that spanned generations. Here, I think it will be more a case of outsiders wishing to present students that can be trained by the Congress as Diplomat/Warriors, as well as perhaps organizing themselves for the next generation."

"Similarly, we have two options on in vitro fertilization," Dan added. "In the case of Sterling and Anari, for instance, Sterling and a Human woman might agree to bear a child that would be raised by both, while he and Anari remain wed. And she might do the same with the right Emro male, once we go looking for one that meets our standards."

"Ours?" Tiny asked, maybe shrinking in on herself a bit.

"Ours," Dan agreed. "That is something that will include the whole of the Congress in deliberation, because such outsider men will need to be screened for a variety of things. I don't want to have to deal with some punk for a decade or longer."

"And I won't want to have to kill him," Suka Kuri added in that subtle boop on the nose that caused eyes to blink and water.

Everybody thought her a harmless old woman. Dan knew better.

"What about you and Uly?" Tiny asked, turning to her.

"I'd like the rest of you to get busy locating potential donors," Dan replied. "That way he and I can get serious. Perhaps having several, just as Solomon and Jacquel have started."

"Oh, she's pregnant?" Tiny perked up.

"It's not generally known, because she's not that far along, but she'll begin showing in a few months," Dan nodded. "Our Human colony thus expands. And I'd like more. And more Samuur cubs running around. And more kits. More guppies. More big green kids. I would like this palace to have to turn into something of a nursery, because that means that we've achieved enough peace now to manage it. Then we can worry about what kind of galaxy we'll be leaving for our children, and not just everyone else."

"Can we do it?" Tiny asked.

"Uly can move civilizations," Suka Kuri said bluntly. "Dan isn't perhaps his level, but the gap is smaller than most appreciate. You are of the Congress now, so you will be Uly's hands in doing things. His reach. His ambassador. The fact that you can introduce yourself as one of his many Wives will impact certain cultures in a manner similar to what happened to the Isann."

"The women suddenly refused to let the men have all the adventures off-world," Tiny noted. "Because Uly had broken them free of the old ways."

"As he does," Suka Kuri replied. "As you will do, too."

Tiny nodded. Sipped her tea.

Dan watched. Waited.

"What's out there?" Tiny finally asked, looking up.

"That, my sister, is why you are here," Dan smiled.

ONE HUNDRED TWENTY-THREE

Lukyan sprawled on the couch. That was the word for it.

Sprawled.

It had been a lovely dinner. Triple date with Anna, hosting Maks and Chervonya, Harald and Sibylle. Fantastic food, using some Human/Mazhin recipes Vahid had assembled into a cookbook, once enough blackmail had been brought to bear.

But he was exhausted.

Anna walked in with a glass in each hand, giving him one as she snuggled up against him and worked on stealing all his heat. She was like that.

He sipped and let the day kind of wash off him.

Time passed.

"Who replaces Pasternak?" he finally asked.

They'd chewed on it over dinner, the six of them, but not reached any solid conclusions. Bakhtiar Teke had functionally vanished, never leaving his estate for any reason, last Lukyan had heard. Nihal Pasternak had been Teke's sidekick and co-conspirator for so long that everyone had turned to look at him as soon as Teke had finished announcing his formal resignation from the council.

One step ahead of a posse, but Anna had worked a deal with him where Bakhtiar shut up and never bothered her again. And she'd be watching.

Nihal had taken a hint and announced his formal retirement, but given them a month to find his replacement.

Chervonya had taken Teke's spot, pretty much on acclamation.

Things had gotten weird.

"You want it?" Anna asked quietly.

"Absolutely, freaking not," he told her. Again. Since she maybe hadn't heard him the first time. Or had been ignoring him. "Happiest as your Plus-One, thank you."

And his brother wouldn't want the spot.

A thought struck him. So ludicrous that he couldn't help but snort.

"What?" she pressed, sipping.

"Wondering if you should lean on the Zehlennko," he offered.

"Katya's cousins and kin have never forgiven her for marrying Uly and bringing them to my attention," Anna laughed back.

"I'll notice that they've done pretty well for themselves anyway," he said.

"And resent being thrust into the middle of Horde politics," she countered.

Lukyan shrugged. Messy. Like everything was when you had a mass of Ononguli involved.

He paused. Sipped. Considered.

"You honestly think that the war is over?" he asked her. Here, in the privacy of their chambers.

"Uly thinks that the Empire will be a decade analyzing everything he's done over this previous decade," she replied. "Then a while plotting how they might react and counter his threat. So yes, I think we can buy ourselves a space. Not sure if I can keep all these damned pirates from running off and hitting Auga shipping and pissing them off, right about the time Uly has lulled them to sleep."

Lukyan pursed his lips. Didn't think he'd made a sound, but she'd come to know him pretty well by now.

She sat up and turned to look at him, not quite in his lap but close.

"You had an idea?" she asked.

"Maybe," he drawled it out in five syllables.

"Talk."

"Imperial Sector Thirty-Two," he said. "Sector Twenty-Two to a lesser extent, because we know some of what's over there, but still wondering who's behind us, so to speak."

"And?"

She could be fierce when she wanted. The *Vatazhko* would suddenly come to the fore and growl at him.

Like now.

"And I had an idea on how to mess with your pirates," he said.

"Our pirates, you pirate," she countered.

He grinned. Their pirates, since he was kinda her sidekick these days, for reasons he STILL had never figured out, and wasn't about to argue with.

"Kit Simonson is building better life support systems, per Maks's latest," Lukyan told her. "Bigger crews for the same hull, or smaller crews for much longer missions without resupply."

"Go on." Damn, her eyes had gotten hard suddenly. That dangerous twinkle he loved so much.

"What if you hired a group of Isann and Samuur conductors?" he offered. "Specifically no Ononguli conductors in the first round. Bought or leased some new explorer design you caused Maks to build. Mixed up the crews instead of keeping them distinct. Sent them into Thirty-Two to explore for new worlds to colonize and places to trade. Even Sterling's maps are blank when it comes to knowing who might be back there."

"And forcing Ononguli crews to serve under foreigners?" she asked.

He noted that Anna hadn't said aliens, so her own thinking was breaking down along Uly's new lines. That brought him joy.

"Lots of Ononguli in the *Spinward Reaches*," he pointed out. "Don't want them losing contact with the homeland in all this. And it gives the hotheads something to do besides go back to the old ways."

"And it will work," she agreed, smiling. "Sneaky."

"Sneaky would be making sure the Zehlennko were in charge," he grinned.

"Oh, that's rude," she laughed. "Because then Uly's involved to some extent as well, forcing everyone to behave and work together."

"I never said it was a nice idea," Lukyan pointed out.

She leaned in and kissed him with passion.

"No, but that's why I keep you around," she said.

He nodded.

All this, because of a *Tuesday*.

ONE HUNDRED TWENTY-FOUR

Ethir leaned on the big conference table and scowled mightily at his three cousins, back along the wall right on the verge of fucking around and trying his patience. Well, Ralphye. Hobse was napping and Waltin had his nose in a book.

Ethir cowed Ralphye anyway, then turned back to everyone closer.

The Legal Department. He still laughed at being in charge of something like this, but Rabiu was a better accountant and Haydar was gone too much. Piruz was a Used Camel Salesman, in every sense of the word.

That left one Thogin ex-pickpocket running things.

You people are doomed.

"This meeting is called to order," he told them. "First order of business is the treaty language for new planetary systems wanting to apply for membership in the government of the *Spinward Reaches*. Thoughts?"

Adylet the Isann nodded. He turned to the woman.

"We've created two paths," she said. "One for people wanting to mostly just trade on favorable terms, while maintaining local control. The second one is a path to full membership over twenty years, as the Warlord takes a larger slice of operational and executive control annually. I see the former as having the most benefit short term, but it leaves folks on their own in the event of trouble. Why would they take it?"

"That's for folks like Rayzian or Z'Gosza," Haydar noted dryly. "Where they have two masters and don't need our fleet protecting them from pirates and trouble. Most folks will be guided into the second. The twenty-year lag lets us bring them along slowly, or kick them out again before they complete it, if they turn out to be assholes."

"What about planets, somewhere in our Core, that refuse to do anything?" Kaarina the Samuur asked.

"They are subject to the depredations of piracy and other criminal elements," Piruz replied in a sing-song that suggested all manner of innocence, without ever committing. "Without Uly doing anything about it if he doesn't want to. Carrots and sticks, as it were. You pay full tariff on trade. Our fleets don't respond to anything but a distress signal after the pirates have left."

"Assuming Uly doesn't crush the pirates responsible."

"Oh, he'll probably do that," Ethir offered. "Or Sterling. Point is, that's after you've lost your ship and cargo, and we're under no obligation to return either, either."

He smiled at his play on words. The others just rolled their eyes. About usual.

He paused.

"Is the language good enough to put in front of Uly for signature?" he asked.

"I think so," Rabiu replied. "We've adapted a lot of Chandlery Court stuff Uly already worked out previously, with some of Maks's meaner ideas. The full Conclave should look at this draft, I think, and start poking holes in it if they can."

"Next full session after the holidays," Haydar said. "Send it home with the representatives and let them chew on it for a month. That should be good enough."

Ethir nodded.

"So moved," he said.

"Second," Kaarina replied.

"Nays?" Ethir asked. "None appearing, motion is approved. Waltin, write that down."

"Already did."

Ethir rolled his eyes, but he'd known his cousin their whole life, being only a few months apart in age.

"Next order of business?" he asked.

"We need an Ononguli lawyer," Waltin replied.

"Didn't ask you," Ethir snarked.

Waltin shrugged.

"No, he's right," Haydar said. "Maks is up to no good, even more so today when he's not trying to build up naval forces as fast as he can. And Chervonya is one of the Lords of the Endless Plains now, per latest report."

"Ask Maks to nominate a member?" Piruz asked. "We've got Rabiu, so we do need balance there."

"Yes, I think so," Adylet agreed. "It will draw Anna and Lukyan closer, since so much of Maks's business will take place outside of Sphere space."

"Okay, Rabiu, you handle that," Ethir decided in his executiveness. "What else?"

"Inheritance law," Kaarina grinned.

Ethir groaned. He hated keeping wallboard charts with strings running back and forth, and that was exactly the only way his brain had found to do some of the things Uly was up to. And Maks, though Maks only had one spouse that anyone knew of and wasn't AS LIKELY to be adopting kids from other species.

Ethir didn't put it past him, though.

"Fine," Ethir succumbed to ennui. "What do you have?"

He sat back and listened as the two women at the table began explaining, but understood that none of the men present had spouses, let alone kids.

"We need a Human lawyer, too," Ralphye yelled from the corner.

"Didn't ask you, either," Ethir yelled back.

But he wasn't wrong. Everyone had kinda turned to look at the Cousins, causing a long moment when Ethir thought they might break for the door. Might not be the worst outcome, either, but they did have a point.

And Ethir didn't want to have to chase them all down.

"Who do we recruit from the newcomers?" he asked his two women experts.

"I'll check around," Kaarina replied.

"Okay, so what else have you got for me today?" he asked.

Then sat back and tried to keep his eyes from crossing as these two enormously dangerous lawyer women explained what they were up to.

ONE HUNDRED TWENTY-FIVE

Gennadi watched Emil climb up on the stool next to him and settle in, a mug of beer magically appearing from the hands of the Samuur publican.

"You ever think about going home?" Gennadi asked.

Emil ignored him and sipped.

"Am home," he finally replied. "Weird, looking at Human women again, but still think I'll end up with Fiona."

"You barely come up to her boobs, Emil," Gennadi said.

His partner in trouble just grinned.

"Samuur are more fun," Emil said. "When was the last time you met a woman that could bench-press you?"

"Okay, fair point," Gennadi said.

And it wasn't like he hadn't *meandered* around his options, since *Nubia* had an interstellar crew. And traveled a lot.

Smorgasbord, but that was what Uly was all about, from the first time Gennadi had looked at the young pup about to take them across the gap to a dead *Danumash* ship.

"What about retiring?" Gennadi asked.

"Don't know anything useful besides shooting people," Emil replied. "Suppose I could buy a bar and sit in the corner watching sports on the screen or something. Maybe beat folks up when they get rowdy. I could be my own bouncer."

Gennadi fell silent and sipped, thinking deep thoughts. Emil was right. They were home.

Weird to think of it. And there were Humans around these days, besides the group of them from the beginning. And he supposed that he'd be an uncle soon enough, though Gennadi wasn't sure which way Emil and Fiona would adopt. Or maybe both.

And maybe he needed someone. He and Emil had been thick as thieves for a decade, but they were getting old enough to know better, according to regulations.

Probably time to grow up.

Or something. He had money. And connections.

Now he just needed to dream.

And that was a nice thing to think about.

ONE HUNDRED TWENTY-SIX

Suka Kuri laughed as she watched Delphine Zahra go through her kata. The Human woman was rather accomplished as a performer. Well on her way to becoming someone in the Moss School.

And had decided that, like Anari and Yanouk, she wanted to also learn Sabre.

Suka Kuri wondered if it was a Human thing. She had four hundred new Humans to meet, so her understanding had grown far wider.

Delphine came to rest and Suka Kuri nodded.

"Getting there," she said. "Watch your feet and your distance, which is what we tell every student for the first year or three."

Delphine nodded. Bowed to the front of the room. Moved to sit next to Suka Kuri with the tea service between them.

"How may I broaden your mind?" Suka Kuri asked.

Delphine fixed tea as a way to organize her thoughts, a thing Suka Kuri appreciated about the young woman. Creatively brilliant, but able to come to rest and think, which was much more rare.

"Everyone is convinced that Humans are too dangerous to be unleashed on the wider galaxy," Delphine finally said. "What needs to change?"

"They need to grow up," Suka Kuri proclaimed sagely. "They have technology far in advance of their civilizational achievements."

"The result of them possibly being one of the Lost Tribes?" Delphine asked. "Ancient religions have such stories, but they generally assume boats on water, rather than starships. I suppose if you fell far enough, you might have to change those tales to make them make sense."

"I think they have been isolated for too long," Suka Kuri replied. "And have gone a little sour as a result. Uly and Dan just reinforce that lesson, when I look at the median among the new colonists. But at some point, someone will make that voyage again. Possibly to one of the *Seven Crowns*. Hopefully, Uly, in a fleet powerful enough to make them listen to reason. *Batyr* probably would, but *Danumash* represents some of the worst tendencies."

"Jacquel is so different from what I was expecting," Delphine said. "But I suppose that was what made her flee from her upbringing."

"Rightly so," Suka Kuri agreed. "She is the exception to many rules, by her own admission. But I think she and Solomon make a good pairing, as he can socialize her better into Uly's ideal. Her intellect and charm will serve her well. And she might be one of his Ambassadors."

"Would she join the Congress?" Delphine asked, eyes a little crossed.

"Not as a Wife," Suka Kuri said. "But Anari is not Uly's. There are many options, and we have specifically made a place where binary logic is not necessary. One can be many things to many people, such as yourself, still working as a waitress when not training."

"It brings me joy to serve," Delphine smiled. "As does learning. And performing."

"And thus, you can expand in as many directions here as you wish to explore," Suka Kuri said. "That is what Uly is building. And it is a new thing, so you will have to carry that message outward yourself as one of his ambassadors."

"Me?"

"You," Suka Kuri grinned. "You are well on your way. And have the talent and skill to reach people in much the same way as Nasrin."

Delphine nodded. Suka Kuri could see the wheels turning in the young woman's mind.

It would be good.

"What happens next?" she finally asked, turning serious.

"The learning never stops," Suka Kuri told her, laughing. "Even when you reach my age and station in life. That's the secret. That's what keeps me young."

They fell into silence and Suka Kuri wondered if she might live long enough to see Dan and Delphine as the first Exemplars of Human origin.

Anything was possible, though the road was long.

She wouldn't have it any other way.

ONE HUNDRED TWENTY-SEVEN

Uly pulled Dan into his quarters, looked both ways to make sure she was alone, and locked the hatch behind her.

Much necking ensued. The calendar rotated through his wives, and all of them were interesting and fun people, but he still held Dan as the highest.

Best.

His other half, and the reason that the Corsac Fox could do all the things he did.

They did. That was the secret.

Finally, they came up for air, merely wrapped around one another. They'd only made it one step into the room.

"Miss me?" she asked.

"Possibly," he grinned. "It finally feels like I have gotten everything moving enough that it can run without me cracking the whip."

She laughed and Uly sighed.

"Yes, I know," he told her. "It has been like that for a long time. But I'm not currently stealing starships and having to scrounge to find enough crew to run them. Or colonizing empty systems and trying to draw in farmers and merchants to make it work. We've reached some critical mass."

"Need a vacation?" she asked.

He smiled.

"I'd ask how you can read my mind like that, but it's you," he said. "Like me and the Mazhin, I suppose. I'd like to take a trip. Somewhere. No responsibilities. No treaties to be negotiated. No wars to be fought. Just explore."

"Good practice to get everyone else into the habit of thinking for themselves," Dan nodded. "They do that now, but neither of us is immortal, and the *Spinward Reaches* needs to last long after we're gone."

Yes, that was it. *The Reaches* had become a thing. Formally. Officially. Legally.

Borders. Trade agreements. Political intrigue would no doubt follow. Possibly Auga assassins for hire.

Something.

Tonight, he didn't have to do anything but enjoy being pressed up against his favorite person in the universe. It was good.

But something niggled.

"Yes?" she asked, still holding him, but leaned back and watching his face.

"Had a thought," Uly said. "Pardon me while I handle business for five minutes?"

She separated to just a hand held and followed as he moved to the couch. Comm was sitting on the end table. He sat with her turned sideways, her legs over his, watching.

"Yes, Uly?" Aibek answered immediately when he called.

"I have an assignment for you, Aibek, if you're interested," Uly replied. "I need you to work with Kadyr and Maks to build and modify one of those patrol Strikers for an exceptionally long mission."

"Okay, where are you going?" Aibek asked.

"We're going," Uly corrected him. "You'll be in command of the ship. I want Zhyrgal as one of your officers."

"My daughter?" Aibek asked, confusion evident.

"Yes, and Maksat can come if he desires, though he always seems more of a homebody," Uly said.

"Agreed," Aibek replied. "She's the adventurer in the family. But I can ask, and Ainura might wish to not be left out."

"Agreed as well," Uly grinned. "But Zhyrgal is key to what I have in mind on our trip."

"Our trip? Where are we going?" Aibek asked. "That lets me figure out various things in the short term, so we can plan for something bigger."

"I want to sit down with a copy of the *Karaŋgılıkka*, Aibek," Uly told him. "And trace all the places Zamir Aytiev went in his various travels. See all those worlds. Maybe not get into nearly as much trouble, but take a crew, heavy on Isann but including everyone, and go see what's back there in the darkness of Sector Fourteen. We've barely started exploring, but I want this to be an adventure."

Silence greeted him. Uly wasn't surprised. Aibek probably had to find his breath again.

"Yes," Aibek finally managed, hardly anything more than all that breath rushing out of his body, but Uly understood.

The Isann had only recently returned to space. And not had anything even as sophisticated as modern ships to try a voyage like that.

And Uly knew that the Isann would have to hold a lottery for crew, because most of the planet would demand to sign on, letting him be choosy.

But yes, he needed a vacation. What better way to do it than the *Karaŋgılıkka Reborn*?

"I will bother you in a few days for an update, Aibek," Uly said. "Good night."

"Good night, Uly."

He set the comm down and Dan's eyes were probably as glittering as Aibek's.

He got that.

It was a dream that could move nations, because it already had with the Isann.

What was out there? Who?

And how could they make the galaxy a better place?

He started to speak, but Dan leaned in and kissed him instead, still grinning, because she got it.

She got him.
And she was the other half that made him possible.
As Suka Kuri said, they could move the galaxy.
Together.
"Enough," she whispered in his ear. "Take me to bed."
"I thought you'd never ask."
How had he ever gotten so lucky?

READ MORE

To read more of my fiction, sign up for my newsletter. You'll also get a free book!

http://www.blazeward.com/newsletter/

ABOUT THE AUTHOR

Blaze Ward writes science fiction in the Alexandria Station universe (Jessica Keller, The Science Officer, First Centurion Kosnett, etc.) as well as The Corsac Fox and several other science fiction universes. He also writes action-thriller (present day as well as historic). In addition, he's the editor and publisher of Boundary Shock Quarterly Magazine and Thrill Ride Magazine. You can find out more at his website www. blazeward.com, as well as Bluesky, Goodreads, and other places.

Blaze's works are available as ebooks, paper, and audio, and can be found at a variety of online vendors (Kobo, Amazon, and others) as well as the Knotted Road Press website directly. His newsletter comes out monthly and you can also follow his blog and his Patreon on his website. He really enjoys interacting with fans, and looks forward to any and all questions—even ones about his books!

Never miss a release!

If you'd like to be notified of new releases, sign up for my newsletter.

http://www.blazeward.com/newsletter/

Buy More!

Did you know that you can buy directly from the KRP website?

https://www.knottedroadpress.com/shop/

Connect with Blaze!

Web: www.blazeward.com
Boundary Shock Quarterly (BSQ):
https://www.boundaryshockquarterly.com/

ABOUT KNOTTED ROAD PRESS

Knotted Road Press publishes dynamic fiction set in exotic locations. Our authors cover a wide range of genres including science fiction, fantasy, mystery, literary, and poetry. We also have unique non-fiction voices in genres such as autobiography, business, cookbooks, and how-tos. We offer both DRM-free ebooks and print books for a global readership.

www.KnottedRoadPress.com